DOT.CON

For Greg Kahn —

Ken Layne

DOT.CON

KEN LAYNE

DUFFY & SNELLGROVE
SYDNEY

Published by Duffy & Snellgrove in 2001
PO Box 177 Potts Point NSW 1335 Australia
info@duffyandsnellgrove.com.au

Distributed by Pan Macmillan

© Ken Layne 2001

Cover design by Dolores Haynes
Typeset by Cooper Graphics
Printed by Griffin Press

ISBN 1 875989 97 8

visit our website: www.duffyandsnellgrove.com.au

1

So this was the centre of the New Economy? A stinking mess of industrial parks? It was Larry Jonestowne's first visit to Silicon Valley and he wasn't impressed.

The famed Sand Hill Road, home of the big Venture Capital firms, was just another grocery-anchored strip-mall boulevard, with bits of garbage and discarded diapers collected in the scrub brush, Mountain Dew cans and Starbucks cups. The architecture was 1970s suburban bank branch: cracking non-union stucco and brown-painted wood and smoked glass.

He drove past dusty lots and Spanish-style mini-malls of cell-phone stores and franchise diners and young sick trees lining drives into massive asphalt prairies, each with a three-storey corporate headquarters of a Sun Microsystems or Apple or Hewlett-Packard or Oracle or 3Com or Novell, no signs of human life save for the janitors waiting at the distantly spaced bus stops and the programmers from India nervously walking back to their corporate housing blocks.

None of the New Paradigm HQs had opening windows. The executives and code-slingers were hiding within, air conditioning blasting, massive arrays of servers locked in bunkers beneath the administrative floors. He found

MicroTorrent Systems after many wrong turns. It was on MicroTorrent Avenue.

There was a guard box, also air-conditioned. Larry told his name to the rent-a-cop and sat for five minutes as the guard made calls, spoke to his cop radio, checked a clipboard and pressed a series of ominous buttons on the booth's console. The guard's arm reached out with a LIMITED GUEST PARKING pass and the barber-pole barrier lifted. Larry's little rental car stalled and the gate swung down. The guard scowled and lifted the robot arm off the car's roof.

Larry parked, scanned his background material, and locked the car. Looking up, he saw surveillance cameras hidden among the amber light fixtures.

In the lobby, a receptionist sat within a horseshoe desk. A uniformed guard stood beyond her.

Larry said hi and she slowly looked up.

'Can I help you with something?'

'Yeah, I've got an appointment with Thomas Sanders.'

'I don't *think* so,' she said, thin lips drawing up around the canines.

'Um, yeah, I do. *InterWorldNet* magazine.'

'Do you have a photo ID?'

He pulled the passport from his shoulderbag and put it on the counter. She took a long time with the photo, nine years old, and began flipping through the pages, staring at the old stamps and transit visas.

'It's me,' he said, forcing a polite smile.

She scowled and jabbed the passport back. Another clipboard, another sign-in, another series of hushed phone calls and buttons.

'Someone will escort you to the executive floor. Please wait.'

Twenty minutes passed and Larry had flipped through a dozen technology magazines when a fidgety young man in

Dockers and a button-down shirt arrived to lead the guest to the secret elevators.

'What do you do here?'

'I'm not authorized to speak to the media.'

The doors parted on the top floor, the third floor, and Larry faced yet another reception area, with another smug secretary behind another horseshoe-shaped desk of blond fake wood.

An hour after parking, he was finally led into a guest lounge outside the executive offices. Tom Sanders was huge, at least six feet tall and 300 pounds, maybe more, shrouded in a massive yellow button-down with a tiny embroidered company logo on the chest. Sanders stuck out a thick hand.

'I appreciate your visit,' he said. Larry nodded and waited for something, not knowing the protocol. Sanders finally plopped into a beige leather armchair and stared at the reporter through his bifocals, perched on a small nose, over blotchy red cheeks.

'Well, thanks for having me.' Larry smiled and sat again. 'The magazine wants a profile on you, about this technology and the, uh, new system.'

Sanders frowned. Larry couldn't remember the name of the thing and felt doomed, already. But he needed the money this assignment would bring. Plenty of his kind had become technology reporters. Some were even getting wealthy. It couldn't be that hard.

'Everything you know about telecommunications changes right here,' Sanders said. It was MicroTorrent's current slogan.

'Sure. But I don't really know much about telecommunications, so do you mind sort of sketching it out for me?'

'As soon as we take care of legal.'

'Legal?'

'The forms.' A young-looking guy in a Wall Street suit

walked into the lounge and patted Sanders on the shoulder. Sanders smiled and said, 'Morning, Henry.'

'I'm Henry Arellanes.' He stuck out his hand and Larry stood to shake it. 'Is Larry your legal name, or Lawrence?'

'Lawrence,' Larry said. 'Why?'

'Oh, just for the forms.' Arellanes had a leather satchel in his left hand. He opened it on the coffee table and began sorting through files. When he finished, there was a two-inch stack of paper on his lap.

Larry said, 'These legal forms, I'm not, uh, familiar with this sort of thing.'

'Non-Disclosure Agreement, that's this one,' Arellanes said with a pleasant grin. He handed it to Larry. About twenty pages, stapled, with a law firm's name on top. 'And this is the Embargo Agreement, of course. This one here is the on-line Embargo. Finally, we have the standard pre-publication review contract, and that's that.'

Larry looked over the stack and shook his head. 'No offence, but you want to *approve* the article before it's published?'

'Of course,' the lawyer said.

Sanders forced a grin. 'That's the only way I do interviews. I was told you were experienced. Was I misled, Larry?'

2

Larry stomped past the *InterWorldNet* Media Ventures receptionist and into the editorial offices. The big windows faced the Bay Bridge and the long room was filled with designer office furnishings, a fancy new Macintosh poking up from each cubicle. Denisa Moss had one of the bigger cubes, near the executive suites to show her ranking of Assistant Managing Editor.

She said into the phone, 'Yes, he's here,' and hung up.

'Yeah, I'm here. We need to talk about this MicroTorrent – '

'Don't come barging into my office. Can't you use a telephone?'

'Did you tell this Sanders guy he has full approval of my damned article? That he can *sue me* for asking questions about him?'

A few meek heads popped up from various cubicles. Denisa smoothed her skirt and stood. She pointed to the glass-walled conference room and hissed at him to keep quiet.

Larry followed her inside and she carefully shut the door.

'Don't you dare storm into my office and start yelling at me, you understand?'

'I'm not yelling, I'm asking you a question. Did you or didn't you tell this – '

'Shut up, Larry. I'll be glad to give this story to somebody else if it's too much trouble.' She sat on the black leather sofa and glared at him. 'I guess all that "I'm so poor, please give me some work" crap was just another lie.'

'No, it's not a lie. You want to see my bank statement?'

'Not really.'

Larry cleared his throat and, for the first time, realized the table was a Ping Pong table. A black-matte Ping Pong table.

'What the hell kind of conference room is this?'

'Don't start.'

'Don't start what? Can't I ask *any* questions?'

'Don't start with the Ping Pong table, or the cappuccino machine, or the designer desks, or anything. I'm not at all interested in any of your opinions. This is where I work, and I'm doing you a favour. Got it?'

Larry sat on the edge of the table and yanked the stack of legally binding documents from his shoulderbag. 'I've done some business reporting. I've seen NDAs and once or twice I've even signed them, when it was reasonable. This is not reasonable. It's a damned profile of an executive. I'm not in their research lab or whatever, and I wouldn't know what they were doing if I spent a month there. Do you honestly think the *Economist* or the *Wall Street Journal* would sign this garbage?'

'This isn't the *Economist* and it isn't the *Wall Street Journal*.' Denisa swiped the papers from his hand and glanced over them. 'This isn't even a business magazine, Larry. It's a technology-lifestyle journal.'

'Oh Lord.'

'Listen to me. We don't break news. We don't investigate. We review computer games and Web sites and interview big shots. This is how it works. It's not a scandal to be uncovered.' She stood and went to the door. 'Don't make me regret giving you some work.'

Larry whispered as he followed her back to the cubicle, 'So you want me to sign these things?'

'Yes,' she hissed. 'You better not have told Sanders otherwise.'

'It never came up. They just assumed I would sign everything and send them back.'

'They assumed right. Sign away.'

He sighed and bent over her desk. Five signatures later, Denisa took her pen back. 'When's your interview?'

'Thursday at noon.'

'At the house?'

'Yes, at the mansion. Sanders says the photographer should come an hour early.'

'Fine.'

No goodbye was offered. Larry escorted himself outside

and lit a cigarette. There were expensive cafés and bistros all around him, filled with chattering dot.com workers, the lucky ones who still had jobs. A whole tribe of black turtlenecks, expensive haircuts, cell phones and nose-rings.

The only reason she had even given him the work was an accident. Next month's intended cover boy had been arrested by federal marshals for a few hundred insider-trading violations. Larry was cheap and fast and available, and had accepted the MicroTorrent story planned for the following issue. A life of leftovers. He walked into the little park that divided the street, San Francisco's 'Multimedia Gulch', and sat on a park bench. A wino appeared in seconds and bummed a smoke.

3

He took the 101 south, out of the fog and onto the winding faux-country roads and store-bought mini-estates of Los Altos Hills. After dozens of circular driveways of imported flagstone holding the same Lexus sedans and BMWs and SUVs, he found Sanders' house.

The numbers 1317 were rendered in expensive tile on a stucco gateway. He skidded into the drive. There was a helipad to the left and a spider-like Bell executive chopper, surrounded by artfully trimmed trees. Fake gas lanterns marked the way to the residence. A gardener wielding a leafblower motioned to the seven-car garage and watched Larry park the little Daewoo.

'Hi. Here to see Thomas Sanders.'

'Mr Sanders' inside,' the gardener yelled over the leafblower.

Larry was admitted into the climate-controlled drywall foyer with the kind of generic marble flooring and fake art prints one sees in a chain hotel aimed at middle managers. The house stretched in ten directions: lowered living rooms of shag carpeting and beige leather couches, stairs leading to darkened halls above, a formal dining room holding an unassembled exercycle and computer boxes, a monstrous fluorescent kitchen, giant flat-screen teevees everywhere – two in the kitchen – all of them tuned to CNBC, all at top volume.

A Salvadoran maid directed him outside, to the largest redwood deck, where steam rose from a hot tub and a eucalyptus grove rose beyond the decking. Sanders nodded hello and beckoned Larry over. A platter of breakfast pastries sat beside the tub.

The big man rose, naked save for his eyeglasses. His belly flopped over his crotch.

'A drink?'

'Yeah, that sounds fine.'

Sanders sank back into the bubbling water and lifted the chrome whistle hanging from his hairy neck and stuck it between his lips. A shrill sound blasted out and another maid appeared.

'Get Mr Jonestowne a drink. What do you want, Larry?'

'Whisky, thanks.' He set up the tape machine – the contract demanded the interview be recorded – and readied the notepad.

'What we're doing is nothing short of changing how people think forever.'

'Well, that's a nice goal,' Larry said.

'And what people like *you* do is make sure our message gets across. See, that way we all benefit. Some punk writes trash about Steve Jobs. He had a daughter out of wedlock. So what? What does that accomplish? But we don't have to worry about that with your magazine.'

Larry felt his stomach tighten and was glad to see the maid return with his drink.

The tape recorder listened for two hours – cross-platform strategies, the early days of Silicon Valley and how Tom Sanders was the only real innovator, irrational exuberance, survival of the fittest, etc. It was a lecture instead of an interview. At 2 p.m. exactly, Sanders stood up, shook his massive body and waddled to the wall, where a red silk kimono hung. The contract stated that Larry would not 'describe Subject's physical appearance, including but not limited to weight, clothing, hairstyle, mannerisms …'.

Sanders walked Larry to the deck's steps and pointed to the glossy new Bell 407 chopper with its MicroTorrent logo across the doors.

'Fly this myself, you know?'

'Yeah?'

'Sure do. Massachusetts National Guard in sixty-six, certified chopper pilot.'

Larry smiled and nodded. Sanders had kept Massachusetts safe from the Vietcong.

'Still fly on weekends, but my pilot shuttles me to headquarters and back.' Sanders stuck out a wet hand and said, 'Looking forward to seeing your story.'

Larry drove away, feeling tired. The $1500 would be enough to pay two months' rent in his leaking dump of an apartment, a two-room unit chopped from a once-grand Victorian in the wastelands of Haight and Fillmore, the end of the road for anybody with too many problems.

4

He found a loading-zone space only a few blocks away from home and avoided eye contact with the dirty street kids and spaced-out old black men selling bits of junk taken from the neighbours' garbage. One of these guys, a forgetful little drunk named Charles, sold everything for a dollar. Broken aluminum chairs, soiled lampshades, CDs stolen by crackheads from parked cars. If Charles found a $20 bill he would sell it for a dollar.

There were cop cars outside Larry's apartment building. And a coroner's van. Larry lifted the yellow tape and put his key in the gate. A blonde cop came down the steps and said, 'Help you with something?' She looked about twenty.

'Just coming home.'

'We're investigating a fatality.'

'That's about normal for this neighbourhood.'

'It's apartment D. You know him?'

'I've only lived here a month. I don't know anybody.'

She opened the gate and let him pass. 'Go on in. The detectives will probably want to talk to you.'

He marched up the stairs, saw a detective working inside D, and unlocked his apartment. Curiosity got to him about five minutes later and he rapped on the open door of the crime scene.

'Yeah?' A young Chinese homicide detective, dressed too fancy for his profession.

'Live across the hall here,' Larry said. 'What's the story?'

'The story? Somebody called from a pay phone on the corner, said his "friend" was in here, not breathing. We came up here and found this guy, been dead a few days.'

Larry glanced around the flat, identical to his but a lot more decoration. The coroner had already taken the body away.

'You know this guy?'

'Nah, told the woman downstairs I don't know anybody. It's better that way.'

'I bet.' The detective took in Larry's tie and haircut and probably the bags under the eyes.

'Short term,' Larry said. 'I can't afford anything pleasant in this town.'

The detective nodded and walked over with his notebook and took Larry's name and number before jabbering any additional details.

'Latino guy, about twenty-two. Skinny little guy. Has a closet full of ball gowns.'

'Methamphetamine?'

'Probably. So you've seen him around?'

'I've seen a couple of guys around here, dressed up on Friday nights. They seemed harmless enough. But lots of disco pounding at 5 a.m., that sort of thing.'

'Techno,' the detective said, pointing at the stereo in the built-in shelves.

'I can't keep track. So what's homicide doing here if he did the Speed Kills thing?'

'Robbery, maybe. Some sort of motive.' He stared at Larry again and said, 'You used to be a cop?'

Larry laughed. 'Hardly. Used to do the police beat, for newspapers. I'm a regular Curious George.'

'Landlord says he rented to a light-haired white guy, never seen our boy.'

'Well, there were a couple of them. Maybe three? Maybe they didn't want to talk to you and got out of here.'

'With his wallet. Nice friends.'

'Summer of Love was a long time ago.'

Larry went back to his apartment, sat at his homemade kitchen desk — the pantry door set atop a pair of rusty two-drawer file cabinets bought from Charles for the usual dollar apiece — and fired up the old laptop. While the machine booted, he uncorked the wine and stared sadly at his bottle of Tijuana diet pills. Only six left.

He filled a coffee mug with red table wine and lit a cigarette. Nothing sadder than a blank new document in Microsoft Word. He paced around the kitchen and flipped through the unopened mail, all junk plus one bill. He looked out the window, to the trash alley below. There they were — his rat buddies, big as footballs, chomping through the Hefty bags and pizza boxes. Some people complained about rats, but Larry liked them just fine. They kept the alley clear of humans.

Just type it up. Quit thinking. Nobody gets paid to think.

After making a few innocuous phone calls to verify the dates and official job titles from Sanders' sterling career, he began transcribing:

'Let me make it clear, Larry. MicroTorrent Systems doesn't need press. We're not some IPO-bound half-baked idea looking for a business plan. MicroTorrent Systems, we've been here since 1974, before Apple, before *any* of these Internet firms going broke every day. We don't go hustling for capital. We are *profitable* …'

The thing was mostly finished by late afternoon, 1500 words of celebrity propaganda. He felt dirty and stared at the phone, wishing somebody would call, some diversion to clear his mind. It took about an hour of staring to get his wish.

'Yeah?'

'You're off the story, Larry. Nice going.'

'Denisa? What're you talking about?'

Dot.Con

'I'm talking about you violating the contract. Sanders' lawyers just called.'

'Lawyers? What the hell for? The thing's done, I'm sending it over – '

'You called companies he used to work for.'

'Well yeah, just to get his job titles and – '

'You violated the contract. Thanks for embarrassing me … again.'

'Come on! It's done, written, just what you asked for.'

'No, Larry. It's not done because I'm doing it myself. Goodbye.'

5

**From: Terrance Copeland
(tcopeland@innerknife.com)
Subject: Free Booze**

Larry – Good news for you. I'm at the Mark Hopkins. Internet conference at Moscone Center. Four days & nights, all expenses paid. Free booze/food for you, as long as we discuss business. Surely you can find a few women willing to take my money. We need to drink at Top of the Mark, for starters. Meet me up there at 9. Then Mexican food, drugs, fights, orgies. – TC

Terrance Copeland couldn't turn on a computer last year if you held his finger on the button. Now he worked for some fraudulent NYC Web consultant firm, in something called 'Silicon Alley'. The plague swept the nation, the whole world.

Larry had few friends in this town, just some Eurotrash trying to cash in on the last days of dot.com fever. Werner, for one. A German hacker-type, via the slums of London. Larry dialled and left a message, demanding the German collect any girls up for free drinks and meet at the hotel lounge.

He shaved, showered, even flossed. Special occasion. A night out. He sifted through the closet and found the last clean dress shirt, still folded nicely from the laundry. His pants seemed mostly clean, especially in the dark. He spat on the boots and wiped a dull shine into the leather. Shook the wrinkles and ashes from the sports coat, loaded smokes and keys and lighter and comb into proper slots, and stepped into the kitchen to shut off the lights.

Hearing noise in the hall, he flung open the door and saw the imp rummaging through the crime-scene apartment.

'What the hell are you doing, Charles?'

'Huh?' Sheepish and smiling, jabbering in his East Texas bayou accent. 'Aw man, the guys here said I could take whatever I needed outta here, they said it's cool, yeah. Chinaman too, he says I can clear it out.'

'They're all gone, Charles. One's dead. The Chinaman will have your ass if he catches you up here.'

Charles stood from his junk-skimming crouch and backed away, one hand behind his back.

'Oh yeah, we don't want that.'

'What're you hiding?'

'Hidin'? Oh, yeah, just this,' he said, flashing a brown wallet. 'Oh, I *been* havin' this, it's my own wallet.'

'Yeah?' Larry swiped it. Driver's licence inside. Driver's licence for one Jesús Peña Ramirez. 593-D Haight Street.

'You don't look so Hispanic, Charles. I think I'll hold onto this. I'm sure he's going to come looking for it.'

'Oh, well, uh, I don't think so, I don't think *he's* a-comin' back.'

'Why's that?'

'He the Mexican fella, the one always dress up like ladies with them white boys, them boys who run off. The Mexican fella, he dead.'

'I'll keep it for Mr Teng, then.' Larry stood there a second, something on his brain he couldn't quite tackle. Charles slowly took a few steps down.

'I ain't a thief, now, I'm just wantin' to sell this old stuff nobody want, that's honest, man, I'm an honest man, just tryin' to make a buck, you know what I'm sayin'?'

'Right, whatever,' Larry said. 'When Mr Teng gets back I'll tell him you'll get rid of this stuff. So you talk to him. And don't sneak into my damned building.'

'Okey, I'll be doin' that, come by later, see the Chinaman.'

Charles reached the landing and opened the door, watching Larry, who stayed in the hall until the imp was shuffling down the sidewalk.

The detectives hadn't worked too hard searching the apartment. Couldn't blame them. Just another John Doe, another unidentified corpse that nobody loved. Larry sat down at his desk, removing the billfold's contents and considering the fate of poor young Ramirez, only twenty-three. How'd he get mixed up with these losers in a Haight Street dump? Another refugee from Latin machismo? The methamphetamine must have killed him. Weak heart. Speed kills. These boys got carried away, forgot to sleep every few weeks. Just two dollar bills inside. A book of free taxi coupons, courtesy of a 'disabled' pal in the city. No bank card, a pocket bus schedule for the *Tres Estrellas de Oro* routes to central Mexico, an expired green card, a tiny ziploc with a bit of meth at the bottom, bits of paper with scribbled first names and local numbers, and an official U.S. Social Security card. He stashed the wallet in the freezer and locked up.

No cabs in sight. Larry walked downstairs and took

Haight to Church, hoping to grab a taxi in front of the supermarket. Along the way, a filthy street woman pushing a trash-filled baby carriage pointed and cackled, 'Repent!'

6

He stepped out of the creaky elevator and into the plush, jazz-age world of the Mark Hopkins' expansive lounge on the top floor. It was early yet; a pianist played a few bars of 'In the Wee Small Hours', doing the Sinatra vocal with a cigarette rasp. Later, hopefully long after Larry and his companions had departed, a full swing orchestra would take the bandstand and mobs of goofy 25-year-old couples would fill the dance floor, clumsily aping the moves they learned from musty films rerun on the American Movie Classics cable-teevee channel and perfected with $30-per-hour lessons from a gay dance instructor who really only wanted to deal with Bob Fosse routines, stealthily adding 'Chicago' flourishes to the Lindy Hop or whatever. Not that the dot.com kids knew the difference, or even cared. When the hair started thinning and the hips began blossoming, these former members of the alt-rock scene traded their Doc Martens and piercings for Zoot Suits and petticoats, gulping martinis in place of beer.

But it had made the old hotel lounges a very profitable business, and the bow-tied waiters didn't complain – not to the new clientele, at least. A silver-haired guy came to Larry's table and presented a cocktail menu.

'That's fine,' Larry said, waving the menu away. 'Vodka martini up, three olives, don't bother with vermouth.'

'Fine, sir. You'll be joined by your friends?'

Larry glanced at the sofa-filled alcove he'd chosen. Of

course, the frauds would be filling the place before long, and a waiter couldn't give such prime real estate to one guy who didn't even possess dress shoes, let alone a Zoot Suit.

'Yeah, yeah, certainly. Party of six,' he said, expecting three. 'Mr Copeland and his young ladies … Mr Copeland of InnerKnife Consulting, Manhattan.'

'I'll let the hostess know you're waiting.'

The man returned a few minutes later with a fine beverage, not a hint of vermouth. Larry shook one of his last Camel Lights from the pack and lit it, leaning back against the sofa pillows and taking in the view. Russian Hill behind him, the wharves, the well-lit phallic majesty of Coit Tower – built by some rich harlot to commend the many firemen with whom she shared coitus, as Larry recalled – the fine homes and apartment buildings littering the hill down to Chinatown and North Beach, the wind-blasted concrete canyons of the Financial District, the Bay Bridge, the twinkling ferries taking the day's stragglers back to Oakland.

He blew a cloud of R.J. Reynolds and sipped the cocktail and felt a bit like a convicted felon enjoying the final hours before incarceration. It was pleasant up here. Larry found it tragically unfair that such evenings were not routine.

A huge laugh echoed through the lounge, fouling the last lingering note of 'I Cover the Waterfront'. Larry leaned forward and saw Terrance Copeland, right hand on the hostess' shoulder, head bobbing, eyes bulging. She nodded politely and quickly led him to the alcove. Larry moved his drink to a safe table at his side and stood to receive the violent bear hug and the monstrously loud voice.

'Larry!' Terrance bellowed. 'You loser!'

'Hello there, jackass,' Larry said. 'Sit down before they throw you out.'

They ordered a pair of martinis.

'How's the trade show?'

'Stupid. We've got a little curtained salon, right off the main concourse, three stalls down from Microsoft, next to Macromedia, fine furnishings, Oriental rugs. Our own sushi chef, sake, gorgeous little tramps delivering drinks and reading business cards with little electronic gizmos hanging from their hips.'

'That sounds awful. What, exactly, are you selling?'

'Beats me! Just learn the code and jabber along. Broadband. E-commerce. Real-time tragedy. Does it matter?'

'No,' Larry said, draining his cocktail. 'Not to me.'

The new drinks arrived.

'Here's to your new gig, whatever it might be.' Larry lifted his fresh martini and Terrance met it with the rim of his own glass.

'It's good to see you, for some reason.'

'You too,' Larry said. 'Sorry I haven't answered your idiot e-mails or anything.'

The piano player said it was his last song, and that the Royale Swing Symphony would be playing next. Larry flagged down the waiter and said, 'We'd like to express our appreciation to the pianist.'

Terrance scowled and dug a $10 bill from his wallet. The waiter smiled and delivered the money to the piano man.

'You could ask, at least.'

'And you could learn to appreciate a working artist. That guy doesn't have an investment package. Most of the world doesn't.'

'Whatever, Lenin.'

'Whatever, Goebbels.'

Terrance grinned. 'What exactly are you doing in this city?'

'I don't know. Thought I'd do some of this computer

writing you hear so much about, get some money for once. Didn't work out.'

'Work for me. Put you in marketing or something.'

Larry winced and said, 'Wouldn't be much different than these magazines. They treat these tech CEOs like *People* magazine treats Tom Cruise. Total approval, contracts that keep me from talking to anyone about him. It's incredible. I searched that Dow Jones database and found a couple of old articles about this guy, patent disputes, semi-dirty stuff, and I couldn't even ask him about it. Lost the whole thing for asking what his official job titles were.'

'It's normal.'

'Until the new depression hits its stride.'

'I'd rather not talk about that. You starving yet?'

'Pretty much. Was thinking of trying a newspaper.' He took a long hit off the drink. 'I don't have very good references.'

Terrance gulped half his drink and slapped the table. 'How about this, Mr Ethical? You start up a Web site, expose all these CEOs for whatever they've done.'

The waiter brought fresh drinks and a small bowl of what looked like candy-coated dog chow. Spare no expense, etc.

'Yeah, that would work great. They'd sue immediately. Like what's-his-name, the semen-on-the-dress guy. Didn't he get sued by … ah hell, the White House guy, Clinton's buddy.'

'Blumenthal,' Terrance said. 'Thirty million bucks. But who cares? You wouldn't actually use your name.'

'There's a certain elegance to such a plan,' Larry said, and yanked his notebook from the sports coat.

'What?'

'Oh, just thinking of a nom-de-plume.'

'Aye, Jonestowne, what's doing?' Werner yelled in his

fake-Cockney accent from across the room. He made his way to the table, pale arms waving, black bowl of hair half covering the shifty eyes, a size extra-small Joan Jett T-shirt and leather jacket on his scrawny frame.

Terrance stood up and grasped Werner's shoulders. 'Nice to see the rotten German! What're you up to?'

'Jonestowne says you're buying drinks, right?'

'Only if you brought women.'

'Done me best. Got a Soviet.' The ex-Soviet was Suzie, from some Black Sea republic nobody could remember. She made it to the table a minute later.

'The lovely Suzie,' Werner said to Terrance. It wasn't a lie. She was tall with a messy pile of black hair, big grey eyes and the usual fine Slavic skin that needed no makeup.

'What's your story?' Terrance asked.

'I'm a very bad actress.' She sat on the arm of the couch and waved for a drink. Nobody really knew what she did, since her alleged movies all went straight to video, but her family's post-USSR economic shenanigans seemed to cover living expenses.

Larry realized he was already drunk. Should've eaten today. It was bad to be drunk around Suzie. Always led to some awful pass at her, always swiftly rebuked.

'Let's drink up and get out of here, eh?' Werner said, watching as the pompadoured musicians messed with their instruments. 'Dreadful swingsters filing in.'

Terrance waved his Platinum corporate card at the waiter and Larry excused himself while they gulped the last drinks. In the men's room he splashed handfuls of cold water on his face and decided to go home. To avoid trouble, he skipped the farewells and took the stairs two flights down, ricocheting off the walls and gulping down his nausea.

7

He jumped a cable car headed west and rode down California Street until the ticket man got close, hopped off and walked down Van Ness, unable to afford another taxi and unwilling to ride the bus with the other cretins. Everybody needed standards. The stroll did him good, breathing the fog, avoiding maniacs reaching out from every darkened vestibule, covering his ears as endless ambulances and police cars and fire trucks sped by in different directions, all headed to pointless emergencies.

He stopped at O'Lowney's Market and got a bottle of wine and a pack of cigarettes on credit – thanks to Nadeem, the charitable Palestinian proprietor – and crossed the street. On the sidewalk, a crazed old woman was beating a pit bull with a folding chair, the dog fatally chained to a No Parking sign covered with gang graffiti. Larry struggled with the lock on the gate, getting inside just as a crack addict tried to grab his arm. As he locked up the lobby door behind him, he saw an acid-case hippie across the street, sitting on the roof over the liquor store, filthy bare feet hanging off the eaves, screaming the word 'Time!' over and over.

Larry was not fond of the neighbourhood.

At 5:04 a.m., according to the clock radio, he woke, fully clothed. The paper bag of wine and smokes was cradled to his chest. His jumbo bottle of aspirin lay open on the pillow, which explained why he didn't have a hangover. But he had an idea.

He got up, brushed his teeth and went to the kitchen to

put on coffee and turn on the computer. Was there anything dirty on this Sanders? Would have to be. Why else would his lawyers keep the magazine from even poking around? Sanders had gone to Harvard and then moved west, that much was in his official biography. The patent dispute Larry read about in the Dow Jones archives involved IBM's New York headquarters. Maybe that was worth a look.

His closest thing to an Ivy League source was O'Leary, an alcoholic business reporter he'd known in Budapest. Larry hadn't seen him in two years, not since the mistake of letting the drunk rent a room. Shameless vice, Hungarian hookers, many complaints from the neighbours. Larry dialled Boston.

'Lawrence? What's the occasion?'

'I need a favour.'

'I'm on deadline. Lemme call you back tomorrow.'

'Look, I can still get you arrested in seven or eight countries, so be nice. Check out a guy named Thomas R. Sanders, Harvard '63.'

'Okay. Who is he?'

'One of them Internet billionaires. I know he had some kind of patent trouble. Want to see if there's anything else.'

'You're into this stuff now?'

'Oh, sure. Market forces, focus groups, consumer empowerment ... How's the paper?'

'Bad. I got thrown off the police beat.'

'No. What'd you do now?'

'I did my job, that's what I did. Some freak up at MIT, futurist guy, big celebrity among those people. He got caught in one of those Internet child-pornography stings, and I sort of broke the story.'

'Terrific!'

'Hardly. His family is real tight with the publisher's family. So guess what I do now?'

'Obituaries?'

'Worse. I'm a media reporter.'

'What?'

'Like Howard Kurtz or something, but all local crap. You know, so-and-so columnist invents the news, somebody plagiarizes somebody, that sort of thing.'

'Oh Lord, that sounds awful.'

'It is. Listen, I'll call some court clerks and check his school records if I can. I don't know too many people around Cambridge. But I'll e-mail whatever on this guy.'

Five years late, Larry jumped on the Web-site bandwagon. He dialled up, opened Internet Explorer and searched Yahoo for 'Web site tutorial'. Hundreds of matches. He scrolled through a few pages and selected something called 'The Moron's Guide to Building Web Sites'. It was nothing but a rant by an illiterate Web designer from Stanford, but one sentence caught his eye:

'In a age when any stuped looser can hit "save as html" in microshaft word and post there web site, good designs are in short supplies.'

'Save as HTML, eh?' Larry mumbled. He clicked Word and opened the Sanders propaganda. Sure enough, he could 'Save as HTML'. How easy is that? The computer moron was right about something.

The document was now a Web page. He went back to the Web browser, opened the file, and laughed. This is how people got rich? The Web page looked just like his piece: plain typewriter font on a white background. Toying with the formatting commands for a few minutes, he added a headline that Thomas Sanders' lawyers would not approve: The Shameful Rise of a Silicon Valley Fraud. O'Leary would come up with something.

Now, how to get the thing online?

Larry found the Web-name registering place and considered various monikers for the publication. Had to consider Ben Franklin, Tom Paine, St Paul, Mark Twain, all those maniacs forced by circumstance into the role of publisher. He consulted the reference library in the living room and flipped through a terrific old book about an earlier Gold Rush. There were dozens of daily newspapers just in San Francisco, one called 'Sluice Box' – named after the screened-tray gizmo prospectors used to filter the gold from gravel and mud.

Not a bad name for a modern Gold Rush paper. And for those who couldn't be bothered to know the definition of 'Sluice Box', it had a marketable tone of vulgarity. He typed 'SluiceBox.com' into the registry and found it taken – by an actual gold-mining concern. SluiceBox.net? Available. Fine. It asked for billing information. Larry took the dead man's wallet from the freezer and typed:

Jesús Peña Ramirez
593-D Haight St.
San Francisco, CA 94117
sluice_box@hotmail.com

He opened another browser window and went to Hotmail, that stalker's paradise, and registered an account for Mr Ramirez, quickly clicking 'I Accept' to whatever insane demands were contained in the user contract. For a phone number, Larry got O'Lowney's from a piece of paper taped to the fridge (for emergency liquor-and-ice orders). Nadeem could be trusted to take a message, if necessary. Always trust a man with three passports.

Then came the horrible news: Larry needed something called a Web server IP address. And a 'secondary address'. And the new name wouldn't work for twenty-four hours.

He disconnected and called Terrance's cell phone. It rang

four times and the voice-mail message answered. He hung up and tried again, and again, until a very damaged throat answered.

'Wha?'

'Terrance? How do I get a Web thing on the Web thing?'

'Christ, what time is it?'

Larry glanced at his scarred Seiko watch: 5:37 a.m.

'Where the hell are you?'

'Home. Working for the New Paradigm. How do I get this Web buddy on the Internet?'

'I can't talk now. Where'd you go?'

'Bastard. You're with Suzie, aren't you?'

'No, no! They blew me off. At three in the morning! They, uh, where'd they leave me?'

The voice trailed off.

'Terrance! Keep it together! This is important.'

'Yeah ... uh. I'm in a bed with some ... yeah, a girl.'

'How do I get this Web friend on the worldwide system dot-org?'

'Let me sleep, man. We'll talk tomorrow. Why'd you leave?'

'Early to bed, etc. Tell me how to do this and I'll hang up. Otherwise I'll kill you.' One had to be firm when dealing with degenerates.

'Dammit Larry ... just put it on InnerKnife's server. Use FTP – '

'What's that?'

'File Transfer Protocol. Download it. Called WS_FTP. The server is, uhm, innerknife.com. Login is *Terrance*. Password is *werewolf97*. I gotta go back to sleep ... No! I have to get to Moscone Centre. Where am I?'

Larry scribbled the information.

'Where am I, man? Hang on.' Muffled noises, a drunken girl's voice muttering drunken girlisms. Yelling. Then, 'Where's Merritt Lake?'

'Lake Merritt, jackass. You're in Oakland. Go to the BART station and take it under the bay to San Francisco, Market Street stop. Get a taxi to the convention centre.'

'Okay ... What time is it?'

'Quarter to six. What's the IP address?'

'Just put innerknife.com, they'll figure it out. Put it in my directory, do one of those Mexican squigglies – '

'A *tilde*?'

'Yeah, sure ... And then *tcopeland*. I'm hurting. Don't you care?'

'No. Who's the administrative contact? And the technical contact?'

'Please, my head is exploding ... me, I'm both of them. Tcopeland@innerknife.com.'

'Fine. It says you have to reply before the thing works, so don't forget. Can I use your credit card?'

'What?'

'I don't have a credit card. It's thirty bucks, I'll give you cash.'

Terrance didn't feel smart enough to fight. Larry wrote down the number, hung up and got the computer online again. Got everything filled in, clicked 'submit' and had three cups of coffee, waiting for the automatic reply. In twenty minutes, he had the confirmation notice. Everything fine. Now to the special server things.

WS_FTP ... There it was, free download, share the wealth. He tried to hit InnerKnife's server. Clicked through the subdirectories until /~*tcopeland* opened on the other side. Wonderful. He zapped the Web page across the country, for practice.

The ease of online-business transactions was a revelation to Larry. Maybe Señor Ramirez needed some credit of his own?

Larry smiled and thought this over. What had the banks

ever done for him? It was a series of bank-related failures that led him to this filthy town. When the wire service in London was closed by the banks, he was owed $5250, for six months of Balkan dispatches. Instead, he got a letter showing the priority of his long overdue paycheck – No. 347 on a list of 352. Then the glossy lads' magazine went bankrupt, and his $2000 plus expenses became a $150 kill fee. And the banks had judged him unfit to hold a credit card, thanks to a few small accounting errors a half decade ago.

Had Mr Ramirez gotten around to ruining his personal finances? Larry slipped the Social Security card from the dead man's wallet and found a bank online, offering robots to open an account – he ordered the standard checking and discovered he could make the initial deposit by ATM once the card arrived. Curious about the consumer habits of Mr Ramirez, Larry requested a trio of credit reports from the major agencies and applied for three Gold cards: a Visa, a MasterCard and an American Express. And an extra card from each company, for a family member. Mr Ramirez's occupation? Computer consultant. Salary? $97,000 per year. Employer? Werner Enterprises, Inc. Nobody would possibly fall for such flimsy information.

A final search brought him to an Internet Advertising network, one of dozens floating around the Web, waiting to go under. He happily accepted the many conditions and chose an exclusive six-month contract giving him about half a penny per 'page view'. No humans involved. Take the HTML code from the 'Welcome to FlyRight Advertising' Approval e-mail and paste it into the Web pages. There would only be significant money if the readership was outrageously huge, but people were making handsome livings off game plans far shoddier.

8

Nothing to do but wait. Wait for the credit cards in Ramirez' mail slot (or polite letters of refusal), the news from O'Leary's sniffing, and finally the unwelcome debut of SluiceBox.net and whatever might be on it. Larry was broke and nervous, and everybody took their sweet time. He was standing in the bay window watching a couple of winos wrestle outside when the phone finally rang.

'You'll like this,' O'Leary said.

'I better. My new career depends on it.'

'Then you'll really like this. Your man Sanders left Harvard under a cloud of sorts. A minor scandal at the time. Seems his dorm buddy tried out for Sanders' fraternity. The ritual hazing got a bit out of control. The buddy died.'

'Oh Lord. That's a bit beyond patent disputes. Was George W. Bush involved?'

'Wrong college. But here's the dirty part: days later, 21-year-old Sanders registers a patent for some kind of, uh, stacked memories or – '

'Memory stack. I've read up on this stuff.'

'Right. Computer thing. Very valuable. Sells it to IBM for a fortune – same year some Stanford guy patents the mouse, by the way. Then the dead dorm boy's family sues Sanders, claiming patent theft. They say their boy invented the whatzit, and Sanders settles out of court. He cancels MIT plans out here and heads West. From a really moneyed clan already, Martha's Vineyard compound, the whole works. The settlement info is sealed forever, but I found the police report on the kid's hazing death – Sanders took part, with his other frat boy pals. There was a bit of coverage in the papers.'

'Nice work! Take much trouble?'

'Yeah. I had to actually walk into three offices and ask to look at the files. This guy's been floating for what, twenty-five years? Somebody running for sewer commissioner gets more scrutiny.'

'There's no such thing around here.'

'I'm e-mailing all the stuff. Our intern just scanned all the official documents. Trying to teach these kids a work ethic.'

'Wonderful.'

'Let me know when you want some hype in my famous media column.'

O'Leary hung up and Larry switched the phone cord back to his computer. He dialled up and checked for new mail. Usual porn ads, forwarded jokes, nothing important. He started a pot of coffee and read the AP wires until it was finished. With a fresh cup of caffeine, he checked mail again and got a huge message from joleary@bostonsun.com.

Just as promised, it was dirty.

Larry spent the next few days calling various people, most of them dead and unable to come to the phone. There was no money to do anything in person. Massachusetts was six hours away by jet. But it worked out okay, for an experiment.

Some 2500 words and many pots of coffee later, it was in good enough shape. For Jesús Ramirez, at least. Larry wrote it in a faux-*Esquire* style, circa 1975. Lots of cheap drama and melodramatic prose, exactly the kind of writing he had always avoided. As an appendix, he inserted the scanned police records and court papers sent by O'Leary. Anybody doubting the sordid tale could read the original documents. For decoration, he borrowed many photographs from the MicroTorrent Systems corporate site. Lacking expensive graphical software, he doctored the pictures with his word processor's simple tools: crude devil horns drawn on Sanders, cartoonish ghosts hovering over the headquarters, etc. The effect was primitive and almost funny.

But the story wasn't.

By Jesús Ramirez
SluiceBox.net

MicroTorrent CEO Thomas Sanders has an interesting method for getting patents in his name: he kills the rightful owner.

Sanders says he's going to change everything you think about everything. And he's in the position to do it: an executive helicopter parked next to his typically vulgar McMansion in the swank dusty suburbs of Silicon Valley, servant-refugees from four Latin American wars, not one but three satellite dishes, a paper worth of $284 million, and his hands gripping the reins of a Net-Web-TeeVee monster poised to wreck anybody south of Bill Gates.

Sanders is a big man — a big, fat, crude man. His height does little to disguise the rolls of lard on his torso, which he delights in parading naked around his home, visitors be damned. And his lawyers have a nice system by which journalists are not even allowed to physically describe him.

But what makes the CEO of MicroTorrent Systems truly stand out is that unlike most of his equally amoral contemporaries, Tom Sanders has actually been caught in his epic graft. Nearly three decades ago, when he was an already beefy young computer genius doing undergraduate mathematics work at Harvard, Sanders had a very smart boy sharing his dormitory room.

Dot.Con

    The boy was Gilliard Tyler Seacroft, and he died in the night on October 12, 1962, stuffed into the tiny boot of Sanders' sleek Triumph Roadster, his buttocks crusted with blood from what the coroner's report said was more than a hundred lashes with a bullwhip, his molars jolted loose from being dumped down a Massachusetts hill into a sewage lagoon, his mouth frozen in a final scream forever preserved in the hardened plaster bandaging wrapped tight around his face by his tormentors. Seacroft wanted to join Sanders' fraternity — and gave his life that fall night for the effort. In an Ivy League land of constant, brutal hazing, a Massachusetts homicide detective called Seacroft's death 'the ugliest thing I've ever witnessed'. There was an investigation, but no charges were filed. Frat boys have a way of circling the wagons, and none would dare implicate another. A tragic mistake of youth, nothing more. Sorry about the dead guy.

    Sanders' grief, if there was any, did not stop him from applying for a patent the following Monday. He had the right lawyers, and the paperwork made its way swiftly through the Patent and Trademark Office in Washington, D.C. Less than three months later, Tom Sanders held the rights to a supercomputer memory-stack improvement that would drastically change the way such machines handle tasks, and would help pave the road for a new generation of smaller, faster computers that used half the energy and could fit in a closet — and eventually on a dinner tray in coach class.

    The patent quickly won the attention of International Business Machines, which paid the young undergraduate $1.8 million for the rights in February 1963. An already wealthy boy became not only a millionaire, but a rising star in the world of

1970s technology. Never missing an opportunity, Sanders turned that early windfall and reputation into a series of ever more lucrative positions in the once-desolate industrial/defence valley north of San Jose, California. In time, that nameless patchwork of towns and suburbs between San Francisco and San Jose would become the most famed spot on the business map of Earth, and Sanders would become one of its elder statesmen before he had lived 60 years.

But in the Lowell, Massachusetts, home of the Seacroft family, Sanders was not known as a techno-visionary. He was known as a crook and a killer. The Seacroft family filed suit in civil court just days after Sanders' IBM deal made the local papers. The lawsuit was for patent theft and the wrongful death of their genius geek boy. The family claimed Sanders stole young Seacroft's memory-stack invention, complete and ready for submission as a sophomore computer-science project, and encouraged the fraternity brothers with booze and sadistic weapons when they embarked on the night's hazing. Additionally, the suit claimed Sanders refused to call police — despite the pleading of his drunken cohorts — when young Seacroft lost consciousness after being dragged from the sewage pool. Instead, the family claimed, Sanders personally stuffed his buddy into a canvas laundry sack, forced the still-living body into the trunk of the car, and then rode with the fraternity brothers in another car back to the dormitories, where he finally forced another frat brother into calling police, with instructions to say a Greek stunt had 'gotten out of hand'.

Two local papers gave brief notice to the suit, but there was no coverage when attorneys for Tom Sanders made a settlement sometime in

March 1963. The case never saw a courtroom. Seacroft's parents, who were in their 70s at the time and had adopted Gilliard a few years after their first son drowned during the Lowell flood of 1953, seemed to have little fight left in them. They were old, and they were not especially wealthy, Joseph Seacroft being a mathematics teacher at a small prep school and his wife Gloria being a music teacher who gave private lessons. Certainly, they were of the blood and community stature that can get a child into a fine college, but their riches belonged to ancestors, many of whom went down in the Great Depression.

Both Joseph and Gloria Seacroft are dead now. As is their boy, Gilliard. All three are buried in an Episcopalian cemetery close to where they once lived. There is no one to tend the graves, so all three are a bit overgrown with ivy. Nobody delivers flowers to the humble plots. Tom Sanders has fresh flowers delivered to his generic mansion each and every day.

Of the fraternity brothers with Sanders and Seacroft that October night, only one — Brendan D. Pierce, Jr — is still alive. The rest died in rich-people crashes: a corporate jet crash, an America's Cup crash, a hang-gliding crash and a downhill-ski crash, to be precise.

Pierce, reached at home on Martha's Vineyard where he was recovering from lung-cancer surgery, sounded relieved at being asked about the fate of Gilliard Seacroft. 'So somebody's finally on to Sanders,' Pierce rasped. 'Well, sure he did it — killed that Seacroft kid, I mean. We'd never seen that boy before that night, we just meant to scare him. I remember hearing about the family, the lawsuit, that whole patent thing, then it made sense. Tommy Sanders squirreled out of it, of course. We're born with lawyers around here. I guess I shouldn't talk, but I've already cheated death once this year ...'

9

The next morning, Ramirez' e-mail hit the computers of some 200 editors and reporters in the English-speaking world. Represented amongst the addresses were daily papers, technology magazines (but not *InterWorldNet* magazine), CNBC, Bloomberg, BBC, *The Australian,* Reuters, AP, CNN, MSNBC, *Wired, Newsweek, Time,* the *New Yorker, The Economist, Fortune, Money, Forbes, Red Herring*, the business newsletters, and sundry other publications and news services. About half the addresses were culled from Larry Jonestowne's private stash – colleagues, friends, ex-friends, ex-girlfriends, editors who once fired him – while the others came from the 'Contact Us' pages.

Most of the recipients deleted the message without reading it, but some did not.

> From: Jesús Ramirez (sluice_box@hotmail.com)
> Subject: The Terrible Truth About MicroTorrent's Tom Sanders
>
> Esteemed Colleagues,
>
> Some of them, they are not what they seem. Take Thomas Sanders, chief of MicroTorrent Systems. The man has not only presided over an Empire of Shame, but he is a thief and perhaps a murderer. Of course, you doubt my accusations. I ask only

that you visit http://SluiceBox.net and read the story.

May Our Father Guide You In Your Duties, Jesús Ramirez

Patrick Chapman arrived late to his job at Reuters in Manhattan, thanks to a suicide in front of his train, and found fifty messages waiting. A young graduate of Columbia's journalism school, he was doomed to re-write wire copy and translate stock tables into snappy prose. Chapman sipped his coffee and clicked through the mail, ignoring a note from his mom, a dozen offers to lose weight through revolutionary new programs, three psychotic notes from people who objected to his story regarding lawsuits against pit-bull owners, a dozen forwarded jokes, various CCs from his co-workers, and one strange message from a guy named Jesús – claiming MicroTorrent's kingpin was a murderer. He laughed, but opened the Web page. Anything to delay the day's dull work. He read the tale and printed a hard copy to take to the midday news meeting.

Sarah Richard returned from a pointless news conference closing the MacroNet convention in San Francisco and flopped into her office chair at C|Net's newsroom, exhausted from the walk and the drunken hoots of podiatrists leaving their own convention. She scanned the In-Box, read the message from Jesús, and followed it to the long article on SluiceBox.net and immediately called MicroTorrent's headquarters.

Kip Boer spent three hours drinking whisky at a Brussels tavern and staggered back to his desk at the Dow Jones News Service. That morning, he was told by an editor – a pasty-faced Englishman who spent all his office time viewing

Japanese bondage pornography – that his business stories lacked 'the human factor'. He slumped into his chair and checked e-mail, finding much garbage and one intriguing note from a Mr Ramirez, indicting the star of MicroTorrent Systems for a savage and horrible murder, not to mention intellectual-property theft. He got on the phone and called his old friend O'Leary at the *Boston Sun*.

For the record, the Dow Jones News Service had the first story on the wires, followed closely by Reuters, Bloomberg and the ZDNet Web site. Each clumsily reworked Larry's story into standard Associated Press style. Several versions actually credited one Jesús Ramirez, suddenly known as a 'renegade Internet reporter', for breaking the story. The tech-savvy editors included the URL, www.SluiceBox.net, and a few even got the address right.

(The AP itself wouldn't move the story until that evening, due to a newly enforced policy of first checking the facts – fallout from a recent Urgent Bulletin prematurely announcing Ronald Reagan's death. This was a time-consuming policy. O'Leary, trusted to sift through public records without a clerk watching, had intentionally re-filed the various Sanders documents in the 'T' folders to buy Larry some exclusivity time.)

Some twenty-three hours after the first bits of the tale hit the wires and tech sites, the *New York Times* correspondent in San Jose got an urgent message: 'Why don't we have this? Explanations required; file NOW.'

And three days later, the *Los Angeles Times* bureau chief in Silicon Valley received a similar message from her editor.

10

Tom Sanders flopped over on his substantial belly to sun his back. A Thai boy arrived with a sugary, milky cocktail of iced tea and a bowl of sweet oranges in custard. Sanders grumbled and tried to get his big head comfortable on the beach chair, already stressed to the point of collapse. This trip was going to hell. His young companion begged off at the last minute, citing a business situation. There were always business situations. He was bored.

The Khmer Retreat resort, an hour north of Bangkok on a gorgeous fine-sand beach, had invested millions to make the modern executive comfortable. A small forest of satellite dishes behind the compound delivered news and entertainment and direct-satellite links for the computers. A huge health spa took up half the resort, with the latest electronic exercise devices, lap pools, mud baths, squadrons of traditionally clad Thai girls to pound the flesh on Italian marble massage tables under thatched roofing, a *Business Traveller* award-winning restaurant with a four-star chef lured from the most expensive and therefore most famous Los Angeles Pacific-fusion kitchen, and a team of former Thai intelligence agents serving as a private army for the paranoid CEOs who frequented the place.

Sanders grunted as he rolled himself again, this time to try to read. Problem was, he didn't like books. Other than software manuals and corporate reports and the business page, he didn't read. Anything other than business news seemed irrelevant to him, boring and useless. He tossed the volume into the sand, Hemingway or something from the resort's library, and rose. Time for lunch, although it would technically be his third lunch today, not including one mammoth breakfast and a bigger brunch.

Before he reached his 2000-square-foot bungalow, a boy ran up and breathlessly said, 'Mista Sandah, you got conference call!'

Sanders spat and followed the boy to the Business Centre. The hostess, in an elaborate silk gown and thick straw flip-flops, led him to the biggest of the meeting rooms. A bank of teevees hung from the ceiling, with one giant screen at the foot of the long table. Sanders was led to the huge wicker chair at the opposite end. The woman pushed a button to raise the console, which contained a miniature video camera, a keyboard, and a small condenser microphone. He asked to have his next meal brought to the room.

On the big screen, MicroTorrent president Harris Taft, a fit man of forty-one, appeared from his office at headquarters. He was dressed in a polo shirt bearing the company logo and khakis, and he looked troubled.

'Tom? You hear me?'

On Taft's monitor was what appeared to be a gigantic pink Elephant Seal with tiny red eyes.

'Yeah, go ahead Harry. What is it? I'm trying to take a vacation for God's sake.'

'I know, I know. Sorry to disturb – '

'Goddamned doctors say my heart's going to stop if I don't rest now and then. Told me to eat this rabbit food.'

'Yes, Tom, sorry to bother you. We have, ah, a business situation.'

Another business situation. This trip was going to hell.

'I'm listening.'

'Some, ah, well I don't know how to tell you this so I'll just tell you.' Taft picked up the *San Jose Mercury News* and displayed the front page. 'I don't know if you can see this –

it's all being faxed over right now – but the press has some crazy story about you ... ah, it's about some patent you apparently sold to IBM in the sixties, and a lawsuit filed by the family of a kid you roomed with, at Harvard. A kid who died, family claimed he invented the memory-stack patent and ... ah, Tom, it looks kind of bad. We're taking a beating.'

Sanders felt the sweat trickling down his flabby arms. He looked at the bank of teevees and saw, on CNBC, his photo suspended next to the announcer. Taft continued, but Sanders was watching the ticker at the bottom of the business-news screen. There it was: MicroTnt, -12_.

'We still going down?'

'Huh? The price, yes Tom, it seems to be going down. We're trying to get a freeze.'

'Who did this?' There was a remarkable calm to Sanders, Taft thought. A remarkable concern for the company. Anybody else would take this pretty rough – patent theft? And maybe a murder?

'Ah, well, we're working on that. It made all the wires, Tom, and it made the Journal this morning. And it's all over cable, and it's the top story on Bloomberg right now. We have to say something quick, Tom. I'm afraid you need to get back here.'

'I asked you who did this.' Taft saw the Thai woman deliver a huge platter to Sanders. It looked like a buffet for a dozen people. Sanders began feeding off a plate of fried spring rolls.

'Well, Tom, obviously we're working on it. See, it's just some crazy Web site. I don't know how anybody even found it. Just this one long crazy thing, with scans of these police reports from, what is it? 1963 or something. The New York lawyers are on their way to Boston right now. I'm sure it's just some crazy nonsense, right Tom?'

'Find out who put this crap on the Web. Get the guys on it, now.'

The guys. MicroTorrent Systems' corporate espionage goons. Contracted from Business Intelligence Partner Services in Menlo Park. Started in 1985 by a former CIA section chief and manned by everybody from Air America pilots to 'military advisers' who overthrew Caribbean governments for sport, the firm was notorious for overlooking any law to stop a leak, silence a disgruntled employee, or disable a competing tech company's R&D – especially if that research-and-development operation involved a product similar to the client firm's specialty. An executive only called BIPS in *extreme* emergencies, for very specific assignments, as the last thing a CEO wanted was a bunch of amoral corporate spies sifting through his secret plans.

'We're considering that, yes. We have to be careful with those guys. You know what they did to us on the Oracle thing.' When Sanders hired BIPS to bug the phones and sift the dumpsters for anything on Oracle's network-PC project, they got wind of it and hired BIPS to counter-spy – which wasn't revealed until Oracle released a network-PC nearly identical to the one being developed by MicroTorrent.

'Screw Oracle. I'll leave in the morning. Have Sandy get my flight arranged.'

Taft nodded and watched with concern as Sanders tore into his next plate of food.

'Ah, Tom? This is a bunch of garbage, right?'

''Course it is,' Sanders said through a mouthful of Shrimp Pad Thai.

'Because, well, heh heh … I don't need to tell *you* this, but we've lost about $150 million this morning.'

'We lost more in March. It came back.'

'Right. Okay, I'll see you tomorrow. We'll get this straightened out, right Tom?'

Sanders ended the video conference and slammed the table console back into its hole. He grabbed three shrimps and sucked them into his mouth, staring at the gentle waves outside, the greasy little shrimp tails locked between his fingers.

11

Terrance Copeland trudged through the dirty New York slush hours after he was supposed to be home. The cab dropped him a block away, due to the snow. He wrapped his scarf tighter around his neck and stomped along the Gramercy Park fence to his building, just a few yards from the gated refuge. Waiting at home were two ridiculously expensive reds he had bought at a Christmas auction, but it seemed terrible to drink those alone when he was already drunk. Fuck it, he thought. I'm rich.

The flight back from San Francisco had been dismal. Which made sense, since it was a United flight. There was the usual two-hour delay – 'Weather,' the agent said, despite beautiful clear skies that would make a San Franciscan dance with joy. They finally got him on a flight, in coach. He tried to relax in his tiny seat and suffered as the jet sat on the runway for another hour: no cocktails until the captain has turned off the no-drinking light. Then, three hours into the flight, the real lies began. Something at Kennedy – monsters, fog, poison sleet – possible trouble, we'll get you there as soon as possible folks, sit back and enjoy your flight. A mysterious landing in Indianapolis, sixty-three minutes grounded, no drinks and no exit, we'll get you back in the sky as soon as possible folks, so we won't be going to a gate, then a sudden takeoff, lighting thrashing the DC-10, we're all out of Chivas Regal I'm terribly sorry sir. The plane circled New York for an hour and finally landed in New Jersey. Terrance waited in the cold for a taxi with all the other furious United passengers. Finally got one – fifty bucks to Manhattan, not including a friendly tip.

He yanked the clotted mail from the lobby box and took the stairs to his flat and parked his suitcase. It was a fine place, for New York, but it disturbed him to pay $1650 a month for a studio. And not even a key to the fabled private park. He cranked up the radiators and rubbed his hands together. A fire would be nice tonight. Too bad about not having a fireplace. He slid into the coffin-sized kitchen, considered calling Sushi Boy for dinner delivery, and took the 1978 Bordeaux from the special shelf. Turned on his Macintosh PowerBook on the miniature coffee table and searched the pillows for the remote. He put on CNBC out of habit and checked e-mail while uncorking the famous wine. Multi-tasking, they call it.

It was a repeat of the closing-stocks program, for the Wall Street stragglers who took a happy hour and never came back. The announcer, who dealt with business news like a sports anchor, was jabbering about a scandal in Silicon Valley. Terrance filled his glass and took a moment to enjoy the bouquet. Hint of oak and raspberry and four hundred bucks.

The sports/stock announcer was now jabbering with one of the many analysts always ready to take the desk: 'And you know, Gary, this is exactly the danger of this new medium – especially dangerous if you're a business leader with something to hide.'

'Thomas Sanders must be feeling a little ambivalent tonight about this new medium he's championed for the past five years.'

'That's right, Gary, and Thomas Sanders may be the first

of many executives who find their Wall Street fame is a magnet for this kind of ... Well, for lack of a better term, let's call it *media outside the media.*'

Christ, Terrance thought. That's certainly for lack of a better term.

'There's quite a lot of speculation about the journalist — if he's even a journalist — who posted these charges, isn't there, Lou?'

'Oh yes. Silicon Valley is absolutely buzzing today. I mean, this has already gone far beyond a business story. A Boston paper is planning to report tomorrow that the Massachusetts attorney general is actually looking into this case, if it is a case, and considering an inquiry. This looks very bad for MicroTorrent.'

'It certainly does, Lou. MicroTorrent Systems is down seventeen-and-a-half as the closing bell rings, and that has got to have investors worried. The era of the celebrity tech executive may have claimed its first victim. And speaking of victims, commodities were hurt early today as profit-takers — '

Terrance hit the mute button. Something stank. The New Mail flag popped up on his laptop and he scanned the messages. The most recent was from Ian McWhorter, the systems guy at InnerKnife. The subject wasn't good: SANDERS THING ON OUR SERVERS???

To: Terrance Copeland (tcopeland@innerknife.com)
From: Ian McWhorter (ian@innerknife.com)

Terrance — Servers crashed this morning. I checked from home and saw 40,000 hits in an hour. We're not set up for that. I traced the traffic, and it's all going to something in YOUR directory. It's this MicroTorrent Sanders thing all over the news. What is this doing here? Plz tell me somebody hacked us. Call me at home. Best, Ian

43

No ... The Sanders puff piece in the magazine ... Jonestowne. Terrance got his cordless and dialled San Francisco.

'Yeah.'

'Goddammit, that's your Sanders story.'

'Terrance? You back in New York?'

'You put that thing on *my* company's server? You broke the servers, psycho. Forty-thousand hits in *one hour.*'

'You told me to put it there. You gave me all the passwords and whatever.'

Terrance gulped his auction wine and cried, 'You want to get me sued?'

'Of course not. Nobody knows where it is; it's all billed to a, uh, fictional person.'

'It's on *my* server ... on *my* credit card. You don't know how any of this works, do you? Never mind, I don't care. It's off my server as of now. I did *not* give you permission to put that on my company's machines. You understand that, right?'

Laughter on the line. 'Sure, you know nothing.'

'You're goddamned right I know nothing. As far as I'm concerned, and you're concerned, InnerKnife was hacked. I never made this phone call. I don't know you.'

'Relax – '

Terrance hung up and dialled Ian.

'Hullo?'

'Ian, Terrance here. I don't know what the hell happened. Well, yeah, I know we got hacked, but I don't know why he ... they ... hooked it to my directory. Get rid of it.'

'Yeah, I did that an hour ago, after you didn't call.'

'My flight was delayed. United.'

'You want me to call the FBI?'

Terrance stared at the teevee screen: it was filled with a shot of the Sanders hit piece on the Web. From *his* Web server. Wasn't there any other news today?

'No, don't worry about that. I'll take care of that in the

morning ... I mean, I already called them, from the plane. The airplane phone. Change everybody's password. They can get the new ones in person tomorrow.'

'No problem. The weird thing is, I don't see any evidence of a break-in. Whoever got through got through on the first try, with your login. Four days ago.'

'Probably that Kevin Mitnick.'

'Isn't he in jail?'

'I'll see you in the morning.'

Terrance drained the bottle and fell asleep on the couch.

Larry heard the phone go dead and placed the handset in the cradle. He had just returned from the Salvadoran take-out place on the corner at Fillmore and checked Jesús' mailbox downstairs. A letter from Chase Manhattan. Expecting a politely worded refusal, he took it inside and slit the envelope with his Swiss Army knife.

> Dear Mr Ramirez,
>
> Thank you for applying for the Chase MAGIC GOLD Visa®. Unfortunately, that card is reserved for our customers with higher incomes and a more established credit rating.
>
> However, you do qualify for our premium MAGIC STANDARD Visa®, at a low introductory A.P.R. of 18.9%, and we have issued a card in your name which will arrive in the next three business days. The MAGIC STANDARD Visa® features many of the benefits of the MAGIC GOLD Visa®, with a generous credit limit of $5000 and a low annual fee of $39, which is waived if you transfer the balance of another card ...

He dropped the letter atop the day's business sections and smiled. This was getting interesting. Time to take care of the

Web server problem. Time to see if Werner actually knows anything.

''ello?'

'Yeah, it's me. I need some technological expertise. You busy?'

'Not really. Thinkin' about dinner.'

'Well come over, we'll figure it out.'

Larry hung up and went to the kitchen desk. Checked his advertising statistics online. Somehow, he – or Mr Ramirez – was already due $2231.29 in banner-advertisement revenue, subject to end-of-month auditing, of course. In less than three days. Amazing. Nobody was supposed to make money from Web ads. Then again, he had no overheads.

He typed SluiceBox.net in the browser and the '404 Not Found' error appeared on his screen. Nervous Terrance.

The Hotmail account had 219 new messages. One from O'Leary, claiming credit for everything. Scrolling down, he saw the first few dozen were from various media concerns, followed by several legal-looking messages, then a long batch of e-mails from ... Well, mostly from other Hotmail accounts. He opened a few and became giddy.

From: cubicle_loser@hotmail.com
Subject: pointcrash.com CEO is coke fiend

Dear Jesus,
I think you shoud know about my boss Gerald Tompkins who is a KNOWN COCAINE ADDICT and has a Black Guy who brings him COCAINE each day to his office. The guys name is Hasbro and he drives in a red mustang ....

From: pearljam97@hotmail.com
Subject: stolen software

Mr Ramirez: I apologize for this anonymous

message but SoftBack Industries uses *all* stolen software, in total violation of the software-piracy laws. They buy *one* copy of Word or Excel or PhotoShop and install it individually on each desktop computer ...

From: xena_princess@hotmail.com
Subject: tim murphy is convicted rapist!

Hi Jesus, just want to say I love your website and tim murphy who is ceo at terrawhirl microsystem is convicted rapist i know this because he tried to rape me and i called the police and then his lawyers give me 10,000 dollars so i would not tell the police and ...

The bell rang and Larry buzzed Werner inside.
''ello matey.'
'Hey there. Here, sit down.' Larry got up and, like a gentleman, took off Werner's jacket and took the wallet from the side pocket.
'What's this about?'
'Don't worry. You look thirsty. I'll treat you to a thousand drinks next month.'
'Won't hold me breath.'
'Meanwhile, here's the problem. This little Web site I started? Well, it's getting a hundred-thousand hit buddies a day.'
Werner twirled in the chair to face Larry.
''ow's that?'
'A scandal of some kind. The papers are in the other room, everything's documented. But I got kicked off Terrance's Web server – his company's computer, I guess. You need to find me some place to put it. And have some offshore credit card take over the domain, quick.'

Werner nodded. 'You want to keep certain people from knowing where it is, eh?'

'That's the idea. Put it in Afghanistan, the Democratic Republic of Congo, on Mars, anywhere out of the way. What to drink?'

Werner answered 'Booze' and spun back to the machine. Larry trotted down the stairs, stopping at his own mailbox to remove the 'L. JONESTOWNE' tag. For safety. When he returned, Werner was typing nonsense at a high rate of speed. Larry uncorked the red and filled both coffee mugs.

'Here you go. Find anything?'

'Ah, lovely wine.' Werner reached into his jacket pocket and pulled out a rolled copy of *InterWorldNet* magazine. 'Almost forget your cover story. It's got a truly cruel thing on poor Kevin Mitnick, as well.'

'Who?'

'Don't you follow this stuff at all?'

'It's not my story.'

Werner's nail-polished fingers handed over the new issue of *InterWorldNet*. There was a horrible airbrushed photo of Sanders on the cover, little teevee things with fiber-optic wires orbiting around his gut, the headline 'Why Tom Sanders Will Change Your Life', something about 'The World's Worst Hacker', 'Wiring Africa', the usual crap.

Larry took a gulp of wine and flipped past fifteen pages of colour advertisements for various dot.coms he'd never heard of, all burning through their investment money and certain to never see next year except at an assets sale. Finally, the contents page. He shuffled through sixty more pages, found another huge picture of Sanders. Larry read a few words in the tiny futuristic font and tossed the magazine on the desk.

'How's it?' Werner asked.

'Terrible, as expected.'

The German retrieved the magazine and said, 'Listen to this.'

'No thanks – '

'"An elder statesman of Silicon Valley already knows your future, by Denisa Moss. His hands on the controls of the new century's entertainment, business and shopping desires, MicroTorrent Systems chief Tom Sanders not only has one of the most enviable positions in the Way-New Economy, he also has the total respect of everyone from the White House technology office to the titans of Wall Street. In the case of Tom Sanders, believe the hype …".'

Larry swiped the magazine and tossed it out the kitchen window, raining chaos on the rat city below. 'About my technical problem?'

'Yeah, I've an idea. Some Swiss guys I know, they've set up an operation on Tonga or something. For Internet gambling. What's that Al Gore used to say?'

'No controlling legal authority. Wonderful.'

Larry sat on the edge of the door-desk and watched Werner do his shady magic. The Swiss were actually Germans living in Zurich, it turned out, originally from Werner's own village near the border. Werner chatted with them in a little window and they seemed happy to provide the space … if Larry would put a small ad-button at the bottom of his pages directing visitors to the International Sport Book Casino.

'All rightie, then. It'll take the usual day for the DNS servers to record the change, then you'll be back online.'

'Whatever you say,' said Larry. 'What's your fee?'

'You could buy the drinks for once. There any cash in this racket?'

Larry pointed Werner to the FlyRight Advertising window.

'Bollocks! That's not bad money.'

'That's after they take a 40 per cent commission. We'll lose a bit with the changeover, but I figure Monday will be really nice, when all the newsweeklies hit the stands.'

'And for your next trick?'

'I'll need a volunteer. Luckily, I seem to have a few candidates.' Larry opened the Hotmail window and went through a couple of tips from disgruntled employees.

'Brilliant! Let's celebrate.'

'Well, I won't see any cheques for another month.'

'I'll bill you.'

Werner flagged a taxi, stuffed Larry inside, and asked for the Brazen Head.

The cab stopped at the Fillmore light, the intersection blocked by a silver BMW. There was honking and yelling while a skinny black kid ran from the flophouse doorway on the northeast corner next to the Salvadoran café, pulling two tiny heroin balloons from his mouth and grabbing the folded twenties, more honking as the light turned green, with the No. 71 bus stalled, its driver outside brandishing a pole, reconnecting the metal stalks to the electric lines above. A crack addict staggered between cars and a stray dog got smacked by a Miata. It wasn't unique enough to get a comment from the cab driver.

North on Fillmore and through the shoddy malls of Japantown, they were suddenly in the Rich Neighbourhood, scraping the Marina District, with buildings of the same style as the slums, but gilded and clean, $70-haircut joints, African art, sushi. The cab stopped and Werner showed his usual affinity for the working class with a 30 per cent tip. Yuppies were crowded around the Brazen Head's door and Werner moved through them, slipping a twenty to the host.

They were led to a nice table by the stained-glass window. Werner whispered to the host, 'When you can, two vodka martinis, extra dry and don't skimp on the olives.'

The host nodded, smiling.

'How'd you do that?'

'Cashed a nice consultant cheque today. Shared a bit of it with our man here.'

Menus and martinis were delivered with a flourish. Werner studied the fare.

'I heartily recommend the Petite Filet Mignon, rare, and the Dungeness crab cakes with the pepper oil.'

'Fine.'

'S'pose we need a decent wine?'

The order was made, a Shiraz demanded, and salads with *bleu* cheese appeared on the red cloth. Eating silently, generic jazz on the sound system, they worked through the greasy crab slabs, then the plump little steaks, seared and bloody and delicious. Buttered broccoli beside them. Warm sourdough bread. Another bottle. Whisky for dessert.

Full and drunk, slurping coffee, Larry said, 'I'm feeling like a little vandalism tonight.'

'What sort of vandalism?'

'Something ... Luddite. Maybe pay a visit to the editorial offices of a certain magazine that likes to ruin me.'

'Seems unwise. Why don't we just keep drinking?'

12

Darren Borman and Scott Charlton were scared and tired from the long walk from the BART station on Market Street, through spooky warehouse districts and dark freeway underpasses. They weren't used to the city, and the street people seemed menacing. Especially the one who raised his arms like King Kong and threatened to eat the brains out of Darren's split skull.

Both were seventeen, both from the dusty suburb of Walnut Creek, a stucco grid of ranch-style family houses a good thirty miles east of San Francisco. While proficient at maths and fanatical players of computer games, they were hardly hackers. Yet they greatly admired those trouble-causing geeks. Since he was fourteen, Darren had courted the local hackers through Web bulletin boards and e-mail, but they ignored his pleas to join the cause. He read the encryption and security debates in the tech magazines and breathlessly followed the chase of Kevin Mitnick, a hacker so infamous that the *New York Times* assigned a reporter to his capture. Now a gawky six feet tall, skinny, somewhat prone to acne and cursed with a squeaky voice, Darren loved the hackers specifically because they seemed just as socially doomed. But they were famous and powerful, and many of them achieved this notoriety from suburban bedrooms just like his. Scott, for his part, didn't know a whole hell of a lot about hacking, not even from the media. But in the Darwinistic world of high school, he was even lower than Darren: bumbling, barely 5 feet 6 inches and unlikely to shed his alleged baby fat unless a famine hit northern California. He generally did whatever Darren thought was clever.

To become true hackers would change their lives. Although they hadn't worked out the particulars, Darren knew to achieve this status was one of the only ways to be different in an acceptably Bay Area fashion – and one of the only rebellions available to straight white suburban high-school boys equally scared of drugs and violence.

Darren saw the angry computer messages about the new Mitnick article. The hackers were calling for a full assault on *InterWorldNet* magazine, to teach those media yuppies to treat Kevin with more respect. Lacking the skills to even break into his sister's computer, Darren convinced Scott they should vandalize the magazine's physical offices, maybe do some computer damage once they were inside. When the news broke, they could honestly claim a part in the phreak revolution, using their cyber codenames. Darren was sW0rdph1sH and Scott was p1NGw3n, which wasn't exactly his choice. They picked up the new issue at the 7-11 while walking to the BART station. The address was right there in the magazine: 24 S. Park St.

'What's it look like?' Scott asked, squinting for addresses. The fog was settling in. Fog was rare in Walnut Creek.

'I don't know, idiot, I've never been here.' Darren would have to lead the way. An architecture firm, an art gallery, a Web design shop, a coffee place.

'Look, it's MacroTek!'

'Keep it down!' Darren hissed. Somebody was moving in the park, maybe another crazy homeless person. They rushed back to the sidewalk. And there it was. *InterWorldNet* Media Ventures, fourth floor. How to get inside? They hadn't planned this very well. A security guard was in the lobby, reading or something.

'Shit,' Darren said.

'What do we do?'

'Give me a minute ... he sees us!'

The guard seemed to look up for an instant, but the boys were too far from the lobby's light for him to register anything. They backed deeper into the fog, Scott tripping on the curb, and retreated to the frightening strip of park.

The cab headed toward South Park. Werner slurred, 'What's the point, again?'

They got out and walked through the wind and fog, nobody around at 12:30 a.m. except a few bums collecting cans from the trash bins.

'Really, now, what're we doing here?'

'Dunno,' Larry said. 'I forgot they're on the fourth floor.'

The *InterWorldNet* suite was in a standard old building with the standard designer retrofitting. Werner jabbed Larry in the ribs and whispered, 'Who's that?'

Two kids jumped out from behind a park bench, one of them ringing the night buzzer and the other hiding behind the potted palm tree. The security guard rose from his desk, sullen and sleepy.

'What's the trouble?' he yelled through the glass.

'They're busting in!' Darren shouted, not needing to fake his fear. 'Stealing the servers, computer stuff!'

'Where?'

'In the alley!'

The gangly kid ran around the corner with the rent-a-cop, as the squat one jolted out from the huge potted plants, stumbling inside the door before it electronically bolted shut. A minute later, the tall one was back, buzzed in by his partner. On the fourth floor, the fluorescent lights blinked on and what seemed to be a wrestling match began.

'Don't believe this,' Werner said. 'Boys have beaten you to it.'

'Balls. They're not vandals, they're just burglars.'

An SFPD car rolled up, lights flashing, and Werner and Larry ducked behind the park bench. They watched for a few minutes, hiding their lit cigarettes. The kids must have left through the back. Not a good move. A quartet of uniformed cops came around the corner with the kids in handcuffs.

Larry and Werner took the long way up to Bryant Street.

'Let's take a bus, right? Got whisky at home.'

'Yeah, that sounds fine.'

It was almost 1:00 a.m. and they were forced to take the Nite Owl line, five stops to Werner's block.

'Satisfied with the evening?'

'The steak was nice. But what the hell were those kids doing? That was *my* vandalism.'

'Told you, matey. Your magazine did a mean thing on Mitnick, king of the hackers. Retribution from the disciples.'

'It's not my magazine. I've started my own, remember?'

13

Thick haze over the eyes. And brain. Where was he? Right, at Werner's lousy studio apartment. The German snored a few feet away. Larry was on the couch, both boots secure, necktie tail looped around his sweaty neck. He sat up, slowly, careful with the cerebral damage. Everything in moderation.

Nothing in the fridge, not even coffee. Ice and vodka in the freezer. Sink full of horrors. Larry found a dubious dishcloth, turned on cold water, closed his eyes and made five quick splashes on the face. Stand tall, he ordered himself, swallow that vomit, be a pro. Better now. Better all the time. He considered sitting down and reversing socks, but that seemed an unnecessary gamble. Outside, he bashed the top of his skull on Werner's midget basement door. He kicked one of those yellowed free community newspapers into the doorway to keep it open. Give a hoot, don't pollute.

At the corner market, he purchased bottled coffee beverages and cigarettes and grapefruit juice and the *Chronicle*, but lacked the concentration to read while walking. He stepped back into Werner's musty cube and threw a small bottle of Donald Duck grapefruit juice at the German's head.

'Wanker!'

'Brought you a little bucket of healthy living. Drink it.'

'Get coffee?'

'Only these processed buddies.'

Larry opened the one window, over Werner's head, and sucked in the allegedly fresh air. The paper was hopeless. Downhill ever since Herb Caen croaked. Downhill twenty years before that. The front page featured an interest-rate cut, a plane crash somewhere, and down below the damning headline: 'Web Magazine Raided; Cyber-Terrorists Blamed.'

'Whoops.'

'What's that?'

'Listen.' Larry turned to the jump on page A-17:

```
Two suspects were arrested outside the office
building, police say. Darren Borman and Scott
Charlton, both 17-year-old seniors at Walnut
Creek High School, reportedly confessed to the
vandalism and break-in immediately after their
arrest and several times after being brought into
custody. The self-described 'cyber terrorists'
claimed to be part of a worldwide movement to
protest the parole conditions of infamous hacker
Kevin Mitnick, police said.
   The suspects would only identify themselves
as 'Swordfish and Penguin', police said, but were
revealed by school IDs found in their wallets.
   InterWorldNet editor LaRouche Melville, speak-
ing at a news conference outside his vandalized
headquarters this morning, said the hackers were
'misguided youth who do not comprehend the
fantastic opportunities of the super-new econ-
omy' and said his company would sue the boys'
families for damages.
```

14

The last-minute requirement for a flight meant Sanders had to take Singapore Airlines to Honolulu and then transfer to United, which led to the usual delays. He could've taken Thai Airways straight to SFO, if he would have – or could have – fitted into a coach seat.

In Honolulu's United Red Carpet club, Sanders called MicroTorrent. Had the site been shut down?

'Well, Tom, sort of,' Taft said over the speakerphone. Two of the goons were in his office, listening to his every word, along with MicroTorrent's chief counsel. 'It seems, well, it seems the original site was hosted on a consulting firm's machine in New York.'

'What? Sue them. Put a Writ of Seizure on the bastards. Who are they?'

'Nobody we know of. They put out a statement on Internet Wire this morning saying they'd been hacked. They're just a nothing consulting firm, Tom. They don't even deal in our business. It's, hell, it's four guys, none of them over thirty-five. They make Web sites and billing systems for small businesses. We've hunted down all their contracts – they don't even make their own software, let alone compete in the interactive-television market.'

'I want everything on all of them. Maybe one of these punks ... So it's offline, at least.'

'Well ... no. It's back, in the last hour or so. We can't trace the IP address. Must be offshore somewhere.'

'Call Network Solutions then! Stop it.'

'We tried that, Tom. Network Solutions has, what'd they

say? Right, here it is, "no controlling legal authority over the content of sites registered. Network Solutions provides Domain Name Server information for its clients under federal law and international treaties – "'

'You tell me we can't stop a *slanderous* Web site from staying online?'

'No. Well, actually ....'

'Mr Sanders? This is Byron Addis, your assistant chief counsel here at MicroTorrent Systems? And one problem we're having, beyond the physical jurisdiction of the Web server, regards the alleged libel and/or slander contained within said Web pages.'

'Get to the point,' Sanders growled.

'Well, Mr Sanders, there is some unflattering insinuation within the description of the public records, but our team's come back from Massachusetts, and the documents described and exhibited by the, er, journalist ... The documents are public record, sir. Rather ancient public record, if I might say, but ...'

The loudspeaker above Sanders' head blurted something about the delayed flight to San Francisco now boarding.

'I've got to get on my plane,' Sanders said. 'When I get to headquarters, I want to hear a lot less of this kind of bullshit.'

'Ah, Tom? Harry Taft here. The, ah, board met this morning, and ... Well, we'd like it if you didn't come straight to headquarters. Obviously, we have shareholder concerns to address, and the problem of these media people and their cameras all around the perimeter of the property, and, well, the board has decided that you're not to come onsite until further notice.'

'What? You don't tell *me* what to do with *my* company.'

'With, ah, all due respect and whatnot, the board runs the company, not me ... and, ah, not you. We're doing our best to put this behind us, Tom. I'd appreciate you not making this more difficult on me. We'll speak soon … have a safe trip.'

Sanders left the lounge and went to the gate. He tried to relax; some garbage from a quarter-century ago was not going to ruin Thomas Sanders. The guys would take care of it. The guys always took care of things. MicroTorrent had been through more than a hundred intellectual-property lawsuits and had smashed through every one as a winner, or at least as a non-loser, thanks to hefty settlements and silence agreements. He boarded and took his aisle seat and reached for a glass of champagne from the stewardess' tray. As he turned to grab the drink, across the aisle he spotted Josh Cavanaugh from SysTechno and waved. 'Heya Josh!'

Cavanaugh frowned and turned to the window. In his lap was yesterday's *Financial Times*, with a front-page box all about Thomas Sanders' fraternity days.

15

Over coffee they'd discussed the implications of this new venture. The implications were good, if a little dangerous. Werner paid for a cab home and Larry had a few hours' decent sleep.

By noon the street noises woke him. It took another two hours for him to go downstairs for the *New York Times*, mercifully still sitting on the porch in its blue home-delivery condom. He drew a hot bath, put Bach on the boombox and poured a cup of coffee. Submerged in the clawfoot tub, he flipped through the news pages without paying much attention to the latest Washington chaff and then focused on the business section. There was a front-page brief in the left-hand column, saying the Massachusetts attorney general was scheduled to make a statement early next week regarding the Thomas Sanders affair. See page B-4.

A Web Site Renews Interest in a Harvard Death:
MicroTorrent's Sanders Could Face Charges
By FELICITY DENTON

BOSTON — A 25-year veteran of Silicon Valley may face criminal or civil charges regarding the death of Gilliard Tyler Seacroft, the apparent victim of a fraternity hazing accident in 1962.

Thomas Sanders, CEO of MicroTorrent Systems, is being investigated by the Massachusetts Attorney General's office in response to a Web page — and the resulting media coverage — that claims to detail Mr Sanders' involvement in the death of his Harvard roommate. Attorney General Ronald Callaghan said today his office would soon make a decision on whether to re-examine the incident.

Also at issue is an alleged patent theft raised by Mr Seacroft's parents shortly after the death — and shortly after Mr Sanders made a lucrative licensing agreement with International Business Machines Corp. for a type of computer-memory patent the Seacroft family claimed in court was the invention of their late son.

Complicating the investigation, sources close to Mr Callaghan said today, is the fact that Mr Seacroft and his parents are deceased, as are many of the judges, police officers and university officials who took part in the shrouded proceedings of 1963. Attorneys for IBM and Micro-Torrent Systems arrived in Boston yesterday to review the old documents.

Scores of media reports regarding Mr Sanders' alleged involvement in the affair and the result-

> ing concern among investors have battered Micro-Torrent stock, which closed at $42 today, down $26 since the Web site gained attention early this week. MicroTorrent had been among the few stocks to avoid this year's NASDAQ turmoil.
>
> Among the bigger mysteries in this case is the self-proclaimed journalist who made the charges public in a crudely illustrated article posted to a Web site, www.sluicebox.net. Identifying himself as 'Jesús Ramirez', the writer has remained silent since alerting reporters to the site by e-mail …

He soaked until the water grew lukewarm, shaved, brushed his teeth, and dressed in clean khakis, an old Izod tennis shirt and war boots. While headed downstairs for a dollar cup of coffee, Larry checked his alter-ego's mailbox and found a thick yellow envelope bearing a P.O. Box return address from New Jersey – two days early. And a thick plastic envelope from Wells Fargo. And another yellow envelope, also from Wells Fargo. He took these up to the kitchen desk and reviewed the contents: a Chase MAGIC STANDARD Visa® (the letter inside stated that a cash-advance chequebook would arrive in the regular three business days), a batch of Wells Fargo cheques for Mr Ramirez, and an ATM card. Not quite financial independence; he needed a way to get money off the credit card, and the Personal Identification Number would arrive by separate envelope. No matter. His own Bank of America account contained another hundred bucks. It no longer seemed an emergency fund.

To think that speed-freak Mexican drag-queen hadn't managed to ruin his credit. Poor bastard didn't live long enough to realize the American Dream.

Feeling slightly paranoid, Larry got online and found a local ISP he'd heard about from Werner: Anonymous-

Web.net, specially formulated for criminals, $14.95 a month. It promised to scramble his Web browsing, e-mailing, whatever one does with a computer. Mr Ramirez signed right up with his new MAGIC STANDARD Visa®, which would help build a healthy credit record. Larry wasn't sure exactly how, but he figured MicroTorrent's people might want to find Jesús. And crucify his ass.

He walked to the Safeway and withdrew sixty bucks from the cashier, along with two packs of Camel Lights. Life was good again.

Strolling through the Mission, hurling a friendly *Buenas Tardes* at the Mexican schoolgirls headed home, it seemed time to finally get that meal at Puerto Alegre.

'Tell me you've got the shrimp soup.'

'We've got a big pot,' the waiter said. 'It's your lucky day.'

'Good. All right, could I get some coffee and a big glass of ice water, and a margarita with the soup? And a bunch of corn tortillas?'

The coffee was fine, the chips and salsa were better, and both the final-edition *Chronicle* and *Examiner* sucked. Except for the stories about Jesús Ramirez and Tom Sanders. The *Chronicle* now said Sanders had arrived back in San Francisco, following an aborted vacation in Thailand. Several reporters met him at the gate and were brushed away by MicroTorrent security, who took Sanders home in one of the company's black-windowed SUVs. The soup arrived, beautiful shrimp swimming in a tongue-burning red broth, loaded with garlic and onions and health. And then the margarita, a big glass of delicious lime juice and tequila on the rocks, the perfect breakfast cocktail.

Suzie stomped in, spotted Larry in the window booth and sat down beside him.

'I knew I'd find you here.'

'I'm happy right now. Don't hurt me.'

'Don't be stupid. Listen, we're going to a rave in the desert.'

'Good luck.'

'No, listen! You have to come with us. I've got drugs and liquor. Werner's waiting on the corner. All you've got to do is rent us a camper-van.'

'How's that?'

'Werner says you've got money now.'

'Hardly. I've got a credit card.' He ate another spoonful of shrimp and said, 'A *rave*? Do I look like somebody who goes to raves?'

'It's in the desert, stupid! You love the desert.'

'Not with people on it.'

'It'll be fun!'

Larry considered his obligations, realized he had none, and lifted a spoonful of shrimp soup to Suzie's lovely lips.

'We don't go 'til the soup's gone. These shrimp died for your sins.'

Larry fed half the remaining *caldo de camarones* to the Soviet, finished the rest by tipping the bowl to his mouth like a common swine, and left $13 on the table, for good luck. 'Perfect as always, Felix,' he called to the waiter. Felix smiled and nodded, mostly at Suzie.

They ended up in Daly City with an awful motorhome. Not particularly big, but of very recent vintage. Werner and Suzie thought it was fantastic. Larry wondered if he should make some American friends. Investigate the soft bigotry of lowered expectations.

It was one of those huge parties in the Nevada desert. Larry sunned himself on the camper-van's roof to avoid contact with the hippies below.

There were thousands of them, dancing half-naked in the afternoon dust, turning red from the sun and green from the body-painting booths, clumsily dancing to the combined sounds of cars, motorcycles and a hundred overlapping techno records. He tried to read yesterday's newspaper but the wind and the sand and the exhaust fumes were winning.

His kidnappers were under the camper's retractable awning, drinking margaritas and jabbering in Eurotrash Esperanto: mostly English, with bits of French and Spanish and their own guttural tongues. He folded the paper and climbed down the ladder. Despite the heat, Werner was in his regular Keith Richards' costume of leather and frayed Levis and sneakers. He reached for the blender and poured a drink for Larry.

'Given up on the roof, have you?'

'It's just as bad up there,' Larry said. 'You people have rotten ideas.'

'But it's famous!' Suzie was barely covered in a tank-top and black safari shorts, tanning one leg at a time by sticking it under the blazing sun.

'Must admit, these people are a bit goofy,' Werner said.

Larry cleaned his sunglasses with the tail of his tennis shirt and scanned the immediate crowd, blinking. 'All crowds are goofy. Hitler loved this kind of mob.'

Werner spat on the sand and said, 'Stop insulting my race, wanker.'

One campsite over, a slurred voice yelled, 'Narcs! Lay off, man!' Larry craned his neck and watched two young ravers arguing with a tall guy in a dark suit. He flashed some sort of badge and spoke quietly, too quiet for Larry to hear from a dozen feet away. People started noticing this exchange – just about all of them were holding illegal drugs.

A second cop-suit walked into sight and grabbed the young girl sitting in the doorway of the ravers' camper-van. He was louder than his partner. 'Which one of you is Jesús Ramirez?'

Larry sat his drink on the folding table and said, 'Let's take a drive.'

'Drive where?' Suzie asked.

'Come on.' Larry yanked the poles from under the awning and cranked it back into the camper's side. 'I'll tell you later.'

Werner watched the scene with vague interest. 'Don't think they're interested in us, matey. Relax.'

Larry yanked the German's arm and hustled him around the camper. He pointed to the licence plate.

'Oregon?'

'Right,' Larry whispered. 'I switched plates with our hippie neighbours.' He went to the table and struggled with it for a moment before deciding it wasn't worth the trouble.

Werner whispered to Suzie and she stood, looking confused. He led her inside and shut the door.

Larry got behind the wheel. The loud Narc turned his way and shouted, 'Need to talk to you!'

'Sorry,' Larry shouted back. He shifted into drive and stomped on the accelerator. The blender, abandoned on the card table but still plugged into the motorhome, went airborne and dumped its contents on the Narc's legs. Through the dust, Larry thought he saw the man raise a gun.

Honking and swerving around packs of drugged kids, Larry aimed for the highway, some ten acres to the west. It was like driving through a fog bank and a hell of a lot hotter. He made it without hitting anybody, but the two-lane escape from the festivities was clogged with slow-moving VW vans, smoking old station wagons and sunburned fanatics riding bicycles.

'Can somebody tell me why we're leaving?' Suzie was in the back, bouncing in the miniature dining booth. 'They're burning the big robot guy tonight.'

'Watch it on the news,' Larry said. 'Those cop guys were after us.'

'Why?'

'Tell you later, I promise. Once we get away from these hippies and this heat and this dust.'

'Sounds nice,' Werner said from the passenger-side bucket seat. 'And how do we do it?'

Larry yelled instructions, pulled into the opposite lane and shot past a mile's worth of vehicles, until a sheriff's deputy waved him over from the opposite shoulder.

'What the hell are you doing?' the deputy yelled.

'Emergency. My wife's having a baby.'

The deputy considered the situation. Larry looked vaguely respectable, meaning he looked like a cop himself, with his quasi-West Point haircut and alligator shirt. Suzie was in the passenger seat, Werner's lumpy leather jacket stuffed under her tank-top, moaning in fake pain.

'Where the hell you gonna go?'

'Reno!'

'You'll never make it! Shit ... All right, keep going. I'll get on the radio, get an escort for you. Go up to the 31, there's ambulances up there.'

'Ambulances?' Whoops.

'For these dopers. Just go!'

Larry yelled thanks and sped down the highway, staying on the wrong side, shooting past a traffic-jammed exodus of West Coast degenerates. Suzie was laughing now. Larry demanded quiet, seeing the sign that read, 'Highway 31, 1 mile'.

Another deputy stood at the junction, his partner sitting on the hood of the cruiser parked across the highway. Both young guys in pilot shades. When the junction-cop spotted the Vagabond Express camper with Oregon plates, on the right side of the road with the other cars, he ran up to the driver's side.

'You're supposed to be in the left lane, we blocked

traffic ... The ambulance ...'

Werner was driving, Larry riding shotgun.

'Don't need an ambulance,' Werner said. 'Just headed home.'

He took another look at them and frowned. Unsheathed his radio and said, 'Hey, what sort of motorhome am I looking for again?' He held the brick-shaped device to one ear and nodded.

'I saw a camper pulled over,' Larry said. 'About a half-mile back.'

The deputy waved them away.

'Close one,' Werner said. 'What exactly are we running from?'

'I didn't rent this camper.'

'Who did?'

'A dead Mexican. Mr Jesús Ramirez.'

'Right. So we're being followed?'

'Took 'em two days to find us here. Let's clean up and move along.'

The Pepperwood Hotel-Casino looked good – it looked old, forgotten, maybe a bit slow with the electronics. Larry didn't have any choice but the Ramirez credit card. He would demand an early wake-up call.

They entered the lobby and Larry went to the counter, wearing Werner's sunglasses, Werner and Suzie working the lobby slot machines.

'*Buenas Tardes. Habla Castellaño, senorita?*'

'Uhm ... you mean Mexican? Uh, ahm sorry, I can't speak Mexican, if you'll wait just a moment I'll get one of the housekeepers – '

'No, ees fine,' Larry hissed. 'Me and mi seesters, we need a suite. Yer biggest suite. We are here for ... for the Internet convention ... from Boleeevia.'

The dyed-blonde reception clerk, who probably hadn't been called a *senorita* in twenty years, took all this with utmost seriousness.

'I see, sir. Your English is very good, you know!' She tapped away at the computer. 'Well, our presidential suite is reserved this week – we've got the rock group the Spin Doctors here this week, playing at eight and eleven. The American kids just love 'em.'

Larry nodded gravely.

'Well, let's see, I've got the three-room Jacuzzi King, our next biggest suite, for one-ninety per night. It's got a lovely view. For how many nights, sir?'

'Oh, uh, just for one night, *senorita*.'

'But you're here for the Computer Convention, you said? It doesn't start 'til tomorrow.'

'Oh, well ... not *this* computer convention. Ees the one in San Francisco.' She stared politely, and Larry felt a vague sense of doom. 'Ah, you see, my seesters' – gesturing to Suzie and Werner far off in the lobby – 'they want to see the, uh, the UFOs.'

'I see! You've driven up our "E.T. highway," have you? That really brings people in from all over the world! They watch that X-files.'

'Yess.'

'You see any little green men?' She winked comically.

'Oh ... ha-ha, yess, we see very many aliens who try to, uh, abduct us. I mean my seesters.'

'I bet! Well let's get you set up. Do you have a major credit card, seen-yor?' Another wink.

Larry smiled and flapped his wallet open on the counter, removing the MAGIC STANDARD Visa® and handing it to her with a flourish. She took the card and slid it through the keyboard's magnetic reader. He winced.

'Very good, Mr Raymeress. And look at that, your first

name is Jesus! You know in our country, Jesus is what we call God.' She reached under the counter and handed Larry a little card. 'If you'll just fill out this guest form, we'll be finished. You must be tired from driving up that highway.'

'Yes, *yo tengo sueño*.'

'It's such a romantic language! My first husband spoke Mexican.'

He smiled and filled out the card as follows, half remembering the address of a South American hotel he once visited:

Dr Jesús Ramirez y familia
Callejón del Gato 7, 1°
La Paz, Bolivia

'Well thank you … oh! You're a doctor!'

'Ah, ees but only a title of academics. *Soy*, uh, I am only a doctor of the computer science.'

'Do you have luggage to bring inside?'

'Of course, *senorita*.' He took the camper keys from his pockets and slapped them on the counter. 'If your gentlemen would be so kind as to bring up the bags from my motor-campo …'

'Certainly, Doctor.'

She nodded and produced three keycards – 'for all your sisters' – and Larry bowed thanks. Shit, Japanese bow, not Bolivians. Whatever. He walked to the slots and grabbed Werner by the neck.

'Come on, Nazi. Luxury awaits.'

Werner scooped up his winnings and flagged down Suzie, who had moved to the craps tables. She scowled and abandoned her dollar bets. In the elevator, Werner said, 'What in hell was that act all about?'

Larry smiled and distributed the plastic key cards.

'Since we're being chased and all … From now on, or at least until we check out of here, *amigos y amigas*, I am Jesús

Ramirez. Famed Bolivian doctor of the computer sciences.'

'I figured this was criminal,' Suzie said. 'Why else would you have money.'

'Silence! The only crime here is a lack of faith. Besides, if anyone asks that gal, all she'll remember is somebody from Bolivia speaking "Mexican". With two seesters. But watch your back.'

They emerged on the twelfth floor and entered the suite. It was obscene. Beyond the foyer, the kitchen, and a giant living room with a sunken heart-shaped whirlpool bath, there were two massive bedrooms, three grand bathrooms and a sort of salon around a red metallic cone-shaped fireplace – red like the whole place. Windows everywhere, facing the Reno skyline and the Sierra Nevada beyond, the snow-capped peaks twinkling in the afternoon light.

'Y' know, except for the bad taste, this is lovely,' said Werner. 'Have they a fitness room?'

'Yeah, I imagine,' Larry said, grabbing the Guest Services book off the coffee table. 'Sure, basement level, racquetball courts, Nautilus machines ... and saunas. Let's take a sauna.'

'I'm too filthy,' Suzie said, shaking road dust from her hair. 'Let's bathe first.'

Sure, the usual torture.

Larry shuffled over to the mini-bar fridge but there was nothing inside but beer and soda and a very tiny bottle of bad champagne. He picked up the phone and demanded two magnums of Moët Chandon from room service. Right away sir, anything else? Yes ... some guacamole. And cigarettes. And candles.

Werner started the gas fire. The sun dropped below the peaks, leaving a brilliant purple panorama. Suzie tossed off her clothes and dropped into the giant tub, followed by Werner. Larry changed into a complimentary red terrycloth robe and smoked a cigarette, waiting for room service to knock. The bell rang and he opened the door and the man rolled in the cart, jabbering in rapid-fire Spanish. Larry nodded along for a bit, catching two out of nine words, answering non-questions. Right when the guy was looking suspicious, Suzie rose from the tub like Athena and said in what sounded like decent Spanish:

'Please forgive Dr. Ramirez. He is suffering from laryngitis and must save his voice for the Internet conference.'

The waiter smiled and thanked them all and wished good health to the doctor. Larry understood that much, signed the check 'Dr J.P. Ramirez,' And slipped his last twenty to the man. The door shut and Larry placed the candlesticks in strategic places, lighting them as he moved through the room.

'You speak Spanish?'

Suzie was in the whirlpool again.

'In my country, Jonestowne, we speak five languages in *high school.*'

Larry uncorked a magnum and filled three glasses from the silver tray. He delivered the champagne, slipped out of his robe, dunked into the bubbling water and said, 'So how'd you lose that Cold War, again?'

Larry switched licence plates with another camper and met Werner at the $5 table, a series of Heinekens at their elbows. He hit a streak and had a pile of $25 chips next to his beer. Werner was doing better, with $100 chips stacked all around him. A hippie guy, with a backstage pass stuck to his tie-dye shirt, sat down at the end of the table. Werner grunted.

'How's it going, brothers?'

'Winning for the moment,' Werner mumbled, not looking up.

'You see our show?'

'No,' Larry said. 'We don't see shows. We're ... Amish.'

'Amish?' The hippie stroked his wispy beard. Werner and Larry were clean-shaven.

'Oh, not your kind of Amish.' Larry crashed on a foolish twenty-two and tossed a few chips to the dealer. He gathered his tokens and wandered around the casino, through a slow Sunday crowd, and found the gift shop. A few copies of the *Chronicle* and *USA Today*. He took one of each and paid with his winnings. Asked for the coffee shop. Around the corner, past the boutiques.

Nobody in there but a tired waitress. He ordered coffee and orange juice and went straight to the business section of the *Chronicle*: 'Witness to Sanders Incident Found Dead.' Not a very encouraging story. The corpse of Brendan Pierce – the guy who very recently pinned Seacroft's murder on Thomas Sanders, according to a 'renegade Internet journalist' – was found alone at his island house when Massachusetts investigators arrived. Didn't recover from the lung-cancer surgery so well – if, by 'didn't recover', you meant his oxygen tanks were full of nitrogen.

The Massachusetts attorney general said there was no point in reopening a quarter-century-old case when everyone involved was deceased. Everyone but Sanders. Larry began to shiver.

The boat, ski, hang-glider and jet crashes that killed the other four witnesses were starting to sound less like Karma and more like murder. Had Sanders been picking off his frat brothers for twenty-five years? Ah, that seemed insane. Even sickly Pierce might have just died from a tank error. Larry made a note to check the safety records of those things: 'Call Ralph Nader.'

Maybe Nader should just take over this whole mess. Demand congressional hearings on the safety of fraternities and murderous CEOs. Let Jesús Ramirez lead migrant-worker protests or whatever.

USA Today had a short article inside the Money section. Thomas Sanders spoke to the press from his driveway. Blamed the trouble on 'competitors who can't produce innovation and are reduced to terrorism, which I guarantee we will retaliate against with our full legal powers.' Nothing in either article about the validity of the Ramirez story and its scanned evidence. The stock was still hurting, but it had regained five bucks.

Were they *that* good? Could they kill off a witness and do a Ken Starr press conference and start going up again? Larry didn't like the sound of that 'retaliate' bit. They must be shaking down every Jesús Ramirez in Northern California. Especially the one supposedly living on Haight Street, since that's the one Larry used to register the Web address. He made another note: 'Try to be smarter.'

Only one good development from the *USA Today* article:

> Attorneys for IBM, however, announced today they are investigating the company's purchase of a Sanders patent in 1963 — a patent the Seacroft family long ago claimed was the invention of their son, Gilliard. Their civil complaint, filed in 1963 and later withdrawn, could be resurrected by IBM, chief technology counsel Lindsey Crane told USA Today. The company's patent attorneys in New York state are now investigating the possibility of filing suit against Sanders regarding the 1963 contract, although legal experts told USA Today that the statute of limitations in both states may limit IBM's recourse. IBM and MicroTorrent are bitter corporate rivals in the interactive-television and E-commerce sectors.

Maybe the IBM sharks would keep Sanders busy a while – long enough for Jesús Ramirez to find some new targets. And change his address.

Werner stepped into the coffee shop and asked for a coffee. He sat across from Larry.

'Something wrong?'

'Ah, this looks bad.' He slid the papers across the formica.

'Woof! You think they iced this guy?'

'You learned English from Raymond Chandler books, didn't you?'

Werner shrugged and took his coffee from the waitress.

'You know, I sorta did this Jesús Ramirez thing like everything else. I didn't think it through, other than the basic philosophical considerations.'

'Matey, I don't think you'll be murdered, if that's your concern. Unless your Denisa talks, there's nobody dangerous who'd ever connect this MicroTorrent thing with you. Is there?'

Larry drank his orange juice and looked at Werner.

'Well, there's you. Luckily I don't worry about you, not too much. Denisa ... she doesn't know anything. I was just another dupe sent to write a celebrity CEO profile. Terrance knows, but he'd be screwed a hundred ways if he admitted anything. InnerKnife.com was hacked, blah blah blah – if it's on Internet Wire it must be true. That's everybody, except our Soviet gal. Oh, and Charles.'

'Charles?'

'That little imp who sells junk on Haight Street.'

'Ah, the one with the jaunty cap. How's he know?'

'Well ... he doesn't, specifically. But he knows our Mr Ramirez is dead. Did I tell you how I got the ID?'

Larry told him. Werner thought it was a sloppy way to do business.

'Doesn't matter,' Larry said. 'Charles just appears every

week or so, goes through the garbage and re-sells the stuff to the tenants until he's got enough to get dumb for another week. His memory doesn't tend to survive those sessions.'

This was true enough. Not long ago, Larry gave Charles a hideous lamp otherwise headed for the trash, went across the street for wine, and returned to his gate two minutes later. Charles was there, trying to sell Larry 'a real nice lamp I been havin''.

'You might want to take care around your neighbour's mail slot.'

'No shit. I could be gunned down in that lobby and nobody would look up from their crack pipes.'

Larry asked the waitress for more coffee. 'We might be fairly safe if all this offshore anonymous crap actually works. But this old dude — far as I know, I'm the only one he ever talked to about the horrible night with Seacroft — I'm guessing they killed him off. Tough to prove from a Reno hotel.'

'Your mate in Boston, perhaps he can check it out.'

'Maybe. I'll call him in the morning.'

'All right, cheer up,' Werner said, rising from the booth. 'We're gonna have a sauna.'

'Maybe in a few minutes.'

Werner slapped Larry's shoulder and headed out.

For a decade now, Larry had been trying to figure out what it was he *did*. And here it was — he wrote damning Web tracts against the wobbly New Economy, masked by the offshore identity of a secret Mexican currently claiming to be Bolivian. There would be no fame or fortune in this life — well, maybe a few bucks — but it was *virtuous*, wasn't it? As long as he stayed alive. And didn't get nailed for the mail fraud.

He paid for the beverages, gathered the newspapers and walked slowly to the elevators. Nobody around. He pushed 12 and shot up the tube. Walked down the hideously wallpapered hallway and stuck his plastic key into the slot. Green light.

The candles were still burning. Made the ugly suite kind of pretty, with the lights of Reno out there. Larry picked a champagne flute off the coffee table and filled it with lukewarm Chandon. Must have left the stereo on. U2's 'Achtung Baby' played at a pleasant volume. He sat on the plush carpet near the glass and watched the city twinkle in the desert air.

He finished the bottle and fell asleep on the carpet.

16

An hour after the camper crossed the California state line, two men in simple dark suits entered the Pepperwood's lobby. One strode into the casino. The other stepped to the counter.

'Can ah help you?'

'Yeah.' He flashed some sort of badge-type thing. 'We're investigating an incident, and it might involve some guests here in your hotel.'

'Oh my. Perhaps you should speak with the day manager – '

'No no,' he said, fake smile. 'That's fine. We'll speak to the manager later. Just tell me if there's a guest here by the name of Jesús Ramirez' – pronouncing the first name *Hay-Zeus*.

'Hmm. Doesn't really ring a bell – '

'J-E-S-U-S, like Jesus, Jesus Christ.'

Her eyes lit up. 'Oh, *them*. You're looking for Dr Raymeeress?'

'Yeah, yeah. We've … got a package for him. What's

the room number?'

'Oh, ahm sorry, Dr Ramirez and his family checked out this morning, for that computer convention, I believe.'

'What computer convention?'

'Well, I don't quite know.'

'You have an address for him?'

'Well, just his home address here – ' she tapped at the computer. 'Cally-john dell gatto seven, then a one and a little zero, La Pass, Bolivia.'

'Damn.'

'Excuse me?'

'Uhm, forget about it, that's fine.'

'Y' know ah should really ask my manager before I release guest information.'

'No, no. It's fine, miss. We're … I'm … these people might be drug dealers, and we're trying to find them.'

'Well you must have the wrong people, sir. Dr Raymeeress was just as nice as can be, a very nice Mexican gentleman, with his sisters y' know? I didn't meet them, but he seemed a very nice man. Certainly didn't look like a drug dealer.'

'You ever seen a drug dealer, ma'am?'

'Well sure. Everybody's seen them drug dealers on the COPS show.'

Jack Rosso met his short plump partner, Nick Collins, in the parking lot.

'Anything?'

'This is mucked up. Woman in there says Jesús Ramirez is a Bolivian doctor, was there with his sisters, for some Internet convention.'

'Bolivia? She describe him?'

'A "very nice Mexican man" and his sisters.'

'From Bolivia?'

'Look, that's what she said. I saw the screen. Address in La Paz, Bolivia.'

Collins took a pack of Doublemint from his pocket and offered a piece to Rosso. They stood in the parking lot chewing gum for a while.

'This Jesus character, isn't he pulling all this crap on the Internet?'

'Yeah, that's what the office says,' answered Collins, tossing his foil wrapper.

'Sure. He's pulling some stunt at this Internet convention.' A security golf-cart came by and Rosso waved it down, quickly flashing his badge-type thing.

'Yessir, help you gentlemen?'

'Where's the Internet convention?'

'Hmm. Don't know about that … There's a computer show on Sundays at the Lucky Seven.'

'Where's this Lucky Seven?'

'Just take South Virginia Street, straight up on the left, can't miss it.'

Rosso and Collins got into their grey Ford Taurus and sped through downtown Reno. At the edge of town, surrounded by mini-malls and discount outlets, was the Lucky Seven, a two-storey motel, empty pool out front, yellow cardboard signs saying 'Computer Show This Sunday'. At the far end of the parking lot was a big circus tent of sorts, with a few families paying the $2 admission at the entrance flap.

'Circle the premises,' Rosso said.

Collins trotted away and Rosso cut the line at the front.

'Hey!' A burly guy in a western shirt and Lee jeans grabbed Rosso's arm. 'Get in line.'

Rosso flashed the badge and turned to the admissions girl.

'Excuse me, miss. We've got a suspect inside.'

She screamed, several people in line screamed, and Rosso went inside. Not quite the San Jose Convention Centre. There were long folding tables spread in two aisles, with western-attired men selling discount PCs and ergonomic chairs and pirated software and a country station playing on a bad loudspeaker. Rosso ran down both lanes, seeing nothing but middle-aged white guys behind the tables. Then, an apparent Mexican, boxing up a generic computer for a family of four. Rosso tackled him. They rolled into the next space, collapsing an elaborate pyramid of 'Wing Fighter IV' cellophane-wrapped boxes. The matriarch of the family assumed this was a heist concerning her $672.89 home computer and kicked Rosso in the head, hollering for the police. Collins ran in through the loading-entrance flaps, pulling his Glock 9mm. The sixty or so browsers inside began noticing the ruckus and the gunman and joined the screaming. The Salvadoran beneath the boxes tried to get away from the man in the suit, but got caught in the canvas divider between the aisles. The whole pipe-frame construction tipped over, causing more yelps of terror. Collins sprinted to the other side, gun held high, looking in vain for Mexicans, and the freaked-out crowd ran for a clear-plastic section of the tent wall that looked like an exit. It wasn't. There was a scraping of metal on asphalt as the entire portable structure pulled in the direction of the mob. Rosso got his hands around the Salvadoran's throat as one wall of the tent collapsed on top of them. A flap of official fireproof canvas came to rest on a tattered orange extension cord and small blue flames erupted.

Rosso pushed the heavy canvas from his head and pulled his own Glock, the barrel against the Salvadoran's temple.

'We got you, Jesus.'

'Get off me, man. What in fuck you talking 'bout?'

And a huge piece of stainless-steel pipe dropped thirty feet and smacked Rosso on the back of his skull.

The next thing he remembered was being led away by two Reno cops. There were fire engines around the catastrophe, a horrible wet burning smell in the air, and paramedics standing at the doors of an ambulance. But the cops took Rosso to a squad car. Collins was in the back, yelling through the mesh-metal divider.

'Let me go, you fucking hillbillies. We've got a suspect in there.'

'I don't think so,' the taller cop said. He reached into Rosso's jacket pocket and retrieved the badge thing. 'What in hell is B.I.P.S.?'

'BIPS. Business Intelligence Partner Services, Menlo Park.'

'Well, sir, I don't know what this BIPS is, and I don't know where Menlo Park is, but you're under arrest for assault and illegal possession of a semi-automatic handgun.'

Rosso jabbered about his concealed-handgun permit, but the cop just shook his head and said, 'You don't get it, do you? This is Nevada. Your California licence don't let you jack off in Nevada.'

In the parking lot, around the smouldering imploded tent, merchants were loading their battered boxes into pickups and yelling vulgarities at Rosso. He wanted to rub his throbbing head but couldn't, with the handcuffs and all.

'Where's that goddamned Mexican?'

'Sir, you've got the right to remain silent …'

Sitting on the back bumper of the ambulance, Carlos Medina drank a cup of water.

'Who are these crazies? INS?'

'Nah,' the paramedic said. 'Just some crazies.'

'Why they attack me? Just 'cause I'm Latino? I got civil rights. I got my green card.'

'I don't know. Don't worry, they're going to jail.'

17

'Let me out by Walgreen's.'

'Why?'

'Because I'm out of floss. Just let me out here and turn in this filthy camper in the morning.'

'Don't be a dick, Jonestowne.'

'Sorry. Just want to have a look at my place before I get killed. Thanks for driving ... and everything.'

'It's okay. Watch yourself, stupid.'

'I will.'

Werner got off the beige-carpeted floor between them. 'You want me to come along?'

Larry looked out on Haight Street. The standard night-time madness.

'Yeah, maybe. You mind going 'round the block and meeting me at Steiner?'

'Fine.'

Larry hopped out the passenger door, followed by Werner and his overnight bag.

'All right. I'll just walk to the flat. If anything's weird – '

'You'll go to the Midtown and get a drink.'

'Right.'

Werner heroically marched through a throng of gang kids and headed south on Fillmore, past the bad coffee shop and hair salons. He took a right, going past the row houses, scanning every shrub and fence for trouble.

Larry waited for the light, ignored a bum wanting money, and passed the metal-gated health-food mart. The Jordanian place was open, doing good business with a bunch of teen punkers in their 1978 safety-pin best. He was hungry from the drive and slipped in to ask for two felafels, to go. Stepped outside again to survey the street. There was Nadine the schizophrenic pushing her shopping cart, jabbering secret conversations to the ghosts in her head. And the poor loser who claimed to be in the Village People, crouched on a stoop with his crack-pipe, sure that somebody was going to buy the rights to his life and make a movie. Two red-headed Irish guys drunkenly fighting outside the Tornado beer hall. Another two Irish guys fighting across the street, in front of Mad Dog In The Fog. The Jordanian gave Larry a white-plastic sack in exchange for six dollars.

Larry approached the gate to his apartment. Nobody around. He produced his key and jammed it in the lock, looking over his right shoulder. No sign of Werner. He stepped into the lobby and reached for the light switch, finding somebody's belly instead.

'Don't move.'

'Not moving.'

'Shut the door.'

'Sure.'

A cold metal tube pressed against Larry's neck.

'What's your name?'

'La … LaRouche.'

'LaRouche?'

'Lombard. Lombard Franklin.'

'What's your business here?'

'I live here.'

'Where?'

'Right here.'

'You know anybody named Jesús Ramirez?'

'The lady?'

Larry saw the goon's eyebrows raise.

'Knock Knock!'
The goon whispered, 'Who's there?'
From outside: 'Pizza!'
'My pizza's here,' Larry explained.
'Fuck.'

A leather-jacketed fist burst through the door's upper window and smashed the goon in the jaw. The man fell to the battleship-grey floor, glass shards digging into his scalp, and got a boot in his head from Larry Jonestowne. And another in his gut. And another in his crotch. And, in a very hazy moment, the handgrip of his pistol smashed against his face.

'Where the hell were you?'
'Over the porch, mate. You all right?'
'Yeah, fine. You?'

Werner nodded and shook the glass from his leather jacket.

'I got you a felafel.'

'He one of them?'

The goon was on the floor of Larry's tiny living room, face down on a fake-Turkish rug bought from Charles for a dollar. Larry rummaged through the man's coat and found Ramirez' new mail. Looked like more credit cards, and a packet of cash-advance cheques. And two credit reports for Mr Ramirez, who apparently was a good consumer risk. For a dead guy.

In the back pocket was a leather case holding a BIPS badge, and beneath it a business card identifying the unconscious goon as Phillip Trageser of Business Intelligence Partner Services, LLC, Menlo Park.

'Yeah, I'd guess he's one of them.'
'Neighbourhood's going to hell. You should get a new place to live.'
'Been thinking about that.' Larry looked around the living

room for a place to stash the Glock. 'Where do people hide guns?'

'Dunno. Never had a gun.'

'Aha – inside the plastic owl, of course.' He forced open the window and reached for the neighbour's plastic owl, supposedly there to scare pigeons. It was crusted in pigeon shit. Larry wrapped the gun in the felafel bag and twisted off the bird's head. The gun fitted nicely and he returned the recapitated owl to its grimy perch.

'Now what you want to do with *him*?'

'Something special. Eat your felafel.'

Larry left the apartment and crossed Haight Street. Passed numerous shuttered businesses and came to the Crossroads hippie-coffee shop. He stepped under the bus shelter and a mustachioed old freak said, 'Doses?'

'Is it good?'

'This shit's good, man.'

'How much?'

'Five apiece.'

'Wonderful. Give me ... three.' Larry dug the last fifteen bucks from his wallet and made the exchange.

'You oughta cool out with this stuff,' the hippie said. 'One's enough.'

'Certainly. Always cooling out.'

Larry slid the tabs behind his ATM card and walked back to the apartment. He put Ramirez' mail in his shoulderbag, along with the computer and his Day Timer. Might need to avoid this place for a few days. Grabbed his toothbrush from the bathroom and jammed it down with the computer's power cord. Werner was finishing off his felafel.

'Good felafel!'

'Yeah, them Jordanians ...' Larry removed the tabs from his wallet and rolled the goon over, shoving all three down his mouth.

'You're *dosing* the poor bastard?'
'He tried to kill me.'
'Nah. He's just looking for the dirty Mexican.'
'Same thing. Hand me your beer.'
Werner handed over his Pacifico. Larry drizzled a little beer into the goon's mouth and rubbed his throat, the way you get a puppy to swallow medicine.
'Now what?'
'Let me eat my damned felafel, then we'll get rid of him.'
Werner put on the Replacements, 'Don't Tell A Soul'. Larry washed the pigeon crud from his hands, got a Pacifico from the fridge and finished his meal.
'You didn't see anybody else around?'
'Nah. Usual freaks. I've finally bought drugs on Haight Street, just like a normal citizen.'
A cell phone chirped. From the belt of Phillip Trageser. Larry and Werner were silent through the four rings.

'Best be getting out of here, matey.'
'Seems like a good time.' Larry took the phone, shut off the power and clipped it to his own belt. Then he went through the goon's wallet, transferred $117 to his own wallet, and found a key-ring. A Ford, with one of those fancy unlock buttons. Probably a Taurus.
'All right. I'm gonna find his car,' Larry said, hanging the laptop bag on his shoulder. 'Get our boy ready, would you?'
Two blocks up Steiner, using the key-button like a metal detector, Larry saw the tail-lights blink on a grey Ford Taurus. He slipped inside and circled back to Haight, passing six SFPD cruisers on the corner of Fillmore, lights flashing and various suspects on the sidewalk. Good, keep those boys busy. Werner was behind the gate, holding a slumped figure and his overnight bag. He dragged Trageser to the car and Larry opened the rear door. Together, they stuffed the guy inside.

Nobody on the street looked twice – this was the normal way of loading passengers in the Lower Haight. Werner got in and Larry took the wheel, up Divisadero and left on Geary. They rolled through the foggy Avenues, KCSM playing bebop Miles Davis. Near the end of the drive, the man lifted his head and whimpered 'Lookit the pretty angels, mamma,' but Werner smacked him on the ear and he sank again.

They parked behind a dumpster by the Cliff House, saw nobody around, and dragged Trageser down the stairs to the sea, tossing him on the cold wet sand by a particularly vicious gang of sea lions. Larry removed the man's shoes, pants and jacket.

'He looks about my size, you think?'

'Oh Lord,' Werner said.

'What? I *need* one of these cop suits.'

The goon seemed to be suffering stomach spasms, all that lysergic acid playing rude games with his muscles. He looked cold in his jockey shorts and black socks and white shirt, jerkily curling into fetal position. Larry briefly considered how awful those barking sea lions must sound to someone on acid.

Back at the car, Werner rummaged through the glove box and actually found gloves, along with a lock-picking kit and a GPS unit. Everything but the black leather gloves went in the dumpster.

'One for you, one for me,' Werner said, slipping the right on his hand.

'Why do I get the left?'

'Because you're a communist. Get rid of all your filthy fingerprints.'

'Right, fingerprints. We're getting pretty good at this.'

Werner didn't bother answering. He hopped out and circled the car, wiping the door handles with the edge of his T-shirt. Larry rubbed down the wheel and myriad knobs and levers with the stolen pants. He reached under the steering column and awkwardly turned the ignition with his gloved hand.

'Any ideas about the car?' Werner asked.

'No, you?'

'I say we give it to the first bum we see.'

Two blocks from the beach, Werner spotted a stinky old wino sprawled on the flip-up seats engineered to keep bums off the bus benches. Larry stopped and Werner jumped out, rousing the bum with gusto.

'It's your lucky day, mate!'

'Wha?'

'Can you drive, mate?'

'Sure I drive ... used to be a ...'

'Fine. Get in.'

They stuffed him behind the wheel and gave him twenty bucks for the journey. He seemed to perk up.

'Straight down the road, buddy,' Larry said, snatching his computer bag and new suit before slamming the driver's door.

'Who ... Who're you boys?'

'I'm a Mexican,' Larry said.

'I'm a kangaroo,' said Werner.

'I ... use to drive Greyhounds.'

'Sure,' said Larry, backing away from the Taurus. 'They're right down the road.'

The bum took off, a bit uncomfortable with power brakes, but he recovered and the tail-lights vanished in the fog. Larry and Werner walked down Geary laughing, carrying their belongings like nice hoboes.

'How we getting home?'

'A taxi, of course.' Larry turned on the cell phone.

'Probably a bad idea – '

'Oh, we'll flag a taxi. This is for something else.' He

glanced thoughtfully at the keypad. 'Is it necessarily wrong to falsely report a sex predator on the beach?'

'Nah, not in emergencies.'

'Hello, 911? I've got to report something really filthy ... Well, I was just at the beach with my, boyfriend guy, and a terrible, crazy lunatic tried to rape me. Where? Near the Sutro Baths. It was horrible, horrible. Yes ... oh, you'll have no trouble finding *him*. He's running around the beach in those jockey deals ... you know, those tight white things.' Another pause, and Larry barked, 'Briefs, for fuck's sake,' and ended the call.

'Something's not right about you,' Werner grumbled, flagging a passing Veteran's Taxi. The cab kept going.

Larry wiped off the phone and tossed it down a sewer drain. There was a little blue fish painted on the concrete over the words, 'Save Our Ocean Friends, Give a Hoot!'

18

'Harry, this over yet?' Sanders' bare feet flapped on the redwood as he paced around the hot tub with the cordless. He was naked again and the housekeepers tried to avoid looking outside.

'We're working on it, Tom. It's good news about Massachusetts – '

'The board had best quit screwing me around. Who do they think I am, Gil Amelio? What'd the guys find? I don't want to see that Web site again.'

'Well, we've got it blocked on our network, so at least the employees – '

'Screw the employees. What'd the guys find?'

'Tom, maybe I better come over.'

A half-hour later, Taft pulled into the drive and parked the Jaguar, leaving another man in the passenger seat. A maid opened the door and led him through the foyer, the walls loaded with framed magazine covers featuring a smiling Thomas Sanders: *Business Week*, *Forbes*, *Fortune*, *InterWorldNet*, *PC World*, *Money* and *Interactive Week* among them. The *Economist* cover didn't make the gallery; instead of a photo, the cruel English had used a caricature showing a bloated Sanders monster trying to eat a mouselike Bill Gates.

Sanders was still pacing around on the deck. A maid led Taft outside and returned with a tray of tropical cocktails and the usual snacks.

'Morning, Tom.' Polite pause. 'Let me get your robe here.'

'Don't bother. If I can't go to my own office I'm not getting dressed.'

'Ah, sure Tom.' Taft pulled a chair near the tub — not too near — and sat down.

'Have a drink.'

'Ah, no thanks. Little early for me. We called BIPS like you wanted, they've been handling the whole thing. They have a few encouraging leads, but there's been a few problems.'

'Like what?' Sanders took a drink and sank into the hot tub, which Taft appreciated.

'Like ... they went off the Web site registry to start. Jesús Ramirez, whoever he is. I've got Owen Lindsey in the car if you want to talk to him, because frankly, it's a little confusing.'

'First tell me what in hell happened.'

'This Ramirez supposedly lives in San Francisco, and they found he has a few credit cards, so they traced one to some hippie thing in Nevada, and then a hotel in Reno. It must've been some sort of mix-up, because that Ramirez had already checked out, and apparently he's some Bolivian.' Taft took his Palm Pilot from his belt and nervously reviewed the notes, avoiding Sanders' glare. 'BIPS had two guys there, and they got a lead that this Ramirez, or maybe a different Ramirez, was up to something at an Internet convention down the street. One of the guys, Rosso, tried to apprehend that Ramirez, and it led to an altercation of sorts. The tent apparently, well, collapsed. And caught fire.'

'Tent? We don't have trade shows in goddamned tents.'

'I guess it was more of a retail computer fair. I guess they have it every third Sunday in the winter.'

'Who?'

'The, ah, Reno Computer Merchants group.' Sanders threw his drink over the rail and snorted.

'And, well, the guys were arrested.'

'The BIPS guys? What in hell for?'

'Ah, arson. And assault. Some other minor charges. But any litigation will be directed at BIPS, Tom, not MicroTorrent.'

'Swell. The guys in the city find anything?'

'They sent two guys to check out this address ... on Haight Street, sort of a rough area. I guess they looked around, and the apartment's empty. Looked like it's being painted and whatnot. One left the other for a dinner break ... Trageser, that's the one who stayed to keep an eye on the place. But he, ah, it's really peculiar, Tom.'

Sanders snorted again and said, 'Get Lindsey out here.'

Taft got the Nokia off his belt and speed-dialled Owen Lindsey's Nokia. 'Come out to the deck, Owen.'

'So where's this Trageser?'

'He ... Well, like I said, it's very peculiar. He was arrested on the beach across town. For suspicion of, ah, forcible sodomy and public indecency or some crazy thing. They've got him at San Francisco General now, because he might have, ah, gone insane.'

Lindsey came through the house and went to shake Sanders' hand. Sanders spat in the hot tub.

'Mr Sanders, you're understandably concerned about these mishaps.'

'Concerned? Who are these clowns? Rapists? Arsonists? Lunatics?'

Lindsey looked distinctly out of place, wearing his usual cop-suit and standing over an obese naked man.

'I can't give you a good explanation of what happened in Reno and San Francisco, Mr Sanders, because I wasn't there and the men who were are in custody. But our lawyers will be talking to all three men today and we *will* find out what happened. Frankly, I think we may have all underestimated this Ramirez character. I hope you'll accept my apologies – and I assure you MicroTorrent's name and your name will never be associated with these events.'

'Sure, Owen. I'm starting to question your competence, to say the least. Your jackals screwed *me* on the Oracle job, and now? Where'd you get these idiots?'

'All of our men are highly regarded veterans of this country's intelligence agencies, Mr Sanders, and you know that.'

'And how'd these morons win the Cold War?'

'There can be complications, but I assure you we'll find this Ramirez and stop this assault on your character and the damage to MicroTorrent Systems. The scope of the investigation has been drastically revised, Mr Sanders. It's no longer our belief that this Ramirez is, as originally thought, some disgruntled psychotic.'

'So who is it?'

Lindsey glanced at Taft and said softly, 'It may well be IBM. They've pulled dirty tricks in the past. Nothing this ... bizarre, but the stakes are certainly higher these days.'

Sanders pulled himself from the water and his haunches

smacked onto the decking. He grabbed a pastry and ate it in two bites, looking pensive.

'And, Mr Sanders, despite what happened yesterday, you know I *personally* took care of the Massachusetts situation, and if need be I will personally resolve the Ramirez situation, wherever it may lead.'

Sanders nodded.

Taft didn't like where this was going. 'Owen, what, ah, exactly is the "Massachusetts situation"? You're aware, of course, that I'm responsible to the board for whatever, ah, services contracted to BIPS, and that *anything* you do comes from my directive – '

'Aw, Harry, shut up. I asked him to check for leaks around Harvard. Stay out of it.'

Taft stood up and said, 'Please don't put me in an uncomfortable situation with the board. I want this to go away as much as you, Tom.'

'Then get the lawyers on IBM. Let BIPS do what has to be done. Owen, don't screw up again.'

Sanders oozed to standing position and walked into the mansion, slamming the french door behind him. Lindsey's Nokia rang. He walked to the wooden rail and seemed, for a moment, to lose his CIA cool.

'I need to get back to Menlo Park.'

Taft stood and asked, 'What now?'

'The car assigned to Trageser. A drunken bum just crashed it into a clam-chowder stand at Fisherman's Wharf.'

'Ah, Owen, this is ridiculous. You've got the homeless stealing your cars now?'

'Told the cops he didn't steal it – that it was *given* to him. By a kangaroo.'

19

It seemed best to sleep at Werner's.

Larry woke early and showered. Sifted through the German's closet and found exactly one proper dress shirt. He put on the suit – fine in the legs but a bit short on the sleeves – and the wingtips, which felt a little loose but pretty good. Should get a pair of those insoles from Walgreen's. At the bottom of the shoulderbag was an emergency tie, a habit he began a decade ago, when his beeper would go off in a bar and he needed to look respectable for a murder scene.

'*Danke*, baby,' Larry whispered as he left, stealing another pair of sunglasses from the table. Werner would be out for a while, having taken a few valiums and a glass of whisky before bed. Nervousness.

It was not a bad day outside. Clear, almost warm. Wouldn't last. Larry walked up to Castro, feeling sharp in the cop suit, and crossed Market. He sat outside at the little Mediterranean place and ordered eggs scrambled with feta cheese and olives, coffee, water, orange juice, and an ashtray. Trotted to the market next door for the papers. Need to put a vacation stop on the NYT, he thought. Maybe donate them to the Newspapers in Education fund for once.

He sipped the coffee and scanned the papers. New low for the Dow and NASDAQ. Train derailed someplace. The usual troubles in Kashmir, Israel, the Balkans, Russia, Central Africa, Indonesia, Belfast. And in the local section, 'Rape Suspect Nabbed on Ocean Beach'. Just a brief, bad writing and reporting, but interesting:

Ken Layne

> An anonymous 911 caller led San Francisco police to a delirious man wandering the beach south of the Sutro Baths ruins late Monday night. The suspect, a well-groomed white male about 40 years old, was clad only in underwear and socks when officers apprehended him at 11:50 p.m., police said.
>
> Sgt Luís Hernandez said the man may be the 'Ocean Beach Rapist', blamed for several attempted sexual assaults on gay beachgoers this year. The man has yet to be identified and was reported in stable condition at San Francisco General Hospital this morning, where he was admitted after arrest for multiple abrasions and observation. 'He was either out of his mind on drugs or just insane,' Hernandez said. An officer is standing watch in the suspect's room and charges are pending.

Arrested for multiple abrasions, eh? New laws all the time.

Nothing thrilling in the business sections. MicroTorrent Systems up a dollar, but still way down. Larry ate his eggs and went through Ramirez' mail. One letter advising Mr Ramirez that he'd been approved for an American Express card. And, in an envelope postmarked two days later, a lovely green bit of plastic stating that Jesús Ramirez shall be afforded all the privileges of membership. The extra card for a family member to Henry Hornberger in Budapest. O'Leary would soon receive a Ramirez-family Visa®. Both could be trusted to make occasional purchases in their respective lands, which Larry hoped would keep the goons confused.

Now to the credit reports: not much to report. A revolving credit line for a local furniture store, balance zero. A Nordstrom account, $42 in the 60-day column. Should pay that off. Employer listed as 'Screamin' Scissors' on 14th Street. Predictable. And terribly out of date, since Jesús worked for

Werner Consulting or something.

Larry paid for breakfast with the Visa® and found a shabby little place called 'Mail and More' down the street. He inquired about a post-office box. Forty bucks a year. Would have to be careful. The MicroTorrent goons found the Haight address without much trouble. But there was safety in numbers — twice a month, this place would be swarmed with shady boys getting their General Assistance cheques. And that's when Larry would retrieve his mail. He filled out the card, asked for a roll of stamps, paid with the American Express. At a smaller counter by the window, Larry wrote change-of-address forms to Jesús' creditors and banker, and another one to the Postal Service. Dropped them in the mail slot and went to the ATM across the street. Deposited a $4000 credit-advance cheque to Jesús' account, $300 cash back. Walked into the bank and deposited two hundred of that into his own account. Repeat as necessary, Larry figured.

He strode into the Beck Motor Hotel lobby and saw a Latino behind the desk. That won't work. He headed east on Market to the TravelLodge. Not a pretty place, but he was tired of lugging the computer bag. Nice dumb white girl inside, no trouble.

'How many nights?'

'Ah, yess. For *mucho* nights. I am a consultant of the computer, *senorita*.'

The girl didn't smile, but she didn't do anything else, either.

'My stay, it will be for eleven of the nights, that is my belief.'

'Well if you wanna stay longer you gotta tell us. There's that pride parade coming and this place gets full.'

'Parade?'

'Yeah, I don't know what it's called. Lesbians and stuff. Bikers.'

Larry slapped the AmEx on the counter, remembering the annual Gay Pride Weekend was coming up. Another 'Look at Me' gimmick in a town of gimmicks. She ran the card through an old-fashioned carbon thing and wrote '$537' in the amount box. 'They make us put it for fifty dollars more than the bill, in case for telephones and stuff.'

'*Muy bien*, fine.' He signed for Ramirez and took the key, a nice old-fashioned metal key. Upstairs by the ice machine.

Typically ugly motel room: lumpy queen-sized bed with a cigarette hole in the covers, yellowed curtains on the lone window, flickering fluorescent light over the bathroom sink, miniature coffeemaker with 'Folgers singles', a 15-year-old teevee chained to the ceiling, remote strapped to the end table, vomit-orange carpet. This was the office. Time to go to work. He uncased the laptop and set up on the shaky round breakfast table by the window. Opened the window to the street noise and fresh air. Put the teevee on CNN. Started the coffee. Unravelled his telephone cord and plugged it in the lone jack, taking the yellow touch-tone from the bedside table. Sat it beside the computer and plugged the phone and modem into his trusty Radio Shack line splitter. And turned on the computer for the first time in five days.

Some renegade Internet journalist ...

The Hotmail account was full up. Another hundred new e-mails of the 'My boss shoots smack' variety. He searched the news sites and gathered the MicroTorrent stories for later reading, the Internet Explorer windows collecting at the bottom of his screen. Then he opened Eudora and got his own mail, hoping this anonymous ISP actually did the job. He remembered to change the Internet-advertising account to the P.O. box – wouldn't want to miss those fat cheques. At least FlyRight Advertising let him choose to hide the address. Couldn't figure out how to do that with the Web-domain registry, so he changed Jesús' address in that wretchedly public database to the fictional apartment in Bolivia.

He disconnected the computer and dialled O'Leary at the *Boston Sun* with a pre-paid calling card.

'Nice work.'

'Yeah, thanks for plunging me into a national kill spree.'

'It's beautiful, man. Where've you been?'

'Got hauled off to the desert with the Eurotrash.'

'I'm on the story.'

'What story?'

'You see the papers? That old frat dude you found, he's dead.'

'Yeah, I saw that. You know anything about the reliability of oxygen-tank regulators?'

'They killed him, Jonestowne. It was a nitrogen tank *labelled* oxygen. Where the hell are you, anyway? Seems this has gotten dangerous for those involved.'

'Careful what you say. I'm somewhere, that's all. Who killed him, and what's going to be done about it?'

'All right, I know the homicide guys who work Martha's Vineyard. I'm not supposed to be out there, right? But I hear this and it all fits together. And this final witness dies ... you're not at home, are you?'

'No. I'm somewhere else.'

'Because if there was ever a time somebody would tap your calls, it's now.'

'Yeah, I'm getting that idea. Hang on.' Larry poured a cup of coffee and lit a cigarette. 'Okay. So what do these cops know?'

'Pierce's nurse is clear. She's been working the Vineyard for twenty years, all old-money families, everybody loves her. She's one of these freaks who likes helping people – her husband's a real-estate guy, no lack of money. So I checked the oxygen suppliers. They're fine, half-century in business, medical stuff, referred by all the hospitals, etc. They log these tanks going out, check 'em at the truck dock.'

'I was planning on calling Ralph Nader about that.'

'Don't bother. The guy who delivered the tanks is close to needing oxygen himself. He's old, no record, house and wife and a little boat. Knows plenty of the geriatrics on the island, cops aren't interested in him at all.'

'So?'

'So, the AG investigators show up to question Pierce and find him uncommunicative, due to being dead. He talked to them the day before, on the phone, said come on over. Seemed happy to get it off his chest. They'd asked if he talked to a journalist about the Sanders thing. He said yeah, but *didn't remember the name*. This part's important for you.'

'Wonderful. Unless ...'

'Unless they — whether Sanders or the cops — can go through the Bell-Atlantic records and find out who called Pierce. But don't worry about that for now. You must've talked to him a while before the thing ended up on the Web site, right?'

'No bills to me, anyway.'

'How's that?'

'Pre-paid calling cards. All the dope dealers use 'em.'

'Thing is, it probably doesn't matter how the call was billed, because it was still made from your phone — '

'Right, next door to Jesús himself. Let's hope they won't see a reason to go through months of incoming calls.'

'So they're headed over in the morning to interview him, see if he'll agree to these quotes in your piece, or Jesús Ramirez' piece. About ten o'clock that night, the neighbours see a plain, dark-coloured four-door pull up in the driveway. They're worried about old Pierce because of the surgery, so old Mr Wilkins walks outside. Sees a tall slim guy in a dark suit get out of the car. And get this: the guy puts gloves on before going to the door.'

'Dear God. So why's this not in the papers? All I read was that your fine Massachusetts legal system wouldn't reopen the Seacroft case.'

'You read the AP story?'

'I don't know, it was in *USA Today*.'

'Bastards. AP took my story on it, *USA Today* just re-typed it.'

'All right, so you did a story that says nothing happening, cancer guy croaks maybe because of a nitrogen tank but who cares. What else did you leave out?'

'Well, everything I just told you, so don't pass it around. And, that the neighbour got a partial plate number on the car. Matched up with a rental from Boston. Rented by somebody who flew direct from San Jose.'

'Sanders?'

'Nah. Not if Sanders is the Jabba the Hutt you described. He paid cash and showed a California driver's licence, but there's no such driver registered in California.'

'Don't you generally need a credit card to rent a car?' Larry had suffered this humiliation enough times to know.

'Not at Rent-a-Heap. They're the only ones at Logan who let you pay cash.'

'These people are going to kill me, aren't they?'

'Not if they can't find you … or Jesús.'

'I guess I'm impressed by your sneaking around. What happened with the media beat?'

'I'm listed on Romenesko's Media News now. Didn't you send him the Sanders stuff?'

'No. Romenesko won't take anything until it's in a legit paper. I figured I'd let you legitimate reporters do that for me. Your boss know you're fooling with this cops story?'

'The city editor likes me, lets me do it on the side, hoping it gets uglier. And since I live on the Vineyard – '

'Since when?'

'Tell you all about it later. She's got Kennedy blood. Call me tomorrow.'

Larry hung up and got the laptop online again. Figured he should adorn SluiceBox.net with link-buddies to all these MicroTorrent stories, especially O'Leary's stories about Pierce. As usual, the working press had done a poor job of putting these new developments in context, so Larry decided to do it himself. Write better headlines, keep score. He found an HTML editor through Yahoo and downloaded it, thirty-day free trial. Not any harder than using the clumsy word processor, especially once he discovered that coding a Web page was about like formatting text on an old typesetting machine.

In three hours of annoying labour, he created a fresh front page that would have put a grin on William Randolph Hearst – it even looked like a turn-of-the-century yellow daily, with a fine new masthead, elegantly huge headlines and columns of smaller type leading to the many MicroTorrent items available to the curious reader. The now-famous Ramirez investigation was linked to a banner headline, 'THE MURDEROUS RISE OF THOMAS SANDERS'. He linked the other articles – from the *NYT*, *Boston Sun*, *Boston Globe*, *San Jose Mercury News*, the business wires – beneath his own. And, for the hell of it, he linked to the local story of the alleged beach rapist, under a clip-art cartoon of a paddy wagon.

The disgruntled dot.commers should really be heard. In their own passionately illiterate words. He made a headline that read, 'Dark Dispatches From the New-Economy Collapse', and linked it to a ridiculously long collection of letters, all copied straight from Ramirez' Hotmail. No use worrying about libel now.

Larry brewed the last Folger's Single and zapped his labours to Tonga or Switzerland or wherever the servers lived, and then reviewed the work with some amount of pride –

especially the ugly flashing banner advertisements that earned him a half-penny for every page read. Hearst became an American Caesar selling entire *newspapers* for a penny.

Larry Jonestowne's vision was, admittedly, far more modest.

20

Terry Texas, Western Commandant of the Fat Lovers Acceptance Vigilante Army, did not like the looks of this hate-language. Not at all.

The alert was in FLAVA's newsgroup, alt.fat.anti-fat-media.reaction – a national clearing house for the constant slurs against fat people produced by anti-fat corporate media. Terry, who had taken Texas as a revolutionary last name to better reflect her big-is-beautiful philosophy, spent her days seeking evidence of this bias. And part of that mission was checking her comrades' messages on their own Usenet group, a pre-Web messaging system that had devolved over the 1990s from a programmers' bulletin board to the final haunt of the fanatic edges of society. There was a newsgroup for every perversion, crusade and pseudo-philosophy, from Japanese pet-sodomy aficionados to furious critics of The Simpsons' new season to Male Wiccans for the Gold Standard.

None of this concerned Terry Texas. AOL tech support had walked her through the use of these newsgroups, and this was her lone stop on the Usenet list. Here, she found the only people she could tolerate: those who fully agreed with her.

The new outrage, according to someone who called herself Sheeba Maximus, was outside FLAVA's usual realm of

Hollywood movies and stick-figure fashion models and fitness centres and the evil medical associations that constantly issued alleged health reports attacking the obese. This latest assault involved the chief executive officer of an important Silicon Valley computer company.

> From: Sheeba Maximus (Sheeba298@aol.com)
> Subject: WE MUST STOP THESE IDIOTS!!!
>
> Yesterday on Dr Laura I heard a caller tell about a web site called sluce-box.com and it is an ATTACK on SUCCESSFUL FAT PEOPLE who don't buy into *Vogue*-Calvin Klein anorexia. Inside this web site is this, which makes me SICK:
>
>> WHALE OF SILICON VALLEY
>> Sanders is a big man — a big, fat, crude man. His height does little to disguise the rolls of lard on his torso, which he delights in parading naked around his home.
>>
>> It is DISGUSTING to ATTACK a VERY SUCCESSFUL RICH PERSON who fight anti-fat HATE every day to suceed!
>> Here is the web site & you should go to it RIGHT NOW and write to the Corporate Media who insults ALL FAT PEOPLE with this hatefull kind of 'reporting.':
>> http://SluiceBox.net/sanders/index2.html
>
> This makes me FURIOUS :^(
> —Sheeba

It made Terry Texas furious, as well. She looked over her wall of famous fat people: magazine pictures of Roseanne, Mama Cass, Rush Limbaugh (although he sure didn't help the cause), President William Howard Taft (from *National Geographic*), Chairman Mao, the King of Samoa (also from *National Geographic*) and Pavarotti. She would get a picture of this Thomas Sanders man. And she would get rid of this foul Web site.

Terry was not only determined, she had all the time in the world to pursue the cause. Thanks to her dismissal from the San Francisco Public Library, where the haters fired her because their skinny-people elevator was too small for her to reach the special-collections basement, Terry got her full salary every month. Of course they wouldn't just give it to her – the case got tossed between the local courts and the state-disability board and various other bureaucracies. But she won, and at that moment she dedicated her life to the Fat Revolution.

The local support groups and national organizations had let her down; they talked about legislation and public-service announcements. She wanted action, now, and she wasn't going to wait for a bunch of politicians to set things right. Not when they were all in the pocket of the fascist phony diet-industry thieves.

Terry also made a little cash posing for obesity fetish magazines, which seemed to all be published in the Bay Area. She saw the pictorials as political statements, especially the ones where she got to sit on the face of a sickly little skinny guy.

Terry typed the URL into her America Online browser and there it was, another assault, another civil-rights case to be tried in the court of consumer action. She printed the offending page. It would accompany her to the FLAVA meeting that night.

FLAVA rented specially priced office space in a non-profit political-action co-op on the south end of Berkeley, a block from her ground-floor apartment. The FLAVA space, not coincidentally, was also on the ground floor. There were many such co-op leftist spaces in the area, because nobody else really wanted the property. And the wealthy denizens of the good neighbourhoods liked to toss a few city grants around here – it made them feel better about abandoning every aspect of their 1960s' idealism. Despite the real-estate boom from Petaluma to Gilroy, this rump of Berkeley was doomed by its shared municipal border with Oakland's worst ghetto. The Great Internet Bubble had its geographical limits.

Terry took off her giant bathrobe and changed into her public costume: size 56 Russian army surplus pants, size 10 combat boots, and a tablecloth-sized black T-shirt that read 'FAT RULES'. She gathered the new evidence and put it into an army surplus duffel bag and left the apartment, stopping at Flints BBQ for a triple order of Memphis ribs with extra bread and a large RC Cola. She was the first to arrive, which provided time to obliterate the take-out and hang the latest clippings on the bulletin board – the 'Wall of Shame'.

At 7:20 p.m., the FLAVA troops began settling inside. All but a few were women, and most wore *Sandinista Grande* outfits similar to Terry's. It hadn't been easy to furnish the place for meetings, due to the general size of the membership, but Terry had dealt with this manufacturers' racism by collecting La-Z-Boy chairs from local thrift shops. This created a curious look to the meeting room, with the big tattered recliners orbiting a large lectern generally used by Terry, and facing the Ché Guevara-style banner on the back wall, illustrated with a silhouette of a large person brandishing a machine gun and the FLAVA logo. The usual fluorescent light fixtures hung above, with the usual call-to-action leaflets spread over a second-hand folding table.

The final FLAVA attendees arrived and sank into the

remaining armchairs, and Terry Texas began the weekly session.

'Comrades, I welcome you to this session of the Fat Lovers Acceptance Vigilante Army.' She raised her fist in salute and several members returned this gesture from their chairs. 'First, I want to commend those of you who took part in our protest Saturday. We made the evening news on two channels and the Monday *Examiner*. And, that terrible hate-filled health club, which had the shameless nerve to run that horrible, hurtful advertising campaign – '

A hiss rose from the FLAVA troops. The television commercial in question was run by a local gym, a low-budget spot showing aliens invading Earth. The punchline was, 'When the Martians arrive, they'll eat the fat ones first'.

'That disgusting piece of skinny propaganda has been *pulled* from two stations already!'

Hoots and whistling.

'But the battle has just begun! Let's give the FLAVA call to arms!'

A rumbling chorus chanted, 'We got the Flavour! We are the FLAVA! Death to the Skinny!'

'I was alerted to an especially despicable piece of media garbage today, from a comrade on the alt.fat.anti-fat-media. reaction newsgroup on the Internet. There's a printout on the Wall of Shame – '

'Boo-o-o-o!'

'– for you to read when we're finished. But I'll tell you a little about it – a *racist* and *hateful* Internet magazine called "Sluice Box" is attacking a *hero* of our revolution, a fat and proud president of a software company!' Hoots of approval for the new hero, boos for the alleged Internet magazine.

Scott Charlton, formerly known as p1NGw3n to himself and fellow Walnut Creek High School student Darren Borman, shifted in his recliner. He had been quietly attending FLAVA meetings for the past several weeks, following his sudden release from San Francisco's juvenile-detention facility – and since Darren abandoned him and joined a Concord-based skinhead movement.

After their arrest, many bad things happened, some that Scott didn't ever want to think about. But the worst – if there could be a worst – was his release. After three days of tortuous questioning, interspersed by three days of savage abuse by the gangland regulars of the centre, Scott was told to go home. He would not become a famous hacker.

His confession, the prosecutor said, was nonsense. His vivid recollections of destroying *InterWorldNet* Media Ventures had nothing in common with the actual crime. He excitedly told of shooting a fish tank with his Uzi and watching all the anti-hacker-media fish die on the carpet, but there was no fish tank in the offices, no evidence of gunfire, no gun, and no carpet. His tales of 'wiping out the secret memory globe' had no earthly meaning, while his description of a space-age rooftop headquarters sounded like something from a James Bond movie and suggested that he had never set foot in the rather bland offices of the computer magazine.

His mother, from whom he'd inherited his bulky frame, picked him up at the San Francisco juvenile jail and didn't say a word the whole way back. His father, a nervous little man, sat in the ranch-house living room until they arrived. Then he read the statement Mrs Charlton had prepared, because it's better for a boy's father to say these things. Scott was grounded for six months. He would finish the school year at an Altamont pseudo-military academy, an hour away by private school bus – a school bus with an armed Vietnam vet as driver. No more Internet, no more computer games, no socializing with anyone.

That last part would be easy, as Darren had been his only friend.

Darren's version of the terrorism was slightly more realistic, so he was held another few days, until he swore that he'd burned a truckload of fresh *InterWorldNet* issues on a nonexistent shipping platform and 'stopped the Internet' for two days. When a cop told him he'd be sued for wasting city resources, he started crying and admitted the great 'Swordfish' had barely entered the building and done little more than knock some monitors off desks. But, coming from a looser family structure than Scott's, Darren wasn't punished in any useful fashion. His sister had suddenly moved to San Francisco to become a lesbian and dance at the Lusty Lady – taking her computer and his interest in being a hacker – and Darren now lived alone with his alcoholic CalTrans highway-engineer father. Mrs Borman had mysteriously vanished in 1992, and he didn't much remember her. Darren dropped out of school and began hanging around with other idiot suburban dropouts who had come to the amazing conclusion that everything was the fault of the Mexicans. And maybe the niggers, but they hadn't seen many black people.

Scott saw Darren exactly once after their release. He was in the driveway, washing his mom's minivan. Darren bicycled past with his new skinhead acquaintances. Scott waved and said hi. Darren stopped, threw a rock, and called his former pal a 'fat pussy.' Scott ran to the garage crying, a big welt forming on his gut. Yes, he had gained a little weight since his release. More than forty pounds. With nothing else to do at home, he took to eating full-time, and his mother always had a big plate of something waiting in the kitchen.

When Scott's loneliness and weight got to him, he begged for clemency. His mother's compromise came from a small display ad in the *Contra Costa Times*: 'Skinny fascists got you down? Join the Fat Lovers Acceptance Vigilante Army! Meets Thursday, 7:30 p.m., 6513 Shattuck #101, Berkeley.'

'You only got into trouble because those rail-thin people made you feel bad about yourself,' Mrs Charlton said. 'If you could accept that you're just a bigger boy, you'd be fine.'

He cried, as was becoming common, but his mom said there was 'more to love' now, and she agreed to amend his house arrest for the weekly FLAVA meetings. She would drive him there and back to make sure he didn't get into any more trouble.

So here he was, four weeks later. He hadn't exactly made any friends, since the rest of the FLAVA troops were about twenty years older, but he was feeling a little better about himself. He'd even taken to wearing the massive army surplus pants and combat boots, thanks to his mom, who drove down to Oakland to buy his new outfit. But Scott was still uncomfortable about the jellyfish growing under his chest, and wore a raincoat even when Walnut Creek was sweltering.

'Uh, Miss Texas?'

'Huh? Who're you?'

'Uh, I'm Scott. Scott Charlton. I've been coming all month.'

'And? We're having a meeting now.' Which meant, Terry was speaking.

'Well, uh, this Internet magazine thing? Being mean to this guy and all?'

'Yes?'

'Well, I'm, uh, I'm a hacker. A computer hacker.'

A gurgle of surprise from the La-Z-Boys.

'Yeah, and, well maybe I can teach these people a lesson, about being nice to fat guys and all.'

Terry draped her torso over the lectern and sized up the kid. She hadn't noticed him, since she really didn't notice anyone unless they disagreed with her. But he looked safe. A little young, but certainly fat. Even wore fatigues.

'And what would you do with this hacker equipment?'

'Oh, uh, well it's not equipment. I mean, you just use a computer. On the Internet. We'd shut down this Internet site. Maybe put up our own, uh, revolution thing.'

'You're really a hacker? One of these kids who breaks into the FBI?'

'Yeah, that's me,' he lied.

'You could break into the Centres for Disease Control's Web page?'

A round of boos; every FLAVA member hated the CDC for its constant propaganda equating obesity with heart disease, diabetes, etc.

'Yeah, I probably could.'

'Good. We'll talk after the meeting.' And Terry Texas ranted for another hour. Her targets were many, but all were thin. The girls on *Friends*, Kate Moss, Madonna, etc. Oprah Winfrey had been on FLAVA's good side, but she'd recently gone on a successful diet, and this did not sit well with the Fat Revolution.

As the sermon ended, Terry told everyone to copy down this Web site's address and send complaints to the editors. If the offending article wasn't gone by next week's meeting, a boycott of the advertisers would begin.

The closing chant was called and the revolutionaries got out of the armchairs with various degrees of effort.

Scott stood by the window to look for his mom's minivan. Terry stomped up to him and said, 'So when are you going to hacker these sons of bitches?'

'Well, it's sort of, uh, complicated right now.'

'Why?! Are you with us or against us?'

'No, sure, I'm all with you. It's just that ... Well, I got caught. By the cops. For hacking this place in San Francisco.'

'Oooh. So you've gone to jail for the revolution?'

'Well, for a little while I guess. My mom, she won't let me have a computer now.'

Terry stared at the boy. The revolution *always* attracted counter-revolutionary demons.

'Where's this mom of yours?'

'She picks me up. She'll be here in a minute.'

'Yeah? Well then I'll talk to her.'

Mrs. Charlton pulled up at 9:30 p.m. exactly. She waved to Scott and Terry marched to the minivan, prepared for trouble. But Terry saw the woman behind the wheel was hefty.

'Hello, you're this boy's mother?'

'Yes, I'm Scott's mother. Who are you?'

'Terry Texas, FLAVA.'

Scott came near the window, trying not to get in Terry's way. 'Hi mother,' he said.

'Well hi Scotty! Who's your lady friend?'

'I told you, Terry Texas. Scott is doing some … extra work for the group. He needs to use my computer.'

'Hmm. Well I don't know about that, Miss Texas was it? You see, Scott got into some trouble with these computers and he – '

'Do you care about your son's well-being? Do you want him to be a self-hating fat person?'

'No, no, certainly not! I've tried to tell him – '

'Then he needs to make a difference. Do you want him to make a difference?'

'Of course! I only want the best for Scotty.'

'I'll make sure he gets home early. The only way to stop the oppression of fat people is to do something about it.'

'Well, I guess you're right, Miss Texas. All right, Scotty, you help the nice lady with the computer and then you come *straight home*, you understand?'

Scott nodded and said, 'I promise, mother.'

'And you know our address, don't you now?'

He nodded again. Lived on ButterFlower Court his whole life, how could he not know the address?

'Okay, well you call if there's any delay, and I'll wait up for you. Now give momma a kiss.' Scott gave her a peck on her hamster cheek and she drove away, waving out the window.

'You better not be bullshitting, boy.'

Scott swore he wasn't. He told himself, *I'm a hacker*, and that helped him not cry again.

Terry nodded to the FLAVA troops exiting and locked the meeting-room door. 'Follow me,' she commanded. He did. They were at her apartment minutes later.

Scott was led to the computer desk and told to sit down, although it really wasn't a computer desk. It was a dining-room table in the living room, with savagely scissored fashion magazines all around the keyboard. She asked if he was hungry and he said 'a little'. And she picked up the phone, ordering a double-deal triple-meat special from Dominos. And that pizza bread with sauce. And a two-litre bottle of Coke.

'Okay, I'm off the phone. Do your hacking.'

'It's, uh, going to take a little while.'

Terry growled and went to the couch and turned on the teevee. He was relieved, until she started cussing at the fitness infomercials and music videos and everything else. At least she stayed away from the PC. He found the America Online shortcut and logged in, thankful her password was saved. Then he typed in a few spelling variations of Sluice-Box.net until he got it right, and looked over the page. On top was that story about the software boss everybody seemed mad about. And beneath that, all sorts of crazy stuff. Letters from computer people, maybe hackers. News stories about computer companies. A bunch of things written by somebody named Jesus, with a Mexican last name. These were kind of funny. One about a computer bigshot who got caught with child pornography at an airport in England. Another saying a software millionaire had lied about getting some fancy college degree and how the company was going broke. Maybe this Jesus guy was some kind of hacker? Scott wasn't sure of the qualifications involved.

How would he hack this? Scott typed yahoo.com and then the question, 'How do I break in for Jesus computer?' Yahoo not being an ask-a-question search engine, it returned everything from ABBA lyrics to a collection of T-shirts printed with the slogan, 'What Would Jesus Do?' He tried again, simple this time: 'Hacker.' That was better. He found some articles on a Web site called 2600.com, and some things from a school called MIT. They were all kind of complicated. But there was a flashing banner advertisement that caught his eye: *Register your Web site today! Do it now!* He clicked, and was taken to the Network Solutions page. He saw a little magnifying glass graphic that said 'Who Is?' He entered SluiceBox.net and found it was registered to somebody named Jesus, with a Mexican last name. In a country he'd never heard of – Bolivia.

Maybe another hacker would help. He found one of those bulletin boards Darren used to talk about, and typed this question:

Hi. I'm p1NGw3n. Could anybody of you guys help me break into a bad corporate internet web site that is against hackers? I would appreciate it if you would tell me. Thanks alot. P1NGw3n.

That didn't sound right. Maybe use those weird spellings like the other hackers?

Dot.Con

H1. I'm p1NGw3n. Coul2 anyb0dy 0f U gUyZ help m3 break int2 a b@d corpor$te 1nternet web s1te that 1z aga1st h@ck3rz? 1 wouLd @pprec1ate It 1f U woUld teLL m3. ThanXs al0t. p1NGw3n@aol.com

There was a knock at the door. Dominos.

Scott realized his mom hadn't given him any money tonight and felt bad that he couldn't contribute, but Terry didn't mention it. She put the pizza box on the coffee table, and told him to come eat. He sent the message – hoping Mrs Charlton had forgotten to shut off America Online's monthly charge to her Discover card – and closed the search-engine windows so Terry wouldn't see his incompetence.

'Gettin' cold, come on.'

He nervously went to the couch.

'Sit down. What's wrong with you?'

'Nothing, Miss Texas.'

She opened her pizza and began devouring the pepperoni-ham-ground beef pie. Scott was pretty hungry himself. He finished before her, and she got a weird look in her eyes.

'You're a hungry boy, aren't you?'

'Sorta, yeah.'

'You want a little of Terry's?'

He nodded and she lifted her last slice to his tomato-sauced mouth. He took a big bite and mumbled thanks. She leaned next to him and put the slice to his mouth again.

'You like Terry feeding your pretty face?'

'Uh, sure, yeah.'

She put the cheese-filled crust between her teeth and straddled young Scott, her massive breasts resting on his shoulders. He didn't know quite how to react, but she seemed nice, if a little scary. Like his mom. His jaws reached for another chunk, tearing off too much because of his overbite, and a big glop of hot tomato sauce fell down her T-shirt, sliding into her cleavage.

Terry Texas moaned and clamped her mouth on Scott Charlton's, the remaining bit of crust lost between their bellies. Her bulk smashed against him and she whispered in his ear, 'This is for the revolution, fat boy.'

When the violence ended, the couch's little wooden legs had collapsed and the coffee table was in splinters. She was atop him on the carpet.

'You like how Terry Texas takes care of you?'

'Yeah,' Scott said, in shock from his first sexual act involving another person.

'And you're going to hacker this racist bastard, aren't you?'

He sort of nodded.

'And once we've shut down this fat-hating magazine, you and me are going to find this hate-filled piece of garbage who wrote this crap about Thomas Sanders. And we're going to teach him a lesson.'

'My mom's gonna be real mad if I don't get home soon.'

21

'Rise and shine. Somebody's trying to snoop around your offshore business.'

'What time is it?'

'Ten.'

Larry groaned and sat up. The bedspread was tight around the window specifically to prevent his awareness of the daylight.

'Did it work?'

'Course not. These boys preside over a gambling outfit hated the world over. They're used to it.'

Online casinos were not very popular with the folks who ran gaming towns like Vegas and Atlantic City and Monte Carlo. The governments didn't like it, either. No regulation, no lucrative tax payments. What good was grease-palmed legislation allowing a riverboat casino when the chronic gamblers could sit at home and play the sports books or piss away their money on Web blackjack? Worse than the Indian reservations. And, in the case of Werner's pals, the companies and computers were spread around the same countries famed for tax shelters and no-question banking.

'How you know these boys, exactly?'

'We've talked enough crime on the phone, don't you think? Time to expand.'

Larry put the handset down and struggled out of bed. 'Time to expand' was special code for 'Meet you at the Expansion Room', a saloon at Market and Church actually called The Expansion Bar, but like many bars it developed a slightly different name among the clientele. The code wasn't originally devised to evade prosecution; it was simply useful whenever they wanted to ditch a crowd and have a drink in peace.

But not at 10:12 a.m., for God's sake. Larry brushed his teeth in the shower, towelled himself alert and put on the cop suit. He'd been wearing it all week, and had finally retrieved his original filthy clothes from Werner's so the suit could make a needed visit to Leng's 1-Hour Cleaners behind the TravelLodge.

Stubble on the chin and out of shaving cream. He knotted his tie and locked the room behind him, flipping the Do Not Disturb sign to Please Clean Room. Another day on the job for Jesús Ramirez.

Werner was at a table by the jukebox with two Bloody Marys and his PowerBook. Larry asked for coffee and sat down.

'Lookin' sharp, Jonestowne.'

'I know.'

'Could use a shave, though.'

The bartendress delivered Larry's coffee and he said thanks. Werner spun the computer around to display the evidence: an e-mail from the Swiss Guys showing the recent sniffing from machines belonging to MicroTorrent Systems and bips.net.

'But they failed?'

'I told you, matey, they deal with such intruders all the time. This is just for your paranoia.'

'Thanks so much.' The caffeine began working its daily magic. 'They still happy with the arrangement?'

'Yeah, seems so.' Werner opened a window with another message. 'Says they're getting plenty of traffic from your little nightmare. You've a gambling readership.'

'Wonderful. And here's something for your many troubles.' Larry took out his Day Timer and removed a cheque to Werner for $2207.55. From the account of Mr Ramirez, for services rendered.

'Never thought I'd see the day,' Werner said, tucking the cheque into his jeans. 'Cheers!'

'Cheers. That's your half of the first advertising payment. Figured you've earned it, what with the multiple criminal acts committed in the name of Jesús.'

'No trouble collecting the mail?'

'Nah. Just as planned. There was a line outside, all the boys collecting their free money.'

'Poofters ought work now and again.'

'What'd I tell you about tolerance, Nazi? Besides, most of 'em go on to become productive citizens of this fine city. And a few drop dead in my building.' Larry waved for more cocktails and coffee. 'Unfortunately, I'm missing one of the credit-card bills. Must've went to Haight Street before the change-of-address got through.'

'Should make a final visit to the old flat.'

'I'll go today. Been putting it off, due to terrible fear. You were going to tell me how you're involved with these gambling titans.'

'Right. Met 'em in London. They ran a pirate radio outfit offshore. Fine station, all the records banned by BBC. Did a bit of freelancing for 'em.'

'You're building up a nice résumé.'

'For deportation.' Werner glanced at Larry's watch and shut down the PowerBook. 'Got some honest work to do now; off to Santa Clara to milk more money from these clowns. Sorry I can't join you at the flat.'

'Yeah, we had so much fun last time.' Larry finished his drink and chewed on the celery, a good source of dietary fibre. 'Maybe I'll ask Nadeem to keep a lookout while I collect my personal effects. If these goons are chasing the Bolivian-Swiss-Tongan Ramirez now, let's pray they've given up on Haight Street.'

'Praying didn't help Jesus of Nazareth, now did it? I'll be home by five.'

Werner reached for money but Larry shook his head.

'Let Jesús pay. We discussed business, didn't we?'

Larry walked up the street to the wine shop and paid for two cases of Australian Shiraz, to be delivered to his motel. Yes, that's right, the TravelLodge, to Mr Ramirez' room. He considered some other errands, but the apartment problem had to be faced.

It was good to stretch the legs a bit, fighting the wind gusts, maneuvring around the homeless. He was weary of whistle-blower e-mails and research and typing – six new mini-articles posted this week, covering the Oakland drug arrest of NetWhere.com's CEO, the rumoured insider-trading charge against Clomp Macro's president, an ugly sexual-harassment situation at Oracle, the foul mistreatment of Indian guest-programmers at Paradigm Shift, Inc., a bootlegged software scandal at PeeCee-People.com, and the sudden closure of *InterWorldNet* Media Ventures.

The *InterWorldNet* collapse was Larry's favourite of the week. His site had become popular with the editorial grunts at *InterWorldNet* — especially among the drones who ran the magazine's unreadable Web site. These anonymous youngsters provided a regular stream of office doom, including news of the fledgling book-department's collapse and the awful new subscription numbers. Once posted to the Sluice Box, these revelations stoked investor nervousness, duly reported by Jesús and then the business media. In turn, Jesús linked to the tech-news coverage. It was a dirty little circle, and in four short days *InterWorldNet*'s editor, LaRouche Melville, was forced to announce yet another 'brief delay' in the public stock offering. And, shortly thereafter, an announcement of the magazine's death after talks with several potential buyers went nowhere. That finished that. Ought to call Denisa and ask about her stock options, Larry thought with a smile.

Unfortunately, Sanders seemed to be squirming out of trouble — ZDNet said he was scheduled to speak at the Vegas COMDEX next week. 'A major address on MicroTorrent's interactive-Net-television strategy', according to the news brief. COMDEX was the biggest of the tech shows, attracting thousands of journalists. And this ZDNet story gave only a passing mention to SluiceBox.net. Larry would not be a footnote. He added a little blurb to his front page, getting a bit carried away with the 1980s' headlines:

JESÚS TO APPEAR AT COMDEX!
Excitement Grows as the Famed and Mysterious Journalist Announces His On-the-Scene Reporting

Dot.Con

From the World's Biggest Computer-Industry Extravaganza! <u>Snake-Oil Vendors and Other Frauds Had Best Take Note!</u>

That last bit linked to the news of Sanders' COMDEX speech.

Having no plans to go anywhere near that awful circus, he registered for press credentials on the COMDEX Web site – Jesús Ramirez, Correspondent, SluiceBox.net. Just to keep things interesting.

Larry strolled through Duboce Triangle – between frisbee-chasing dogs and pasty Speedo-clad boys hoping for sun but getting the first drops of rain. The sidewalks were damp by the time he reached Haight, the capital of filth and human wreckage. The regular hoodlums blocked the entrance to O'Lowney's Market, until one of the kids saw Larry and whispered, 'Vice!'

'Hey Nadeem.'

'Where you been, man?' Nadeem kept working this lousy store while his investments matured. Of course his family owned the store, and three others like it, and the buildings above.

'On assignment.'

Nadeem got a pack of GPCs from the rack, looking at Larry's suit.

'I told you, I'm on assignment.'

'You know what? A buncha guys been hanging around, dressed just like you. You guys start a band or something?'

'No, nothing that bad. They been around lately?'

'Mm-hmm. One came in for a Coke yesterday.'

'Can I get some Camel Lights instead? Oh, and how much I owe you?'

'Man, you must be on assignment. Lemme check.' Nadeem grabbed the spiral notebook hanging by the condoms and flipped to Larry's page. The sign on the cash register was clear – 'Sorry No Credit, Don't Ask' – but he made a few exceptions. Larry always paid, eventually.

'Let's see ... six bottles of that French table wine, nine packs of GPC, two packs of Camels, a can of coffee, a litre of Jack.' Nadeem tapped the prices into the register: $96.74.

Larry peeled five twenties from his wallet. 'With the smokes, this should do it.'

Nadeem tossed over the Camel Lights and leaned his head to Larry. 'You're not selling dope or something, because – '

'Oh come on, for God's sake. Of course not. By the way, you get any weird phone calls this month?'

'Yeah, every day.'

'Specifically, you get any calls about Jesús Ramirez?'

'No ...'

'Yes.'

'Man, I've been going crazy over this. Whyn't you tell me?'

'Haven't been around, as you've noticed.'

'This almost makes sense now. I should've guessed. Aw, this is too much. I've been reading you every day, man!'

Larry arched an eyebrow and rapidly smacked the top of the cigarette box against his palm. 'You're taking investment advice from me?'

'It's all panned out fine, man. You probably saved me a grand on Clomp Macro. Where you getting this stuff from?'

'First of all,' he said, lighting a nicely packed Camel, 'it's not *me*, and it's very important nobody ever, ever gets the idea it *is* me.'

'Shit,' Nadeem laughed. 'You sound like my uncles in Gaza.'

A local drunk slipped in, headed for the beer cases in back.

'HEY! You got money, Ray?!'

The drunk mumbled something and lurched for the 40s shelf. Nadeem said 'Excuse me' and leapt over the counter, shooting down the aisle. He returned with the drunk in a headlock, tossing him through the doorway.

'I fuckin' told you, Ray, don't come in here without money.'

Ray the Drunk got up, brushed off his knees and wandered away, mumbling insults. Nadeem walked behind the counter and shrugged.

Larry grinned, glad to see the store operating as usual.

'So where you staying?'

'Around. Actually, maybe you can help me. I've got to get in there and divest, as it were. And for reasons we don't need to discuss, I'm a little concerned about these guys stealing my fashion sensibility. Delivery coming soon?'

'Yeah, beer's coming pretty soon.'

'Lovely. Somebody you know?'

'Well yeah, a cousin.'

'Of course. If you could run a brief blockade, that might at least keep me from vehicular abduction.'

'Blockade? Shit, that sounds kind of fun. Lemme get my mom to watch the register.'

22

The first peculiarity of Larry's homecoming was the blond man in the cop suit, staring out the third-floor window of the neighbouring building. Larry jaywalked between a honking MUNI bus and a growing mob of bicyclists from the weekly 'Critical Mass' protest. Cops must've forced them off Market Street. He kept an eye on the window. And just as he let himself inside the gate, the man's gaze went down to 593 Haight Street. Both wore dark suits, wearing police-style sunglasses in the rain. Here goes, thought Larry, giving the man a friendly cop wave.

Thrown off by Larry's own BIPS suit, the man gave a terse wave in return. Dry cleaning pays.

Larry calmly and frantically got in the lobby, noticing the door's glass pane had been replaced. Mr Teng taking care of his investment. Nobody in the lobby or on the stairs. Larry checked both mailboxes, a new Cantonese nametag on 593-D's slot. He stuffed the few letters and bills into his jacket pocket and took the stairs quietly. A Post-it note on his door: YOU PAY <u>RENT</u> – MR. TENG.

'Make this quick,' Larry told himself. Somebody had been inside. Books knocked off the shelves, sofa cushions on the floor, fridge door open along with the back window. He glanced down to the alley, bid silent farewell to the rat buddies, and closed the squeaky window. Pulled the giant duffle from the closet and stuffed his minimal clothing inside. His shaving kit and washcloth from the bathroom – never know when a motel won't provide washcloths. The zippered binder of music CDs. Whoops ... The newspapers piled around his armchair were loaded with MicroTorrent stories. Then again, any pile of recent papers was full of MicroTorrent stories. A rushed selection of books. A bulging folder of selected Jonestowne clips from the pantry, a manila envelope of personal photographs, his lucky National Security Agency mug, the Sony ICF shortwave and the midget boombox. With a little tugging, it all fitted into the duffle bag. A corpse could fit in the duffle bag.

He took a final look around the one-bedroom flat, wishing good luck to the hundreds of orphaned books, the homemade desk, the loyal coffeepot, the various furnishings and awful artworks bought from Charles.

Honking outside. Screaming of bicyclists. Blockade in progress. Larry hoisted the huge bag and reached for the doorknob. It turned from the outside. He dropped the duffle at his feet — on his feet, actually — and put his full weight against the door, struggling to get the key from his pocket and into the deadbolt.

Through the door, a cop-style voice yelled, 'OPEN UP!'

No need answering. The bolt went home just as the top panel of the door splintered. He grabbed the duffle again and lugged it to the living room. The window stuck. Larry heaved the 200-pound sack through the glass and it plopped on the shingled ledge. He stepped outside, really pouring now, careful of the rain-rotted eaves. On the street, the beer-distributor truck had westbound traffic blocked, while Nadeem's '67 convertible Mustang took care of the east. Haight Street was never meant to be a thoroughfare. Car horns and curses down there, headlights turning on as the sky darkened. Larry caught Nadeem's eye and pointed to the colossal duffle balancing on the edge.

'Toss it down!' Nadeem yelled, squinting under a Giants cap. 'Back seat!'

Larry gripped the window sill with one hand, gashing his palm on a chunk of glass, and launched the bag. It landed a bit short and with a terrific thud, on the windshield of an illegally parked Plymouth K-car.

Nadeem cursed and dragged it off the injured vehicle. He got it into the Mustang's back seat and saw trouble: two of those cop-suit guys, blocked on Steiner by the traffic, getting out of a grey Ford Taurus at the intersection. The bicycle protesters were riding in circles, kicking at the paralyzed cars, chanting 'Clean Transportation Now!' From the south, sirens.

'Get down from there, man!'

'Trying!'

Larry shook off the sunglasses and transferred his grip

from the sill to a flagpole, a rainbow flag jutting from the neighbour's apartment. The cop shoes didn't have much traction; he skidded twice and nearly dropped. That's when his doppelganger appeared in the busted window.

'Don't move!'

'I ... I'm with you!'

'What?'

It was creepy. Same jaw and build and height and nearly the same white-blond hair. Maybe a few years older. Same as all the agents. These BIPS goons must've come off an assembly line.

Larry used his free hand to pull the badge from his pocket. He saw the goon pulling something different and let the badge cover flip open.

'Phillip Trageser!'

'Trageser?! Didn't you ... you're not ...?'

Larry steadied into a crouch and let the flagpole hand reach behind him, to the plastic owl, sticky with wet pigeon crud.

'Yeah buddy, I'm back on the case.' Back from the acid nightmare of the sea lions.

The honking was deafening. Confused, the goon stepped through the window, his right hand still inside his coat, left hand gripping the sill and hitting a chunk of jagged glass.

'Damnit!'

'Careful, that window's broken,' Larry said. The owl head was off now, and his fingers searched for the opening of the felafel bag. There.

'I know Trageser!' the goon yelled. 'I worked with Trageser! You're not Phil Trageser!'

Larry pointed the Glock at the goon's chest.

'Whatever, jackass. Don't move.'

The goon moved. Larry fired – not a bad shot for someone whose most recent target practice was six years back, aimed at the dockside rats on Bratislava's riverfront. The bullet sank into rain gutter, two buildings down. But the goon slipped. And a rotted eave gave way. The BIPS man grabbed at a glistening shingle. Both the shingle and the goon went down, his drop cut short by the spiked gate installed to prevent exactly this kind of intrusion.

Larry glanced down and saw the wet iron tips protruding from the man like the dorsal fins of a stegosaurus, from the lower back to the skull. And just beyond the carnage, Nadeem, yelling something. Larry was having trouble concentrating with all the noise and blood and the numb feeling in his right hand from the shooting. He grabbed the flagpole and dragged himself to a steadier chunk of ledge. Put the gun back in the owl's belly and screwed on the head, tossing it to Nadeem, who caught it and tossed it to the beer-truck driver.

Seeing the cop-suit guys knocking bike riders aside, Nadeem left his precious Mustang and worked his way through the protest, waving to the goons. 'One of your guys is down, in the alley!' He pointed to the rat world behind Larry's building. They went for it, turning back on Steiner and fighting through the bicyclists.

Larry eased down, scraping hell out of his back, and landed feet-first on his porch. This is interesting, he thought – a dead guy pierced on a fence and nobody paying the slightest attention to anything but the bike lunatics and the traffic. And scattered on the stoop in front of him, the dead man's wallet, car keys, cell phone, gun, BIPS badge and Life Savers. These items might be useful someday.

He gathered the evidence and loaded it into his own suit, the Glock stuffed down his belt. Unhooked the shoulder holster and slipped it off the impaled torso. As an afterthought, he emptied his own wallet of everything but his driver's licence, reaching up to stick his calfskin trifold into the goon's damp back pocket. The man's pale skin peeked between his shirt and belt, revealing an old surgical scar.

Nadeem came around the corner, looking a bit tense.

'Get in the truck!'

Larry opened the gate and stepped through, the dead man's left hand slapping his head. No wedding ring. Nadeem jabbered something in Arabic to the beer-truck driver, who hopped in the Mustang and ended the eastbound traffic blockage by burning an enviable amount of rubber and speeding away.

'In there!' Nadeem yelled, pointing to an open rack. Larry squeezed between the cases of Budweiser and pulled the rolling door down. Nadeem blasted the truck horns and tapped the accelerator. Cop cars from every direction, their lights bouncing off the Victorian houses. The goons came out of the alley, saw the approaching SFPD army, and in cowardly fashion got back in their Taurus to make a violent U-turn through the bicyclists. 'That's fucked up,' Nadeem muttered.

Larry ate a Life Saver and bounced in the dark with the bottles and cans. The ride lasted an hour. Nadeem rolled the panel door open and started yammering.

'I seen a lot of Clint Eastwood movies, I seen a lot of *Miami Vice*, I've worked on Haight Street since I was fifteen, and I ain't *ever* seen anything like that.'

Larry stretched his arms and blinked in the afternoon sun. They must have come south; the rain had a near-exclusive love for the city.

'You mind if I open one of these beers?'

'What is all this, man, the mafia?' He pulled off the baseball cap and dropped it, checking his hair in the truck's side mirror.

'Okay,' Larry said, twisting the cap of a Bud. 'First tell me where we are.'

'San Mateo, at my cousin's warehouse. Hope to hell he

doesn't wreck my 'stang.'

'I'm sure it'll be fine. Any more bastards in these suits see what happened?'

'They tried, man. They were stuck at the intersection with those bicycle protesters. I saw that guy fall on the gate and ran over to 'em, told 'em to go in the alley, that one of their boys was hurt.'

'Perfect. *You* ought to be in an Eastwood movie, my friend. Dirty Nadeem.'

'Oughta not be involved with this ... Why're you wearing one of their suits? Who are they?'

'They seem to work for MicroTorrent Systems, some sort of corporate intelligence squad. You want a beer?'

'I don't drink man, I'm Muslim. Fine, gimme one.'

'Here. So you know about the Jesús Ramirez thing. They're after *him*. He ... Well, he used to live in my building.'

'This is messed up.'

Larry told a quick version. 'And these corporate spies from MicroTorrent have been after Ramirez' head, or my head, ever since.'

Nadeem took a sip and considered this outrage. Having grown up in East Jerusalem during the *intifada*, he'd seen many ugly deaths and wasn't particularly troubled by the day's bloodshed – it was the convoluted background that disturbed him. Then again, he'd made a grand off Ramirez' business tips ...

'So how do they know it's you?'

Larry finished his warm beer, replaced it with another, and lit a cigarette.

'Maybe they don't. I hope they don't. A few things connect it all, if they ever figure it out. Doesn't matter, now I'm dead.'

'Dead?'

'The guy stuck to my gate? It's Larry Jonestowne. Most

accidents happen at home, you know.'

'You're dead?'

'Looked enough like me, especially with his face troubles. I had a moment to trade IDs with him.'

'What made you do that?'

'Honestly? I don't know.' Larry sat on the footboard of the truck and examined his cut hand.

'Man, they've got DNA and all that stuff now. They're not gonna believe that guy is you.'

'Well, who's going to argue with the cops, or the coroner? Not this spy shop – it can't be good for business to have your dead private eye all over the papers. And the cops can collect all the fingerprints and skin flakes and stray hairs they want – some will match our clumsy dead friend Larry Jonestowne, and some won't match anything at all.'

Nadeem considered the story's many holes – he learned English watching *Columbo* and *The Rockford Files* on Israeli teevee.

'What about fingerprints? Don't they fingerprint you for a passport?'

'No. Maybe they do now, especially for dangerous foreigners like you.'

'And the guy really looked like you?'

'You saw him. Yeah, he looked enough like me, maybe fifteen pounds heavier.'

'What about the guy's family?'

'No wedding ring. Let me see your cell phone.'

'What's wrong with yours?'

Larry had the dead man's phone clipped to his belt. Next to the Glock.

'Wouldn't be wise. Let me use yours.'

'Press "end" when you're done. Who you calling?'

'Myself.' Larry dialled his voice mail and hit 4 to 'change personal options'.

'Hi, this is Larry. Uh, I can't take your call, and, well, I just can't take it any more. The voices, the vampires in the walls, the miserable horror of it all ... That goddamned Yugoslav war, I can't get it out of my head. Make the shelling stop! If only I had a gun ... Well, to hell with it, I'll just jump out the window. Uh, goodbye forever. Leave a message at the tone.'

Larry smiled and handed the phone to Nadeem. 'This cell in your name?'

'Well, not exactly. One of those bums gave it to me for a six-pack. They always come in with these things; I use 'em 'til the phone company turns 'em off.'

'That's a crime,' Larry said, taking the phone again. 'Now, do me a final favour. Tell the cops you're my buddy, and it sounds like I left a suicide message on my voice mail.'

'What?'

'Just do it. Otherwise the cops might never think to check it.' Larry dialled 911 and held the phone to Nadeem's ear.

'Hi, yeah. I want to ... uh, I want you to check on my friend, Larry. Larry Jonestowne ...'

'With an E,' Larry whispered.

'Yeah, J-o-n-e-s-t-o-w-n-e. I'm worried, I guess, because his answering machine, I mean his voice mail, it says he's gonna kill himself.'

Larry grinned and nodded.

'On Haight Street.' Nadeem mouthed *What's the address?* and Larry whispered it.

'Yeah, it's 593 Haight Street, apartment C ... No, C, like casualty. Yeah okay, thanks.'

Larry hit the 'end' button.

'C as in casualty?'

'I don't know what I'm supposed to say.'

'Don't worry, that was fine. Now, about the phone.'

'Aw man, I just got this one.'

'I'll buy you a real one, in your own name.' Larry dropped the Nokia to the concrete, stomped it good, and kicked the remains into the weeds.

23

Nadeem let Larry stay in his family's San Mateo house. A fine house, with one side for the women and another for the men and a lovely patio for summer dining. To avoid additional witnesses, Larry stayed in a guest room on the men's side, where Nadeem's girlfriends were sometimes hidden. In the morning, the Mustang was back. Both agreeing the cop-suit should vanish, Nadeem loaned Larry a pair of jeans and a Sierra Nevada Pale Ale T-shirt and drove him to the TravelLodge – 'Keep your damned blond head down,' he said – and they unloaded the duffle and owl and plastic bag of BIPS paraphernalia in the Ramirez room.

'Well, that's a lot more than I ever intended to ask you for, but thanks a lot.'

'No problem. Dudes had me nervous all week.'

Larry gave a hundred to Nadeem. 'Get yourself a new phone. And tell your mom that hommos was delicious. Not that I was at your house or anything.'

'Yeah? She's proud of her hommos.'

'Wonderful stuff. I'll see you in a while, when things cool down. I'm here if you want to stop by. *Assalaamu alaykum* and whatever.'

They shook hands and Nadeem sped down Market in his convertible. That afternoon, a plainclothes cop stopped by the liquor store – Detective Coulter Stevens, who knew Nadeem as one of the few sane people on the block. The

Lower Haight was a death magnet. Homicide, suicide, dope overdose, exposure, liver failure ... When a week passed without a corpse, Stevens got nervous.

'See anything yesterday?'

'Oh yeah.' Nadeem hopped over the counter and walked to the doorway with Stevens.

'Make a statement?'

'Not much to state. Crazy dude jumped through that window, speared himself on that fence.'

'Know him?'

'He came around the store. Larry something.' Nadeem lit a cigarette and offered one to the detective. 'Crazy dude, always wearing that black suit like an undertaker or something.'

'You see him jump?'

'Saw enough. I was in the street helping the beer guy unload. My mom was at the register. All these bike protesters riding around, breaking shit, screaming and hollering.'

'Yeah, they're real charming.'

'I heard the guy's window go CRASH! Look up and see him land on that gate. Made me want to throw up.'

'Well, buddy, maybe you just closed the case.'

'What case? Freak killed himself.'

'Yeah, seemed that way. But somebody showed up with a security-guard badge or some horseshit, said the jumper was his "partner" on a "stakeout". They told him to wait for a detective and he walked off.'

'This street's full of freaks.'

'No kidding. Anyway, no witnesses as usual, nothing else about mysterious stakeouts, so I thought I'd come see my regular witness.'

'Ain't nobody wants to talk to cops around here.'

'Don't I know it.' Stevens tossed the half-smoked cigarette in the gutter. 'Take it easy.'

Nadeem waved, strangely exhilarated by his twenty-four hours of death and intrigue. Maybe he would take that police exam after all.

Larry locked the door and dumped the plastic sack on the bed. Another Glock. He forced it inside the owl – these owls weren't really designed to hold *two* guns – and put his loose credit cards and money in the new wallet. Would have to do something about a driver's licence, someday. He examined the dead man's ID: Richard S. Welch of Palo Alto, age forty, one inch shorter, same eyes and hair, allegedly same weight. Liar.

After tucking Welch's licence, concealed weapon permit and sundry plastic cards inside the BIPS badge cover, Larry stuck it all into the lightweight shoulder holster, considering his options. He lifted the mattress and saw the usual abandoned porn magazines. Too obvious. Under the sink? The toilet's water tank? He paced around the room, frustrated, and kicked at the wall. The cheap drywall gave way, a perfect little hole. He jammed the holster inside and refitted the loose chunk of drywall, using Crest Tartar Control as cement. Wiped away the plaster dust with a wet towel. Then he pushed the two cases of Shiraz in front of the patch job. Perfect.

He rolled a chair outside and climbed onto it, reaching over the eaves with the owl. Pigeons everywhere. 'Move, filthy birds,' Larry whispered. They didn't move. He waved the plastic owl, saying 'Flee! I am a bird of prey,' and they just made pigeon noises. He left the owl among them.

Time for the news. Larry bought the papers outside the lobby and took them upstairs. There it was, bottom of page four in the *Chronicle*:

```
HAIGHT ST. MAN PLUNGES FROM WINDOW

In the midst of Tuesday's Critical Mass bicycle
rally and a massive traffic jam in the Lower
```

Haight, a 34-year-old man fell to his death outside his apartment.

Lawrence L. Jonestowne, 34, died immediately after falling from his second-storey window onto a security gate along the sidewalk, police said. Medical examiners at the scene said Jonestowne's apartment was in disarray and that the death was being considered a suicide. There was no note, police said, but the man's answering machine message said he was depressed over the fighting in the former Yugoslavia and would take his own life.

The death occurred as more than 300 bicyclists stopped traffic on the street, stranding commuters on MUNI bus lines 7 and 71. City medical examiners said the man's street-facing window had been shattered, leading them to believe he had leapt through the glass and onto the iron gating below. No witnesses to the death have come forward, and neighbours had no information about the man or the incident.

'That's it?' Larry said, throwing down the newspaper. 'What about my work? Three California Newspaper Publishers Association awards? The Gulf War, folks?! A year's reports from Sarajevo?! Fuckers.'

He flopped onto the bed and turned on the teevee. Regis, CNN, soap operas, sporting events, Mexican soap operas, cartoons, CNBC. That's it. Larry Jonestowne was dead, and nobody cared.

Well, that was the idea, wasn't it? He got his Day Timer off the table and flipped through the address book. Must be a relative in here somewhere. Sure, Earl Jonestowne in San Antonio. His methadone-addict half-brother. Dialled the number, not bothering with the PacBell card. The following number has been changed, please make a note of it. Larry made a note of it and dialled again.

A very young Texan voice answered, 'Hullo?'
'Who's this?'
'Lauren.'
'Lauren Jonestowne?' Jesus, a niece.
'No. Lauren Banner.' A half-niece?
'Is Earl Jonestowne there?'
'Who?'
'Never mind. Bye.' No niece. Maybe Earl was dead, too. Good riddance.

He called Suzie.
'Yeah?'
'Hey, it's Larry.'
'Bastard, you haven't called me all week.'
'I know, I'm sorry. Things got difficult.'
'I don't even know where to call you. You don't answer e-mail – '
'Need you to do me a favour.'
'Why should I?'
'It's important. I need you to go to the coroner and identify my body.'
'What?'
'Just call 'em up, tell them you read about my suicide – it's in today's *Chronicle*, page four in the front section.'
'I'm supposed to tell somebody you're dead?'
'No, no, they already know I'm dead. Just say you want to see the body, and when you see it, say it's me. You know what an appendectomy is?'
'I'm not stupid.'
'Of course you're not. My corpse has an appendectomy scar, make sure to tell 'em that. And it wouldn't hurt to cry or something.'
'Ha! Why would I cry? I deny everything.'
'Yeah, well *admit* everything to these people. Or make something up. Tell 'em you're my girlfriend, my fiancée.'

'You wish.'

'Come on, it's an ugly situation. I need to be cremated. Tell 'em that was my desire. No family, no arrangements, just cremate me.'

'That costs money.'

'Fine, write a cheque. I'll pay you tonight. And I'll buy you as much sushi as you can eat.'

'Sushi? The good place?'

'Mm-hmm, that's the one. Seared ahi, soft-shell crab, sashimi of every variety, eel – '

'Spicy tuna rolls?'

'You bet. And sake. Oceans of cold, delicious, premium sake.'

'Yum. But I'm only eating grapefruit this week, my diet – '

'Will you quit with these freakin' diets.'

'I guess I can eat fish for one night. Hey, why'd you kill yourself?'

'I've been depressed about all the wars.'

'Hah!'

'Just tell them what I said. They won't care. Meet you at nine?'

'I want the seared ahi on the table when I walk in.'

'Of course.'

Larry hung up, smiling. Why couldn't every woman be just like her? He thought about this a moment, and figured it was probably best that every woman in the world couldn't be lured into terrible perjury with a sushi dinner.

He showered and remembered he'd forgotten to get shaving cream again. Five days' growth ... Why not? Dressed in khakis and a button-down from the duffle, he headed out for a coffee. While sitting outside at the Cup o' Joe, the mobile phone rang. He let it ring, finished his coffee, took the Nokia from his belt and turned it off. Should get rid of this thing. He stuffed the phone into his empty cardboard cup, snapped the plastic lid on top and dropped it down the café's trash slot with the *SF Weekly*. Then he visited his personal bank, passport in hand, and closed the account. Who knew how fast the machines of mortality churned? Yes, very sorry, moving across the country, must withdraw everything. A manager had to approve the cashout and Larry was aware of the security cameras. He took the envelope of hundreds and tucked it in his pants pocket. Looked like he was carrying a burrito. Went to Bank of America on Castro and bought a $4000 bank cheque to the order of Jesús Ramirez. 'Buying a car from this guy,' Larry told the teller. 'Hope I'm not getting ripped off.' The teller didn't care.

A new image was required. He walked down 14th Street until he found a 'unisex salon' called Screamin' Scissors, filled with talkative young homosexuals. Flipped through *GQ* and *People* and *Out* until he was called to the chair.

'And what can we do for you today?'

'I ... I want a new look.'

'And pray tell, what would that be?'

'Mexican.'

'Mexican?'

'Dye my hair black, give me a shave and leave the moustache. And dye that black, too.'

'Hmm, Mexican? That's a new one.'

'Yeah, novelty all around.'

'Don't know if you've got enough whiskers for a moustache yet.'

'Deal with what's there.'

In a huff, the stylist applied the hot shaving foam and carved a moustache from the stubble. Then he applied the colour to Larry's hair and upper lip, which burnt like hell. The purgatory ended with a rinse and shampoo and another rinse.

'All right, there you are. Like it?'

'Sure.'

'Here's something to keep the moustache dark as it grows in.'

Larry accepted a packet of beard dye.

'Shampoo normally, and come back in a week so we can re-do the roots.' The stylist ran his fingers through Larry's newly dark hair. 'It looks much better on you than I thought it would. Really brings out your suntan. Do you want styling gel?'

'Thanks, but no.' Larry lived in San Francisco; he had no suntan. 'You know Jesús? He used to cut my hair.'

The stylist seemed to back into the mirror. 'Jesús?'

'Yeah, he worked here, didn't he?'

'He used to. He sort of disappeared. You're not a cop or something?'

'No. Why would I be?'

'Some creepy detectives have been coming around all month, looking for Jesús. I figure he got in some trouble, speed or something.'

'Well, I hope Jesús returns. No offence, you did fine. It's just that he cut my hair for a long time.'

'Did he? I thought Jesús only did transsexuals.'

'Well ... I was considering it for a while ... a sex change, I mean. What I owe you?'

The stylist walked Larry to the register and wrote out a bill for the shave and colouring. 'That's thirty-five dollars and five for the moustache dye.'

Larry gave him fifty, promised to return in a week, and got the hell out of there. So the BIPS boys had learned of Jesús' former employer. Best to be extra careful with the charge cards. The motel ... nah, that was fine. The dumb gal hadn't run his card through the computer. Just a primitive carbon slip yet to create a digital trail. He hoped.

At the Van Ness/Market BofA, the black-haired Larry

used the outdoor ATM to deposit a $4000 bank cheque to Ramirez' account. Try putting *that* together, he thought with amusement.

24

Terry Texas struck a deal with Mrs Charlton: for the sake of young Scott's self-image and recovery from juvenile delinquency, he would spend the remainder of the school year at FLAVA's headquarters, doing educational projects for the fat revolution. Mr Charlton wasn't convinced this was a substitute for education, but as usual he kept silent.

Scott's hacking efforts, such as they were, had yet to destroy the Sluice Box. He made many excuses, and Terry accepted them – she liked the sex part. But she was not amused by this Jesus character's response to FLAVA's letters of protest. Their impassioned calls for fat tolerance were all reproduced on the Web site, followed by savagely mocking replies by Ramirez. The worst was his answer to Terry's own letter, which she had spent hours crafting.

> **Dearest Miss Texas,**
>
> **We are grateful for your third-rate Symbionese Liberation Army prose. It is unfortunate that such an idiot outfit doesn't exist today; your skills would be much in demand. And, with the wonders of the digital world to service even your kind, you could merrily compose such dispatches without ever lifting your arse from whatever rent-controlled hovel you call home. Let us take a prejudiced guess – Berkeley?**

You say, 'There are more FAT consumers than sickly skinny consumers', and based on sheer consumption, we would have to agree. Luckily for this newspaper, your angry demographic is not exactly our target audience.

Additionally, you say we must 'apologize to FAT people everywhere or PAY THE PRICE'. We are charmed by your upper-case threats, but in the end, we shall remain among those of lesser heft, and await your imminent demise from diabetes, or heart failure, or ham-sandwich blockage of the trachea, or some such thing.

**Bon appétit,
J. Ramirez**

'We've got to make an example of this evil hater,' Terry said. Scott was at Terry's computer, checking his AOL mail for help from the hackers. None had appeared.

'Maybe we could, uh, kidnap him or something.'

'That's not a bad idea, Scotty.' On her personal Wall of Shame, she thumbtacked the printout of Ramirez' response. 'But I don't think we should try that in Bombay.'

'Uh, it's Bolivia.'

'Don't talk back, boy.'

'Maybe we don't have to find him. Look at this.'

Scott opened SluiceBox.net and pointed to the 'JESÚS TO APPEAR AT COMDEX' headline.

'It's the big computer show in Las Vegas,' Scott explained. 'Even this Thomas Sanders guy is going, to make a speech or something.'

'Hmmm. So this skinny little racist has the nerve to show up at this convention with our fat and proud executive ... Scotty, this is when the cowardly fat people are separated from the *real* fat people – the revolutionaries. Are you ready to kidnap the enemy?'

'Yeah, sure.'

What their plan lacked in elegance, it more than made up for in stupidity. Terry, claiming her FLAVA position made her 'too famous' to perform the actual kidnapping, decided Scott would attend the convention as a proudly fat computer person. This would require a slight change of image, so she sat at Scott's side and directed him to find a proper executive-clothing store – he would pay with her Discover card, and the salesman could call her for approval if necessary. For obvious reasons of despising the self-hating Big and Tall clothiers, she wanted Scotty dressed by whomever dressed the other executives. They tried many searches – 'fat and beautiful CEO suit', 'handsome fat executive', 'proud fat businessman' – but eventually found the shop by reading the *Chronicle*, to which Terry subscribed for the sole purpose of disfiguring the Macy's bra ads. In the business section was a feature about the 'sloppy dorm-room apparel' of young Silicon Valley pirates undergoing a fashion upgrade at an elite Union Square men's boutique.

Scott was horrified of going to the city alone, and less than happy about the shopping spree, having never been to such an establishment. Terry laughed off his concerns, and when he began to cry she raped him on the kitchen floor. So he took the BART and got off in the city.

Larry went to a fancy men's shop in Union Square. His old friend Tim Bollingsworth managed the place and looked smashing in a custom four-button suit.

'Larry? What happened to your hair?'

'Glad you like it. I need a quality suit, something subtle, yet flashy – diplomatic ball in Mexico City, that sort of thing.'

Tim nodded and looked over his friend's frayed khakis and cheap war boots. 'You need more than a suit. I can give you my 40 per cent discount, but this is still going to cost some bucks. You get a job or something?'

'Sort of. Set me up. Forty long, thirty-two waist.'

Tim went to the racks, saying 'Italian' to himself. He had been a skilled graphic artist, but when the computer people seized the whole industry, he quit and took this lucrative day job. The computer people returned to haunt him: the boutique had recently become known for making sloppy tech millionaires look respectable.

Larry stood in the doorway smoking until Tim returned with several suits draped over his arm.

'Now, for your frame you need a fuller cut. Probably a double-breasted jacket. This one – '

'Nah, too Superfly.'

'Okay. What about this? It's earthier, glen plaid.'

'Nah, looks like a bagpipes player.'

'Give me a chance. Now this one, it's a dark pinstripe, very tiny stripes, you see?'

'Mm-hmm.'

'You don't want wide stripes, those are for fat guys.'

'Don't want any pinstripes.'

'Fine. This one is what we call a windowpane pattern.'

'Bad luck.'

'How's that?'

'Reminds me of window panes. What's this one about?' Larry lifted the last suit from Tim's arm. A good grey flannel.

'It's a Canali, nice Milano suit. Has a vest, see?'

'Nah, don't like vests. You got something like this in a double-breasted?'

'I think so. Figured you'd want the Italian.'

Tim went back to the racks and a squeaky voice said 'Sir?' from the dressing rooms. He came to the door.

'How are those looking in there?'

'I don't know. The pants are all really long.'

'I know. We'll hem the pants to fit you, that's what we do.'
'Oh.'
'Why don't you let me see how those are working out?'
'Uh, in a minute. I have to put the pants on.'

Tim shook his head and brought over the double-breasted Canali for Larry's inspection.

'Yeah, yeah. I like this. Let's do it. And I'll need some shoes, like yours.'//
'We don't have shoes, Larry.'//
'What the hell kind of place is – '//
'I'll call Neimans to bring some over. Eleven?'//
'And a half.'

And a half-hour later, Larry was standing before the three-way mirror, Tim making chalk marks for the cuffs, the new Allen-Edmonds shoes shining.

'Beautiful, just beautiful. I like this shirt, too. Won't you pack me up three of these, in whatever shades work best? And pick out some nice ties, muted colors, and a belt. I'll need a raincoat, too. Something dark.'

'I've got a good Burberry that'll look nice with the suit.'//
'Perfect.'//
'What's the occasion, really?'//
'Just dinner tonight. One of those places where you need a tie.'

At the counter, Larry produced an American Express.

'This isn't yours.'//
'Yes it is. Look,' he pulled a payment envelope from his khakis, stamped and ready to go.//
'What is this, your *nom de plume* or something?'//
'Exactly. I'm undercover. So if anyone ever asks who bought this suit …'//
'Right. You better pay the bill, Larry. I don't want this coming back to me.'//
'*Jesús* pays the bills.'

'Right. I'll have the tailor get it ready. You want to pick it up today?'

'Actually, just have it delivered. To my motel.' Larry scribbled the address. 'And, if it's no trouble, don't run this charge 'til the end of the month. I think I'm over my limit.'

'I don't like the sound of this.'

Larry pointed to the old credit-card machine behind the counter. Tim grumbled and put a carbon over the AmEx, made the imprint, and Larry signed it with a flourish.

'Just want this payment to get there first,' he said, waving the envelope. 'Trust me, Timmy. Take a look at my Web site, and I'll take questions tomorrow. Meet me for beverages at the Fairmont.'

'Okay ... I'm off at seven. I expect to hear the whole sordid story.'

They shook hands and Larry strolled away.

'Nice doing business with you, Mr Ramirez! Come see us again!'

The kid finally emerged from the dressing room. Tim walked around him, looking concerned.

'I still look fat, don't I?'

'Well ... I don't know. This suit looked great on Marc Andreesen.'

The fat kid sulked back to the dressing room and put on his street clothes — huge army pants and a cheap raincoat.

'You have any better suits coming? I need this quick.'

'Sheesh. Look, I've got some things coming in tomorrow, I'll see what I can do. Write your name and number down, I'll call if there's anything better for your, uh, frame.'

The kid wrote 'Scott Charlton, (925),' and then dropped the pen. Above his childish handwriting was this:

Jesús Ramirez, TravelLodge on Market,
SF, Room 217
plz visit us @ SluiceBox.net.

The salesman ... hadn't he just yelled 'Mr Ramirez' to somebody? Scott ran out of the store.

'Hey!' Tim yelled. 'You just wrote the area code! Jackass!'

He returned to Berkeley sans suit, but with exciting news.

'I found him!'

'What do you mean, you found him?' Terry had the E! channel's fashion show on the teevee, the outrage highlight of her afternoons.

'That Jesus guy, Jesus Ramirez! He was in the suit store!'

'He was?'

'I couldn't find nothing, but the salesman guy wanted my name in case they got a bigger suit – '

'Racists.'

'And this guy in the store, he bought some stuff to be delivered, and he's the Jesus guy. At a hotel, the TravelLodge on Market Street in San Francisco. I got the room number!'

'Good work, idiot. So what are you doing here?'

This stunned him. He'd done so well ...

'I, uh, I thought you'd wanna be there, to tell me what to do.'

That was better.

'You did well for the revolution. We'll kidnap this skinny piece of hate after the meeting.'

The Thursday FLAVA meeting. Scott had fifty-two hours to develop courage. Terry ran him away from the computer so she could work on her new leaflet: 'The Ignorant Hate of Jesús Ramirez.' These would be distributed throughout Berkeley before the meeting, fighting for windshield space with the leaflets from another dozen causes.

25

Larry saw his reflection in the lobby's glass doors and gasped in delight. He looked like Carlos Fuentes arriving to accept a literary prize. Sweet.

Suzie had a different idea.

'Oh my God, you look like Saddam Hussein.'

'Shhh. Eat your ahi.'

They feasted on sea creatures and Larry explained his death and Suzie described her comical visit to the morgue. She cried on cue, kissed what remained of the corpse's lips, and waited for the detective. Sadly, she was the closest thing to family Larry had. Yes, he had been very depressed. He wouldn't leave the apartment for weeks at a time, had threatened to end it all, even refused to make love to her.

'That's highly unlikely,' Larry said. She was in a black sleeveless suit, a silver choker around her throat, thick hair piled on her bare shoulders.

'Shut up, dead guy.'

'You're the one who kissed a corpse. How much was the cremation?'

'I got something called the Nautilus Society to do it, three hundred bucks. You burn in the morning. So pay up.'

Larry gave her three crisp Franklins.

Suzie put the bills in her purse and said, 'I like it when you've got money.'

Much later, they closed the place, and when the dining room lights switched off, downtown and the bay sparkled below. This was the San Francisco rich tourists loved — beauty, fine dining, a sense of wonder in everything. Larry poured Suzie the last of the cold sake, half of it landing in her wasabi dish. They both found this endlessly humorous. In the elevator, she leaned against him, drunk and beautiful.

They admired their reflection in the brushed steel of the elevator doors for the twenty-floor ride down. They strolled through the highrise lobby bumping against each other. The usual Montgomery Street squall was waiting outside. She hid beneath his new Burberry, her clean fragrant hair blowing against his face. They caught the last cable car east and huddled in the wind, alone except for the conductor and brakeman.

'I'm leaving tomorrow.'

'What?'

'I said I'm leaving tomorrow. For Croatia.'

'Ah, the miniseries.'

'Yeah. But I won't miss you.'

''Course you won't. You'll have Mel Gibson or somebody to keep you amused.'

'It's a TNT miniseries, Larry. Jimmy Smits.'

'A real Mexican, at least.'

'Shh. Why don't you kiss me for once?'

They passed Grace Cathedral, but didn't look up to admire its neo-gothic belltower. At the end of the line, the ticket man tapped Larry's shoulder.

'Sorry, people. Far as we go.'

There were cabs on Van Ness. She took one and he walked, trying to think of something other than how nice it would've been for her to spend the night. He unlocked his room, finished a bottle and sat on the floor, staring out the window. He finally slept, feeling rotten and alone.

26

'This is purely unacceptable.'

Tom Sanders was back in his clothes and back in his office, the media having abandoned his crimes for newer offerings from Jesús Ramirez. Owen Lindsey sat across from the desk.

'Again, Mr Sanders, nobody knows anything about it.'

'To hell with that. Your idiot cornered this Mexican and *vanished*?'

'Unfortunately, it's complicated. Richard Welch has been with the company since – '

'Yeah, it's complicated. It's getting more complicated all the time with you. Look here.'

Sanders clicked his Netscape bookmarks and called up SluiceBox.net.

'Still there!'

'Uh, Mr Sanders, your intranet is supposed to block that site.'

'Yeah? Well I'm the CEO of this company, Owen, and I don't use the peons' intranet.'

'Yes sir. At least he's targeting other executives now.'

'Bastard says he's coming to COMDEX. You know what happens when you click this, Owen? It goes to a story about *my speech*. Your one and only job was to get rid of it, get rid of whoever posted this. Instead you've got one of your qualified idiots in the madhouse – '

'It must be a bluff, sir. Nobody would show up at COMDEX and admit to being this Ramirez. Twenty corporations are hunting him.'

Sanders snorted and said, 'What about this Trageser idiot?'

'He's at home now, recovering.'

'Recovering? I don't think he'll recover from being a damned idiot.'

Phillip Trageser was sent home after a week in the hospital. Rape charges against him were dropped; a police lineup took care of that. The victims pointed to everybody but Trageser. The 911 call was traced to the suspect's own cell phone, which presumably vanished with his clothes. But freedom didn't take care of his madness. He jabbered incessantly about the sea lions, and the roar of the Ocean Queen, and the horn player leading him down the crystal stairs to an underwater metropolis. His wife, a Nicaraguan he picked up during the covert wars, couldn't take it. She hired a Salvadoran nurse to change his adult Pampers and split town with a guitar player.

'And this one who disappeared? In the middle of some bicycle race?'

Lindsey tried not to squirm. He couldn't tell Sanders what he knew, or how little he knew. The missing man was scouting out Ramirez' apartment, as he had done for a week. His partner, Martin Hickey, was perched across the street in another building, in an apartment seized from a Chinese family without immigration papers. The letters 'INS' – shouted at appropriate volume – were of great value in such situations.

Hickey reported something nobody at BIPS could comprehend: Welch left his post and ran to 593 Haight Street, entered the lobby with his bootleg key, and a few minutes later threw something out the wrong apartment's window. Agents had already searched this unit like all the rest and found nothing of interest – they were only waiting for Ramirez to retrieve his mail. Welch stepped onto the ledge, and then somebody who looked and dressed *exactly like him* came through the broken window. Hickey couldn't tell who was who, even with his field glasses. It was pouring rain, and maniac hippies had blocked the street with their bicycles. A MUNI bus managed to gain a car length and blocked his view of whatever happened next. Hickey called for backup, but the guys couldn't get past the intersection. Then some Mexican in a baseball cap pointed them to an alley behind the building, and with great authority said one of their guys was down. They found nothing but rats and garbage. When they returned to the car, the Mexican was gone and the bicyclists were rioting and the cops were rolling in. Fearing a repeat of whatever happened to Trageser, they got the hell away.

By the time Hickey got outside, the cops had swarmed 593 Haight, taping off half the block, a dark-suited body impaled on the gate. Hickey flashed his BIPS badge and was told to get lost. Headquarters said stay close, so he sat in the bar across the street, watching paramedics pull the corpse off the spikes, having particular trouble with the skull. Then the coroner's wagon parked – his view blocked again. A *Chronicle* reporter and photographer came into the bar to escape the rain. They claimed the tenant of Apt. C, somebody named Larry Jonestowne, had jumped out the broken window. Had his driver's licence right in his pocket.

Hickey couldn't argue. He sat there with a pint glass of 7-Up, imagining all manner of devious tricks, plastic surgery, double agents, mind control. After mentioning these concerns to Lindsey, he was put on sick leave. Such things might happen in the world of political espionage, but BIPS jobs rarely got weirder than sifting through dumpsters and stealing e-mail.

It was turning into a very bad month for Business Intelligence Partner Services. Lindsey investigated the incident himself by paying a quiet visit to an acquaintance at the

Coroner's office. Who would have been glad to show him Jonestowne's body, no questions asked, but it had already been reduced to cinders. Fiancée's wishes. Of course she ID'd the body. Forensics hadn't found anything to argue with the police report – the apartment was a wreck, the victim was an unemployed nobody who seemed to own little more than the clothes on his back and a lot of books, and his blood was on the window sill, from a glass cut on the left hand. The Chinese landlord, glad to have the apartment vacated, agreed that Larry Jonestowne was crazy. So did a shopkeeper who saw the jump.

Lindsey saw the photos. The spikes through the face blurred the features a bit. It was a tall man with short blond hair, that much was certain.

'What's the interest in this nut?' the assistant medical examiner asked. Lindsey mumbled a lie and got out of there.

'As I told you before, Mr Sanders, there is something extraordinary about this case.'

'You ever think you're just wrong, Owen? Barking up the wrong tree and all that? I know about this Haight Street. Nothing but drug addicts and maniacs and gangs. You ever think, for one moment, that your Virginia boys are pansies? In all your years of government work, have you ever dealt with a goddamned *global* situation based in some chicken-shit nigger ghetto?'

'Actually, Mr Sanders, more than a few revolutionary efforts with a global scale were based within very modest quarters.'

'Goddammit, this isn't political! This is business! This Ramirez is a front, you imbecile.' Sanders grabbed a pastry off his desk and pulverized it. Chewing, he said, 'What about the credit cards, anything?'

'Not recently. Whoever Ramirez is, he's not leaving much behind. The mail's going to some post-office box in the homosexual neighbourhood now, but our men haven't spotted anyone checking it. We broke in, obviously – nothing but a past-due utility bill.' Lindsey looked to his Palm Pilot. 'Of course, we're electronically following his actual charges. One to a wine shop in San Francisco, a newspaper subscription in Phoenix, a massage on Long Island, a $200 dinner in Budapest, hotels in five cities ... crazy things, Mr Sanders. Whoever's doing this knows something about how we work, and he is – or they are – specifically trying to throw us off the trail.'

'Get his goddamned cards shut off.'

'That, sir, would do away with our only method of following Ramirez and his associates.'

'Associates, huh? What associates?'

'That's why we're redoubling our efforts regarding IBM.'

'You better. We got hit yesterday. The sons of bitches are suing me for the patent. From 1963, for Christ's sake. They're snakes.'

'Yes sir. I guarantee you, the Harvard situation is gone. IBM can try to make a show of this, but without a criminal case, it's just another patent dispute.'

'Try telling that to the trade papers. Or the fucking stockholders. Or fucking *Newsweek*.' Sanders launched himself to standing position and tossed the new issue at Lindsey.

Lindsey caught the magazine and looked at the cover: a stupid graphic of a masked Pancho Villa character bursting through a computer monitor. And the words, 'The Lone Ranger of Cyberspace: Wreaking Havoc in Silicon Valley'.

'This, Mr Sanders, is an unfortunate development. But you must remember, *Newsweek* is part of the *Washington Post*, and ever since Watergate we've known where their sympathies lie.'

'You guys need to get over Nixon. I've heard enough bullshit for today. You've got one week – seven days – to end this. And then you're off the job.'

The *Newsweek* article, which Lindsey would never read, did not reveal any anti-American bias. Instead, it was the standard brain-dead cover piece, connecting the standard fears of its ageing readership: the Internet, the New Economy, foreigners, free speech and globalization.

In an amusing concurrence recalling the dual Bruce Springsteen covers of 1975, *Time* had also fallen for the Ramirez story: 'The Apocalypse According to Jesús Ramirez', with a pointlessly racist illustration of a dark-skinned Jesus Christ in a sombrero, tapping at a computer. Both stories were hyperbolic, short on facts, and loaded with horrified reactions to the Sluice Box.

The *Time* piece was perhaps the best example, although arguments could be made ...

By JEFF STEUERWALD

SAN JOSE — Not since Mark Twain began publishing his caustic commentaries on the Gold Rush has one reporter caused such consternation in this moneyed capital of the New Economy.

Jesús Ramirez, a phantom journalist publishing whatever suits his fancy on the Wild World Web, is teaching the corporate titans of Silicon Valley a thing or two about public relations. Since his dramatic posting of an incendiary profile of MicroTorrent Systems CEO Thomas Sanders (see Page 24), his Internet site — www.SluiceBox.net — has become the must-see Net destination for millions of investors, CEOs and even the tech-company employees of this strange land where two-bedroom tract homes sell for a million dollars and 'stock options' are discussed at backyard barbecues the way regular Americans talk football scores.

In the past two weeks, Ramirez' Web site has expanded its reach, targeting the executives of dozens of Silicon Valley companies.

Among the revelations of this modern-day prophet: the allegedly racist treatment of Indian software programmers; the drug arrest of a popular Menlo Park CEO; an insider-trading scandal at a major semiconductor firm; and leaked information that led to the collapse of InterWorldNet Media Ventures.

Mr Ramirez — if that is his name — has maintained a low personal profile. Perhaps the first virtual celebrity, he has never been photographed, ignores interview requests and has made no attempt to capitalize on his fame (or infamy, in the minds of many NASDAQ executives). He publishes all correspondence, and if he is the bane of technology executives, he is regarded as a saviour by lesser employees and layoff victims. The only reader complaints on the site are from a self-styled group of 'fat revolutionaries' who objected to Ramirez' portrayal of Sanders as a 'crude, fat man'. His responses to these letters are less than kind.

If this new foe of the money changers in the temple has an Achilles' heel, it is his reliance on a shady offshore gambling concern. Ramirez, revealed by World Wide Web records to be based in Bolivia, runs his scandalous Internet publication from an ever-changing roster of tax-shelter nations, Tonga and Switzerland among them. And these Internet servers — the machines which broadcast individual Web pages such as those operated by Ramirez — are under the ownership of the Mediterranean-Caribbean Gaming Association, an Internet gambling company that

    is the ire of anti-gambling prosecutors from
    Louisiana to Luxembourg ...

Larry threw the magazine to the sidewalk, smacking a chained Labrador's head.

'It's insulting.'

'You're wrong, mate. It's perfect.'

'From the first 'graph, total bullshit.'

'Forget all that rubbish, wouldya? You know what this will do for traffic?'

Werner called the waitress for more coffee.

'The whip's coming down now. Dear God, the cover of both?' Larry couldn't bear to read *Newsweek*'s version.

'Your moustache's coming along nicely.'

'Yeah? I need to dye it again.'

'Not really going to Vegas for this trade show, are you?'

'Nah. Just want to throw the hounds off the scent. Don't need any more Haight Street horror.'

''Least you're dead.'

'There's that.'

Werner sodded off to Silicon Valley and Larry put together an article back at the motel – the new chief technology officer at SeaGull Systems had annoyed his database programmers by trashing six months of development and producing a new skeleton code. It was stolen, of course, from his previous employer.

With mixed feelings, Larry linked the *Time* and *Newsweek* stories to his front page:

INFAMY RAGES!
Even the Technology-
Happy Media Pay Heed
to the Works of Jesús!

27

Jorge Banderas did not like the looks of this hate-language. Not at all.

He'd spent the afternoon writing angry letters to the Democrat governor, who was quickly turning out to be as bad as his predecessor, the Latino-hating chicken-voiced Republican. Jorge stamped the letters and headed to the post office, but something caught his eye along the way. The windshields and telephone poles were all covered in red flyers titled 'The Ignorant Hate of Jesus Ramirez'. Jorge didn't like seeing such words directed at a Latino.

He took a flyer from a Honda Accord and read it as he walked. This Jesús guy was apparently an Internet journalist, and some stupid white swine didn't like it. 'Terry Texas', it was signed. Supreme commander of the Fat Arse Foundation. Based out of the same building as Jorge's non-profit: The Latino Media Revolutionary Council, which had its own Spanish acronym, CRML. He'd seen these fat white women, dressed in boots and army surplus, snarling at him in the hallway.

And Jorge had heard of this Ramirez – there was a big article in *Time* this week, although he hadn't yet read the piece. Somebody needed to write the letters to the corrupt governor.

He dropped the letters and returned to the office. In truth, Jorge *was* the CRML. After being fired from the *Los Angeles Times*' Ventura County bureau for well-documented unprofessional behaviour – Jorge had the bad habit of inventing stories and fiercely defending them – he decided the Anglo media system was designed to destroy talented young Latinos. Only questionably Latino himself, he had few cultural resources to draw upon; his mother was a third-generation Latvian Jew and his father a half-German with vague ties to Argentina. Spanish wasn't spoken at home, because nobody could speak it. His given name was 'George'.

When all doors closed, he did what any deluded activist must do. He moved to Berkeley. While his reporting skills were nonexistent, his factional prose had just the sort of flair required to get a local grant. With e-mail and a fax machine and a Web page, he was a one-man movement, a virtual César Chávez, regularly calling for boycotts and sit-ins and occasionally getting a handful of protesters and the all-important media coverage. The self-made revolution had been recently validated by a new journalism magazine called *Shill's Content*, which offered him a bi-monthly column on the problems faced by Latino reporters.

A few local Hispanic associations had promised to send a representative, yet there was always a scheduling conflict. It was embarrassing, but he made up for the lack of a Board of Directors by inventing one. Their names, assembled from the local phone book, were listed on CRML's stationery.

Jorge flipped through his mail and saw this Ramirez wasn't just on the cover of *Time* – he'd made *Newsweek*'s. This was big. And racist. Both covers were stereotypical anti-Latino insults. Pancho Villa? Christ in a sombrero? He read the articles, astounded by the Gringo ignorance. And this FLAVA group was worse. Calling for a boycott of Ramirez' advertisers. Trying to keep a Latino from earning a living. A real living, in the elite media world of Silicon Valley. These white pigs only wanted the Latino to pick lettuce and clean the swimming pool. And to think these FLAVA swine were planning this cultural war just beneath his tiny office. He decided to beat them to the punch.

Dot.Con

Jorge got a bagel from the office fridge and began work on a leaflet: 'CALL TO ARMS: ANGLO RACISTS WILL NOT MUZZLE OUR INTERNET HERO!' He was still working on the flyer at midnight. It was a beautiful piece of revolutionary literature. When it was just right, he copied the text and ran it through the AltaVista search engine's free translation service on the Internet, English to Spanish. It looked good, whatever it said.

Then he sent an e-mail to the wire-service datebook editors, local television stations (even the Spanish-language channel) and the *Chronicle* and *Examiner*.

From: Latino Media Revolutionary Council (info@CRML.org)
Subject: SF Rally for Jesús Ramirez

Jesús Ramirez, a Latino journalist fighting for oppressed workers everywhere, has been targeted by a Racist Anglo Faction angered by his honest portrayal of corrupt Silicon Valley whites who make their millions from the back-breaking labours of Latinos in this fascist state of California, which was stolen from its indigenous and Spanish owners.

Señor Ramirez, a proud Bolivian who has focused his investigative-journalism talents on the wrongdoing of Bay Area technology criminals, shall not suffer this indignity alone. The Latino, Chicano and Hispanic People, La Raza, will rise up in support of Ramirez on Thursday night at 7 p.m. in San Francisco. Thousands will take part in the protest, which will be held at 16th and Mission streets in the city — a city first settled by the Spanish and then stolen by the Gringo. Scheduled speakers include Ramirez and Jorge Banderas, chairman of the Latino Media Revolutionary

Council, and other leaders of the cause. Banderas can be reached for interviews via this e-mail address.

Yes, that sounded good. He opened an old protest flyer in Adobe Illustrator and changed the date; it said something in Spanish about Governor Wilson's campaign to deny public education and workers' benefits to Latinos. To keep things current, he changed 'Wilson' to 'Gray Davis'. That should get some people to the rally. Tomorrow, he would make copies at Kinkos and distribute hundreds of these flyers in San Francisco's Mission District. All he had to do was tell the shopkeepers and Latinos on the street that the protest would be televised – he'd perfected that sentence in Spanish. Everybody wanted to be on the teevee.

The e-mail to Larry's personal account was brief: 'Dead? Call me now, freak.' O'Leary.

Larry was getting worse at returning calls. Phones had long made him nervous, and now he had a legitimate reason. He dialled Boston with the PacBell card.

'Yeah?'

'It's me, your old dead buddy.'

'Christ, about time. You've seen the magazines, I suppose.'

'Mm-hmm. Awful.'

'Isn't *anybody* going to expose your suicide or whatever?'

'Unlikely. I seem to have less friends every year. Besides, my tragic death barely made the paper here. How'd you hear about it?'

'Kip Boer read it online and forwarded a copy. He's putting it in his monthly newsletter.' Boer, the Brussels financial reporter, had worked with both of them in Prague. He made a noble effort to keep tabs on the crackpots and amateurs who once laboured for the English-language paper. Using his corporate Dow Jones Interactive news-library account, he set up automated searches for all his former colleagues, noting the diaspora's hirings, firings, weddings and other life changes. Larry was the fifth death so far – one exploded in Bosnia, one had a brain tumour, and two had passed on due to drinking-related illnesses.

'I was hoping for an obit in the *Times*. Guess an e-mail newsletter will have to suffice. How's your Sanders deal?'

'Aren't you going to tell me what happened?'

'Not now. I've gotta change motels; some lesbian-Hell's Angel parade has the whole place booked. But rest assured, my early demise had something to do with MicroTorrent and their goons.'

'I figured. Things are getting interesting out here.' O'Leary dropped to a whisper. 'One detective is kind of hot on it, but he's keeping very quiet. They don't want any more conveniently dead witnesses.'

'There aren't any more witnesses.'

'Another frat boy. Freshman pledge or whatever. He wasn't part of the hazing crew, but he was around while they got their story straight. Sanders raised hell, standard ritual threats, and the guy kept quiet. Until our gung-ho detective tracked him down.'

'How'd this cop know?'

'He didn't. He just tracked down the whole '62 frat gang and bullshitted each of them, "I know you're hiding something about Tom Sanders," etc.'

'That's some fancy work.'

'Yeah, and I'm the only one who knows about it.'

'Except me.'

'You and Jesús best be quiet. I'll let you know when it's running – might be Sunday's front page – and then you can do one of your Web bulletins the night before. Make sure to call me a "star reporter". Now here's the good part: They're putting a warrant together tomorrow, talking to the Nevada prosecutors about extradition – '

'Really!' Larry laughed while exhaling smoke and nearly suffocated. 'At COMDEX? Dear God …'

'Yeah, they figure it'll be tough to squirm out of this when he's away from MicroTorrent and their million lawyers. And I'll be right there. Flying out tonight. He's taking questions from the tech press after his stupid speech.'

'This is too good. How I'd love to see it.'

'Thought you were going.'

'Nah, that's just to keep him nervous. It's the least I can do.'

'Well, stay close to your computer. Maybe I'll e-mail some notes from the nightmare.'

'Yeah, yeah, you must do it. Jesús' cousin … Miguel Sanchez.'

'Miguel O'Sanchez.'

'Perfect. The Irish Mexican. Reporting from the bowels of COMDEX as Ramirez lays low. Okay, I need to pack and run before the bikers arrive. And don't forget to make a few charges to Jesús, as long as they're legitimate business expenses.'

'Everything I do is a legitimate business expense.'

Larry hung up, dropped the towel from his waist, dressed in a sports coat and tie, and stuffed his new suit into the duffle, trying not to wrinkle the fine fabric. He trotted down the stairs, a dumb smile on his face, and entered the lobby. It was already filled with leather-clad, spiky-haired bull dykes in full costume. Bored of the Cheech-and-Chong accent, he just asked for his bill.

The day clerk had it ready.

'Don't you need to swipe my card?'

'Nope, all done. Put it through the computer this morning. We call it Checkout Express.'

Whoops.

'Just sign here. Phone calls are itemized on the bottom. Do you have the key?'

'Uh, yeah, but my bags are still in there. Just waiting for my taxi. I'll leave the key in the room.' Larry stuffed the customer copy in his pocket and ran to the payphone outside the lobby. Big bikes growled in the parking lot.

'Werner, emergency. Get a cab and pick me up at the motel.'

'What?' Some hog revving her hog.

'Taxi! TravelLodge! Now!'

Larry took the steps slowly, looking around. Huge loud women loading ice chests into the rooms. He locked the door behind him and turned off the computer. Zipped it into the bag. Peeked out the window. No cab yet. But a grey Ford Taurus pulled into the lot, blocked by a row of Harleys, saddlebags and toolboxes scattered around. Larry grabbed his shaving kit and a complimentary washcloth from the bathroom and forced them into the duffle. Somebody exiting the car, passenger side. No suit, but otherwise looking like a standard BIPS goon on the golf course, headed for the crowded lobby. Larry hoisted the duffle over one shoulder and the computer bag over the other. Standing at the door, trying not to collapse under the weight, searching for that magical taxi. There it was. He opened the door to see Werner running up the stairs, looking worried.

Werner took one end of the duffle and they hauled it to the cab, the driver waiting with the trunk open. Larry took shotgun and slammed the door, the German in back.

'Where to?'

'Just go!'

Blocked by motorcycles. The Ford Taurus on the other side, its driver outside now, scanning the crowd, right hand inside his jacket. The cab reversed onto Market, nearly colliding with another stream of bikers, and headed east. Larry watched the other BIPS man run out of the lobby, looking up to the second floor.

'Okay, got you safe from the ladies. Now where?'

They weren't really safe from the ladies. Market Street was clogged with the riders and would be for days.

'Only in San Francisco,' the driver said, chuckling. He was probably forty, hopelessly good-natured, enjoying the endless freak show. Larry hated it when people said 'Only in San Francisco'.

'Yeah, let's get the hell out of this San Francisco. I need peace, quiet … I want to hear the waves.'

'You wanna go out to Ocean Beach?'

'No, no. Too many … sea lions. Head down to Pacifica.'

'Sure thing. They got waves there.'

The driver got on the 280 South, through Daly City and to the coast. Larry patted his jacket pocket for smokes and realized he'd forgotten them on the nightstand. He looked back to Werner and made the universal peace-sign to his mouth, and Werner checked his pockets.

'Sorry, mate. Left in a rush.'

'Thank Christ. That was excellent timing.' Larry saw a pack of Merits on the dash and asked if he could buy a couple off the driver. They all lit up, smoke filling the car and fog filling the sky.

Larry was almost relaxed when he realized what else he'd forgotten.

'The owl!'

The driver searched the gloom for owls.

28

Werner and Larry walked down the Pacifica pier, ten-foot visibility, waves pounding the pilings, invisible gulls squawking. The luggage was inside the SeaHorse Lodge, a musty little motel among the mobile homes and tiny houses of this strange semi-rural beach town. The dot-fraud people would eventually find Pacifica, mow down the huts, raze the SeaHorse, and fill the foggy shoreline with hideous new condos, one-bedrooms starting at $299,500, pre-wired with DSL fibre optic, the usual horror. Larry liked it fine as it was. A shame he had to go right back to the TravelLodge.

'Maybe let the owl sod off?'

'It's not just the owl, it's that BIPS crap hidden in the drywall.' Larry took a swig from his 32-ounce Bud, cleverly disguised by a brown paper bag. 'I'm going senile. I *planned* to check out first, get the stuff from the wall, grab the owl and leave. Damned "checkout express" threw me off.'

'Good you didn't go back, matey. Those boys almost had you.'

'Yeah, again.' The SeaHorse clerk was paid in cash, under Werner's name and a rock club's address in Berlin. 'They find those Glocks and that rent-a-spy's badge, things become much uglier. Like, murder investigation. By real cops.'

He lit a Camel Light and leaned on the rail. Two old Asians were at the opposite end, fishing in the fog, bait and tackle spread around.

'It's still Jesús had that room, right?'

'It can get complicated. Say these BIPS people decide to

claim it was their guy on the gate, not the suicidal Larry Jonestowne. A plain dead maniac is suddenly a murdered corporate spy. Say a homicide cop talks to the day clerk, tracks down my nice new suit, catches Tim off guard. Or traces the calls to O'Leary. Or follows my Aussie Shiraz back to the wine shop. Or goes looking for my lovely fiancée. Oh, she's in Croatia? That's convenient.' Larry finished the beer and dropped his cigarette butt down the bottle, protecting the ocean friends. 'Real detectives don't have to sneak around like these MicroTorrent goons. They get to put people in jail, just for a friendly lie.'

"Spose your Ramirez shenanigans would make you look a bit suspicious.'

'A bit.'

'Gonna be tough to get in there.' Werner tossed his butt to the sea and Larry scowled.

'You figure they're lesbian photocopies of real bikers? Drugs and weapons and whatever? Maybe nervous about cops?'

'Ah, seems unlikely. Just poseurs like the rest of San Francisco.'

'Yeah, but these gals are out-of-towners.'

'Hence the motel?'

'Mm-hmm.' Larry still had the room key. He dangled it at Werner like a little puppet.

'Don't like the sound of this, Jonestowne.'

They called a taxi from the Sandside Saloon, killing the 45-minute wait with a few games of pool and a few slowly sipped Bushmills on the rocks. Werner loaded the jukebox with T. Rex and Ziggy Stardust, causing the handful of redneck hippies at the bar to grumble and leave. The barman yelled, 'Taxi?' He was glad to see the strangers take off.

A turbaned guy was at the wheel, listening to the AM sports station, no questions. Twenty bucks to Church and

Dot.Con

Market. It seemed best to walk the last couple blocks.

The motel's orange plastic sign in view, Larry stopped at a payphone, wiped off the bacteria and dialled the lobby.

'TravelLodge Market.' A nervous young guy's voice.

'Yeah, this is Detective Kirk Cobain, SFPD. Got a lot of biker freaks in there tonight?'

'Sure do. The motel's full with them. Is this about the noise again?'

'No, no. The patrol officers took care of that.'

'Yeah, they were here. Twice.'

'This is a narcotics situation. And weapons. Some plainclothes officers will be taking a look around. We need you to look the other way, if you know what I mean.'

This sounded like cop talk, although the clerk didn't really know what Larry meant. Neither did Larry.

'Sure, we always cooperate – '

''Course you do, buddy. I'll check in when we're finished. Be careful with those nuts, they're violent. Now put me through to 216.'

Werner, shaking his head.

'What?'

'Be glad when you sod off. You're enjoying this too much.'

'Being effective does not imply personal enjoyment.' The room picked up after three rings. Werner heard awful noises through the earpiece.

'Yeah, this is the front desk. You need to get out of there *right now*, vice cops are about to raid your room ... I don't know! Just get out of there!'

Larry hung up with a grin and headed for the motel.

'That's your plan?'

'This is the last favour I'll ever ask – '

'Bollocks.'

'There's a roof-access ladder in back. The dumpster should be right under it. Just hop up and grab the owl. It's right over my room.'

'Done with this.'

Larry increased his pace. They heard choppers revving.

'Many more dollars for you this month. I get the new cheque, change the addresses, maybe to your Swiss buddies, maybe Bermuda, I skip town, no more troubles.'

'Can't hardly wait.'

A quartet of bikes rocketed past them on Market, headlights cutting through the mist. Werner and Larry separated at the corner, the German cussing to himself, headed for the dumpster. Another stinking dumpster. Larry went straight to the concrete stairs, seeing the clerk peering from the office, feeling grateful he'd only dealt with the day shift. Larry nodded gravely to the fluorescent-lit office and took the steps. Incredible noise from the other rooms. Lynyrd Skynyrd, Motorhead, Melissa Etheridge. Bottles breaking, harsh laughter. No lights in his former room. He jabbed the key in the lock and threw the door open, crouching. Nothing.

On his knees, he searched for the cubby hole. The patch job was too good – he couldn't remember exactly where it was. Igloos full of Coors and mouldy sleeping bags against the wall. Using his lighter as a torch, he rapped his knuckles along. There. Pushed it, the toothpaste holding far better than intended, and grabbed the shoulder holster full of evidence. A horrible noise from the ceiling. The light fixture shook and dropped to the unpadded carpet, bulbs exploding, the loose wires above sizzling like bacon. A final pop and the whole motel went dark, everything but the huge TravelLodge sign on the street corner. Larry jumped in surprise and smashed his arm on the nightstand. A car screeched to a stop outside. More thumps from the roof. He staggered to the bathroom, looked through the louvred window to the foggy blackness. Not a safe drop. Another car, braking hard. Honking. Larry ran for the door, smashing against something huge and alive and stinking of barbecue sauce. It crushed him against the floor.

'It's over now, racist!'

He struggled, getting nowhere. She was massive. He felt the breath being pushed from his lungs. And then an awful thwunk. The head collapsed on his shoulder.

Another furious, deep female voice: 'Fuckin' kill you, traitor bitch!'

Larry pulled himself out and over and away, fingers clinching the threadbare carpet, broken glass slicing his chest, trying hard to breathe silently. Another monster, and a big long pipe smashing whatever jumped him. He scurried under the bed, his shoes catching on the mattress frame.

'It's a setup, get in here!' That awful voice again. 'Vice cops my arse!' The building was shaking from the boots of god knows how many angry biker women. This wasn't going so well.

Under the bed, he managed to get the shoulder holster latched around his chest, losing his sports coat in the process. Not much room under a box spring. His eyes adjusted to the near darkness. More voices, grunts, stomping, kicking, an ice chest knocked over, the awful sound of someone drinking a Coors in a single gulp and then smashing a skull with the empty bottle. He wormed out the opposite side, lying in the bed's shadow, considering the very few options.

He bounced into standing position and yelled, 'Freeze!' Right hand hovering over the holster – which contained nothing resembling a gun, but it made an effective contrast to his white shirt. Three huge biker gals in the doorway, hands up, backlit by the motel sign's orange haze. Another large specimen on the carpet beneath them.

Larry pulled the badge wallet and tried to hold it in a gun-like manner. Only the darkness disguised this particularly pathetic stunt.

'Out the door, all of you. Hands up!'

The three burly bikers took only a second to turn around, walking onto the concrete balcony single-file. The one on the floor didn't move. Larry stepped around her. In the sign's glow, he saw an obese woman spread on the carpet, in fatigues and combat boots. Sticking his head out the doorway, he shouted, 'Keep moving, all the way down!' All the way past the stairs, he hoped. They kept moving, although they lacked a proper regard for the Law. Doors had opened along the second-floor terrace, drunken faces peeking out.

It was clear, sort of. Larry sprinted for the stairs, yelling and twirling onto the steps, barely avoiding a fatal tumble.

And from a room three doors down, 'Hey! That ain't no gun!'

Fifty lesbian bikers came after him.

Things weren't much better on the roof. Werner climbed up just fine, and walked carefully on the gravelled tar to the ledge over Larry's room. There was the damned plastic owl, pigeons nested around it. He got down on his knees, not trusting the flimsy overhang, and reached for the bird. Got it. Damp pigeon shit on his hands. As he rose, something huge tackled him, gravel digging through his leather. In the street's light, he saw a very red, very young, very fat face. It hissed, 'Hello from the Penguin. You're kidnapped, Jesus.'

Werner smashed his knee into the fat kid's groin. A terrible and childish scream followed, and Scott Charlton rolled to the side, hands cupping his crotch. Werner rose, cursing, and retrieved the owl. He was close to the ladder when the kid hit again, knocking the German's head to the roof. Knocking him out cold.

Scott was shaking. His crotch was wet. Blood? He touched it and sniffed. No, just urine. Throbbing with pain, he walked carefully to whatever Jesus was carrying and picked it up. A dirty plastic bird. What did it mean? He fondled it, his fingernails clotting with pigeon filth, and found the head screwed right off. And inside, a gun ... two guns.

Other than his Laser Trigger home-computer gun, Scott had never touched such a weapon. He watched the TravelLodge sign's light glimmer against the black barrel. And despite the pain in his crotch, he felt tough. Screaming from the rooms. He crawled to the ledge, the Glock in his right hand, and peeked below. Three fat women ... They looked sort of like Terry ... but in the doorway, he could see Terry's boots. She was hurt. She *needed* him. He pointed the gun at the women, his aim lacking due to never firing a gun before and having to do it upside down. A male voice shouted. It sounded like a cop. He lifted his gun hand to the roof. The women backed away. And the guy came out of the room, holding ... a gun? Scott couldn't tell. He pissed himself again.

Oh no, Scott thought. What if *that's* Jesus? He always imagined Jesus was a kind of hacker kid, not some big cop guy. And now the guy was escaping, running down the stairs, dozens of women chasing him. Scott had never seen so many huge women, not even at a FLAVA meeting.

Scott plodded across the roof and found the ladder, went down, and ran around the building. *That* must be Jesus. Coming up the stairs, his hand in his suit. Going to the room. Where Terry lay hurt. Scott came up the steps and said, 'Freeze!' He knew that much from the teevee.

The man turned and yanked a gun from the suit. Scott pulled the trigger. It hit the man in the chest, an amazingly good first shot that proved computer games do teach certain skills, and Scott watched the man stagger to the cheap iron railing and tumble over the side, landing with an awful splat on a parked Harley. The bike groaned and fell over, hitting the bike next to it, and the bike next to it, the whole line falling like dominoes.

'Terry?'

She heard something, something far away.

'Terry! Get up! I shot somebody!'

Vague memories of the night. San Francisco. Yes, to kidnap that evil racist. Shot somebody?

'Terry, quick!'

He helped her stand, his groin muscles screaming, and led her down the stairs. She was not easy to hold upright, lurching from side to side, barely lifting her feet. He dropped the gun, hoped he wouldn't have to shoot anyone else, and got her to the sidewalk. There was another guy in a necktie running through the parking lot, along with a mob of biker women and a screaming night manager. Scott saw police lights and managed to get Terry Texas into an apartment doorway, five buildings down the street. She collapsed and the sirens wailed. Scott flapped his raincoat around them both and played dead. Had he spent more time in the city, he would have realized what a perfect impersonation of a street person he was performing – he even stank of urine. More women ran by, then cops in uniform, then the other guy in the tie. Scott didn't move. But he did cry, just a little.

The sound of the gunshot brought Werner around. He grabbed the back of his skull and mumbled, 'Bloody hell.' It was somewhat bloody.

He rose, with difficulty, and saw the headless owl. A gun still inside. He groped for the head and screwed it tight. Dropped it into the dumpster and shakily made it down the ladder. Right, must liberate the owl. Werner reached into the trash, his scuffed hands hitting discarded newspapers and bloody tampons and empty Shiraz bottles. Felt the bird's horns and pulled it free. Some noise out front. Lots of noise out front.

Stumbling, he went down the dark side street, the owl zipped beneath his jacket. Yes, officers, expecting a young 'un. At Guerrero, a Veteran's Taxi sat idle. The driver didn't like the looks of Werner, but he unlocked the doors when the German slid a twenty through the barely open window.

Larry Jonestowne lost the women after five blocks. They did not tire easily. Larry did.

He slipped into an alley off 16th Street, gasping for breath, hurting all over. He plucked a few glass shards from his bloodstained shirt and peeled the shoulder holster off his back. Cursed thing. He wiped his fingerprints from the leather strapping and threw it over a fence. He failed to remember the bulging badge cover was still in his pants pocket.

SFPD cruisers went down the street, just like always. No motorcycles, no sirens. He returned to the sidewalk, walked three blocks without seeing a free taxi. Fine, he thought, I'll take the BART to Daly City and get a cab from there. Where was Werner? Why drag the poor German into this mess again? Didn't matter. Werner was fine, certainly, and Larry would ask no more of his Nazi buddy. Larry was leaving San Francisco for good. No more toying around. Everyone was crazy.

Almost to the station. Puerto Alegre was just across Mission. Wouldn't be bad to have a margarita and some shrimp enchiladas, to calm the nerves. No. Get out of this insane city. He reached the corner and saw chaos.

The 16th/Mission BART station looks like a giant tiled sink, the forever-grimy kind one might find in a Louisiana drunk tank, the drain hole containing double escalators to the train platforms. It is a shockingly ugly piece of public architecture, wasting some 30,000 square feet and the entire southeast corner, and generally serving no purpose but to frighten anyone unlucky enough to depend on the trains, as reaching the escalators requires a harrowing journey through a gauntlet of pickpockets, gang-bangers, drunks and heroin dealers.

Of course, such dismal public spaces are ideal for protests. On a portable stage, a man was screaming half-English nonsense to a crowd. The requisite giant red banner said 'CRML' in standard Havana font. A crowd of maybe a thousand, all Mexicans and Central Americans. A mariachi band up there, playing *Beso Me* something, signs hoisted high, beer bottles smashing in the streets, cops safely on the perimeter. Blocking the BART entrance. Not a taxi in sight.

The next BART station was at 24th Street. Larry couldn't walk that far; he was bruised and exhausted and bleeding. Whatever, just get through the protest, get on the train, get out. He crossed the street, avoided the officers' gaze, and plunged into the mire. What in hell were they talking about? They were giving away free beer. Totally illegal, but a useful social lubricant for a quiet crowd. Little guy on the stage, fist in the air, burly men with television cameras on their shoulders. Larry squeezed past three drunken guys, all short and mean and hissing.

'Excuse me, *perdón, por favour*, sorry, *lo siento*.' Doing fine, getting closer.

'*¡Policia!*'

A beer bottle smacked Larry in the back of the head, bouncing off and crashing on the pavement. He groaned and tried to duck into a family, four or five kids, the angry matron, fists raised everywhere.

From the stage: 'You see an Anglo newspaperman, you tell him Jesús Ramirez is our man! A man for the people! *La Raza!*'

A fist smacked Larry in the ear. Larry sank, on his knees. The people above him pointing and screaming: *¡Rubio!* His dye job was fading fast. Should've gone back to get the roots dyed.

'You see a white cop, you tell him Jesús Ramirez is *our* man! *¡Viva Jesús!* To the Latino technological-media revolution! They want to make you not matter! They take and take, and they never give!' Jorge grabbed the *bajo sexto* player by the shoulders and commanded him to translate. The musician did his best. A circle developed around Larry, boots and bottles raining upon him.

Jorge at the microphone again, pumped up by the ruckus. 'You see this, *la Raza*? This is the Anglo media establishment!' He waved the *Time* and *Newsweek* covers over the crowd. 'They say a Latino can't work in Silicon Valley! Only to clean the white man's shit from a toilet! They say a Latino executive looks like Pancho Villa! They say our Jesús wears a sombrero!' Hooting, boos. Larry dived through a hole in the mob and landed on his back, many shoe soles atop him. This was better; the crowd above didn't know he was there. Just under the din, he heard engines. Very loud engines. Cops closing in? No, those were Harley choppers.

'And you want to see some hate? There are racist white pigs right here, right across the bay, who want to shut down our Jesús! They're boycotting our man!' Drunken rumblings in the crowd; with his anti-Wilson/Davis leaflets, Jorge had convinced two liquor stores on 16th to donate a dozen cases of beer each. Once that was swallowed and the protest broke up, the mob would want more, and these markets would make a bundle. 'I've seen these racist fascist whores! These big gringo women, angry because our Jesús tells the truth! The truth about these white swine who get rich off the computers, who stuff their mouths with the food we picked in the fields!'

The mariachi man gave up. He had no idea what Jorge was talking about. Jorge saw a hyped-up kid by the stage, fist pumping the air, and led him onstage. 'You speak Spanish, man?' Jorge whispered.

'Shit, I speak Spanish. Wassup?'

'What's your name?'

'My name? They call me Little Chuy.'

'Translate for me. Make it loud, dramatic.'

'What the fuck for?'

Jorge pulled a twenty from his wallet and slipped it to the kid, a lean teenager in khakis, shiny black shoes and a wife-beater undershirt.

'Say what I just said, about the white pigs boycotting Jesús, putting him down, all that. How he's our new hero, so we can all get rich, with the Internet.'

'Shit, I'll take that Innernet cash!'

Little Chuy loved the microphone. He took the rapper stance, arms swinging low, bouncing on his heels, and gave the crowd a lot of 'Yo Yo Yo!' and thanked all his homies in the 'hood for stickin' by him and thanked his family and thanked God and then flashed the Mission Street gang sign. Jorge hissed, 'Do the Spanish!'

He did the Spanish, each statement punctuated by 'Ya know what ahm sayin?' Hoots and applause from the mob. Little Chuy smiled, stalked the stage, slapped the hands extended from the crowd. A homey jumped up with a small but loud boombox, taking the mariachi band's mike and holding it to the speakers. Little Chuy started rapping in Spanglish, all about Jesús the pimp, getting all da rich bitches down in San Jose, bringin' down the white niggaz in da World Wide Way.

Jorge watched in envy. Maybe all that Castro and Chávez stuff was out of style. The people loved Little Chuy. Looking over the manic crowd, Jorge saw the local television vans parked at the corner, a line of cops, traffic tied up. This was a real protest. Then he saw the huge women on motorcycles, maybe a hundred, maybe more. FLAVA? Sure looked like it. Were these FLAVA psychos going to attack? Jorge hadn't planned on a violent protest.

A *chola*'s spike heel dug into Larry's belly. He shrieked and knocked the girl over, rising to face a half-dozen men wielding protest signs. Larry punched the closest guy, a tough-looking *cholo* in a hooded sweatshirt and khakis. It took another three punches to get away from the mob, not counting the ones directed at Larry. No safe way to the escalators. He squeezed out, elbows and signs and beer bottles pounding him. Made it through the ragged edge of the crowd, gasping for breath. Cops everywhere, but not looking for him. He hoped. And just beyond the patrol cars, an army of lesbian bikers.

'That's the sonofabitch!'

As the monstrous bikes revved, those at the mob's edge turned away from Little Chuy. The older folks were frightened. Jorge saw the headlights pointed at his protest and swiped the microphone from Little Chuy.

'People! These gringo pigs are here to scare us off! They've been trying to scare us off for 500 years! and we're not scared!'

Jorge turned to give the mike back to Little Chuy for translation, but Little Chuy was gone. Jorge watched the mariachi musicians climb off the back of the stage and head for a safer gig, their velvet sombreros bobbing toward Mission. The choppers poured into the BART plaza, slipping between teevee vans and squad cars, the lead riders – the same three Larry had forced from the motel room – armed with lengths of pipe and God knows what else. Larry spun into the crowd again, another try for the escalators, complicated by the fact that the crowd was moving in the opposite direction, toward the sidewalks, the streets, possible safety. A snorting motorcycle was right behind him, the deranged rider swatting with her lead pipe. Howls of pain as tyres crushed limbs. He fell, took another trampling, and rose to his knees, another biker to his left, gaining speed through the thinning crowd, her furious eyes on Larry. Nowhere to run. As the pipe swung, he jammed a protest sign's stick handle into her front spokes and she catapulted, over the railing and into the drain hole. The bike landed on his calf. Larry groaned, squirming away from the hot engine, leaving behind his left pants leg and a certain amount of skin.

He made it to the escalators just as BART police were closing the gates. He sat on the metal step and rode down and tried to close his eyes. That hurt more than leaving them open. He stood with difficulty at the bottom and saw the huge biker flattened on the floor, BART cops standing around her, telling the departing protesters to keep moving.

At the ticket machines – three out of five bearing 'NOT IN SERVICE' signs – he struggled with his change and got two dollars into the machine. A Bay Area Rapid Transit guard approached and said, 'You all right?'

'Yeah,' Larry said, grinning through his blood and bruises. 'Those maniacs about killed me, that's all. Just trying to get on the train.'

'You want to make a report, or get an ambulance?' The guard's voice was low and soothing, like Billy Dee Williams.

'No, no, that's fine. Gotta get home.'

'You sure? You're looking bad, man.'

'Be fine, thanks.' Larry took his magnetic-stripe ticket and went through the turnstile, blood marking his path along the easy-clean, seldom-cleaned tiles. He sat on the concrete bench, breathing hard, and waited.

'Final train to Daly City,' the walls said. He slumped into the first seats and ripped the sleeve off his right arm, to the elbow, dabbing at the blood leaking from his ears, nostrils, neck, chest, forehead, scalp, legs and hands. Left the bloody cloth on his seat, and left the station not looking any better. He had a hard time getting a cab.

29

Sanders stood in the master bedroom of his penthouse suite, a tailor marking the hemline on his new suit. He had a closet full of custom suits and had brought one to Las Vegas, but the stress of the Ramirez garbage had added to his weight. Significantly. The old suit had no fabric left to let out.

Wanting to avoid the other Silicon Valley CEOs – who were still just barely acknowledging him – Sanders was at the Mirage, a safe distance from the COMDEX show. Harry Taft was next door, Owen Lindsey next to that. A BIPS man was stationed in the elevator lobby at all times; three of them traded shifts and shared a smaller suite one floor below. Lindsey hadn't personally worked an assignment for five years, but Sanders gave him no choice. The MicroTorrent account was important.

The tailor asked, 'And what side do you dress on, Mr Sanders?'

'None of your damned business.' Sanders couldn't stand it. *His* tailor knew better than to ask about a man's business.

'That's fine, Mr Sanders. I'll just measure your old suit. We'll have everything ready by lunchtime.'

'You better.' Sanders kicked off the trousers and put on his kimono. The little tailor packed his things and let himself out with a cheery goodbye. Made Sanders cringe.

The doorbell rang a minute later. Sanders cursed and waddled over, yelling, 'What?'

'Tom, it's me, Harry. And Owen.'

Sanders opened the door and grunted good mornings. Lindsey followed Taft to the living room, floor-to-ceiling windows providing a panoramic view of the Strip and Charleston Peak to the west. They sat around the coffee table.

'Got my speech?'

'Sure do.' Taft took a printout from his briefcase. 'We just changed the release date, and a few minor things about the partners.'

'What changed with the partners?'

'Ah, nothing crucial, Tom.'

'Somebody back out?'

'Well, ah, for the moment, yes. Microsoft.'

'What?!' Sanders reached for the phone, one of five in the suite. 'I'll have Ballmer's head on a plate – '

'Tom, let's not complicate things. We'll work it out. Minor, minor details. They want a little more than we've agreed to, they're just bluffing. Once we get the buzz going this afternoon, they'll be right back onboard, I promise.'

'Better be onboard. What in fuck are we supposed to use for an OS?'

'Well, what I've done in the speech, we're just not mentioning Microsoft by *name*, but we're implying it.' Taft shuffled the pages, looking for the edit. 'Ah, here: "And the MicroTorrent TeleNetVision 1.0 will be powered by a market leader in PC operating systems."'

'Should say *the*, for God's sake. What's *a* market leader? You're either the goddamned market leader or you're not.'

'Well, ah, legal says we've got to go this way.'

'Legal can kiss my ass. I want *the* in there. Microsoft wants to complain, they can drop dead. We'll put freakin' Linux on the teevees.'

'Ah, Tom, let's not say anything like that in public, okay?

I'll put your *the* back in the script. Owen, why don't you talk to Tom and I'll get a new printout.' Taft got up and got out of the suite as fast as possible, without actually breaking into a sprint. He had hoped Sanders would moan about the edits – that way, he could escape while Lindsey delivered the latest bad news.

'You want coffee, Owen?'

'No, thanks Mr Sanders.'

Sanders got up with a grunt and went to the kitchen, pouring a mug of coffee and topping it with Chivas Regal and whipped cream. He sank into the couch again and said, 'Well?'

'Some good news: we've checked every hotel and motel from here to Stateline, and there's no Jesús Ramirez registered anywhere.'

'Yeah, great news. You think the troublemaker would register under his own name?'

'Well, Mr Sanders, it seems he's getting more reckless. We tracked down a Jesús Ramirez – through one of his credit cards – staying at a motel in San Francisco. Our men were there within an hour of the authorization.'

'And got nothing, as usual.'

'They spotted a man, leaving in a hurry. Two men, actually. They got a good look at one.'

'What about the other one?'

'Well, they said ...' Lindsey pulled a report from his briefcase. 'The other was a thin man, maybe five feet ten inches, pale, longish dark hair, sunglasses, jeans and tennis shoes. They don't think he's Ramirez. The one they *do* think might be Ramirez is the same one the clerk identified as signing the bill. He's about six feet four inches, maybe six feet five inches, caucasian, short dark hair, probably dyed, a moustache, jacket and tie. They both left in a taxi.'

'Great, Owen. Real fine detective work. How'd they leave

in a taxi if your guys were there?'

'It, unfortunately, got complicated.' Lindsey cleared his throat. 'Some kind of parade has brought all these motor-cycle gangs to San Francisco. A sort of, well, lesbian-pride parade or something – '

'Oh for God's sake.'

'And the parking lot was full of these Harley-Davidsons, and all these women, blocking our guys. They reported in, directly to me, Mr Sanders. And, well, to me it sounded like this Ramirez left in a rush, perhaps leaving something behind. It seemed prudent to keep a few men in the area, just overnight, just in case. At least to check out the room when the new guests stepped out.'

'Anything?'

'Something, but, well, it's not very good.' Sanders sighed and Lindsey pulled some faxes from his case. Including articles from the *Mercury News*, *Chronicle* and *Examiner*. 'At 20:07, our guys – Jeff Basart and Dylan Bickley – were across the street, on Market, watching from their car. This lesbian biker gang, specifically the three in what had been Ramirez' room, turned off the lights and left. Got on their motorcycles and departed, westbound on Market. Basart called in and said he was going to take a look, standard use of the lock tool, just see if anything useful was inside. He left the car and crossed the street, his view momentarily blocked by a passing street-car. When he got to the motel's parking lot, he noticed the door to this room was open – the occupants had closed it behind them. Before, well, before he reached the stairs, two people, two very large people dressed in a similar fashion to the bikers, took the outside steps in a suspicious manner.'

'Quit with the Adam-12, Owen.'

'Yes, sorry. They looked suspicious, they were sneaking up the steps, glancing around, obviously trying to avoid detection. Basart was on intercom with Bickley's cell phone, that's how we know this much.'

'Complicated, eh?' Sanders finished off his coffee cocktail and glared at Lindsey.

'Unfortunately, yes. Bickley took off when the ... trouble started. To await backup.'

Sanders glared.

'The shooting, Mr Sanders.'

'You morons actually shot somebody?'

'No, not exactly. Basart was shot, shot dead. At this point, I have reason to believe our missing agent, Richard Welch, is working for the other side. I've called headquarters to send out another team of guys to watch IBM – their hotel rooms, their space on the convention floor, everything.'

'What good's that gonna do? Never heard of such pathetic crap. You get a pair of idiots arrested in Reno, another goes crazy and gets hauled in for rape, one disappears and you tell me he's defected, and one gets shot? Meanwhile, this Ramirez says he's here and you can't find him. Yeah, blame it on goddamned IBM, Owen.' Sanders licked the whipped cream off the mug's edge. 'And what makes you think this Welch idiot is working against us?'

'Well, Mr Sanders, ... Basart was shot with Welch's gun. We've got some questions to answer.'

Sanders grabbed the faxes and started with the *Chronicle*. His face turned a deep, ugly red as he scanned the article:

```
Private Eye Killed in Market St. Row;
Police Seek Links to Lesbian Biker's
Gruesome Death at Mission Protest
By THOR WHALEN
Chronicle Staff Writer

A private investigator for a Silicon Valley 'cor-
porate intelligence' agency was shot dead at the
Market Street TravelLodge just before a lesbian
```

motorcycle activist plunged to her death at the 16th and Mission BART station last night. The bizarre altercation involved more than 200 lesbian activists visiting The City for Sunday's Dyke-Byke Pride Parade, along with some 800 Mission District residents holding a rally for a Latino journalist.

Santa Clara resident Jeffrey Basart, 42, was pronounced dead at the scene from a gunshot wound to the chest. Witnesses, including the motel's night clerk, told police that Basart toppled from the motel's second-storey verandah onto a row of parked motorcycles.

What happened before the shooting remains a mystery, police said. Basart, an employee of Menlo Park-based Business Intelligence Partner Services, was apparently on a surveillance assignment. Police found a semiautomatic pistol with the body, along with a private investigator's badge. The man carried a valid concealed-weapon permit, police said.

Even more curious was the discovery of a pistol identical to Basart's, found by police in the shrubbery beneath the verandah. Because the weapon had fallen onto a sprinkler head watering the plants, detectives speaking on condition of anonymity said it was unlikely any fingerprints would be found. Ballistics experts will examine the gun and the bullet that killed Basart later today, police said, but detectives on the scene told the Examiner it 'smelled like' the gun had recently been fired.

Patrol officers had twice visited the motel earl-ier in the evening due to excessive noise complaints. Complicating matters was a statement by the clerk, 27-year-old Wade Schulte, that minutes before the shooting someone identifying himself as an SFPD vice squad officer called the lobby and said he would be raiding Room 216. It was outside this room that Basart was shot.

Police and medical examiners were still at the scene when a riot broke out in the Mission district. A protest was being held by the Berkeley-based Latino Media Revolutionary Council in support of renegade Internet reporter Jesús Ramirez. According to the group's Web site, the rally was called to defend Ramirez from 'fat white fascist women' who have launched a boycott against Ramirez' Web site, www.SluiceBox.net.

That Web site has been the source of much discussion in Silicon Valley, especially after Ramirez published an incendiary profile of MicroTorrent Systems' CEO Thomas Sanders, implying that Sanders was responsible for the death of a Harvard classmate in 1962. Another Berkeley group, the Fat Lovers' Acceptance Vigilante Army, has called for such a boycott on its own Web site, www.FLAVA.org.

About an hour into the rally, police said, participants in the Dyke-Byke Pride Parade rode their motorcycles straight into the protest, leaving more than 30 residents injured and one visiting motorcyclist dead from injuries sustained when she crashed her Harley Davidson into the BART station's concrete railing and dropped more than 100 feet. The cyclist, 51-year-old Tonya Brisbane of Reno, was pronounced dead at the scene from multiple head injuries.

Wanda Simpson, 48, of Carson City, Nev., was arrested at the scene for reckless driving, as were another 14 bikers. Police said when she gave her local address as the TravelLodge on Market Street, they took her to the scene in an attempt to help homicide investigators there piece together the night of mayhem.

'I wish it made sense,' said Detective Coulter Stevens. 'The gal claims she received a phone call from the night clerk, warning of a vice raid. The clerk denies making the call, no such raid was scheduled, and no such raid took place. She then said her friends, including our dead Ms Brisbane, briefly left the motel. When they returned, Ms Simpson claims she caught a woman — described as being five feet nine inches and about 375 pounds — breaking into the room.'

Among other strange details from the night, the motel's master circuit breaker blew out, leaving all the rooms in darkness during the altercation.

'Next, she and her surviving roommates all claim a plainclothes officer appeared at the back of the room,' Stevens said. 'Again, witness reports are limited due to the power outage, which PG&E and the fire department [are] investigating. This supposed officer forced them to leave the room, at gunpoint, and then ran down the stairs, disappearing eastbound on Market. They followed, on foot, now apparently believing the man had lied about his affiliation with the SFPD.'

The biker women claim they returned to the motel minutes later and found the body of Basart on their motorcycles. Schulte, the clerk, agreed with this detail. While Simpson, Brisbane and many other guests of the motel then left on motorcycles to chase the man seen in Simpson's room, five guests remained to await police.

The altercation at the protest occurred about 10 minutes later, police said.

More than 20 patrol units cleared the plaza surrounding the BART entrance, while paramedics took the injured to local hospitals. At least 17 victims were treated at San Francisco General Hospital. Spokesperson Ronda VanDusen said all but one were released this morning.

Detectives said they were disturbed by something they retrieved from the site of the riot: the private-investigator badge of Richard S. Welch, another employee of Business Intelligence Partner Services. The SFPD's Stevens said the badge was found, along with Welch's California driver's licence and credit cards, in the back pocket of a shredded pants leg near the BART escalators.

Reached this morning, the firm's spokesman said Richard Welch was on administrative leave and had been for a month. Calls to his home went unanswered. The spokesman refused to comment on the company's involvement with the incidents.

A police spokeswoman said: 'I've never dealt with these guys, so I don't want to say nothing bad, but I expect the district attorney might want to have a word with whoever runs this outfit. We carefully license [private investigators] in California, especially those carrying concealed weapons.'

The firm's Web site, www.BIPS.net, lists many prominent Silicon Valley technology companies as clients, including MicroTorrent Systems, the company which has lately suffered massive losses in share price, due in part to the exposé by Ramirez, the renegade Internet journalist who was the reason for last night's rally in the Mission district.

Werner tossed the paper on the bed.
'Blokes gone mad, all of 'em.'
'Yeah,' Larry whispered. He didn't feel so great. 'You okay?'

'Ah, bump on me head, nothing. Owl's safe above with the pigeons, minus one gun.'

'The BIPS jackass?'

'Yep. Wanker who hit me must've swiped a pistol. Weird. Told me he's kidnapping "Jesus", said he was a penguin. Big boy.' Werner shook his head and said, 'Can't believe you got pounded at your own protest.'

'What could I do? "Excuse me, I'm the Mexican journalist in question?"' Larry groaned. 'The whole city should be firebombed.'

A blonde woman walked out of the bathroom.

'Come on, bath's ready.'

'Hurts … too much. Sponge bath?'

'There's not a big enough sponge. Get up.'

Amanda was a nurse Werner had met after his motorcycle accident on Highway 1. A healthy northern California girl, dressed in bike shorts and a UCSF sweatshirt, ponytail, charmingly crooked teeth on the bottom. She took Larry's arm and helped him stand. The sheets stuck a bit.

'Bloody hell, Jonestowne. You've ruined the linens.' Werner didn't lie. There were brownish-red stains from the pillow to the foot of the bed.

Larry grimaced and limped to the bathroom. He stepped in the tub, cursing, and slowly lowered into the water.

'Agh!'

'Shh. I'll take care of your various wounds once I can see where they are.'

'I can't *shh*, I'm dying.'

From the bedroom, Werner yelled, 'Give him the pills, already.'

Larry looked at her and tried to grin. 'You have pills?'

'I'm not supposed to, and I didn't give you any.' She shook two Vicodins from a bottle in her purse. 'Werner! Get him some water.'

'How about a beer.'
'You shouldn't take these with alcohol.'
'Beer, please?'
'Werner!' Larry's ears rang. 'Bring him a beer.'
'Thanks,' said Larry, gulping the horse pills and chasing them with almost cold Bud.
'Sure. Soak a while.'

She turned off the light and left him to the tub. The pills did their work in Larry's empty stomach, synthetic opiates reaching his brain, sending false messages of peace and serenity, numbing his mind.

'Get out and dry off,' she said, flicking the light on again. A half-hour had passed. With sterilized tweezers, she plucked the remaining broken glass from his head and chest, coated the endless abrasions with antibiotic salve, and wrapped the uglier wounds with gauze and tape and Band-Aids. The left leg needed a whole roll of bandage.

'You should have someone look at this.'
'You're a nurse.'
'Yeah, but you might have some scarring.'
'I'm not a model.'
'No kidding.' She stared at his swollen face a moment. 'I don't think anything's broken. No swelling of that sort. Your nose already broken?'
'Yeah, a few times.'

A knock at the door. Werner took the new sheets, tipped the maid, and tossed them on the stained motel mattress.

'You should stay out of the sun 'til these things on your face heal up.'
'No sun in this part of the world. Pills?'

She reluctantly gave him another half-dozen – 'Three days' worth, Larry' – and left enough gauze and tape and Neosporin for a week.

30

He slept another hour, CNN rumbling in his head, and sat upright when the name 'Thomas Sanders' was mentioned. The business report, live from the Las Vegas COMDEX trade show. In just five hours, Sanders would be announcing MicroTorrent's interactive-television strategy. The stock was up 4-15/16. Just because the jackass was going to speak at a scheduled event. Seemed a poor way to gauge a company's value. It was 10:30 a.m., time for coffee.

Larry rose, feeling better than he should have. Only tiny blotches of blood on the sheet. He found a plastic bottle of water on the dresser and drank the whole quart. Took another pill and followed it with half a Bud. Needed caffeine. Needed to walk around, get some air. The whole room smelled of death and medicine. Placing the computer on the table by the open window, he hooked up the phone line and dialled in, simultaneously checking Ramirez' Hotmail and his own e-mail. Brushed his teeth, tried not to gag, and rinsed with generic Listerine.

He dressed and glanced at the little hourglass on the computer screen. It would be there a while. The salty breeze outside was an improvement. A quiet town. Small houses in silvered redwood, goofy weathervanes twirling in the sea breeze, very few people around. He headed up the street and found a café, ordered coffee and sat beneath a gas heater with the San Jose paper. It had nearly the same story, nothing on the pending Massachusetts warrant. He drank down a refill and headed back to the SeaHorse.

Another hundred e-mails for Jesús, a few for Larry from

O'Leary. The first-person account from COMDEX was a good read. He posted it to SluiceBox.net and pecked out a quick response to O'Leary: 'Lovely, it's up, send more of the same. Much to tell, once the wounds heal.' But something nagged his semi-numbed brain ... Werner's trouble on the roof. Penguin? Searching the collection of MicroTorrent/Ramirez stories produced no penguins.

He spent forty-five minutes hacking together a pair of new tech horror stories for the site, spurred by the cubicle e-mails as always. JumboNet's president was having an elevator installed. An elevator to transport his Porsche to a private garage adjoining his third-floor office, even as two hundred employees were pink-slipped. And QuestWeb's CEO had been arrested for drunk and disorderly conduct at a notorious drag-queen bar in San Francisco, the same CEO named in a class-action lawsuit by gay programmers claiming vicious discrimination by QuestWeb. Larry made a few phone calls and checked the Internet sites for details – even the complaints were online – reviewed the 400-word pieces, and posted them with the standard hyped-up headlines.

Another business bulletin about MicroTorrent on the teevee. Just four hours until the speech. Letting the stock close high. It seemed wrong to miss Sanders' arrest.

He shut down the computer and gathered pills, bandages, a reporter's notebook, Ramirez' social-security card and the shaving kit. Pulled his canvas shoulderbag from the big duffle and crammed the laptop and everything else inside. Catching his reflection in the dresser mirror, he swiped a pair of Werner's wraparounds. They almost hid his bruised eyes. The trenchcoat looked ridiculous over his sweater and shabby pants. He exchanged it for a green infantry coat liberated years ago from a dead Serb, scribbled a note to Werner, and locked the door.

Luck was with him. A taxi arrived in thirteen minutes.

Skies were clear and windless at San Francisco International, so the United flight was canceled due to weather. Larry cursed and got a refund and bought a ticket from American Airlines, departing in 30 minutes. It would be close. Should've taken Southwest from Oakland, he thought, but there was no time to cross the bay, in the all-day rush hour. He picked up the late edition and sat at the Fog City bar, sipping a Jamesons with water back to prevent dehydration while flying. A few new details in the paper: the bullet that killed this Basart goon was, indeed, fired from the discarded Glock, registered to BIPS and assigned to Richard Welch. District Attorney Callaghan announced a crackdown on 'gun-slinging Silicon Valley rent-a-cops wreaking havoc in our city.' Protest leader Jorge Banderas held a press conference in Berkeley, accusing the fat activists of sabotaging the Latino media revolution or whatever. Ramirez, as usual, could not be reached for comment.

Seat 9-A, emergency exit. In the event of an emergency, he would still have more leg room. Once the captain turned off the No Drinking light, Larry requested three little bottles of Cabernet, 'to save time for us all', and borrowed the airplane phone from the row behind to call O'Leary's room. No answer, press one to leave a message.

He did. 'Jesús has risen, and he is coming soon.'

It was sunny and beautiful in Vegas. A cabbie waved and Larry limped over. As he slid into the back seat, a horrible voice yelled, 'Wait for us!'

Larry turned and saw an obese woman in combat pants bouncing toward his taxi.

'You wanna share?' the cabbie asked.

'Not really.'

'Hell with her.' The cab sped away. Larry kept his eyes on the woman, thinking he'd seen her before. 'Where to?'

'Going to COMDEX, unfortunately.'

'Yeah, so is everybody. Makes it nice for us, but I wouldn't wanna spend a week with those arseholes. No offence.'

'None taken. I'm only here for terrorism.'

The cabbie laughed. 'You sorta look like a terrorist. Whaddya do?'

'Me? I'm a piñata.'

31

Scott ran to the curb a minute later, breathing hard.

'Keep up, Scotty.'

'I'm trying.'

Terry Texas was proud of her agility. Despite her weight, she could trot at a good pace, for fifty yards or so. It was the only physical leftover from junior high, when she was still thin enough to run track.

'Skinny fascist took the only cab. We can't be late.' In three minutes, another fleet of taxis arrived, and the kidnappers squeezed inside a Yellow.

'Take us to the COMDEX,' Terry commanded. The driver nodded, glancing in the rearview at the strange pair. The woman had a black eye and a bandage on her forehead. She was dressed up like a … he was reminded of John Candy in the movie *Stripes*. A lean, mean fighting machine, sure. The kid was almost as big, dressed in some awful suit – like a woman's pantsuit, the kind they wore in the 1970s. And a poorly knotted tie over a shiny beige shirt.

Terry felt awful, but she refused to show it. They had spent hours on that dirty stoop. When she finally came around, they searched for her Isuzu Trooper, but it was gone. Towed from the motel parking lot, since it was blocking the entrance. They waddled to the Civic Centre BART station and returned to Berkeley. It was on the train that Scott started crying. He didn't know exactly how it happened, but he'd caught Jesus, and then saw these other women kicking Terry, and he had a gun, and somebody kicked him in the nuts, and then he really caught Jesus, trying to sneak up on Terry. He didn't remember firing the gun, but he couldn't forget seeing that man fall off the balcony, smashing into those motorcycles.

Still dazed from the beating, Terry didn't scream at Scott. Her eyes seemed faraway, and she smiled and said, 'Nothing wrong with that, Scotty. You killed that racist Jesus. Nothing wrong with that.'

At home, the teevee news didn't say anything about Jesus being killed, just some security guard. Terry screamed and yelled, slapped the hell out of Scott, and then dragged him to the bedroom. Afterwards, she patted his head and said it was fine, they'd just stick to the plan. Go to Las Vegas, kidnap this racist Jesus, and issue FLAVA's demands: replace the cast of 'Friends' with fat people, ban fashion magazines, life in prison for Kate Moss and all members of the AMA and CDC, and no more of those 'healthy choice' symbols on fast-food menus.

At the convention centre, Terry paid the $12.80 fare with $13 – 'You can keep the change' – and they stood blinking in the desert sunlight. She checked the women's briefcase Scott carried, a relic of her days as a library clerk. Inside was a roll of duct tape, a steak knife, and a flashlight. He also carried a musty cloth sleeping bag, rolled up and stowed in its army surplus cover.

'You sure I look all right?'

Terry stood back and nodded in approval. Her convalescence had left no time to buy Scott a suit, so she'd dressed him in an orange polyester pantsuit she used to wear to work, many years ago. The blouse was hers, as well. The tie was bought from a souvenir shop at the Oakland airport. It was decorated with a silkscreen of a cable car, with a little San Francisco skyline above it.

'You look very handsome. Better than all these computer racists.'

'Okay.'

They entered the lobby, confused by the various booths – 'Exhibitors', 'Media', – and finally consulted the information desk. The skinny freak told them they should go to 'Exhibitors'.

Standing in line, Scott felt self-conscious. He didn't see anybody else in an orange pantsuit, but this was no time to cry. The guy at the table asked for their names, and then scanned the printouts.

'Nothing here. Are you sure you pre-registered?'

'Pre-register? Nobody told us that.'

The guy nodded to Terry. 'Well, what's your exhibitor code?'

Terry elbowed Scott and whispered, 'Show him your business card.'

'Oh, right.' Scott took the inkjet-printed card-sized piece of paper from his velcro wallet and put it on the counter.

Charlton Company Inc.
Mr Scott Charlton, CEO
Consulter for the Internet
Berkeley, CA

'Consulter?' the guy asked.

'For the Internet.'

'Well, nothing I can do here. You can buy an exhibit hall pass over there.' He pointed to a row of green booths by the entrance.

'This is discrimination!' Terry spun on her boot heels and

stared at the nervous dot.commers in line. 'Anti-fat discrimination! I'll sue you Comdexes, all of you! Racists!'

'Ma'am,' the guy said, trying to smile. 'Just get a hall pass over there. This line is only for pre-registered exhibitors.'

'Racists!'

Larry glanced at the commotion. Behind him, a pretty young business reporter said, 'What's that about?'

He watched the huge woman stomp away – that woman again – with an orange-clad boy behind her. He shrugged.

'These things get worse every year,' she said. A small girl with efficient dark hair, nice freckles on a strong nose, short professional skirt and a silk blouse, good legs in medium heels, leather laptop case hanging from her right shoulder. Larry noticed appealing things, too. They were in the R-Z line.

'Yeah, I swore I'd never see one of these trade shows in person.' When he reached the counter, he said, 'Jesús Ramirez, SluiceBox.net.'

The girl leaned around him.

'Ramirez? You're Ramirez?'

'Shh. Who the hell are you?'

'Amy Wells, MSNBC.'

'One minute, please?'

Larry produced his social-security card and MAGIC STANDARD Visa® for identification. The bleached-blonde girl at the counter couldn't care less. She gave Larry the press pass, which looked like a credit card itself, and the clear-plastic badge cover with MEDIA printed in yellow on the bottom. The pass said JESÚS RAMIREZ in huge black letters, with SLUICEBOX.NET beneath, in slightly smaller type.

The girl gripped his bicep while she waited for her credentials. Trapped, Larry looked at his watch and scanned the hall, hoping he wouldn't see a familiar face. She took her pass, looped the chain over her neck and walked him away from the line.

'*You're* Ramirez?'

'Sort of ... not really.'

They walked toward the row of glass doors.

'You smoke?'

'I'm quitting.'

'Come outside.'

They went to the plaza's fountain and sat down. A trio of actors dressed like video-game characters ran by, distributing passes for a free-booze press party. Larry took one and filed it in his Serb coat.

'Somebody beat you up?'

'Sort of.' He offered a cigarette and took one for himself.

'I want an interview.'

'You can't have an interview. Jesús doesn't *do* interviews.'

'Does anyone know you're here?'

'I hope not.'

'I love you!'

'C'mon, we just met.'

'No, not *you* – your site. It's fun.'

'Fun?'

She took a long drag and watched the smoke drift away.

'All this stuff linked from your site, these corporate spies, all this chaos ... you're causing it?'

'Not intentionally. I shouldn't even be here. Bunch of psychos nearly killed me last night – '

'Nearly?'

'Whatever.'

'You're not even Mexican, or Bolivian or whatever ... you dyed your hair?'

'Momentary lapse of judgment.'

'You ever take those sunglasses off?'

He lifted them slightly, revealing the bruises.

'God, you're a wreck.'

'Listen, you be quiet and maybe we'll do a little interview. Not that I've ever been interviewed.' He looked at the watch again. 'Obviously, I'm here to see Sanders talk. You do anything weird, and it'll ruin everything.'

'I won't do anything weird.'

'Promise.'

'I promise. MSNBC honour.'

'Great.'

They returned to climate control, consulted the conference schedule, and headed to the escalators, Larry stopping for a $6 double cappuccino. The coffee stop prevented them from witnessing another scene by Terry Texas and Scott Charlton. Their hall passes didn't allow access to the conferences, but Terry screamed 'racist' enough times that the usher let them in, commanding them to stand in back.

Walking into the packed room, Larry said, 'Keep a safe distance, for Christ's sake. Bad things seem to happen around me.'

'Don't run off.'

'I won't run off. Just give me some room.'

Thankfully, there were only solo seats remaining. She found a chair in the sixth row, middle section, while Larry searched for O'Leary. There he was, third row on the left, head bobbing, lockjaw grin, listening to the reporter in the next seat. Larry had flipped his badge, only the magnetic strip showing, hoping to avoid further recognition.

'O'Leary!'

The long neck turned, the grin widened.

'You criminal!'

Larry trotted around the front row, up to O'Leary's seat, second from the aisle.

'What in hell are you doing here?'

'Journalism. What's your excuse?'

O'Leary rose, all six feet six inches of him, and hugged Larry.

'Careful, wounded.'

'Right, sorry' – he spoke without unclenching his teeth – 'Got your message, didn't quite believe it.' His brown hair was prep-school cropped, his tie reflecting the same pedigree, with a rumpled Brooks Brothers' shirt and tan cuffed corduroys. A filthy preppie, head to toe.

There was an empty seat one over.

'Hey there, mind if I sit down?'

The young tech reporter had a mean, snide face, ripe for punching.

'No, I'm saving it.'

'Well, why don't you let the guy sit down until your pal returns?' O'Leary said, smiling and menacing.

'Not how it works,' the youth barked. 'Seat's saved.'

'Well, let's not be rude about it. My friend here will surrender said seat to your pal when he shows.'

'Wrong!' It was a squeaky, hateful voice. Wire-rim glasses tight on the skull, curly hair slicked with some sort of gel product. Larry stood between them.

'I'll just have a seat,' Larry said. He turned to sit, but the reporter pushed him, and Larry had no choice but to dump his hot coffee on the cretin's head, steamed milk clotting in the curls. The glasses fell and the eyes blinked and the fists came up. O'Leary slid over and found the spectacles, muttering something soothing, Larry shrugging sorry to those around them. The conference room's lights went out, and the usual *2001: A Space Odyssey* score rumbled through the public-address system.

'Sorry, dude,' Larry said, helping the snarling reporter back to his seat. 'I'll just find another chair.'

The reporter tried to rise again, but O'Leary politely forced him back into his precious chair.

O'Leary rolled his eyes at Larry, standing in the aisle now. Larry mouthed, 'No worries,' and discreetly pointed to his media pass: 'Mel Greenbaum, *MacWorld* Magazine.'

O'Leary's eyes got wider, his mouth open in silent hilarity. Larry put a finger to his mouth and slipped away. Some flack from MicroTorrent took the podium, science-fiction graphics projected behind him, president of the board William Howard Taft or something. O'Leary waited a Christian interval and glanced at his neighbour, still seething from the coffee incident, a notebook clenched between his fingers, the name JESÚS RAMIREZ hanging from his wet button-down shirt.

Larry went to the back of the room, squinting through his shades for an empty seat, and saw Amy Wells waving, someone behind her yelling, 'Sit down!' Larry grimaced and went down the aisle, pardon me excuse me and past the knees of his alleged colleagues, dropping in the chair beside her.

'Thanks,' he whispered.

'You're welcome,' she whispered back. 'Man, you weren't kidding about bad things happening around you. What was *that* about?'

'Nothing. Old friend of mine up there, he's covering the Sanders thing. Some jackass wouldn't let me have the extra seat.'

'Who?'

Larry pointed to his badge.

'Oh no.'

'Shhhhh,' somebody hissed.

32

'What the hell are you saying?'

Sanders and Lindsey were arguing in the green room.

'What I'm saying, Mr Sanders, is that for the moment, our licence has been suspended.'

'For the moment?!'

'We'll have to talk to some people in Sacramento, nothing major.'

'Christ. For this motel thing?'

'Partially, yes.'

A knock on the door.

'Just do your speech, Mr Sanders, break a leg – that's what they say, right? I'll take care of this. And I promise you, this has no impact on our investigation of Ramirez, or IBM, or any of this.'

'You better be right.' To the door he yelled, 'All right, I'm coming.'

Sanders straightened his tie in the mirror, grunting, and went to the door. Three men in cop-suits were there.

'Thomas Sanders?'

'Yeah?'

'We have a warrant for your arrest from the state of Massachusetts – '

'What?'

'– in the murder of Gilliard Tyler Seacroft.'

'Owen!'

Lindsey ran to the door. He pulled his mobile phone and dialed the BIPS guy waiting down the hall.

'Lindsey. Can you please escort counsel to the green room behind the auditorium? Immediately.'

'What is this? I'm giving a goddamned speech.'

'Mr Sanders, you have the right to remain silent. You have the right to an attorney. If you cannot – '

'Hell with that.'

'Cuff him.'

'Wait!' Lindsey, nervous, smiling. The lawyer, looking like a New-Age gangster in double-breasted pinstripes and oiled hair and a Palm Pilot in his hand, approached the cops.

'Henry Arellanes, Arellanes and Clover, San Jose.'

The cops just stared.

'Gentlemen, Mr Sanders has a *major* address to deliver, one which is crucial not only to MicroTorrent Systems but to the entire technology industry! This is live on CNBC, CNN, the international media are here. Please, whatever the issue here, let the man make his address. Tom, how long's the speech?'

Sanders, red and flustered, said thirty minutes.

'Thirty minutes, gentlemen. Stand in the wings, whatever you like, but let the man make his speech. Believe me, he has a lot more to keep him on that podium than this.' Arellanes swiped the warrant and glanced at the charges. 'He's got thousands of *stockholders* watching. Please, gentlemen, be reasonable. Mr Sanders is among this country's most respected technology executives. We'll take care of *this* once he's spoken. Deal?'

The Boston cops conferenced in a huddle, and the apparent leader turned back to Arellanes.

'All right. We'll escort him to the stage. Don't pull any crap.'

'Gentlemen, we're a Fortune 100 company, not criminals.'

'We'll see.'

The movie music was roaring again as they walked down

the concrete hall, Sanders between the cops, Lindsey and Arellanes tailing them, both on cell phones.

'Ladies and gentlemen, the chief executive officer of MicroTorrent Systems and a 25-year veteran of the Silicon Valley technological revolution, please welcome Thomas Sanders!'

Subdued applause. Three men walked Sanders to the stage's edge, and then Sanders – looking confused, furious, taking a deep breath – stepped to the podium. He stared at the prepared text during the uncomfortable silence and said, 'Thank you for that warm welcome.'

'How do we find him?'

'They're all wearing nametags. Just walk around and find him!'

Scott grumbled and headed down the first aisle, squinting through the darkness, a sea of press badges. Someone yelled, 'Down in front!' He crouched and surveyed another row. At this point, he had no idea what Jesus looked like. The previous night had left him confused and horrified. He wouldn't even be able to recognize the guy on the roof, let alone the guy he shot.

Terry yelled, in a half whisper, 'Flashlight!'

Scott nodded and fished the light from the big purse. He shined it down a row, catching everyone in the eyes. Much displeasure was expressed. An usher grabbed Scott by the arm and said, 'What do you think you're doing?'

'Uh.'

'Turn that light off. Go back to your seat.'

Scott went back to the wall. Terry wasn't pleased.

'They told me to.'

'*They*, Scotty, aren't here to kidnap an evil racist. You are. Now find him!'

'I can't see the nametags.'

Terry considered this for a moment. Sanders was speaking, something about teevee.

'Then go to every row, and tell whoever's in the aisle seat that you've got a very important message, for Jesus Ramirez.'

'You think that'll work?'

'Go!'

Scott went to the far end of the auditorium, hoping to avoid Terry's surveillance. She leaned against the wall and tried to follow Sanders' speech – he *was* a fat and proud executive – but she had no idea what he was talking about.

'Everything you know about telecommunications, my friends, it changes right here.' No response. 'Of course we've been promised much, and we've certainly seen a revolution in the past few years, but ... you ain't seen nothing yet.' No applause. Damned press. 'With the release of MicroTorrent TeleNetVision 1.0, we are truly talking about a total evolution of not only the global economy, but of the very interaction between humans, and not through the business-to-business model but through direct consumer empowerment.'

Terry edged closer to the sound/light booth, and Sanders prattled on, a slideshow on the screen behind him, illustrating whatever.

'As is always the case, when you are an innovator, then out come the wolves, ha ha. We've seen it happen to our friends at Microsoft, we've seen it with ... IBM, and we've seen it at AT&T and AOL and Oracle. Let me make it perfectly clear: Attempts to stain our innovation with half-truths and flimsy alter-egos will do no good at MicroTorrent.'

Amy Wells nudged Larry.

'Watch the bandages,' he whispered.

'How does it feel?'

'It hurts.'

'No, being here. Watching him squirm?'

'I don't know.'

'We're here for the long haul, folks. And when we come back next year, and there's a MicroTorrent TeleNetVision box in half the homes in America, you'll think back to when I said, 'You ain't seen nothing yet.' Thank you, and, uh,' glancing back to Lindsey and the Massachusetts cops, 'I'll take just a few questions.'

The house lights switched on. A hundred eager tech reporters stood, hands stretched high like overeager students.

'Yes, you there.'

'Michael J. Kelso, Interactive Week. Can you tell us something about the OS on this box?'

'Well, sure, thanks for your question. Our release date, as I've said, is August 1st, and we've got a Class-A team working day and night to make sure this system is not only revolutionary, but user-friendly right out of the box. That means a simple, point-and-click interface, from what will seem to the average consumer as easy as changing channels, and ....Yes, on the left.'

'Martin Solomon, Reuters. You mentioned "the" market leader in operating systems, but didn't name the company. Word in the Valley has been that Microsoft was providing the system, a Windows 2000-based hybrid. Is there a reason you're not naming Microsoft today?'

'Well, we're all vicious sharks out here' – some laughter from the media – 'so we're always tinkering with our partner roster, making sure we not only have a market leader onboard, but a team that's going to take us to the next level. Yes, on the left.'

'O'Leary, *Boston Sun*. Ahh, Mr Sanders, do you care to comment on the murder warrant you were just served' – the whole room gasped – 'regarding the 1962 death of your Harvard roommate, Gilliard Tyler Seacroft?'

Silence. Counsel ran to the podium, the Boston cops

stepping closer. Counsel whispered to the clearly shaken Sanders.

'No, at this time, ah, I have no comment – '

'Perhaps a personal comment, perhaps in regards to, ah, a Mr Jesús Ramirez, who, ah, seems to deserve credit for bringing this, ah, situation to light?'

Sanders' knuckles, already squeezing the lectern, went white.

'Yeah? Well that little spic is gonna pay for this bullshit, you tell him that!'

Lindsey and Arellanes ran to Sanders' side, pulling him back from the microphone. He slapped the lawyer away and spoke again:

'Twenty-five goddamned years I've worked in Silicon Valley, and no criminal wetback is gonna change that!'

From O'Leary, a terrible grin stretching across his square jaw: 'Maybe, ah, you'd like to direct some of your, ah, concerns to Mr Ramirez himself?'

'Goddamn right. Coward, lies and libel and slander. Cut him a new – '

'He's right here.' O'Leary grabbed the *MacWorld* reporter by the shoulders and stood him up. Those in the front rows turned and saw the JESÚS RAMIREZ credential, while those in back stared at their colleagues' faces, trying to grasp the significance.

Lindsey and Arellanes were locked around Sanders' big arms, pulling him from the mike. The Boston cops looked nervous.

'You coward!' Sanders yelled, his voice carrying through the crowd even without a microphone. 'You're fucking finished! Finished! Dead!' Lindsey and Arellanes struggled; a BIPS man appeared, adding his muscle to the battle to get Sanders offstage. 'I know who you are, you goddamned fraud! I know who pays you! Goddamned IBM!'

Another mass gasp, as pens danced on notebooks.

'You backstabbers! You're done! I see you, Ramirez! I'll chew your nuts off!'

The *MacWorld* reporter was in shock. He had glanced down at the nametag, after O'Leary boosted him to standing position, and he just couldn't comprehend what was happening. So he stood there, eyes glassy, sweat pouring down his sides. He thought about running out, but his legs were numb. His whole body was numb. A communications graduate from USC – paid for with his father's personal-injury practice – he had got an internship at *BusinessWeek*, briefly held a copy-editing job at *USA Today*, and then went down the ladder to *MacWorld*. He was smug about this career path. He loved Macs.

The house lights switched off. Then the stage lights. Total darkness. There was yelling from the booth, and then the awful sound of a body thrown, echoing through the hall.

A fat kid leaped over O'Leary and yanked the new Ramirez to the carpet, stunned tech reporters watching the shadows struggle, no attempts to save their colleague, or Ramirez, or whoever it was.

A ripping sound – O'Leary thought, 'Duct tape?' – and then Ramirez was gone, hustled up the aisle between concerned voices and a few screams. From the stage, there was the clicking sound of guns shifted from the safety position. And a thud from the floorboards. Muffled yelps from the aisle. Digital-camera flashes made the room look like a fireworks show.

Amy Wells rasped, 'My God, this is incredible.'

'Yeah?'

'Yeah!' Frightened media representatives rose from their seats, feeling their way down the rows, bumping into each other. She slid out of the way and made for the aisle.

Light. Double doors opening. A thick figure dragging

something away. Another thick figure following.

Backstage, Thomas Sanders was face down, two pistols at his head, somebody tightening cuffs on his wrists, a mini-Mag-Lite shining at his eyes.

'Nice try, fat boy.'

'What are you talking about?'

'Shudup. Save it for the judge.'

'Walk faster. Who's she?'

Amy Wells had a strange look in her eyes.

'Later,' Larry said to O'Leary. The shuttle driver slid the van door back. They climbed in, watching the Vegas police park by the doors, COMDEX closed for the day, tech reporters blinking in the sunshine and terrible confusion.

'You see it?' O'Leary couldn't stop smiling.

'Of course I saw it. Prison forever, for all of us.'

'Not for us. Those cops took Sanders by the neck, down the long dark hall.'

'Let's hope. Where's the schmuck?'

'The accidental Ramirez? I think he was kidnapped. By a couple of huge nuts.'

'Them again.' Larry laughed. It never stopped. 'Where're we staying?'

'We?'

'I don't have a room; just flew in to say hello.'

'Yeah, I presumed as much. Then we're at the Mirage. Her?'

'Amy Wells, MSNBC,' she said, dazed. 'I'm not a *her*.'

'Well, you're not a *him*.'

'She's fine,' Larry said, leaning his head on the window.

O'Leary tipped the shuttle driver and they went to the room, a mini-suite on the eighth floor. Larry collapsed on the couch, eyes closed, and O'Leary turned on CNBC.

'So, ah, you're a reporter?'

'Yeah.' She sat on the edge of the cushion, her fingers in

Larry's wrecked hair. 'Is he on drugs?'

'Probably.'

'I shouldn't be with you guys. What happened?'

'Much happened.' He picked up the phone and ordered club sandwiches, three packs of Marlboro Lights and two bottles of Champagne. 'We, ah, should enjoy the reportorial process now and then.'

She stared at Larry. This was a side of journalism they had never mentioned in college. O'Leary went to his laptop in the dining area and started typing, forever grateful to the Massachusetts detective. He called the paper.

'Oh yeah, incredible, outrageous. Will, ah, get you ten inches for the morning, and ah, I'll really have to insist on the front, with a nice teaser for the Sunday epic ... Fine, you'll have it in an hour ... Huh? ... I don't care about your Web site; just put up some wire copy.'

Brilliant, O'Leary thought, returning the phone to its cradle. The wires and teevee knew Sanders was arrested, knew it was about the frat death, but they knew very little else – he had everything. The girl wouldn't get her story out first, he would make certain of that. Room service arrived. O'Leary distributed the sandwiches and Champagne flutes. He shook Larry's shoulder and said, 'Wake up. Might want to have a sandwich.'

Amy said, 'Who *are* you people?'

'Stop worrying, have a drink.'

Larry pushed his shades back and stared at the food. He took a quarter sandwich and chewed thoughtfully.

'It worked. Everything worked.'

O'Leary laughed and downed half a flute of Champagne.

'Yeah, it worked. Good job, Mel.'

Larry looked at his *MacWorld* badge and tossed it be-hind the couch. 'Yeah. Bitchy little Mel Greenbaum. Great country, America.'

Amy finished her glass and said, 'How's that?'

'Well, just think ... Today, by accident of course, he actually served a purpose.' Larry sipped the Champagne and looked at his bandaged fingers. 'We must've screwed up *something*.'

'Nothing,' said O'Leary, refilling the flutes. 'Sanders is in custody. Our, ah, little jackass vanished with the fat people. There's plenty of cigarettes for you. Marlboro Lights, right?'

'Camel Lights.'

'Same thing.' O'Leary demolished another chunk of sandwich and returned to his story. 'Sunday cover, as promised,' he said. 'Definitely worth the trip.'

'Who do you work for?'

'A paper, Boston.'

'Do you, um, usually cover technology?'

O'Leary laughed and shook his head.

'You knew something was happening, the arrest – '

'I know nothing. When do you have to file?'

'In an hour,' Amy said.

'I'll wake you.'

'Wake me?'

'Go on, have your fun with Ramirez.'

She stood and looked ready to start interrogating, and then she shrugged and smiled – a sweet high-school smile, the kind of girl just begging for the worst sort of corruption.

'Sure, I'll file in an hour,' she said. 'C'mon, Ramirez.' He stubbed out the Marlboro and rose, shakily. Reached for the champagne glass and drank the rest of his serving, the canvas shoulderbag still on his shoulder.

Amy closed the sliding fake-wood doors behind them and pulled down the covers. 'On the bed,' she commanded. He flopped onto the bed. She unlaced his boots, pulled the socks away, unbelted the khakis and slid them over the bandages, carefully removed the sweater and T-shirt, removed the watch, and stared.

'What?'

'My god, you're like a mummy.'

'Mostly the leg.'

'Does it hurt?'

'Yes, it hurts. Everything hurts.'

'You've got medicine?'

'In the bag. Two, please.'

She fed him two Vicodins, tap water from the bathroom to follow, and tossed off her skirt and blouse.

'Jesus,' Larry said. 'That's a lovely sight.'

'Yeah?'

'Yeah. Get over here.'

She kicked off the white panties, unhooked the bra, and curled around him.

'I don't do this,' she whispered, licking his ear.

'Do what?'

'Pick up injured strangers.'

He grinned and kissed her, then dropped flat again, groaning from his battered shoulder and some other injuries he couldn't pinpoint.

Amy said, 'Can't you move at all?'

'Not today. You want date rape or whatever, do it yourself.'

'Yeah?'

'Yeah.'

'Like that?'

'Yeah … certain courts might consider – '

'Quit talking.'

They quit talking.

33

Terry and Scott dragged the squirming sleeping bag to the escalators and through the main lobby. Nobody interfered. They reached the block-long driveway/plaza, full of rolling billboards, a seven-foot-tall Hello Kitty being led around by two Japanese women in foil jumpsuits, a busty model dressed as the CD-ROM heroine Lara Croft and signing 8x10s of the digital character, some sort of insect robot driving in circles, and dozens of pretty girls in green thigh-high boots, distributing press-party invites and pretending to fire phallic laser guns.

Terry waved a cab and they dragged Ramirez to the back seat, passing two young programmers from LucasArts.

'What the hell game are they from?'

The other programmer shrugged. 'Fridge Raider II?'

With the sleeping bag sitting upright between them, Scott sucked in his gut and slammed the door shut.

'Where to?' The cabbie expressed no concern; yesterday, his passengers included three Martian vampires, a midget and his R2D2 costume, a headless cheerleader, and Big Bird.

'We need a hotel.'

'You don't *have* a hotel?'

Scott shook his head.

'Everything's full, people. This is COMDEX.' Now he'd seen everything – damned companies bring these freaks out here without a room? 'I'll take you down to the end of the Strip, maybe one of those motels will have something.'

'Then do it, and hurry!' Terry barked. The driver shook his head; these freaks always had to 'stay in character'.

The Win-Win Casino/Motel was a loser's dump between a used-car lot – 'Need Money? Ca$h For Your Car NOW!' – and a combination liquor-souvenir store. It was a two-storey L-shaped building, dubious pool behind chain link, and an old neon sign flashing 'V_CANCY'. Terry was running low on money, so she didn't tip the driver. He spat and sped away.

Scott stood outside with the captive while Terry got the room. Second floor, on the end, next to the ice machine. They dragged Ramirez up the steps and onto the thin, green-swirl carpet.

Both kidnappers were panting. The sleeping bag was still.

'Terry? You think he's okay?'

'I don't know, check on him.'

Scott unzipped the bag a little, around where the head should be. Ramirez' face was bright red, his curly hair soaked with sweat, the eyes half open and glazed. The duct tape wasn't only tight around his mouth; it nearly covered his nostrils. Terry ripped it away and replaced it, this time below the nose.

'Get some ice!'

Scott opened the door, made sure the coast was clear, and waddled to the ice machine. He held the lid with his head and scooped up as much as he could carry, dropping most of it on the way back.

'What should I do with it?'

'Use the ice bucket! Here, put it on his head.'

Scott dumped a handful of cubes on the captive's forehead. They bounced off and landed on the carpet. Terry scowled and got the plastic bucket from the dresser, saying, 'Watch him close.' Five trips later, they had packed Ramirez in ice cubes, the old cloth sleeping bag soaking up the melt.

Terry peeked through the curtains. Nothing happening. No cops. She arranged the demands list and the photocopies of the press release, 'Hateful Racist Internet Reporter is Political Prisoner of FLAVA', and picked up the phone.

'Are you gonna order us some pizza?'

'No, Scott! We have to tell the police we've got Jesus.'

But she was hungry too, so first they called Dominos, complained when it took thirty-two minutes instead of the promised half hour, ate both large pies, and then called 911.

'Yes, this is FLAVA, the Fat Lovers Acceptance Vigilante Army, and we've got Jesus.'

'Excuse me, ma'am?'

'Jesus! The racist! We kidnapped him at the COMDEX.'

'Okay ... Would this be, uhm, you say Jesus has been kidnapped? As in, Jesus Christ?'

'No, goddamnit, Jesus Ramirez, the hater!'

'Okay, well, let me check on that for you.'

Scott sat on the bed, flipping through the teevee channels, looking for news about the kidnapping.

'Okay, ma'am, uhm, we don't have a missing-person report for, uhm, Jesus Ramirez. Or for *Jesús* Ramirez, if that's what you meant. So, I'm sorry I can't help you.'

'Listen to me! *We* are the kidnappers. *We* just kidnapped Jesus, the hateful racist, the one on the Internet. And if you don't answer our demands, we'll *kill* him, got it?!'

'Okay, ma'am, we'll check that out.'

'Don't you want to know where he is?'

'Uhm, is he with you, this Mr Ramirez?'

'Yes, and we'll kill him if – '

'Okay, ma'am, well we've got your number here. The Win-Win Motel, is that right?'

'How do you know where I am?'

'Thanks ma'am, goodbye.'

Terry slammed the phone down.

'Are they gonna call back for the demands?'

'Shut up, Scott.'

When an hour passed without incident, she found the

Yellow Pages and turned to 'Television Stations'. By the time she'd phoned the last 'news hotline', she was getting the hang of it. The revolutionary fat-acceptance militia, FLAVA, had kidnapped the racist Internet's Jesus Ramirez, who was at the COMDEX to attack the famous fat activist and computer businessman, Thomas Sanders. If the demands weren't met, FLAVA would kill the racist. She then gave helpful directions to the motel and said she was available for interviews.

After the local stations arrived with their gaudy teevee vans, a few financial-news crews were called away from the free-booze parties, and by 7 p.m. the CNN truck rolled up. The police didn't arrive until the motel clerk called, complaining about all the teevee vans. Terry's 911 call had been dismissed as a particularly insipid prank. A producer from CNBC told a traffic cop about the trouble following Sanders' speech.

'So you guys saw somebody kidnapped?'

'All the lights went out,' the producer said. 'Didn't see much of anything. But this Ramirez was apparently there – this CEO was chewing his ass out, from the stage. We looked for Ramirez afterwards, no sign of him.'

'He's a reporter? What kind of reporter?'

'I don't know. These nuts say he's – ' she looked at the press release, which Terry had dropped from the bathroom window. 'He's some racist or something. Was going to kill this Sanders guy because he's fat.'

'The reporter's fat?'

'No, Sanders. He's pretty fat, I guess. They say he's part of this Fat Vigilante Army or something.'

The cop went to his car radio. 'Hostage situation. Say they're gonna kill a fat guy.'

O'Leary rapped on the bedroom door.

'Get in here.'

Larry woke, searching the ceiling for clues, feeling a warm body against him, clean sheets. Right, COMDEX.

'Leave us alone.'

The door slid open.

'I won't be leaving you alone. Come see the news.'

Larry rose, sore all over, and found his boxer shorts. Staggered into them, went to the couch. CNN.

'Fantastic, just fantastic,' O'Leary said, crouched by the teevee. 'You're a political prisoner.'

'The hostage situation just gets stranger, Bernie. Las Vegas police say the kidnappers want, among other things, the cast of the NBC series *Friends* to be replaced by fat people – '

'Now, do we know if this is actually the renegade Internet reporter?'

'That's the opinion of the police, Bernie. They've surrounded this motel, the Win-Win Casino Motel at the far end of the Strip. According to witnesses, these activists kidnapped Ramirez after the speech at the big COMDEX computer show here, a speech by embattled MicroTorrent Systems' CEO Thomas Sanders, who, as we've learned, was arrested on murder charges right here in Las Vegas, apparently right after his speech. We've got some video, and as you can see, it was a tense scene.'

The blow-dried reporter kept talking over the footage, Sanders screaming from the stage, men in suits pulling him away, the camera searching – and there was Ramirez, the face white, glossy with sweat. And, a foot taller, O'Leary, rocking on his heels, head bobbing, a shark's grin.

'Kristine, if we can delve into the background just a little, we're talking about a Silicon Valley executive who was first named in this scandal by the very Internet reporter now being held captive, is that right?'

'It certainly is, Bernie ...'

Amy walked out of the bedroom, the sheet wrapped around her.

'Ah, good morning,' O'Leary said.

'Morning?'

'Figure of speech. It's only seven.'

She plopped onto the couch and lit a cigarette.

'Can I get fired for this?'

'Smoking?' Larry asked. 'Probably.'

She laughed. Tell the truth, they think it's funny. 'I've got to file a story. You promised you'd do an interview.' O'Leary had already filed.

'Did I? Look, they've got old Ramirez.' Larry pointed to the teevee. 'There's your story.'

'You promised.'

O'Leary brought three beers from the mini-bar to the coffee table. He'd finished the champagne alone.

'You, ah, if you promised ...'

'Damnit, O'Leary.'

'That's, ah, what you get, stealing a man's room.'

Larry grumbled and got up, returning with his Day Timer. He scrawled a cheque to O'Leary for $2000.

'Here. Now quit hassling me.'

'Revenue?'

'It's a faith-based donation.'

Amy ignored this exchange, listening to CNN. 'I should take notes.'

'They'll run it again in a half-hour,' O'Leary said. 'Do your interview. Take your time.'

Larry took his beer and the ashtray and went back to bed. She followed, her Budweiser balanced on the laptop, evidence of college-waitress jobs.

O'Leary put on a navy blazer with brass buttons. Standing in the bedroom's doorway, he shook his head. 'This, ah, does not look very professional.'

She looked over her shoulder at O'Leary, but kept typing.

'All right, my workday's over. See you later.'

Larry lifted his head slightly. 'Where you headed?'

'Cultural investigation. Try to find that Mustang Ranch.'

'What about the Kennedy girl?'

'Ah, it's a little iffy right now.'

'Iffy?'

'Well, ah, if she finds out I went to a whorehouse.'

Amy finally looked up from the screen. 'I'm trying to do an interview.'

O'Leary nodded. 'Good luck. He, ah, generally makes no sense. Best to take liberties.' To Larry he said, 'You sound brilliant in the Sunday piece. Almost eloquent.'

'Thanks. Give my regards to the hookers.'

O'Leary lurched out, still grinning.

'He made up your quotes?'

'Well, sure.'

She looked stunned.

Sanders had never been in such a room. The walls were acoustic tile, probably full of asbestos. There was a fluorescent fixture on the ceiling. One table, particle board with wood-style plastic coating. Four blue moulded-plastic chairs, of the free-clinic variety, Owen Lindsey and Henry Arellanes in two of them.

Sanders paced, the crumbs of seven donuts marking his spot at the table.

'At worst, Mr Sanders, we fly to Massachusetts, have a bail hearing, and you'll be back in California for dinner.'

'Can't believe you didn't shoot that Ramirez.'

'Mr Sanders, I'm sure Henry will back me on this. We can't go shooting people at COMDEX while you're being arrested.'

'I'm ... uncomfortable with this sort of talk,' Arellanes said, 'considering our present location.'

Sanders reached for his Palm Pilot. Cops took it. 'Give me your Palm, Owen.'

Lindsey removed the latest model from his jacket and slid it across the table. Sanders took the stylus, clicked 'New Memo', and scribbled. He slid it back.

Find Ramirez. Kill him.
Him & whoever else behind it.
$10 mil for you. Go now.

Lindsey glanced at the screen, exhaled, and deleted the memo before returning the Palm to his suit. BIPS' licence was gone, maybe for years. The lawsuits alone would wipe him out. He'd spent the past decade at a desk, either for the government or for the tech companies, but he still knew how to do a job. He didn't want to, not at all, but he also didn't want to end up poor and disgraced. Five million and disgraced ... That was somewhat better. He rose.

'Mr Lindsey, what's happening here?'

'I'm not counsel, Henry. My job is the same as when I got here: investigate whoever's circulating this slander against Tom Sanders. And I have no particular interest in visiting Boston again.'

Lindsey opened the door, said something to the cop, and disappeared down the hall.

'Our best and *only* recourse, Mr Sanders, is to post bail, get you back to MicroTorrent, get *my* staff on discovery, and get these charges dropped. If this thing is half as flimsy as the IBM suit, it will never see a courtroom.'

Sanders seemed calm, ever since Lindsey left. Arellanes didn't want to know why.

'Fine, Henry. Let's go to Boston.'

One of the Massachusetts cops knocked and came in –

Pat Williams, the secret friend of O'Leary. Williams looked so much like a rumpled Eastern Seaboard big-city detective that people constantly stopped him on the streets, asking if he was on that *Law and Order* show. With him was a Vegas captain on the desk.

'Where'd your rent-a-cop go?'

'Mr Lindsey is attending to MicroTorrent security issues at the convention.' Arellanes was quick that way.

'The convention's over.'

'Hardly,' Sanders said. 'We've got a goddamned exhibitor party at the Excalibur tonight ... I was supposed to be there.'

'And, as a matter of fact, detective, COMDEX runs through the weekend.'

'Fine, excuse-boy. I meant it's over *for the day*, as your disturbance managed to shut the show down.'

'My disturbance?' Sanders spat at the floor. 'How was that *my* disturbance? You guys come in there to assault *me*, while this *terrorist* is ten feet away.'

'You mean Ramirez?'

'Fuck's right I mean Ramirez. Whyn't you do something about *that*?'

'Not our jurisdiction. But it is the jurisdiction of Captain Gonzalez, Las Vegas metropolitan.'

Gonzalez smiled hello, a round guy about forty-five, droopy moustache.

'We've got something at the end of the Strip, one of those little motels.' He took the chair that had been Lindsey's. 'Dispatch ignored it at first, sounded like some deluded nut, but now it's a hostage situation.'

'What does this have to do with my client?'

'Well, these people say they've got Jesús Ramirez held hostage, and they say they're part of the "fat revolution", working for you, Mr Sanders, their fat spokesman.'

'What? You calling me fat, you sonofa – ' Arellanes shook

his head and tapped Sanders' shoulder.

'I'm not calling you anything.' Gonzales patted his belly and smiled. 'I'm telling you that something called F-L-A-V-A, one of those Berkeley groups in your part of the world, is dropping statements to the teevee news crews from a bathroom window, saying they've kidnapped this Ramirez because he insulted you. Because he called you a fatso.'

'And,' Williams said, 'If you've got *anything* to do with it, you get to deal with Nevada for a few years, then we'll come back to talk.'

'Gentlemen, Mr Sanders is a Silicon Valley executive, a famous man in the business world. Famous people attract every sort of nut, as I'm sure the Las Vegas police can confirm. I can assure you he has nothing to do with some Berkeley radicals and their kidnappings. This sounds like some ridiculous Patty Hearst stunt, and personally I take offence that you would – '

'Look, we're just trying to get this guy out of there, if he's even up there,' Gonzales said. 'What do you know about him?'

'Read the fucking Internet, you'll see all you need to know.' Sanders slumped in his chair. 'I want to get this over with. When we going to Boston?'

'First flight in the morning,' Williams said. 'Unless something changes in the next few hours … I'm gonna take a look at this motel.' He smiled at Gonzales. 'With the captain's permission.'

'I'll give you a ride. You can meet our local hostage negotiators.'

'Psychologists?'

'UNLV's finest.'

They left, and Sanders was led to his cell, bitching and moaning the whole way. Arellanes promised to work all night and be back in the morning.

34

Lindsey drove to the Mirage, changed into his idea of street clothes – a Woodside country-club polo shirt and pressed slacks – and turned on the teevee while he ate a quick room-service omelet, tomato and American cheese. His doctor said lay off the eggs, but he was hungry.

'Nash Bridges' was interrupted by the local news. Hostage situation in North Las Vegas. Famed Internet journalist Jesús Ramirez, being held by a fat revolution army, all because Ramirez insulted Thomas Sanders, a fat activist who ran MicroTorrent Systems, in town for COMDEX.

With his spook's compartmentalized brain, Lindsey ignored the 'fat activist' part and focused on the kidnapping. Was Ramirez there? He'd seen the kid – really, just a kid, a short stocky kid, probably a Jew, maybe one of those Mexican Jews, untrustworthy in any case – but was unable to do anything, after Sanders went berserk and got roughed up by the Massachusetts cops. A BIPS man searched the hall, but as usual came up dry. Lindsey had started to hate his entire staff, these soft, post-Reagan agents. Always scared, always going crazy, always ending up in jail or the morgue. For a corporate account.

Lindsey loved the old world order, the George Bush Snr CIA, even the William Casey CIA. The only time he'd ever felt truly alive was in Central America, poisoning communists, exposing their dirty secrets to the pro-democracy forces. In his mind, he was still fighting the Cold War, but these days the enemy was Washington, not Moscow. All the same to him.

He didn't like the sound of this kidnapping. Radical Berkeley group? As if Tom Sanders, a lifelong Republican, would have anything to do with some feminist nuts from Berkeley. Why would *they* be after Ramirez? Why would they be calling Sanders a hero and threatening to kill some Mexican? Those people loved Mexicans, would change the national anthem to Mexican if they could.

Lindsey put on his shoulder holster and loaded the Glock. It was Lindsey's favourite gun, and he required all BIPS agents to carry one. He fitted the silencer around the barrel, tucked it inside the quick-release holster, and put on a plaid blazer. It had been a normal, post-agency life this past decade. But the enemy was always there; it just changed guises. Today, the enemy was out there, trying to destroy American capitalism. Trying to destroy Lindsey's very comfortable existence. He examined himself in the mirror and thought he looked very normal. And maybe he did, for brunch at a country club back in 1962.

The sleeping bag convulsed. Terry was at the window, steak knife and leaflets filling her hands, and told Scott to check on the racist. He unzipped the top of the bag. Ramirez was almost blue now, snot dripping from his nose, glistening against the silver tape.

'Terry? I think he's sick.'

She kneeled beside the captive and looked at the hater's pasty, swollen face, resisting the urge to punch him.

'So what, he's sick.'

'Terry? What if he dies? Then what do we do for a hostage?'

That would be bad. Terry ripped the duct tape from his mouth, and his eyes opened slightly from the pain. She pushed the tip of the steak knife against his neck.

'What's wrong with you?!'

'Ungh ... cold.'

She touched his forehead. It wasn't cold at all, burning up.

'He's not cold.'

'Maybe he's got fever or something?'

'What are you, a doctor? You joining the AMA now?'

The ice had just about melted, but the sleeping bag was soaked through. Terry liked the air conditioner at full blast; it was about 60 degrees in the little room. The hostage sneezed again, and began shuddering.

'We kidnapped you, racist. And if these fascists don't meet our demands, you're dead. Dead, Ramirez, you hear that?!'

'Ungh ... I'm ... I'm not Ramirez.'

'Bullshit.' She slapped him, hard.

'I'm Mel ... Mel Greenbaum.' He coughed again. '*Mac-World*, the magazine.'

Scott looked nervously to Terry.

'Who is this, Scott?'

'It's Jesus! I swear!' He unzipped the bag to the chest, showing the media badge.

'It's ... no, I'm ...'

Terry slapped the hostage again. The eyes closed. 'But I guess he's no good dead. Make a hot bath, Scotty.'

He nodded and went to the tub. She held the knife to Ramirez' throat – he didn't notice, being unconscious again – and peeled off the cold, wet sleeping bag. She duct-taped his arms to his side and his ankles together, then yelled at Scott.

'Bath ready?'

'Almost full.'

She dragged Ramirez by his feet to the bathroom, steam pouring from the door. 'Help me put him in!'

Scott lifted around the shoulders, and they dropped him into the scalding water. Ramirez screamed and screamed.

Gonzales and Williams parked the cruiser behind the local FOX affiliate's van. They'd driven through for hamburgers and had a friendly talk. Both old-school cops, both sons of immigrants, both past the age of brutalizing suspects for fun.

'Over there,' Gonzales pointed, walking past the car, pointing to the distant lights of his suburban development, Adobe Springs. No springs, no adobe.

'What do houses cost out there?'

'Got mine for ninety thousand. Before these freakin' tech companies pushed up the prices. Three bedroom, two bath, third of an acre with "desert landscaping", got a swimming pool, whole fucking deal.'

'Nice.' Williams lived in a cramped, drafty row house. Charming if you like that sort of thing. No yard, ancient plumbing, rot in the porch columns. 'Maybe I'll move out here. I like this air.'

'Gets hot in summer.'

'Gets hot in summer in Boston, too. How's the department?'

'Pretty good, not bad. Better than Los Angeles.'

A reporter and her cameraman ran up to the pair. Blinding light atop the lens.

'Officer, do you have any information on the kidnappers?'

'This man's a captain, lady.'

'Yeah, a captain with no information on anything.' Gonzales smiled and looked at the shoddy motel. 'We just saw the teevee vans and wanted to see what's going on ... same as you.'

Yellow tape blocked the steps. The other guests had been evacuated, sent to an even seedier motel in North Vegas.

Beside an unmarked GM, three bookish fellows stood, one talking to a mobile phone.

'Yes, I empathize with your concerns ... yes, these empowerment issues ...'

'Idiot shrinks,' Gonzales whispered to Williams.

The one on the phone, a short balding guy in a blazer and worn slacks, turned to the new arrivals as he ended the call.

'Jerry Gonzales, how are you boys?'

The man extended a limp hand. 'Dr Robert McWhorter.'

'Can you treat wounds?'

'Well, no …'

'Pat Williams, I'm here from Boston. These people up here, they say this CEO is their leader?'

'No, not really. Apparently they feel *solidarity* with the man, Thomas Sanders, because he's taken a public stance in regards to his weight.'

'Bullshit. Tom Sanders is a money-grubbing computer executive. We're taking him to Boston in the morning on murder charges. Sleazebag killed his Harvard roommate in 1962, cashed in on his buddy's patent, came out West and avoided the whole thing 'til this Ramirez showed up and put it all on the Internet.'

'I see. It's important – Mr Williams, was it? – that in these situations we avoid stock generalizations.'

'Ah, save it for the kidnappers. They got this Ramirez or not?'

'They have somebody. I asked that they put him on the telephone. He sounds frightened.'

'No shit!' Gonzales laughed. 'Some nuts gonna kill you unless *Friends* gets a new cast of fat people, you gonna be happy?'

Williams put his arm around the psychologist's shoulders.

'Listen, it might do these people some good to know that Sanders is in custody, right? For murder. Anybody got IDs on these losers?'

Another psychologist said, 'One goes by the name "Terry Texas". That's been traced to a Web site, one that states some generally similar demands regarding the media's use of abnormally underweight fashion models – '

'Right, and we hear there's another one?'

'Yes,' McWhorter said. 'He calls himself "Penguin". Beyond that, we've not much information. But by his voice, I would hypothesize that he's a young man, perhaps eighteen to twenty, and suffering a combination of delayed adolescent anxiety and weight-related self-esteem – '

'Jesus and Mary, cut it with that. What's their weapon?'

'The male, he claimed to have several machine guns.'

'Machine guns? What kind?'

'He refused to elaborate, other than comparing them to machine guns used in what sounded like a very aggressive computer game ... Death Brigade VI, he said.'

Williams laughed.

'If I may be so bold, doctor, get on that phone and tell 'em Sanders is locked up, police don't make the teevee shows, and that if they don't get the Ramirez guy out of there, we're gonna blow up their fucking room.'

'I ...'

'Nice plan, detective.' Gonzales flagged one of his own. 'Detective Williams here is working on the Sanders thing, from Boston. Tell your negotiators to do what he says.'

35

Lindsey drove past the Win-Win Casino/Motel, keeping with traffic, and saw the police and teevee trucks in the parking lot. He turned right at North Bruce Street, drove one long block southeast, and parked on the street behind a medical-supply warehouse. No guard around.

He got out of the car and pressed the alarm button on the key, hearing the double beep as the doors locked. The street parallel to the Strip was just a street, concrete and asphalt and gutters and a sidewalk on one side, desert and brush on either side. When he was opposite the back of the motel, he veered off the pavement and through the sagebrush. One cruiser back there, two uniforms a dozen yards to the right, watching the side of the building. Thanks to the teevee, he knew it was the room on the second-floor corner. The bathroom light was on.

Hiding behind a dry little mesquite tree, he waited for the closest uniform to walk to the column of light made by the parking-lot fixture and the teevee vans. Then he sprinted to the car's bumper. The only holes on the back side of the motel were tiny ventilation windows for the other rooms, already cleared. Hence the lack of cops. A few feet from the cruiser was a roof-access ladder. He jumped through the shadows and caught the bottom rung, scaling up to the tar-gravel roof.

Lindsey was gloating on these local cops' stupidity when a chopper appeared, spotlight shining around the motel. He ducked between two Carrier air conditioners – for the lobby, he guessed – and waited for the helicopter to make another circle and leave. Then he scrambled to the end of the L, finding the bathroom fan's vent pipe. The desert had done a good job sealing the roofing tar. He pulled, cutting his hand on the sheet metal, and yanked again. It came out with a grating, scraping noise. Through the hole, he saw a kid, unconscious or close, in the tub. Fully clothed. It was Ramirez. Lindsey squinted through the hole and saw the COMDEX press badge hanging from the neck. No doubt about it. He thought about that ten million. Sanders couldn't screw him; to do so would be inviting another murder charge, murder for hire. The money was as good as in the bank – an offshore bank.

He slipped the Glock from the holster and pointed it down the ventilation hole. And a fat woman moved in, her massive backside blocking Ramirez. A few splashing noises later, and they were both gone. Lindsey reholstered and considered the options.

'They can't see shit.'

'Nope.'

'Let's get up there. Demand they put Ramirez in the window, prove he's there.'

'Anybody know what he looks like?' Heads shook. Gonzales smiled. Incompetence amused him. 'Go ask the teevee people, they got him on tape.'

A psychologist and a uniform headed for the NBC van, both looking disappointed with the errand.

Gonzales turned to a detective, Phil Larabee. 'You sure there's only two of 'em?'

'Sure? No, not sure. But the clerk has one fat gal getting the room, and a fat boy waiting outside with our guy in a sack or something. Pizza guy came, but he left, we checked.'

'Look,' Williams said. 'They've got this guy, probably knocked out. Gonna take both of 'em to drag him to the window.'

'Maybe,' Larabee said. He just wanted to go home and drink nine beers and watch whatever soft-porn showing on HBO. 'Fuck it, why not? We'll get the snipers ready, you guys give it a go.' He radioed the gun boys, on the roof of the Courtesy Used Cars building across the street, various other sharpshooters hiding in the brush and atop the liquor/souvenir store.

'You people be nice to your visitors and don't shoot me, all right?' Williams grinned and walked away.

Gonzales slipped a black bulletproof vest over his gut and patted Larabee on the shoulder, following Williams, headed for the shadows beneath the verandah. McWhorter shook his head, hating this macho aggressive behaviour, and dialled the room on his mobile.

'Hi, yes Terry, it's Rob, Rob McWhorter ... No, I told you, I'm not a policeman. I'm a psychologist at UNLV, and when they have difficult situations, sometimes they ask me to talk to those involved ... No, Terry, I'm not trying to analyze you. My concern is for your safety, and your friend's safety, and the safety of Mr Ramirez ... Yes, yes, I *know* you regard him as a prejudiced individual ... right, a racist.'

He looked at Larabee and shrugged. Larabee grabbed the phone, watching Gonzales and Williams tiptoe up the stairs.

'Listen, lady: Here's what's happening. You've got a bunch of tired cops out here, and everybody wants to go home. You fuck around, these cops are gonna do what they do, and that's shoot ... No, lady, this ain't Berkeley, we don't burn the cops in the schoolyard or whatever. So here's the thing. I'm sittin' out here, looking at this motel, thinking you're a fraud, you get it? I'm thinking you don't have no Jesus Ramirez. We got no Jesus Ramirez missing, you understand? And we're gonna be very, very pissed off if you're just up there wasting our time. So right now, you open those curtains and show us this Ramirez, or I'm sending fifty cops, guns blazing, right into your goddamned room. 'Cause no matter how fat you people are, we got enough bullets.'

Terry dropped the phone and ran for the tub. Scott was sitting on the bed, hungry again. 'What now?'

'They're attacking! They don't believe us!'

She dragged Ramirez from the tub, not bothering to consider how terrible he looked.

'Help me! They want to see it's him!'

Scott got up and sighed, walking to the window. She pulled back the curtains and they pushed Ramirez' face against the glass, an old steak knife against his throat.

Lindsey cursed – a rare occurrence – and looked down the hole. He could hear them, in the room. He tugged at the roofing. It was thin, just a double layer of tar paper. Baked and brittle plywood beneath it. A big chunk gave way. He set it aside and continued, through the asbestos insulation, until there was a human-sized hole over the bathroom. Widely spaced 2x4s, chalky drywall, a coat of latex over that. Grasping the gravelly surface, he lowered himself, landing in the still-warm tub with a quiet splash.

He glanced up, making sure it would work as an escape route. Fine. Stand on the edge of the tub and pull right up. With the Glock again unholstered, he checked the fit on the silencer and peeked around the doorway. Both of them at the far side of the room, hoisting Ramirez to the glass. Some hostage-proving tactic?

Lindsey aimed at Ramirez' back. Two-thirds up from the waist, left of the spine, there was the heart. His finger curled around the trigger.

The motel room's door flew open with a bang. Lindsey flinched, the finger pulled inward, and he fired – hitting Scott Charlton right in the ass. He dived back into the bathroom, hearing official shouts, and scurried up the hole. He was halfway down the roof ladder when another cruiser appeared, and he dropped, an awful crunch from his ankle, and ran into the scrub, one leg dragging.

'Hands up!' It sounded small in the desert air.

He didn't put his hands up. A bullet whizzed past, then another, then another. He stuck to the ground. And felt a slug sink into his own ass. Owen Lindsey kept crawling.

The street was a problem, as cruisers were going back and forth. He lay in the weeds for five minutes – teeth clenched, remembering all his training in Virginia – and when he saw nothing but tail-lights, sprinted across the pavement, ignoring the ankle, his right buttock on fire. He jumped into the creosote just as another pair of headlights hit the street.

Desert survival training, he'd taken a three-month course in that, for Afghanistan. So he was totally prepared to limp through a mile of brush and arrive at a new development called Mesquite Ridge. He broke into a model home and pulled off his bloodied slacks, turned on the shower, and hosed off his wounded backside.

Gonzales spun into the room – he had the bulletproof vest, after all – and aimed his revolver at the sorry trio. Terry Texas launched herself at the captain and he smacked her in the temple. The barrel left a big red splotch aside her left eye and she sank to the carpet. The hostage fell with her; he was out. The other terrorist was huddled in the corner, crying like a baby.

The captain kept his eyes on the trio and said over his shoulder, 'Come on in.'

Williams smiled to the crowd below, saluted the snipers, and entered the sorry room. He saw blood on the fat boy, but heard the wimpy crying and figured that wasn't a problem. The alleged hostage, he was a problem. He looked close to dead.

'Get the paramedics for this guy?'

Gonzales spoke into his radio, 'Victim in trouble up here, let's go.'

The paramedics arrived thirty seconds later, rolling Ramirez onto the stretcher. Williams kneeled beside the fat boy and said, 'What in hell do you think you're doing?'

Scott didn't answer. They took him next, then Terry, huge and unconscious.

'Better than the 24-Hour Fitness,' Gonzales said as the paramedics stumbled out.

Williams and Gonzales decided to follow Ramirez' ambulance. They were curious. He was rolled into the emergency room and a handsome young intern looked the hostage over. Checked the pulse, the eyes, the breathing, the temperature.

'Glucose,' he barked to the male nurse. 'Get the wet clothes off.'

The doctor-in-training came into the hall. Gonzales looked at him.

'Hypothermia ... in Vegas. And, for fun, scalding of the extremities. Some contusions. He'll be fine.'

'You do me a favour?'

The intern smiled at Gonzales. 'What's the favour?'

'Just see if the boy's got a wallet.'

He returned to the little room, padded at the hypothermia victim's pants, and returned with a moist leather billfold.

'There you go.'

Gonzales said thanks and the intern trotted off to another emergency.

'Melvin Greenbaum, 25, Burlingame, California.'

'Bay Area?'

'Yep. Here's a business card. Mel Greenbaum, staff writer, *MacWorld* Magazine, San Francisco.'

'Think that's the famous Ramirez?'

'Probably not.'

'Jesus and Mary.' Williams laughed, watching the gurney holding Terry Texas roll by. 'Think I'll get some sleep. Take this Sanders to Logan in the morning.'

'Think I'll sleep, too. Where you staying?'

'Mirage.'

'Come on, give you a ride.'

'What's the charge on these nuts?'

'I dunno, we'll make up something.'

36

MSNBC Exclusive:
Renegade Internet Reporter Goes Public;
The First Interview With Jesús Ramirez
By Amy Wells
MSNBC Staff Writer
LAS VEGAS — Who is Jesús Ramirez?

    For months, that has been the biggest question in Silicon Valley.
    From his Web site, SluiceBox.net, Ramirez has left the titans of the computer industry scared of something other than NASDAQ, hoping his muckraking would spare their companies. And on Friday at the COMDEX show, it seemed the secretive reporter had gone public, when his prime target — MicroTorrent Systems' CEO Thomas Sanders — was arrested by Massachusetts police in connection with the 1962 murder of Gilliard Tyler Seacroft. The arrest came moments after Sanders abandoned a disastrous press conference, when a Boston newspaper reporter asked about the warrant.
    [Click Here for Full Story]
    It was this long-forgotten death that Ramirez brought to light in an article posted to his site.
    On Friday, television cameras showed a young man wearing Ramirez' media credentials, and in a bizarre altercation in the auditorium, members of a self-proclaimed 'fat liberation army' kidnapped the man, leading to a four-hour standoff outside a seedy motel on the famous Las Vegas Strip.
    The hostage was not Ramirez.

The Internet journalist was in the auditorium, 30 feet away, and claims he has no idea why the kidnappers chose another reporter, or why another reporter was wearing Ramirez' press badge.

'Mistakes were made, I guess,' Ramirez said Friday, from his hotel suite. 'These people, they're all insane — medical tests would prove it. I'm just trying to do my job, just wanted to sit quietly and watch Sanders get arrested.'

Asked if he had advance knowledge of the Massachusetts warrant, he laughed and said, 'People like to tell me things, they send e-mails confessing all sorts of information.'

It is the first time Ramirez has spoken to the media. The subject of hundreds of newspaper and tech-magazine articles and a cover story for both Time and Newsweek, the reclusive Web journalist says he has neither read nor responded to the countless e-mailed media inquiries he has received since launching the site.

'I am very busy, with work and whatever, and it seems dirty to spend my time talking to other reporters. They should be doing better things, like exposing frauds, or rescuing puppies from floods.'

This self-employed journalist — SluiceBox.net is whatever Ramirez wants to publish online — claims to be the target of violent corporate spies employed by MicroTorrent Systems. He refused to discuss any personal or professional details. Ramirez is a tall, light-haired man, perhaps 25, perhaps 40. His ancestry is a mystery, as well.

'My uncle was Mexican,' he says, and then changes the subject. And the Web site registry listing his address as La Paz, Bolivia? 'I frequent a hotel there. No different than George Bush Sr listing a Houston hotel as home.'

What prompted Ramirez to start his own Web newspaper, targeting the golden heroes of the Internet Revolution?

'Disgust. Disgust with the way things are going. Used to be, smart people wanted to do something interesting. Write a book, start a cult, make a record, grow a beard. Now? Now they want options. Damned reporters want stock options, not that they're worth anything anymore. They'll gladly take stock in the very companies they're supposed to be covering. That's not right.'

Ramirez watched his reported kidnapping on CNN from his own hotel across town, cursing at the correspondents for jumping to conclusions. He claims to have little patience for television news, business-wire services and almost all American newspapers.

'Halfwit bloodsuckers,' Ramirez says. 'Vampires with baby teeth. They lack the most basic reportorial skills, and for some reason, they're smug. Smug! Ignorance and arrogance, all coated in Teflon.'

Asked his reasons for targeting the CEO of MicroTorrent Systems, Ramirez compared Sanders to Richard Nixon.

'They leave horror in their wake, but we are stronger for destroying them, or something. Maybe we're not. Maybe we're just weaker, and stupider, and then we die, slip in the bathtub or whatever. Choke on a microwaved burrito, alone, watching infomercials.'

Some have questioned his association with an offshore Web gambling operation, which provides the servers for his site. He claims the gambling firm's owners are 'acquaintances, I think from a war,' and that no money has been exchanged. There is banner advertising on each page, through a San Francisco-based network, FlyRight. Ramirez says the income is 'nothing big, enough for a night out now and then.'

'The servers are wherever they are because certain corporate-espionage goons make things difficult. These people are skilled at many things, whether crushing the competition with bogus lawsuits or using CIA-style violence and intimidation to silence critics. Have you studied the railroad monopolies of the 19th century? They would be laughed out of Silicon Valley, dismissed as kittens and wimps.'

FlyRight would not reveal information about Ramirez' contract, but a representative said the company has no responsibility for the content of its network affiliates. However, the representative, who would not speak on the record, said any site attracting the wrong kind of attention would be bad for network sales and such sites would have their contracts cancelled.

Ramirez expressed little satisfaction that Sanders had been arrested in connection with a 1962 murder, or that IBM — which purchased a computer patent from Sanders that made his early reputation in Silicon Valley — had filed suit against him last month. That complaint alleges that Sanders sold IBM a patent that actually belonged to Gilliard Tyler Seacroft, who roomed with Sanders at Harvard.

'He'll probably squirm out of it,' Ramirez said. 'Be on the cover of *Fortune* or *Forbes* next year, "Tom Sanders: Back On Top."'

'Like it?'

'Well … sure, it's fine.' He closed the laptop and put it on the carpet.

'You don't like it.'

Larry took his coffee from the nightstand.

'Some errors, nothing huge ... Should've let me edit the damned thing.'

'That's unethical!'

'Please.'

37

Everybody had lots of fun in Las Vegas. It is, after all, America's Favourite Family Fun Destination.

Mel Greenbaum spent three days in the hospital and several hours being questioned by the LVMPD. Young Greenbaum was accompanied by his father, the personal-injury attorney, who threatened to sue everyone he saw. When Mel got home to Burlingame – a short commuter-rail ride to the San Francisco office – there was a letter from *MacWorld*. With his final cheque.

Owen Lindsey limped to his car the next morning. He drove straight from Nevada to Menlo Park, making one brief stop at a Criti-Care franchise clinic in Bakersfield, to have the bullet pulled from his backside. Hunting accident. 'With a 9mm?' the doctor asked. Lindsey paid cash and left.

Sanders was escorted to the airport in the morning, Arellanes at his side, Williams taking particular pleasure in leading the suspect through a gauntlet of business-news teevee crews and reporters – O'Leary among them, bobbing and grinning, giving a clandestine wave to his detective pal.

Harry Taft flew to San Jose, business class, Sanders' empty seat beside him. By airplane phone, he was named the acting CEO of MicroTorrent Systems.

Terry Texas was charged with kidnapping and resisting

arrest. She was released on bail, after nearly convincing the prosecutors it was Scott Charlton and a mysterious ringleader who forced her to take part in Greenbaum's capture. There were health considerations, as well – in the hospital, Terry was diagnosed with obesity-related diabetes. Police reports said the previously nonexistent 'ringleader' escaped through a hole cut from the bathroom's ceiling and vanished into the desert.

Scott Charlton was treated for a single gunshot wound to his right buttock and, having passed his eighteenth birthday, was booked into the grownups' jail.

Amy Wells' exclusive interview was reprinted or substantially quoted by dozens of newspapers and wires. Brian Williams even mentioned her by name on the MSNBC newscast. She went home to Seattle, having learned many new things.

And Larry Jonestowne spent the weekend at the Mirage, charging wine to the *Boston Sun* and watching movies on Showtime from the bathtub, epsom salts healing the wounds. He did very little work, just some headlines linking to O'Leary's story and even the MSNBC interview. By Monday he felt repaired and used the return ticket to SFO without hassle.

In Pacifica, the sun was shining. Really shining, with only a few grey clouds up north, the air warm and salty. The room was made, a note from Werner on the pillow: 'Enjoyed the show on the telly. Give a ring.' In paper bags aside the Igloo cooler, four bottles of Chianti. Larry changed into shorts and Converse and took a two-mile run up and down the beach, if you count the mile of walking and gasping for breath.

The Castro theatre was showing a Bette Midler concert film that night, and a line of truant employees waited for tickets. Larry stood at the queue's end, wasting time, watching the

Mail and More entrance. At 4:30 p.m., a short young man walked out, gym-earned muscles bulging from a white T-shirt. Larry abandoned the line and walked up beside him.

'Hey there.'

The guy looked over, still walking.

'Yeah?'

'I've seen you, working in that mail place.'

'Sorry, got a boyfriend.'

'No, man, I want to talk to you about my mail.' Larry had a hundred folded in his hand. 'Here. Listen.'

The guy glanced at the bill and stuffed it into his stone-washed pocket.

'If you want a drug partner – '

'No, nothing like that. Buy you a drink?'

'Headed home.'

'Come on, one drink.'

The guy glanced at Larry's crotch.

'For God's sake, a *drink*.'

They walked south on Castro until Larry spotted a bar he knew. 'Tables upstairs, on the loft,' he said.

'You hang around here?'

'Not really.'

They went upstairs and took a table by the window. Happy hour starting. Larry asked for a glass of red wine. His companion ordered a whisky sour.

'It's pointless to explain why, but some freaks are hanging around my PO box. I need my mail.'

'Those cops?'

'Not cops, I promise. Silicon Valley goons … I'm a former, uh, programmer. Caught 'em doing bad things. Theft, software, whatever.'

'Really?' The guy had small dumb eyes, a very square jaw, a flattop haircut and bushy moustache.

'Really. I ask a small favour. Get the mail from Box 988,

give it to me. Another three of these hundreds for your trouble.'

'You sure this isn't a drug thing?'

'No, sniff the envelopes. You seen these guys around?'

'Yeah, sure. Every few days they come in, asking about *your* mailbox.' The guy ate the candied cherry from his drink and scowled. 'How do I know you're this Ramirez?'

'Keep it down,' Larry said, producing his wallet. 'Look.'

'That's not picture ID.'

'What the hell are you, a bartender? Here's my mailbox key.'

'I don't know.'

Larry sighed and handed over another hundred. The guy stuffed it inside his jeans.

'You know how these tech companies react, when somebody blows the whistle?'

'No.'

'You should read a magazine article or something, fascinating stuff.' Larry offered the guy a Camel Light and he refused. 'Whatever, just grab my mail. Make sure nobody's watching.'

'I'm the only one there 'til four-thirty.'

'Fine. Shouldn't be anything else coming. After tomorrow, you can proudly tell these goons the box is empty and Ramirez has never returned to check it.'

Larry had changed addresses again, to a Bahamas PO box the Swiss Guys promised to manage. Just deposit the new FlyRight cheque, get those last bills, make the minimum payments – Ramirez had turned out to be an excellent credit risk.

'Where?'

'Where? Drop it off at my motel.'

The guy latched his hand onto Larry's thigh. 'Do you like me?'

'No!'

'No? Then why'd you take me here?'

'They serve drinks, don't they?'

'Okay, sorry.'

'Yeah, sorry.' Larry stubbed out his cigarette. 'Thought you had a damned boyfriend.'

'We're having problems.'

'Everybody has problems. Talk or something.'

'He's so sweet. I just feel too young for him, like I'm missing out on life.'

Larry waved for the check.

'Where's your motel?'

'I'm staying in Pacifica.' Larry peeled two twenties from his wallet. 'Taxi down, after work tomorrow. I'll give you the three hundred then.'

'You're not trying to rape me or something?'

'I'll be in the parking lot.' Larry scribbled the SeaHorse address on a napkin. 'Don't come anywhere near my room. Go home to your boyfriend. Get married or something.'

'You're a rough-looking guy.'

'Bullshit.'

Larry put a ten on the tray and got up. 'See you tomorrow ... in the parking lot. Mail, just my mail.'

He went down the stairs and called Werner from a pay phone. They met at the Fish Market on the avenues. The usual wait for a table, but free wine in the meantime. They stood on the corner, drinking in the mist.

'Terrific show on CNN.'

'Accidental, like everything.'

'Didn't know him?'

'Nah. Tried to sit with O'Leary and this twit punched me. In all the confusion ...'

Werner smiled. He'd been witness to such confusion.

'How's your Amanda?'

'Lovely gal, bit athletic for me.'

'You should marry her. Big old house in the English countryside, border collies running around, all creatures weird and small.'

'Not quite time for all that.'

A woman stuck her head into the fog and yelled, 'Ramirez, two.'

Sticking to the program, they ordered cold Napa Chardonnay with the fish, grilled rare shark for Larry, broiled salmon for Werner.

'I'm considering a vacation.'

'Couldn't hurt. Join the Swiss?'

'Don't know. Although the Bahamas sound nice. Got a few grand in an official offshore account now.'

'About time. No reason you can't do this shite on a tropical beach.'

'Indeed. Maybe I'll settle down, marry Suzie, get a compound on the shore.'

'This marrying on your brain, ain't it?'

'Mortality beckons. Need to sire a brood, have a sweatshop in the garage, toddlers doing Web design … Besides, I'll need someone to change my adult Pampers.'

'Sod off with that. You're a young man.' Werner dipped his bread into the fish juice and chewed. 'Don't think our Suzie's shopping husbands just yet. How 'bout your MSNBC bird?'

'What?'

'What?' Werner swallowed the sourdough and refilled his glass. 'Exclusive interview? Not that dumb, Jonestowne.'

'She's a sweet girl. Not a bad reporter, considering.'

'Few bruises don't mean you're old.'

'Yeah, but I'm tired.'

'Been tired a while.'

Larry ate a baby carrot and smiled.

'Why don't you come with me? Can't be too hard to take

over one of these Caribbean towns. Do all your Web nonsense, dump it in a tax-free account.'

'Never liked this Web.'

'It's what you *do*.'

'Am still a guitarist.' Werner finished the bread and waved for more. 'Not told you much 'bout London, have I?'

'No, not that much.'

'Headed to LA soon, a mate down there I used to play with. Had a record in the UK, y'know?'

'Yeah?'

'Melody Maker, New Music Express, John Peel and the BBC, all that. Played to twenty thousand at a football stadium. Played the festivals – '

'You don't even *own* a guitar.'

'Got me down.'

'And now?'

'Over it.'

Larry stared at Werner's girly T-shirt, 'The Donnas'. The Keith Richards' hair and jawline.

'What a fraud!'

'Ah, you know. Like tellin' a bloke about the supermodel you used to see. Load of rubbish without the evidence.'

They went to Café du Nord for a nightcap. Plans were made: Get Ramirez a passport, buy the tickets cash, secure an estate. Werner and maybe even Suzie would drop by for a month or two, examine the island life.

The swing band started and Larry stood.

'Don't need this.'

'All right then. Get your passport.'

'Pacifica post office. Drop off the photos, fill in the lies, pay the expedited service fee … and I'll have a lovely new passport just begging to see the world.' Larry glanced at his reflection in the bar mirror. 'Should get the hair dyed again, for Ramirez' portrait.'

'Should have a bloody shave.'

Larry got a cab and relaxed in the back seat. He was almost asleep when the taxi pulled into the SeaHorse lot.

A few minutes of BBC lulled him into real sleep. The last words he heard were, 'Our correspondent in Manila says the cannibals have seized …'

38

He woke to the waves and various honking horns. Put on his swim trunks, and dived into the Pacific. Cold, awful, exhilarating. He did a few painful laps and rode a wave to the sand. Ran to fight the shivers. Ran right over a US Navy medical-waste bag, dumped off a ship. Bastards. What about our ocean friends?

After showering off the salt and toxic waste, he thought about shaving and didn't. The jaw still hurt, sore beneath the whiskers. The bad dye job was gone – just brown tips on his white-blond hair, like some Discovery-channel freak of nature. Must find a stylist, he thought. Every half-arse town has a 'stylist', and Larry found Pacifica's on the walk to the coffee hut. Rosalita's Unisex Hair-and-Nails Salon, closed Mondays. It was Monday.

At the distant Safeway grocery, Larry bought Clairol 'deep natural brown' for the head, and some gunk to cover grey beards. That should work to cover a blond moustache. He picked up more Chianti and a jug of Odwalla orange juice and two packs of Camel Lights. The tabloids at the check-out counter had nothing about Jesús. Just the movie stars and their many problems, 'Tearful Demi: Bruce Stuffed My Head Down Our Dirty Toilet', 'Wedding Bells for Lisa Marie?'

Larry slid Ramirez' Safeway Club card through the device, saving $2.47 on his purchase and contributing to a perplexing database of consumer habits.

A taxi was waiting at the motel. Larry checked his watch, 3 p.m. The mail-boy wasn't expected 'til five. But there he was, sitting in the back, looking around.

Larry scanned the parking lot, same five cars. Nobody in the office; the old man was probably watching teevee in the back. No pedestrians, as usual. A few fishermen way down the pier, rods over the water. He came around the passenger side and said, 'Little early, eh?'

The mail-boy jumped in his seat.

'Problem?'

'This is your mail, that's all of it.' A rubber-banded bunch of envelopes. Larry took them through the window and dropped the bunch in his plastic Safeway bag.

'What's the trouble?'

The mail-boy looked down at his shiny cowboy boots and said, 'Somebody's looking for you.'

'No shit, I told you somebody's looking for me ... You didn't.'

Were those eyes getting damp?

'He ... I'm so sorry, but five-thousand dollars – '

'You fraud!' Larry opened the door and pulled the fraud outside, by the neck of his T-shirt. The cabbie, a middle-aged black guy with a grey moustache and a Giants cap, glanced over his shoulder but kept quiet.

'I'm so sorry!' Sniffling now. 'He followed me, after we left the bar. He threatened me – '

'With five grand. Some threat.'

'I'm *really* broke, I couldn't turn it down.'

'So you told him where I'm staying. Why are you telling *me*?'

'I felt bad ... it was wrong. I *liked* you.'

'Where is he?'

'At ...'

'Stop crying. Where?'

'The Shell station at the offramp.' Five blocks away. 'He told me to drop off your mail, make sure you were here, then I'm supposed to wave to him, when we passed the gas station.'

'We?'

'Me, in the taxi.'

'Right. You got the money?'

'Just half. I get the rest when ...' More sniffling.

'When what?'

'When he arrests you.'

'They're not cops, goddamnit. They can't arrest me or anybody.'

Larry set his grocery bag on the asphalt, careful with that wine, careful with everything.

'I ... I just wanted to tell you, so you could get out of here.'

'Appreciate it. You're a very noble little thief. When's he expecting you to drive by?'

'I told him I was supposed to come after work, that I didn't know if you'd be here yet ...'

'So any time between now and five.'

'I guess.'

Larry leaned close to the mail-boy's ear and whispered, 'It's a good thing you've done, telling me. And it's lucky, because otherwise you'd be dead right now.'

'Dead?'

'Dead. You think those lunatics would let you live after this? You have any idea what sort of international scandal you've opened up?' Larry glanced at a minivan. 'That's my car. You hide in the room and we'll get rid of this taxi. Another twenty-five hundred for your trouble.'

The teary eyes brightened. Larry got his room key and slipped it into the mail-boy's palm. 'Go on in. I'll pay the driver.'

'Really? You're not going to ditch me?'

'No.'

The mail-boy smiled, dabbed his eyes, and went straight for the room. Larry closed the rear door, picked up his groceries, and walked slowly around the car to the driver's window.

'Hey there, sorry about the hassle.'

'No hassle yet,' the driver said, not looking at Larry.

'Well, as you've probably figured out, there's a sort of lovers' quarrel going on.' Larry watched the mail-boy close the door behind him.

'I don't judge people – '

'Great. Now here's the problem. We've been staying down here, the two of us, that sort of thing. He wanted me to leave, now he wants me to stay, I'm not sure … It's, uh, irreconcilable differences or something.'

'Seen plenty of that. Been driving twenty years 'round here.'

'All right, then you know what I mean. What's the meter?'

'Well, we got seventeen for the way down, but this boy says it's round trip, so – '

'So, sure, let's say forty.' Larry pulled three twenties from his wallet and handed them through the window.

'You gave me sixty.'

'Appreciate your honesty. That extra twenty is for a small favour.'

'What kinda favour?'

'Just do me the kindness of driving around the block, wait a few minutes, and come back. I want to make sure things are fine. If he says anything about, uh, anything, I'll grab my suitcase and go back to the city with you. That sound fair?'

'Well, I don't – '

'C'mon, man. I don't want to stand outside in the fog for an hour waiting for another cab, you know? Extra twenty there, just for a few minutes' wait.'

'I guess.'

'Fine. Thanks very much. If I'm not out here, keep going, keep the money.'

Larry took his time walking to the room, watching the taxi drive away. The driver didn't much like the idea, but it was half a day's fares. He pulled behind a parked motorhome that had seen better days. To dispatch, he said: 'This is 352, I gotta coupla homosexuals divvying up the household, so I'll be 10-20 in Pacifica for a few, then back to town with or without 'em.'

'Roger, 352. Good luck.'

He was fiddling with the AM dial when the barrel pressed against his temple.

Larry set the Safeway bag by the door and tried to get a look inside. Curtains closed tight, just like he left them. A dirthead on a motorcycle drove by. No other traffic. On the little overhang above his door, he could just see the owl's plastic horns. He tried to reach it, grabbed a pigeon instead, and recoiled in horror, nearly falling over. Need a chair, a rope, something. He unhooked his belt and made a lasso from it. Three tries – three loud whacks of belt hitting pigeons – and he got the horn. The owl was in reach.

Larry removed the filthy head, stuck the Glock in his waistband, and decided to go beltless, considering all the pigeon crap. He tossed the empty owl back to the overhang and knocked on his door.

'Who *is* it?'

'Me.'

'It's open!'

This was true. Larry bashed into the door as he turned the knob, and both door and Larry flew unhindered into the wall. The mail-boy was sifting through the dufflebag.

'Get up. Against the wall.'

Larry whipped the Glock across the mail-boy's skull. He fell in a heap on the carpet.

'That's for being greedy.' Larry stuffed the gun into his waistband again, planning to return it to the owl and drop it off the pier.

Not much time. In the mail-boy's jeans was a billfold bulging with $2700 and change. Larry put that in his front pocket. He turned off the laptop – choosing not to wait while Windows shut down – and jammed it inside the shoulderbag. He looked around the room. Too much stuff. CDs, newspapers, clothes, wine, a suit in the closet, shoes, a boom box. He dragged the duffle to the bed and started filling it. Again. He threw a bedspread over the body.

The groceries – he opened the door slowly, saw nobody, and pulled the Safeway sack inside. He put the mail and hair dye in the shoulderbag, the rest in the duffle, deciding to leave Werner's Igloo cooler, the candles, the stacks of newspapers. He put on the Serb jacket and a pair of sunglasses.

Ready. He dragged the duffle next to the door, slipped the shoulderbag over his neck and peeked out. The taxi. An honest driver.

He trotted out to the driver's side and said, 'Wonderful. Can you open the trunk?'

Same baseball cap, but not the same driver. A familiar sort of gun jutted from Owen Lindsey's right hand.

'Nice try, Ramirez.'

Larry dived for the asphalt. It felt about as good as all the other times. The driver's door opened and Larry heard a shot zing past. He scrambled around the taxi, heard nothing, got to his feet and raised his head just enough to see through the passenger-side window. The second shot made more noise, as it took out that window's glass, which Ralph Nader would note was of the non-shatterproof variety.

He hopped in front of the tyre and pulled his own Glock – Lindsey's Glock, if you wanted to get legal about it. A horribly loud cement truck drove by. Larry winced in anticipation and glanced under the car. No shoes in sight. Where'd the creep go?

To his right, he saw the old man at the check-in desk, on the phone. Gunfight at the SeaHorse Corral. Nothing happening behind him – the guests were either out or just out of it. Or scared, hiding in the bathroom, begging mercy from the deities. Larry inched the barrel upward, its tip just visible from the opposite side of the taxi. Another shot, slamming into the wall-unit air conditioner behind him, the hiss of escaping freon. Then another, blowing out the driver's side rear tyre. The taxi slumped.

Larry tried to see through the wheel wells. There. Wingtips, behind the minivan. That would be an interesting shot. He aimed through the cables and shock absorbers and fired. And missed. And, apparently, hit the minivan's gas tank. It exploded.

A storm of metal fragments blasted against the taxi, knocking Larry on his back. He got to his feet and saw a fireball from the minivan's tail. Bits of plastic and glass raining down. Larry shuddered, retrieved his shoulderbag, and squinted through the smoke. Might be a good time to leave.

He got about six feet away. Then he got shot.

Larry collapsed into the shrubbery, and some moments later realized he wasn't dead. It was strange, being shot. The thigh, the right thigh. He looked at his khakis and grimaced. A hole in the pants, a little hole like a cigarette burn. And another hole an inch away, already dark with blood. He was still in the dirt, the little bushes all around him, many scratches to prove it. Through the waxy green leaves, he saw those same wingtips walking toward him across the parking lot, past the smouldering minivan and battered taxi, the steps uneven. It took a great deal of concentration to lift the gun, aim, and fire. He was going for the heart, but the crotch works, too.

Really time to leave. Larry pulled himself from the shrubs and saw a man in a tattered polo shirt and pressed slacks, the face darkened with smoke and blood, moaning terribly, his hands on his groin, the gun on the asphalt. Good enough — Larry had reservations about killing people. He limped past the motel, tossing the Glock into a dumpster, getting a block south before he heard sirens and slid between the slats of a crumbling redwood fence. It was a backyard, of sorts. Weeds and sand. A few feet away was a sliding-glass door. A light on. He looked at his leg, blood staining the khakis almost to his ankle. Sirens approaching. He went to the door and slid it open.

39

Taj Mahal was playing low. A bearded, curly-haired young man was pacing slowly through the living room, holding something that resembled a cell phone to the ceiling.

'Hi,' Larry rasped.

'Just lookin' for a signal.'

'Yeah.' Larry coughed, glad to see it wasn't followed by a shower of blood. 'Mind if I, uh, use your bathroom?'

'Well all right.' The man — about five feet eight inches,

maybe a track-and-field sort, wearing a University of Kentucky sweatshirt and jeans – kept pacing around, staring at his device, a red LED flashing from its base. Larry noticed a blue glass bong on the carpet, about two feet tall, and the sticky aroma of cannabis in the air.

'Thanks.' The only light came from a laptop computer in command-line mode, the azure letters glowing on the dark screen. He limped through the small living room to the hall. On the bathroom wall was a large framed poster of some Hindu monkey god, ripping its chest open. Inside was a tiny Indian couple, dressed like royalty. Larry fought with his boots and got the khakis off. It wasn't pretty. Should sterilize this, he thought. With what? There was a big plastic bottle of Listerine on the sink. He sat on the edge of the bathtub-shower enclosure and poured the mouth rinse over the holes. Had he felt better, he would have screamed.

Under the shower nozzle, he rinsed the leg in scalding hot water and followed it with another Listerine treatment. Kill those germs. Then he hosed off the scraped-up palms, the scuffed knees, the scuffed head. Now what? The holes weren't bleeding much. No bones hit. Just some other stuff that hurt like hell. Flesh, muscle, that sort of thing. Sepsis, that was the enemy. If the hole went untreated, evil little bacteria would flood his body, causing chills, fever, blood poisoning and other such horrors. The First Aid booklets mentioned such things.

He wrestled the shoulderbag off and set it on the toilet lid. Gauze and tape and Neosporin inside, thanks to Amanda. Was Neosporin recommended for use on gunshot wounds? The tube was ambivalent. After squeezing a quarter-sized dollop on either hole, he padded them with gauze and more gauze and wrapped the tape tight around his thigh. Covered the whole mess with the Ace bandage. Amy Wells was right – he was a mummy.

No more pills in the bag. This would require pills, many pills. He opened the medicine cabinet. Pepto-Bismol, mint floss, vitamin C candies, toothpaste. And a prescription bottle of Tylenol 3, the codeine variety. He took three and washed them down with tap water. A whole bottle of pills. Prescribed to one Louis Billings, use only as prescribed. Could be useful. Larry opened the door and limped to the living room.

Louis Billings was sitting cross-legged on the floor, tapping at the laptop's keyboard. He didn't look up.

'Appreciate it. Had a little accident.'

'You wouldn't, ah, happen to have one of those, you know, cigarettes?'

'Yeah, sure.' Larry took a pack from his coat and tossed them over. Louis Billings made the catch and slowly looked to his right.

'You know, I don't, ah, ever think … I've seen a guy standin' in my house wearing a, ah, Russian army suit and, ah, boxer shorts with penguins on 'em.'

Larry lowered himself to the sofa, using the armrest for support.

'Serbian, actually.'

'That's, ah, that's cool.'

'I got shot. In the leg.'

'In Russia?'

'No, around the corner.'

'Oh.' He took a drag and looked at the burning tip, took another drag and set the cigarette on a coffee saucer. 'Yeah … I heard that.'

'The gunshots?'

'Ah, heard those.'

The leg throbbed. Larry decided the gunshot hype was true.

'You, ah, want to take a try on this funny stuff?' Louis

motioned toward the giant bong.

'Not generally. Guess it wouldn't kill me.'

Larry took the hippie pipe and the lighter. The sound of a car outside. Footsteps.

'I'll – '

'Just, ah, step in there.'

Larry boosted himself to standing position and hobbled into the walk-in closet. He shut the door halfway and slipped behind a big wool coat. The doorbell chimed.

'Yeah?!'

'Police.'

Louis sprung from the carpet, automatically retrieving the bong and slipping it behind the door as he opened it.

'Hello.'

'You hear shots?'

'Oh, a few.'

'We're looking for two guys, both about six-three, white males, both armed.'

'Ah'll keep my eyes open.'

'Seen anyone, anyone suspicious?'

'Nope.'

'You've been home?'

'All day.'

'Doing what?'

'Oh, you know … just playing, playing with computers.'

The Pacifica cops glanced inside, seeing the laptop on the floor.

'Okay. We're advising people to lock their doors. If you see anything, or hear anything – '

'Nine … one … one.'

'Right. Good evening.'

As he closed the door on the departing cops, he heard one say, 'You smell that marijuana? Jesus.'

Louis returned to his machine, and held the blinking

device in the air again. 'All clear,' he said. 'Uh, by the way ... if you don't, ah, mind me askin' ... Who are you?'

Larry limped out of the closet and said, 'You do this Internet crap?'

'Well, sure.'

'I'm Jesús Ramirez.'

Very slowly, Louis started laughing. A long, possibly psychotic laugh.

'No shit.'

'No shit.'

'Ah, that's ... Whoo! Jesús Ramirez ... Hey Zeus! Ah, that's good.'

'What's that thing?'

'Oh, this? Well ... This, it's a *wireless modem*. Can't, ah, get no signal out here.'

'For?'

'Oh, well ... you know.' Larry didn't know. 'So, how about this? The, uh, president ... of Macintosh Regalia Inc., what's with that?'

'Lost the contract with Adobe. Added half a million in bogus expenses to the Acrobat Reader contract. Layoffs start next week.'

Louis laughed again, shaking his head. 'No shit. So you're Jesús ... Thought you'd use that one. Sent it myself.'

'That was my plan. Toss those smokes over here?' Larry caught the pack and stuck one in his mouth. 'The day got complicated. I was – '

'Shot in the arse.'

'The thigh, actually.' He pointed to the clot of bandage above his knee.

'Little Tommy Sanders?'

Larry lit the smoke and smiled, despite the terrible pain. 'You really read that thing, don't you?'

'Oh ... goddamned *everybody* reads it. That is the greatest journalism, ah, of our time. Jesús is the world's greatest journalist.'

'Yeah, when he works.'

Louis rose again and slapped his stomach and said, 'Whoooo.'

'What?'

'Oh, you know, I'm just thinking about maybe getting some food.'

Larry reached for the saucer and ashed. 'Yeah, go ahead. I'll get out of here.'

'No problem, hang out. Them cops, ah, might be lookin' around.'

'Probably.'

'Was, ah, thinkin' ... maybe get some Thai food. Hungry?'

'Not really.' The pain and drugs made his stomach feel like a bag of gravel.

'Probably, you know, ah, wouldn't hurt. Have some food.'

'Sure.' Larry reached for his wallet, but the pants were hanging from the shower curtain rod. Drip dry.

'Catch me later. Ah, requests?'

Larry fought with his brain, asking it to come up with some food ideas instead of constant pain. It relented, barely.

'Yeah. Some of that Pad Thai, with shrimp. Maybe some soup. Shrimp curry.'

'Okay.'

And the guy was gone. And Larry was sitting in a strange apartment, barely a block from the SeaHorse, where some savage gunplay had just occurred. The BIPS guy – had to be a BIPS guy – was on the run, probably checked into some spook hospital adjoining a secret military base in Monterey. Hopefully suffering at least twice as much as Larry was.

Then again, Pad Thai with shrimp had improved many foul days.

'Ah, not so bad.'

The remains of Pad Thai, some sort of foil-baked fish, shrimp curry, spring rolls and coconut-milk spicy chicken sat on the carpet. And several empty bottles of Pale Ale. Louis took the bong and sucked down a huge column of smoke. It looked like twice as much smoke was exhaled.

'How's, ah, that leg?'

'Better. I can't feel it quite as much. Helped myself to a few Tylenol 3s, hope you don't mind.'

'Me? No, ah, take 'em. Always more.'

'Guess you've got health insurance.'

'Ah, for the moment. Gotta git.' Louis kicked the styrofoam Thai containers toward the kitchen and stood. 'Got to, ah, head to the airport.'

'Going somewhere?'

'No, ah, not me. A girl, ah, we hang out … she's flying in.'

'Maybe drop me off?'

'Well, okay … might want to, ah, put on some pants.'

The khakis were ruined; he unloaded the wallets and dropped the pants in the trash. From the closet, Louis produced a handsome walking cane with an alligator head for the handle and found a pair of twill work pants around Larry's size – 'somebody left 'em, I suppose' – and they got in Louis' ridiculous Trans-Am and headed for SFO. No cops, just the usual fog making dusk seem like midnight.

Larry said thanks, accepted the bottle of pills he'd already lifted, left money on the seat for the food and beer, and limped into the airport, never having the slightest clue about Louis Billings.

He stared at the wall of screens showing departing flights. Where to go? Not having a passport was a small problem. The non-passport options were limited: Canada and Mexico. But *flying* into either required a passport – or a birth certificate and accompanying photo ID. He could get close to a border, that's all. Mexico was easier. No hassle, just drive across. Yes, just drive across, walk across, just bring money, no questions. The San Diego-Tijuana crossing is the world's busiest frontier. Inspection only occurs when you try to come *back*.

Then there was the shootout. Did cops check airports for a common motel battle? No roadblocks leaving Pacifica. If the police put up roadblocks for every Bay Area shooting, the entire economy would collapse. Traffic just barely moved as it was.

Larry slumped. His pain-wracked mind finally decided none of this mattered. The duffle in the motel had all the evidence anyone needed. A whole catalogue of the late, not-so-great Larry Jonestowne. Newspaper clippings, photos, even his real passport. Finished. The ruse would be exposed, at very least. He looked around the terminal, thinking, "This is the last time I'll board a plane in this country."

San Diego, then. Three more flights this evening. All on United. He saw the signs pointing to the United counters and cringed. There were a dozen flights to Los Angeles. Connect to San Diego from LAX? Too much hassle, double the chance of cancellations, and more time for somebody to find out where he was. Flying was the safest form of transportation, but not if the goons were waiting at the arrival gate.

In the ticket line, he stood behind a horrible family, Navy people, the kids eating Ghirardelli chocolate bars, the buzz-cut father grumbling about the faggots, the tight-faced mother nervously quieting the children and anticipating her nightly beating, once they got home. They were headed to San Diego, as well. Of course they were.

Two Middle-Eastern guys stepped behind him. And, immediately, began forcing their car-sized suitcase against his heels. He ignored it for a moment, until it hit his bad leg.

'Stop it!'

'Huh?'

'Stop ramming your fucking suitcase into my leg. This isn't fucking Damascus.'

'What?' The short one, as always. Chest puffed up like a rooster, Adidas track pants, hairy neck.

'Don't push your suitcase into me,' Larry said. It seemed reasonable. There was nobody behind them, and only a few in front of them.

'You!' The short one spit air. 'You are a racist.'

'Get bent.'

'You, what is this you say, this is not the fucking Damascus? How do you know I am Syrian?'

Larry pointed to the Syrian Arab Airlines tags on the huge suitcase and turned back to the counter.

'What you say, it is anti-Arab.'

'Next in line?'

Larry dragged himself to the counter. She was just what you could expect – a mean old troll probably thrown off the stewardess gig a few years back.

'Hi. I need a ticket to San Diego, the 8:18 flight.'

'Do you have a reservation?'

'No. Otherwise I'd just go to the gate.'

'I see. For how many?'

'Well, just me.'

'Very well. And how will you be paying this evening?'

'Card.' Larry reached his wallet with pain and produced the American Express. She snapped it up, the way a big-mouthed goldfish attacks a flake of fish food.

'Seating preference?'

'Emergency exit row, if it's there. Window.'

'You'll have to talk to the gate attendant for that. So window?'

'Well, no, unless it's an emergency exit seat. Otherwise, aisle.'

'So, aisle?'

'Sure, fine.'

'Return date?'

'One way, please ... I'm driving back.'

'I see. All right, Mister ... Ram-er-ess ... and your identification?'

'Excuse me?'

'Your *identification*. Photo identification.'

'Well ... here's my Social Security card. You've got my AmEx.'

'No, sir, we require photo identification, either a driver's license or state identity card or military ID or passport.'

'To go to San Diego?'

'Yes, sir.'

'Since when?'

'Regulations.'

'I don't drive, I don't have a licence ... I just flew to Vegas on Friday, nobody asked for photo ID.'

She didn't budge.

'Well ... What can I do?'

She tapped some keys on her terminal.

'Ma'am?'

'What can you do? You can get a photo ID. Next in line!'

Larry retrieved his card and backed away, shocked. The Syrians took his place. The short one hissed and said, 'Good luck, Zionist!'

He limped to the concourse, everything destroyed again. There was, however, a new addition to his wallet collection. Mail-boy's driver's licence claimed he was five feet ten inches – about a three-inch lie – and had a dark-brown head of hair and that silly moustache. Age twenty-nine. That could work. Even better, the licence was one of those new-fangled holographic watermark deals, with a big California state seal in the middle of mail-boy's face. Tough to duplicate – and even tougher to see the photo.

Walking as normally as possible, he went past the sourdough shops and souvenir stands to the men's bathroom. A few Japanese businessmen slicking their hair, one burnout staggering around the urinals. Larry opened the Clairol and read the instructions. Apply to dry hair, using the included gloves, leave it on for twenty minutes, then shampoo. He saw a middle-manager type approach the sink and empty a shaving kit onto the formica. Yes, shave first, leave a nice Freddie Mercury moustache. Larry removed his own shaving kit and stepped to a sink, swiping his hand beneath the infrared to keep the hot water going.

He filled a flimsy paper towel with water and soaked his whiskers, until he thought they might come off without a struggle. Sprayed a handful of travel-size foam into his raw palm and rubbed it into the beard. With a frenetic waving of the disposable razor, he managed to keep the water on and slice off two weeks of beard, leaving the now-bushy moustache intact. No one seemed to mind this public grooming.

Now, for the dye. Larry took the last stall and sat on the lid, unpacking the chemicals. Various bottles, spouts, confusion. He put on the gloves, rubbed the foul-smelling stuff into his hair and applied the next round. Next, the burning beard gunk on his moustache. At least it was a different sort of pain.

He flushed the plastic gloves. Time to rinse and shampoo. He half-opened the stall door and saw two cops walking through. A knock.

'Yeah?'
'You all right?'
'Yeah, sure. Airplane food.'
'Gotcha.'

They left. Looking for Ramirez? Larry poked his head out again and saw another cop, a big customs cop with a dog. He watched the German Shepherd's snout poke beneath the door, pucker at the hair-dye smell, and leave. Impossible, Larry thought. His scalp was on fire, the bathroom full of cops. And then he did the only thing for which he ever felt true embarrassment. He opened the toilet lid, pinched his nose to prevent drowning, dunked his blackened skull inside, and gave himself a swirlie.

And another one, and another one, and yet another one, until the water ran clear again. Patting his scalp with clumps of industrial toilet tissue, he stopped the dripping, checked the sinks again, and lurched over. A handful of liquid soap was used on his scalp and moustache. Two teenagers came to the sinks and watched him with some amusement. Otherwise, he bathed his head in peace.

It wasn't a perfect job. A few dark splotches, one on the left ear, another on the temple – don't mind me, just skin cancer. After combing the hair down, he examined himself in the mirror. The Serbian jacket was hard to forget. He took it off, rolled it into a ball and stuffed it into his bag. The walking cane went in the garbage. It was a nice old cane, but he couldn't afford the association.

At a souvenir shop, he bought a medium Giants windbreaker, black nylon and polyester, shiny and anonymous. He returned to the United window, behind a tour group from South Korea. The woman was still there, distributing bad service to the travellers. When it looked like she would again be his helpful representative, he asked the couple behind him to go first. 'Waiting for someone,' he said.

'You're so nice! Thank you!'

'No problem.'

'Next in line!'

He got a better ticket agent. Having missed the 8:18, he

asked for the 9:44 flight. Decided it was best to pay cash. She glanced at the driver's licence but didn't bother to look up. Emergency exit? Of course.

Larry dragged himself through the security checkpoint, turning on the laptop to prove there was only room for a small bomb inside. He went to the gate and sat. At 9:01, the first announcement came.

'Attention, passengers of Flight 2179, we have a brief weather-related delay. Shouldn't be more than thirty minutes. Please stay close to the gate and we'll get you boarded and on your way as soon as possible, and thank you for flying the friendly skies.'

Larry looked out the windows. Three-quarter moon, not a cloud in the sky, the vaguest mist close to the ground. He rose with a grunt and walked down the long hall, trying to make his limping seem normal. That mostly required taking very small steps, like a midget. He wanted a cigarette, and a drink, but mostly he wanted a flight south. He settled for a drink.

He took a seat and ordered a Jamesons, water back. A *Chronicle* lay abandoned on the bar. To his left, he noticed two guys sipping Bud Lites, one talking too loud.

'Oh, you'd recognize him,' the talker said, pulling a wrinkled fax from his jacket. 'Big blond dude, heavy whiskers, wearing a goddamned Russian army coat. And bleeding like hell, since he was shot.'

Larry shrank into his shiny Giants jacket.

The bartender glanced at the blurry fax and asked, 'You guys cops?'

'Sort of. Silicon Valley work, corporate espionage.'

'Espionage? Like James Bond?'

Both laughed. The talker said, 'Not that exciting. Computer stuff, intellectual property, software, that kind of thing.'

Larry waved and pointed at his empty glass. The

bartender nodded and made a new drink.

'More water?'

'Nah, thanks.'

The bartender returned to the talker. 'So this guy, what'd he do?'

'You want to know?'

'I asked, didn't I?'

'He shot my boss.'

'What?'

'Yep. Boss had him, outside some motel. The guy was trying to sell some stolen computer crap to Microsoft or something. Boss cornered him, and this guy shoots him!'

'Bad?'

'In the nuts! Bad enough.'

They all laughed. That was bad enough.

'So why you guys here?'

'Can't tell you.'

'Oh come on. Who's gonna know?' The bartender motioned to the empty bar, empty except for Larry, pretending to read the *Chronicle*'s op-ed page.

'All right. About an hour ago, the guy tried to buy a ticket south, and then all the sudden he cancels it!'

'How you know that?'

'Can't tell you that!' More laughing. 'He must've got spooked. Ran off. But he's trying to get to San Diego for some reason. We got the guy covered.'

'You want another beer?'

'Nah, working.' The silent guy pantomimed that he was working, too.

'So why you sitting in a bar?'

'Flight's delayed, all of 'em. We'll be headed down soon – he doesn't have much choice, far as a flight.'

'Yeah, only United this time of night.' The bartender got his 7-Up and took a drink, his brow furrowed. 'Maybe he went to Oakland?'

'Got men there.'

'San Jose?'

'Yep, we're there, big time. This guy isn't going anywhere.'

Larry listened to this conversation with practised disregard. Great editorial about the Presidio or something. He took the empty Jamesons glass and dropped it in the side pocket of the shiny Giants jacket. And waved for the bill.

He paid cash and walked out.

'You guys carry guns.'

The talker got quiet.

'What? How you gonna catch this guy?'

'Generally, yeah, we legally have guns.'

'You don't now?'

'Well, that's not the kind of thing we talk about.'

'Okay. Anything else I can get you guys?'

'Nope, better go to the gate.'

The quiet one broke his silence.

'That guy, just ran off.'

The bartender said, 'He was sitting there half an hour.'

'And now he's gone.'

'Maybe he had to make his flight like everybody else?'

The talker nodded to the bartender and threw down eight dollars. Both goons departed in a hurry.

'Couldn't be,' the talker said.

'Tall guy.'

'Our guy's blond, bearded, limping.'

Their guy was also named Ramirez. They turned onto the concourse and saw Larry, not doing such a good job hiding his limp, turning into a men's room.

'I'll check it out. You go to the gate.'

The talker trotted to the bathroom and went inside, passing a guy rolling a janitorial cart to the next filthy stall. Nobody at the urinals. He got down on his knees and looked under the stalls. No feet. Three down, Larry met the unwelcome entrance with a heavy glass to the skull. The guy wilted.

Larry peeked over the doors. Nobody there. He reached beneath the goon's jacket. Shoulder holster, no gun. Maybe the weapons were checked baggage? No matter. After liberating the $182 from the wallet, he took Warren Burkett's ID and boarding pass and flushed them down. Whoops, bit of a clog. Flushed again. Water rising. Larry pocketed the car keys and pushed the goon's face into the bowl and left.

He limped to the 'people mover' and rode it to the parking garage. Probably a Ford Taurus. Walking through the top level, he pressed the key-button. Nothing. He hobbled down the stairs to the next level. Halfway through the rows, an airport cop in a golf cart pulled up.

'Help you?'

'Sorry, can't remember where I parked.'

'What's the car?'

'Gray Ford Taurus. I think I'm going senile.'

'It happens, get in.'

Larry took the passenger seat.

'People leave the ticket on the dash – '

'That's what I did.'

'Should write down your level.'

'I know.'

Larry held the keychain low in his right hand, repeatedly pressing the alarm button. Finally, he saw tail-lights flash. The guard didn't.

'There it is.'

The cart stopped.

'Should write it down.'

'I will, next time. Thanks.'

The cart whirred away. Larry slipped into the driver's seat. A familiar car. Hurt like hell to accelerate. He tried with his left foot, but that was messy. On the 101 South, smoking and listening to Sinatra on KCSM, he headed to San Jose. If Burkett hadn't drowned in the toilet, the BIPS creeps should be convinced Ramirez was somewhere at SFO. Maybe. Larry was too tired to play Outguess the Spook.

Parked in the metered lot at San Jose International, he limped inside. Only United flights tonight, sure. He paid cash for a ticket, showing mail-boy's licence again, and trudged through the security gate, turned on the laptop, turned it off, walked down the long horrible hall. And sat at the gate, surrounded by a bunch of weeping synchronized swimmers from Rancho Bernardo, shuffled from flight to flight for five hours.

At 10:27 p.m., the helpful gate attendant said, 'Attention, those waiting to board the San Diego flight, weather conditions are preventing us from making this flight this evening.' Cries of sorrow from the swimming team. Resignation on the business-people's faces. Larry gazed around the waiting area and saw a BIPS goon across the way, standing by a Starbucks cart covered with a tarp. Looking right at him.

A swim-team girl sat one seat over, comforting a classmate. Larry tapped her shoulder and she looked over.

'Yes?' She looked suspicious, having probably learned in childhood to avoid wounded winos with freshly dyed hair.

'Southwest, they've got a flight to San Diego. In five minutes.' It hurt him to lie so much. 'But you've got to talk to that guy,' pointing to the goon.

'But, our tickets – '

'He has to accept them. But you have to *run* – all of you – it's about to leave!'

She turned to the swimming mob and said, 'Get up! A flight's leaving now! That guy needs our tickets!'

And two dozen teen swimmers took to the carpet, screaming. They filled the aisles, an ocean of flapping ponytails and calf muscle. The BIPS goon watched in horror as they surrounded him, boarding passes waving in the air. Larry took this opportunity to approach the counter.

'Lady, emergency!'

'Yes?'

'Hi, yeah.' Larry pulled his boarding pass and let her see it. 'Just walked back from the men's room. There was a man in there, with a gun.'

'A gun?'

'Mm-hmm. He asked me if I wanted to make a million dollars.'

'For?'

'Well, I don't know. But that's him.' He pointed to the mob. 'With those school girls.'

She picked up the phone and turned away, mumbling official lingo. 'Please wait here, sir,' she said to Larry. 'Airport police are on the way.'

They sure were. A wave of airport cops ran down the aisle. Larry decided he didn't want to talk to them. He walked away, walked right past them. The goon was on the floor, jacket pulled off, shoulder holster exposed, guns pointed at his chest. The swimmers were delirious.

Larry dumped the Giants jacket and put his sunglasses on. He returned to the Taurus, cursing, and paid the three-dollar parking fee.

40

He went south, down the 101, stopping for coffee at an AM/PM, listening to Art Bell talk about UFOs, trying to ignore the weird throbbing from his leg, trying to ignore the fact that he was driving a stolen car to the border. In Paso Robles, he parked at a Denny's diner and took a walk with his Swiss Army knife. The leg ached; he ignored it. Dark residential street, Spanish-style houses, the windows glowing with teevee flicker. There it was: A late-model Taurus with a faded 'Pat Buchanan for President' sticker. Perfect. He knelt and removed the licence plate screws, put the plate in his shoulderbag, and repeated the operation on the front bumper. The owner would probably drive to work tomorrow and get pulled over and blame it on the immigrants who were ruining this country's heritage.

He washed down a pill with the last of the coffee, drove two blocks to an abandoned fast-food place, parked in back, and screwed on his new plates. Good 'til next year. For tonight, at least. The old ones he threw to the failed franchise's roof, tossing them like frisbees.

Windows down, talking back to the radio to stay awake, he drove a safe and sane 80 mph, the BIPS-issued radar detector glowing green beneath the dash. Probably a GPS unit in the glove box, paranoid goons. He reached over, removed it, tossed it out the window. And the gloves, and the lock-picking kit ... he reached under the seat. Another Glock. And another under the passenger seat. Weird. He switched to the right lane and threw the guns out the passenger window, into the shoulder's shrub. In a few months, some gang kid doing highway cleanup would find the shiny pistol, smile, and tuck it into his orange vest. And ten yards south, a rival gang kid would make a similar discovery. The fun continues.

Coming over the Santa Monica mountains on the 405, Larry smiled. A perfect warm night, the orange grid of LA stretching for 50 miles, and a Warren Zevon song he'd almost forgotten, the Spanish guitars strumming behind the junkie lyrics:

> *I hear mariachi static on my radio*
> *And the tubes they glow in the dark*
> *And I'm there with her in Ensenada*
> *And I'm here in Echo Park*

By the time he stopped for gas in Torrance, he had decided Ensenada was the destination. Eat fish tacos, get some sun, maybe learn proper Spanish or something. But the leg was hurting more, not less. His guts were churning with cold coffee and pills. Hadn't eaten since Pacifica, seven hours back. Medical attention, that's what was needed. Not a hospital. He washed the windshield and drove across to the public phones. Flipped through the Day Timer.

The San Diego entries were all in fine-point black felt-tip, a fancy pen that must've come with the address book. He flipped through the pages, too many journalists and drunks, not enough doctors. Ah, maybe her? Clarke Cartright, Oceanside. If she'd still talk to him.

He limped to the phone and dialled. Number has been changed, etc. Dialled the new one and got a message, 'If this is an emergency, please call my mobile at ...'

This was an emergency.

'Hi, uh, Clarke? This is Larry. Larry Jonestowne. You still a doctor?'

'What'd you do now?'

She was finishing a late shift at the UCSD Medical Centre. A third-year ER resident now, soon to escape to the lucrative world of private practice and specialties.

'This better be important,' she'd said before ending the call and returning to the calamity. Larry had met her in Oceanside, a decade ago, during some anti-anti-abortion riot. She had just graduated med school, and instead of starting the residency ordeal, had gone to work for Planned Parenthood. Not as a doctor, but as a political activist. Governor Wilson was toying with the MediCal abortion payments, the nuts were going nuts, Falwell still had cache, the elder Bush was in the White House.

She was funny – a rarity in activists. And beautiful, in that well-bred California way. Born in La Jolla, schooled back east, horses in Poway. They had dinner, they got drunk, the inevitable occurred, followed by a few weeks of passion and his sudden departure to Saudi Arabia.

Clarke said she lived in Bird Rock, a pleasant beach neighbourhood beneath La Jolla. Larry found the house, the PRO-CHOICE sticker on her Honda, and limped to the door.

'What happened to you?' She was dressed in post-work sweatpants and a flannel shirt and looked a lot better than he did.

'Can I come in?'

'I guess.'

'Lovely place.' It was. A silvered redwood cottage, oak floors, fireplace with a Duraflame burning, Iranian rugs, the furniture all charmingly second-hand. 'You have one of those medical satchels?'

'I've got mine.'

'I've been shot.'

'Sit down.'

He sat. She looked out the big arched window, closed the blinds, and got her bag.

'Right leg?'

'How'd you know?'

'You're limping, Larry. Take off your pants.'

She helped with the bootlaces, tugged the ill-fitting trousers off, and removed the bandages and gauze.

'You sterilize it?'

'Listerine.'

She shook her head and poked the holes. This caused Larry to howl.

'Be quiet. I've got neighbours.'

'It … hurts.'

'Of course it hurts. Anything numb?'

'I don't know.'

'You drove here just fine, so you're probably not paralyzed.'

'Can't you … agh … give me a shot?'

'You take anything else?'

'No,' he lied.

She scowled, went to another room, and returned with a long scary needle.

'You're rotten.'

'There was a war.'

'You could've called.'

'Please? The shot?'

'Didn't seem to have any trouble contacting your newspapers.'

She speared him with the needle. A little harder than necessary. He groaned but didn't otherwise complain.

'Take these.' A handful of antibiotics. He tried to swallow them dry in one gulp, and ended up choking. She frowned and went to the kitchen, returning with a Michelob. He gulped half of it, blinking.

'Thanks.'

'Still an alcoholic.'

'It's *your* beer.'

'Be still. Hmm. It's pretty much cauterized, missed the artery. You're lucky. Bleed much?'

'Enough. What – Ow! – what about that sepsis?'

'Septicaemia? Not yet. Bend your knee. What's this gunk?'

'Neosporin,' he said. The knee worked. 'Did it pierce a muscle or something?'

'Grazed a little muscle, otherwise just fat. Flex your toes.'

'Fat? I'm not fat.' The toes worked.

'Fat, Larry. It's just some normal fat on your thigh.'

Clarke cleaned and dressed the ugly little wound and got a beer for herself.

'I'll live?'

'Unfortunately. You'll have two little scars. Want to tell me about it?'

'This Silicon Valley company is trying to kill me.'

She smiled and took a sip.

'Really?'

'Yeah, really. I'm, well, I'm some kind of Internet journalist now. Posted some stuff they didn't like ... one guy in particular.'

'Usual slander?'

'No, not at all. Can I smoke?'

She got an ashtray from the kitchen and took one of his Camel Lights.

'So, you say a computer programmer shot you ... With what, a nine-millimetre?'

'What are you, a cop?'

'Emergency room. Same thing.'

'Not a programmer, for Christ's sake. Private intelligence squad, former CIA goons, corporate espionage.'

'And they care about you?'

'Yeah, care about killing me. This company, its CEO is in jail on murder charges. Thanks to me.'

'How's the stock?'

'*Et tu?*'

The morphine hit hard. He tried to leave, but she parked the Taurus in her garage and put a blanket on the couch. He was out in five minutes. She had another beer, another smoke, and watched the fire burn down, half wishing these people had finished him off.

'Where're you going?'

'South. Mexico. You look great.'

'I could've killed you. Shot you up with whatever I wanted. Nobody would know, and very few would care. If you're hungry, muffins in the breadbox.'

She vanished; he heard the shower. A while later, she clomped to the living room and returned with an amber bottle of pills. 'Take these with meals, one of each. Change that bandage tomorrow. And have a real doctor look at it someday. I've gotta go, so lock up behind you. The garage key's by the door.'

And she was gone. Larry had another cup of coffee and dialled Werner.

'Matey! Where've you hidden?'

'Out of town.'

'Good. Didn't think you were dead.'

'All patched up. Sadly, I'm screwed.'

'Bollocks, you'll be fine.'

'Nah. Couldn't get my duffle. Full of Larry Jonestowne paraphernalia. Show's over.'

'We got it, it's here in the flat.'

'How'd you do that?'

Werner told the quick version. He and Amanda had

arrived by taxi at the SeaHorse Lodge and found cops, fire trucks, an ambulance, the media, all the official elements of disaster. They were stopping to visit Larry and meet the Triple-A tow truck. The transmission had collapsed in Amanda's rickety minivan – a gift from her parents, after they replaced the lemon with a slick new SUV.

Amanda was surprised to see her vehicle had exploded.

While she waited for her copy of the police report, Werner went to his room, hauled out the duffle and ice chest, and told the dazed man that all those cops outside were looking for him. The man seemed to understand, and took Werner's advice: hide under the bed until things get quiet, and be out before the housekeeping staff arrived in the morning.

'Don't know why you've busted into my room,' Werner told him. 'And I'd best never find out.'

Then Werner told the excited manager that he'd be leaving, too traumatic, all this ruckus. The manager understood. The nice Pacifica cops offered to give the distraught couple a ride to Monterey, to Amanda's apartment. As the officers loaded the duffle and ice chest into the trunk, Werner remembered his lucky plastic owl. The friendly cop backed the cruiser to the door, so Werner could stand on the bumper and retrieve the bird.

'What's it for?' the officer asked.

'Pigeons, they're frightened by it. Got an aversion to pigeons.'

'Wonderful,' Larry said. 'Where's the bird now?'

'On the roof of my flat, attracting dirty pigeons. Looks a bit forlorn without its pistol, but he's safe.'

'Well, my mind is eased. But I feel awful about her minivan. Have to get her a new – '

'Matey, you don't understand. That tranny *collapsed*. Automatic, would've cost a grand to replace. She gets seven grand replacement value on the clunker. We're off car shopping this afternoon.'

'Dear god … you're right, that filthy owl is good luck.'

'Where you headed, then?'

'South. Recuperate, avoid these goons. Send O'Leary all the passwords, tell him to keep the site fresh. You'll hear from me.'

Larry hung up and examined the mail. A nice cheque from FlyRight – $4722.09, proving something about print media driving Web traffic – and a letter saying his site had been dropped from the network, due to objectionable content and reader complaints to advertisers. He was to remove all FlyRight ad code from SluiceBox.net by 12 a.m. Monday.

Nazis. He crumpled the letter. No time to deal with advertising problems. Endorsed the cheque and addressed an envelope to the Swiss bank. Licked two dollars' worth of stamps and wrote 'Par Avion' beneath them. And drew a little airplane next to that.

From Jesús' dwindling U.S. account, he paid the balance on the credit cards – noting a change of address, everything to the Swiss Guys. Great guys, whoever they were.

The rest of the mail consisted of 'You are pre-approved' offers. Enough with the credit cards. He tore the envelopes to shreds, unopened, and tossed them in Clarke's trash with the coffee grounds. He washed the mugs, took a Tylenol 3, went outside, found a mailbox on the corner, stole the plates off a Toyota pickup with a 'Don't Like My Driving? Call 1-800-EAT-SHIT' bumper sticker, put them on the Taurus, pulled into the driveway, locked the garage, and reluctantly left the pleasant bungalow.

The Federales ignored the car as Larry drove slowly across the frontier, under the green, white and red plastic letters that said M E X I C O.

41

The Ensenada-Rosarito toll road, a four-lane divided stretch of Baja California's Highway 1, is a quick left and then another quick left immediately after crossing the border. Many beach tourists miss the little offramp – despite many signs pointing right to it – and spend a confused hour or two in Tijuana traffic. The very unlucky are funnelled into the ocean of cars headed back to the United States. They sit in traffic, cursing, harassed by vendors selling Hello Kitty piñatas and Pokemon plaster statues and colourful blankets. Such trauma has brought a swift, tearful end to countless weekend getaways.

Larry didn't miss the ramp. He drove carefully and with courtesy, to a long boulevard running straight west, along the gruesome fence separating Mexico from its nervous NAFTA partner, *El Norte*. Stadium lights sat atop giant towers, to illuminate the nightly sport: those without papers run through the fence holes, and the U.S. Border Patrol agents – visible on every dry dead hilltop inside their white SUVs – watch through Night Vision goggles. A group of unwanted Latinos, most dark-skinned ancestors of the Aztecs and Mayans, run through a gap. The Border Patrol wagons head over, the dust fills the night, another group runs, and another, and another, and this goes on all night, every night. Most succeed in crossing; a few are captured and returned to the border to try again. These savage invaders were migrant workers trying to return to the produce fields. Without them, California's biggest industry would crumble. White people, no matter how stupid or useless or hungry, will not crouch in the Central Valley sun for twelve hours a day, picking lettuce for a dollar an hour.

Larry slowed down for a group of migrants trotting across the road. 'Good luck, comrades,' he said, and watched the dry hills for action.

The road turned south, along the coast. Clear and gorgeous on the ocean. At the toll booth, he paid the two dollars with a friendly *Buenas Tardes* to the attendant. He was hungry and Rosarito had many good restaurants, but he held out for Puerto Nuevo, the beloved Lobster Village. An actual village now, with streets and vacation homes. He remembered it when there were three lobster restaurants and a curio stand.

Parked at the edge of the dirt lot, next to a convertible VW Rabbit with a 'Mean People Suck' bumper sticker, Larry switched plates and walked into the village, eating an antibiotic and a Vicodin in anticipation of his meal.

'*Buenas Tardes, amigo,*' the waiter said. A safe greeting for all nationalities. 'Just for you today?'

'Just for me.'

'Anywhere is fine.'

Larry picked up a Tijuana newspaper from the bar and sat by the window. Ashtrays on the dining tables, right where they belonged. The order was made – a medium lobster special, with soup and a small margarita.

The margarita came right up, awfully big for a small. He sipped and smoked and tried to make sense of the paper. Something about a narco-terrorist incident, the assistant police chief of Tijuana shot dead, a kidnapping, the Cuban ballet in town, a new Maytag factory in the border zone, columnists with romantic *noms de plume*, stereo sales, a plane crash in Mazatlan, pages of blistering political attacks.

The lobster was huge, glistening with garlic oil, the tail meat flaky. He ate straight from the shell, then took a hot flour tortilla from the basket and made lobster burritos. An hour of eating later, he was headed down the last stretch of highway before Ensenada.

A big Princess cruise ship rested in the deep-water port, and its sun-dazed passengers filled the streets. This was new. They were packed into Hussong's, alleged to be the oldest saloon in the Californias. The Spanish founded the port town four centuries ago, a natural harbour in the *Bahia de Todos Santos*. Larry chose to avoid the downtown tourist shops, but he did need wine. *Bodegas de Santo Tomas* was the place to fill up the trunk. Four cases, two Cabernets, one San Emillion, one Barbera. Larry agreed with the staff that he must be having a very big party.

He left the car on Avenue Miramar and walked to the shopping district. A series of quick transactions resulted in a sack of replacement clothing, swim trunks, a few weeks' worth of groceries from the fancy new Calimax supermarket, and five cartons of Camel Lights.

He drove south, looking for a quiet place to live. So had several thousand other Americans, mostly cranky old retirees. Their mobile homes and dingy beach shacks fouled the bay from Playa Hermosa, which wasn't very *hermosa*, to Estero Beach.

It was better on Punta Banda. A 10-mile-long, phallic peninsula appropriately topped with a spouting ocean geyser known as *La Bufadora*, it had been spared excessive development due to the water problem. There wasn't any. The last time he'd made this drive, there wasn't electricity. Generators had churned behind the few restaurants.

La Bufadora's main road went through lush farms, the usual impromptu trash dumps on the shoulder, abandoned tamale stands, and finally the one-street town of Punta Banda. A lumber store, a dismal computer shop, mini-mercados, beer joints, a *restaurante* or two, and nothing again. A big billboard to his right pointed to the Punta Gorda Beach Resort, rooms

$40. A bit steep. He turned right anyway. The asphalt road curled around a stinking lagoon, big weird cranes and pelicans wallowing in the filth, no traffic. The off season.

As the narrow road veered west and the sun set behind the peninsula's craggy hills, he saw glimpses of a fine beach, lined with semi-handsome homes of recent vintage. They came with the electricity. A gaggle of real-estate signs led him to a gravel turnoff, and then another gravel road running parallel to the beach. He switched on the headlights. Only a few cars around here, a few porch lights burning. Why wouldn't these people live here year-round?

A few had 'For Sale' signs posted. One of these looked especially good. He parked and walked to the front courtyard. A weird little mass-produced fountain in there, no lights, yellow Mexican stucco on strong concrete walls. A peaked roof – maybe open beams? That would be nice. He tried the door then slipped between the walls – these houses were right up against each other – and emerged on the patio. It had a two-foot stucco wall around it, a fire ring and barbecue on the left, some dunes covered in iceplant just beyond the wall, and then the beach. He lit a cigarette and stared. The hoodoo island, *Isla de Todos Santos*, was straight ahead, the twilight catching the strange Monument Valley-style formations. To his right, the lights of Ensenada were flickering on, a cruise ship moving slowly away. The island's robot lighthouse turned on, as well. Not a soul on the beach, the bay-sized waves crashing just a few yards away.

The house itself he could barely see through the big French doors. But it had an open-beam ceiling, a fan hanging from the huge brown crossbeam, rough pine furnishings, big square tiles on the floor. He smiled and nodded to himself and tried the back door. Locked, but willing. The non-union builders had installed the deadbolt backwards; its screws faced outside. He fished the Swiss Army knife from his Serbian jacket and removed the cover, flicked the bolt back, and stepped inside. The lights worked. The place would be just fine. It was, in fact, the finest place he had yet to call home.

There were big Mexican rocking chairs around the fireplace, a fridge and gas stove in the kitchen – along with a Mr Coffee, a toaster oven, and a colourfully tiled island dividing it all from the living room. More French doors opened to the bedroom, its own fireplace sharing the chimney with the living room, a window seat facing the sea, a king-sized bed in the centre. Off this bedroom, a long master bath, with a full-sized tub, a walk-in closet, a tiled vanity the size of a lawyer's desk. In the back, two more bedrooms, another bathroom with shower. Clean towels on the racks. Clean sheets and fat quilts on the beds. A three-disc CD stereo. What the hell was this place? It was of relatively new construction, but it lacked vulgarity. A few geegaws and gimcracks, plastic flowers, two awful paintings begging for the fire ring, but otherwise …

Larry took the front deadbolt apart and opened the door. He backed the Taurus to the courtyard gate and hauled in the wine and other supplies. As he was making the last trip, a blue Dodge pickup stopped, and an old man waved. Larry waved back and walked over.

'Evening.' He was bald, alert and vaguely suspicious.

'Hey there. I'm just moving in.'

'Bought the place?'

'No, no … not yet. Renting for two months. Professional sabbatical.'

'Nice house there. I live a couple houses down from you.' The man motioned behind him. 'Going down to the resort to pick up some beer. Everything closes early on the peninsula.'

'Yeah,' Larry said, looking around. 'I like it. Quiet.'

'Sure is. I moved down here from goddamned LA. Had

it with the traffic, the gangs.'

'Understood.'

'Pete Doran.' He stuck out his right hand.

'Jerry ... Jerry Ramirez.'

'Nice to meet ya. You Mexican?'

'No, uh, not really. My uncle ...'

'Well, I think you'll enjoy it down here. Been here four years, don't plan on going back.'

'Well all right, sure I'll see you around.'

The old man waved and drove off.

Larry sighed, got the last case of wine, and put it in the empty laundry room with the others. He parked the Taurus behind a dead motorhome, wheels deep in the gravel, and saw something gleaming in a potted cactus. The house keys.

'Jackass,' he said to himself, and locked the front door behind him.

A few gnarled logs by the fireplace. With the Metro and Living sections of the *LA Times*, he got a nice blaze going and sat on the Mexican rug with a glass of Cabernet. There wasn't a room in the house where you couldn't hear the waves, but here was best, the doors swung open, a rhythmic pounding from the shore. He fell asleep in his clothes there, by the fire, but several hours later woke to the barking of sea lions and transferred to the grand bedroom.

42

He considered the wound, remembered that pilgrims soaked in the salty Dead Sea to cure all manner of problems, pulled on the new swim trunks, started the coffee, and limped down the sand into the sea. When the water was dangerously close to the gunshot hole, he dove in, feeling only the shock of the cold Pacific water.

Dog-paddling in the mild surf, he looked over to the house. The ceiling fan turning. Rolled onto his back to feel the sun, still low in the eastern sky. There was a chunk of rock about a hundred yards out, strange blobs moving around. He did a paraplegic backstroke and soon heard the gruff dog sounds. Sea lions, about twenty of them, jabbering to each other, warming their blubber in the morning sunshine. Don't worry, cousins, he thought. That rock's for you. Seals might be cute, they might wear birthday hats and balance balls, but sea lions were just mean. Shortly before departing San Francisco, Larry read about a huge, barnacle-crusted sea lion that had become comfortable on the grassy beach park just beyond Fisherman's Wharf. A Japanese couple tried to pose beside it for a photograph, and it nearly severed the husband's foot. A memorable snapshot.

All around him, crazed bluish sea birds dived into the little waves. Pelicans. He watched them hunt breakfast and shoot back into the sky, fish flapping inside the beak-sacks. Then a huge V-formation of the goofy creatures headed south down the beach like a little Air Force, not ten feet above. Nature's Bum: the only animal born with its own shopping cart.

He rode a breaker to the beach and shook off. Light breeze, a few grey clouds far up the coast. Walking along the wet sand, he realized the leg didn't hurt so bad. The only visible people were on a little fishing boat a mile away. Otherwise, birds. Every sort of sea bird: pelicans, gulls, sandpipers, oyster catchers, sea foxes, water snouts, crab suckers, sand hens, tide owls and others. Larry decided to buy one of those bird guides.

He headed back to the house, saw nobody stirring in the neighbouring casas, and drank two cups of coffee. Put on a T-shirt and his watch and tried the new Mexican sandals.

Not bad, a few blisters away from fitting. After collecting wallet and Day Timer and the real-estate agency's number, he locked up and drove to the nearest phone. About two miles by road.

'*Bueno*, Fiesta Realty.'

'*Buenos Dias. Habla Inglés?*'

'Yes, can I help you?'

'Yeah, sure can. You've got some houses for sale out on Punta Banda?'

'Mm-hmm. Seven houses for sale. We built five of them, all on the beach.'

'Terrific. There's one I saw, number 32. Any chance that one's for rent?'

'They're all for rent, until they're sold. They're vacation rentals. Are you interested in looking at that one?'

'Well, I've seen it ... Walked all around, looked in the windows and whatever. I'd like to rent it.'

'For a vacation?'

'Yeah, a vacation. A sabbatical, actually.'

'Oh? Are you a teacher?'

'Something like that. Probably for two months. Is it available? I, uh, see there's nobody in it.'

'Let me check.' She returned a minute later. 'We've got a long-term rental scheduled for May, but otherwise – '

'How much?'

'Well, when did you want to move in?'

'Oh, uh, right away. I just figured I'd drive down and find a place.'

'Well, I think we can do that.' Papers ruffled through the phone. 'Since we had a cancellation and the month already started, we can give it to you for six-fifty a month. For two months. If you want to stay longer, because of summer – '

'Sure, sure. That's fine. Let's say two months, and I'll pay for that, and we can talk about the other stuff.'

'Do you want someone to come down and show you the inside?' Larry had already hung up his clothes, filled the fridge and slept in the bed.

'No, no, that's fine. I've seen it, I want it. Where's your office?'

It was in Ensenada, downtown. First, Larry had two fish tacos and a Pepsi for breakfast, at a little Punta Banda restaurant called 'Patty's Place'. He was downtown in twenty minutes, noticing the streets looked far more inviting without a throng of cruise-ship passengers. Parked a block away, he put on the sunglasses and strolled into the offices of Fiesta Realty.

A painless transaction. He handed the cash to the co-owner, Mrs Sanchez, and she handed him a xeroxed packet of information. Who to call for firewood, nearby restaurants, Please Conserve Water As It Must Be Delivered By Truck, a number for maid service, that sort of thing.

'I didn't see ... I mean, is there a phone in the house?'

She laughed.

'No, no phones. We don't run the lines unless you *buy* the house. You see, these houses are rented for weekends, even overnights, and almost all the people are foreigners.'

'Right, and the scumbags would make a thousand dollars' worth of calls to France or LA or wherever – '

'Exactly. If you need a phone, you should see Baja Cellular. They're right down the street.'

'Great, thanks.'

A cell phone wouldn't help his old computer, unless he had one of those fancy cell-phone modems compatible with Baja's mobile system. He'd inquired about such gizmos at COMDEX, and the grinning shysters just said, 'In six months, a year at most, that will be the most common portable-computer accessory – ' He just walked away. Didn't that guy in Pacifica have a wireless modem or something?

Didn't AP and the military spokesmen have portable satellite hookups in Bosnia? Didn't matter now. He'd figure out something, if he cared to work again.

Mrs Sanchez did not request an ID. He signed the receipt 'Jerry Ramirez' and was told the keys were in the potted cactus.

At the fish market – a thriving bazaar filled with live crabs, trays of fresh shrimp, whole tunas, squirming squid and other such bounty from the sea – he loaded up on food for the barbecue and a kilo of smoked marlin, for snacks, and had a few fried-shrimp tacos and a Dos Equis beer for lunch. The car was on a side street, next to a half-completed mini-mall. A terrible stinking drunk staggered over, his nose bloody from a fall. Larry smiled and pulled the Taurus keys from his swim trunks.

But he didn't give the car to the rummy. The guy was just too drunk, barely able to walk, and a whole classroom of school kids was crossing the street, dressed in their neat little uniforms. He gave the bum some pesos and drove down Costero, wondering what to do with the evil vehicle. Passing a circus being erected south of the cruise-ship dock, *Espectacular del Mundo* painted on the big tents, he saw some gypsy types on the edge of the lot, drinking outside their ratty Airstream. Maybe one of those guys? Seemed sketchy. Then he saw the U.S. Navy boys.

A trio of sunburned guys wearing their Oklahoma street clothes, probably on their first leave from San Diego. Even inside the car, he could hear them, the high-pitched howls of the rural kids who comprised the lower ranks of the U.S. military. They were harassing an old Mayan woman selling cotton candy, one of the jackasses kicking at a pathetic stray dog. Their laughter made Larry cringe.

He got out with his plastic bag of fish and approached them, a no-nonsense cop approach.

'Hey, sailors!'

They turned. The chests puffed right up, just begging for a street fight.

'Captain Mark Bolan, U.S. Navy Intelligence.'

This deflated them a bit.

He flapped his wallet open, but they didn't see anything.

'You boys drunk?'

The tallest one muttered, 'Uh uh, nope.'

'You sure? If you guys are drunk, I'll have your arse. Ages?'

Twenty, nineteen, eighteen. All too young to drink, according to Pentagon rules – no matter what country they were terrorizing.

'Port of call?' Larry was just guessing at this. The Marines and Army he somewhat understood, but he had little experience with Navy people.

'San Diego, sir.'

'What ship you boys on?'

'USS *Natchez*, sir.'

'Why are three seamen of the U ... S ... NAVY harassing this poor woman?' He smiled at her, handed over 20 pesos for a cotton candy and said, '*Gracias, senora. Lo siento ... Adios.*'

They didn't have much of an answer. Larry ate a hunk of the sugar and winced. This stuff tasted like garbage. No wonder he didn't eat candy. He gave it to the dog; it sniffed the fuzzy multicoloured stuff and wandered away.

'That's a very bad answer, boys.'

They reddened. The shortest one was quaking, holding his hands together to hide the fear.

'You know, sailors, you come down here to Mexico, you think you can just act like buffoons, don't you?'

Nods and head shaking and nods again, trying to guess the answer.

'Well, let me tell you something. You come here or any

other country, and you are *cultural diplomats* for the United States of America, right?'

They guessed to nod for this one.

'Right.' Larry lit a cigarette. 'Diplomats. The flesh-and-blood representatives of the greatest – and I mean the goddamned *greatest* – country on this planet.'

They nodded violently. This sounded familiar.

'So! Next time you have shore leave – I should say, *if* you ever get shore leave again – I expect you little pricks to behave in a way that reflects positively on the United States of America.'

'Yes sir, we sure will.'

'Good. You boys love this country?' They looked confused and he grinned. 'Not *this* country, but America!'

They all agreed they loved America.

'All right. I might forget this little incident, if you boys can manage to do one chickenshit errand without mucking it up.'

They were adamant in professing their abilities to perform whatever errand.

'That's my car.' Larry gestured to the official-looking Taurus. 'I'm on RE-CON down here, if you know what I mean.'

They didn't, and he didn't, but they nodded.

'Here.' He tossed the keys to the one who looked the least dumb. 'Get it back to San Diego, 32nd Street Station. See Lieutenant Jagger at the back gate and he'll get you back to your ship. And no fucking around, boys. Straight across the border, no booze, no trouble. I'll be checking with the lieutenant in two hours. I want my car there … and washed.'

The trio piled into the car, made a patently illegal U-turn on Costero, and headed north. He watched them until they disappeared in traffic. Taxis were lined on the corner. He picked the most respectable-looking driver and said, '*Vamos a Punta Banda, por favor.*'

The driver looked back, eyebrows arched, and Larry gave him a hundred pesos.

'*Está bien?*'

'*Está bien.*'

For safety's sake, Larry got out in the village, by the fish-taco place. He bought some cigarettes and a phone card and a sack of mesquite coal, mostly to meet the mini-market staff, and trudged through the La Jolla Beach Campground to the sand. A pleasant mile walk from there, through the big alien clumps of kelp and a few fishermen, dragging their long nets from the waves. Larry watched this process with some interest. These Mexicans were catching fish the same way men once did on the Sea of Galilee, two millennia ago. Waving off the hungry sea birds, untangling the fish from each section of net, and tossing the flopping sea critters into buckets. When Christ approached such fishermen, he allegedly said, 'Follow me, and I will make you fishers of men.'

And they straightway left their nets, and followed him.

Of course, St Matthew left out some political details.

That night he ate alone on the patio. Rare mesquite-broiled swordfish with lime and cilantro, beans, avocado salad, and corn tortillas. He didn't read and he didn't listen to the stereo. He just watched the white foam of the waves as the tide grew closer to the dunes, a half moon behind the house, throwing yellow light on the water.

One clear afternoon many weeks later, sitting on the sand, he saw a distant kayak, a little sea kayak with a white-haired man paddling around the bay. Thinking that would be a novel way of bringing beer home, he walked to the village and posted a note on the restaurant's bulletin board, among the beach houses for rent, Sunday breakfast buffets, and old mobile homes for sale:

SEA KAYAK WANTED
Will Buy Or Rent.
Need For 2 Months.
See J. Ramirez At
Casita #132 Strand

Good enough. He looked to the beach outside and imagined himself riding the waves to shore, a full-scale Marine landing, Wagner blasting, cases of Tecate lashed to the stern. But nobody showed up with a kayak and he continued carrying his beer home.

The new clothes went untouched, other than the swim trunks and Mexican sandals and one T-shirt, which he'd rinse under the patio's faucet and let dry on a chair when it became rank. It was hard to get suntan lotion on one's own back, so after a day or two he quit trying, and the skin reddened and darkened and peeled a little and darkened more.

And one afternoon, six or seven weeks after his arrival, he got up from the sand, walked into the house, looked at his unopened laptop, and said to the open-beam ceiling, 'What in hell am I doing?'

43

The computer, already worn and battered and covered in stupid decals like a steamer trunk, had a new problem. It wouldn't start. Thinking the battery was dead, he plugged in the AC power and typed a while, long enough to charge up. Still no battery power. He flipped the laptop and laughed. A bullet, lodged in the underside. Since his shootout in Pacifica.

He remembered turning on the machine at airport security, in both San Francisco and San Jose. Checking the inside of the shoulderbag, he found poison battery goop clotted on the bottom. There's a consumer test he hadn't seen in *PC Week*: When your laptop takes a bullet, how long until the battery goop leaks out?

There was also a tiny hole in the canvas, barely noticeable. He hung the bag from his shoulder – the hole was even with his crotch. Forget the owl. Larry's new Lucky Hero was a broken laptop battery. It deserved a shrine in Vatican City. If the Pope had such a lucky battery, he wouldn't need that ridiculous Popemobile.

It was strange, going through the saved e-mails. Producers from the teevee networks, editors from dreadful magazines, their messages sent weeks and months ago, from elaborate offices far away. He had no idea what was happening in the civilized world. The stock markets could've collapsed again, earthquakes could have destroyed San Francisco, Germany could be at war with England. But none of this was likely. Real news, despite the huge industry built around it, was very rare.

Larry wrote a column. It was the kind of thing he imagined Mike Royko might type after vanishing for a few months. It wasn't that good, but it wasn't bad, and Royko was dead anyway. He liked being at the keyboard again. It was set up on the breakfast bar, the big tiled slab dividing the kitchen from the living room. It was the perfect height for typing while standing. But his column and personal e-mails would not go out until a phone line came in.

After the morning swim and a big pan of eggs, Larry left through the courtyard and examined the utility poles. He didn't like the idea of taking the bus for an hour and sitting in an Internet café with a bunch of Aussies. He wanted a line into the house, to the bureau set up in his kitchen. A borrowed line.

Unfortunately, all the houses around him were intentionally phoneless. He walked the gravel path to its end, passing five empty *casitas* like his own, then scrambled over the low dunes, following the poles to the paved road. They ended a half-mile north, at Punta Gorda Beach Resort, the end of the line. The end of this little finger of the peninsula.

It was a white stucco two-storey place, the usual L design, maybe forty rooms, a restaurant-bar in the adjacent building, a big round swimming pool, recreation room with ping pong, etc. The beach surrounded it on three sides. A few lonesome cars in the parking lot. Larry had yet to walk to this end, precisely because of the hotel – his stretch of beach was his alone, except for the seabirds and the occasional stroller at sundown. Hotels meant noisy kids, and drunken teens, and hostile military families. But it was the off-season here, as well.

For appearance's sake, he strolled into the restaurant – empty of diners – and sat at the bar. A smiling young Mexican in a black necktie said, 'What can I get for you, my main man.'

'I'm your only man at the moment.'

'Yeah, it's slow. Slow 'til spring break.'

He was the Manager of Restaurant/Catering Services, according to his business card. And, this time of year, the only bartender and waiter. Ricardo Castro Cota – 'Call me Ricky.'

'Jerry, Jerry Ramirez.'

'You *habla* the *español*?' An East Los Angeles accent.

'I don't *hablo* too damned *mucho*. *Entiendo*, that's about it.'

'That's cool. I barely spoke the shit myself, 'til I came down here. My parents own the place, bought it for their retirement.'

'Christ, everybody's retired down here.'

'Not me, man. Just perfecting my skills.'

'For?'

'Cruise ships. See that?' He pointed out the window to a

big white ocean liner heading into port. 'Next year, I'll be working there. But in the Caribbean. Money, rich young girls in the bikinis, and more money.'

Larry laughed and asked for a margarita, rocks.

'What you doing down here? Bring your girl down?'

'Nah. Just resting. A two-month retirement.'

'You surf?'

'Nope.' Larry was getting the salt-crusted look of those California longboard freaks back at Hussong's Cantina. 'I just flail around the water like a jackass. Staying at a house down the beach.'

'Ramirez, right. I seen your thing on teevee, man.'

'Teevee?' Whoops. What thing on teevee?

'For the canoe.'

'What?'

'You put an ad on the teevee bulletin board, said you want a canoe.' Ricky got the remote and flipped through Punta Banda's home-made cable system, rigged off some enterprising senior's satellite dish. There was a channel with local ads – house for rent, motorboat for sale – in electronic text against a blue screen. Then, 'SEA KAYAK WANTED'.

'I didn't put anything on that video deal,' Larry said. 'I don't even have a teevee. I put a note on a plain old bulletin board in the village, couple of weeks ago.'

'Ah, Irma musta typed it in.'

'Who the hell's Irma?'

'Old lady who runs the cable. She's on prescription dope or something, good deeds and all that.'

Larry grinned in relief. 'It's for a *kayak*. Was trying to buy a kayak.'

'Yeah, I was gonna knock on your door.'

'You got a kayak?'

'No, man, I got a jet-ski. Tryin' to sell it.'

'I don't want a damned jet-ski.'

'Sure, man. It's a Kawasaki. The bitch is *fast*.'

'And noisy. Just wanted a kayak, for … exercise. Doesn't matter, I'm leaving soon.' He finished the drink and said, 'How much?'

'On the house, if you buy the jet-ski.'

'Christ. Here, keep the change.' Larry put a bill down and rose. 'Nice to meet you. How late you guys serve dinner?'

'Only 'til seven, until spring break. Then, girls in the bikinis all over the place.'

'Yeah, and their frat-boy louts. See you later.'

On the way out, Larry saw what he was looking for. A maintenance room behind the kitchen. A padlock hung open on the latch. He slipped inside. Tools, janitorial supplies … And a rectangular beige-metal cabinet on the wall. The telephone switch box. Inside, the little wires connected to the various room phones, the connectors with plastic push-buttons like those found on the back of a 1970s stereo. It was old, dusty, easy to exploit. He wondered if anyone bothered to lock the door at night, and decided wondering was a waste of time. He pocketed the padlock and left.

Walking home, he counted 276 yards, a yard per step. The lumber and building-supply store, a short mile east of his mini-mercado, had a charming Spanish name, 'Pacific Lumber'. The lumber section was outdoors, fenced, a tin overhang protecting the finer woods. It didn't rain much in Ensenada – total desert. The longest roll of telephone wiring on the shelf was 250 metres. He took one of those and a 100-metre roll for the balance. And a handful of alligator clips and wire-nuts. And electrical tape. The total was six dollars, a real bargain. But the big plastic wheels of phone wire were heavy; when he reached the village, he didn't stop for beer. Still a dozen bottles of wine at home.

After dinner, he watched the sun sink behind Punta Banda and read. It quickly became very dark, with a new moon and a light cover of clouds. The shoulderbag was loaded with the spools of wire. The clips and wire-nuts and electrical tape and Swiss Army knife and his mini Mag-Lite – with the stealth blue lens cover – went in his pockets. Across the gravel drive was a shallow ditch, full of weeds and Kleenex and other local flora. That's where he began, coiling 30 feet and dropping it. Then he walked, leaving wire behind him. The ditch faded with the end of the gravel, but nobody would notice the wire this far out. The paved road was way off to his right. He could see the glow of the swimming pool when the big spool was empty. Crouching in the sand with the flashlight in his teeth, he slit the thick casing and stripped the blue and orange ends and ignored the barber-pole wires. Only two of the four were needed to connect a phone. This operation was repeated with the 100-metre roll, the wire-nuts screwed tight, and then sealed up with tape.

The hotel was quiet, restaurant and bar closed for the night, the lobby windows facing away. He walked straight to the maintenance room, closed the door behind him, and piggy-backed on Room 240's line. It was the only room lacking an ocean view, and wouldn't be rented until spring break. Binge drinking and date rape don't require ocean views.

Larry wished for one of those linesman's phones, the bulky things the installers use to check for a dial tone in such situations, but he was satisfied the line was live. To prevent detection, or being locked out, he chopped the cable about 10 feet from the box and threaded it through a screened ventilation window near the ceiling. Nobody would look up there. About 50 metres of the second roll remained. He left the spool on a shelf, as a gift.

Outside, another wire-nut operation was performed, and he hiked back, whistling. It took half the day, but now he could work from the house. He had the satisfied feeling of a job well done.

The ugly sound of a modem connecting made Larry smile.

O'Leary kept a CompuServe account, useful to journalists because of the hundreds of local dial-in numbers around the world. O'Leary's account was specifically useful to a dozen journalists who were provided with his password. There was an Ensenada number. A simple local call.

Before checking mail, Larry checked the site.

A JUDICIAL CALAMITY: SHAMELESS KILLER TOM SANDERS IS SENT HOME

At least O'Leary was following the goofy headline style. Ads still on the site ... Viagra ads?

Sanders pleaded out, to involuntary manslaughter, and was released for time served, five years' parole. His plea bargain involved answering questions about the mysterious death of Brendan D. Pierce, Jr, of Martha's Vineyard. Sanders did more than answer questions, he told them exactly how his hit man, Owen Lindsey, did the job. Even though Sanders ordered the murder – a significant charge on its own – and admitted killing poor little Gilliard Tyler Seacroft, he walked. 'Home confinement' for six months, passport seized, but no real punishment. Larry felt like vomiting.

The Owen Lindsey story was happier: Not only did the he plead to second-degree and get fifteen – after being positively identified by the Boston Rent-a-Heap clerk and Pierce's elderly neighbour – but he was rolled to prison in a wheelchair. So *that* was Lindsey, trying to finish the job in Pacifica. And currently recuperating from major reconstructive surgery. Larry didn't just shoot him in the nuts – he had shot off Lindsey's manhood.

The surgeons tried to build a new one out of spare parts, a chunk of arse here, some tendon there. Lindsey was reported to be suffering great discomfort. And BIPS' assets were auctioned off to Pinkerton.

Larry realized he was gripping his wounded leg. And grinning. He hopped from the barstool and poured a glass of red. He clicked around the links O'Leary had posted: a big *New York Times* article, several of O'Leary's own reports, and a lovely *Mercury News* piece. With a photo of Lindsey. Yep, that's the bastard.

To the e-mail. There was plenty, as always. One from Werner high in the list: 'Matey, yr hotmail's full up. Switched the site's contact info to ramirez@sluicebox.net. Setup attached. Cheers.'

Another e-mail account. Larry pasted the info into his Eudora software. Much quicker. The good news continued: the Swiss Guys had found a sympathetic advertising network. Mostly porn and 'Internet pharmacies'. Would he mind if they took a 10 per cent cut? Not at all. Bring on the porn, bring on the Viagra. Good enough for Bob Dole, good enough for Ramirez.

Among the many media inquiries, one subject line caught his eye, sent only yesterday.

> **From: Owen Pike (owen_pike@time.com)**
> **Subject: PLEASE READ,**
> **NOT AN INTERVIEW REQUEST**
>
> **Mr Ramirez,**
>
> I know there's a slim chance you'll read this, but will keep it short nonetheless.
> All too recently, I was plucked from an obscure *Time* franchise in Australia and deposited in New York. Until they understand the depth of their mistake, I am managing editor of your fine country's edition of *Time*. And I am offering you a 1,000-word essay on whatever aspects of the Ramirez Phenomenon, for US$5,000, for next week's

lengthy collection of all things Sanders and Sluice-Box.

I'll get the money sent wherever you like. If this appeals to you, please reply by the 8th — we'll need the piece by the 10th at latest. Yes, a terrible rush, but we claim to be a weekly.

Cheers,
Owen Pike

PS — I can promise a cover blurb, and guarantee there won't be another Pancho Villa illustration. The woman responsible for that travesty has been shot.

Well … Larry sipped his drink. He posted a short version of the 'Ramirez Returns From Exile' column; the rest would be saved for print. Actual print. He had no love for the glossy news magazines, but hell, it was *Time*. He sent Mr Pike a brief reply.

Yes, the exile was over, the trashbuckets had been punished in myriad ways, and he wanted to celebrate. Leave this lovely, lonely house and gather the troops. Enough of this monkish nonsense. The final e-mail he read that night was from Suzie, her Hotmail address. Terse as always. 'Coming home soon, you still dead?'

That was enough to keep him smiling on the brief hike to the resort. He disconnected the wires outside the maintenance window, coiled ten feet around his arm, and dumped it behind a bush in the dunes. Back at home, he hid the length of wire along the gravel path, locked the door, and slept to the sound of the waves.

44

It had been two months. Larry woke to a knock on the door, a helpful representative from Fiesta Realty. Was he interested in staying on? No, no, must return to work, but it's been ideal. Yes, leaving on the eleventh.

Everything reminded him of this departure. Only five eggs left, half a dozen tortillas, the olive oil tin nearly empty. The wine was almost gone. Just enough drinking water. Just enough cigarettes, too. All arranged for a pleasant two days of writing.

After the swim, he made breakfast and turned on the machine and sat down. And stared at the blank screen for seven hours.

It wouldn't come. He smoked, he paced, he drank coffee, he made a fire, he took a bath, he did pushups, and nothing changed.

After dark, Larry walked to the resort and connected his phone line. Maybe *that's* what he needed, a flood of electronic gibberish to get his brain focused. That didn't work, either. He hit the wine, hard, and was almost asleep when he remembered to disconnect the line. That would've been cute: the Federales at the door in the morning, the fraud evidence running straight to the alligator clips on the modem. The walk seemed long and treacherous, windy, dark, cruel rocks slamming his toes, exposed in the sandals. Ominous clouds reflecting the lights of Ensenada.

He slept poorly, jolted awake by horrible nightmares. The next day was worse. Trivial matters filled his mind – the dishes had to be washed before leaving, the hard water burned his eyes in the shower, an ominous pelican corpse had washed up, the last box of orange juice tasted weird. A few hundred words, delete, more words, delete. Attempting to sit outside, he was startled by a pickup driving down the beach. Just two Mexicans inside, collecting kelp, but he was convinced they were staring. He drank another pot of strong coffee, and his pupils grew to the size of hubcaps, the veins on his temple throbbing.

The thing was due, now. Pike had replied with glee, expecting something good in the morning. Not so likely. The sun sank. It was cold outside, the wind harsh, white caps visible in the bay. The tide rolled in, was it getting closer? Would he be washed away tonight?

'You're paranoid,' Larry said to his reflection in the bathroom. 'You need medicine.'

The Vicodin. He'd hardly touched them after the first week. Just needed one, to calm these awful nerves. And a glass of wine. And some music for the soul, courtesy of a classical station in Ensenada. All this helped. Just type the fucking thing, just another SluiceBox.net piece, dumb jokes and strange tangents, just what they wanted. Fine.

He looked at his watch and stood at the computer. More wine. The painkiller was doing its magic, his skull relaxing. A paragraph – hell, a lede. Another graf. And, suddenly, a rhythm. That was the hardest thing, the rhythm. Another smoke, another graf, and then a roadblock. The sentence quoted Mencken, but he couldn't remember the exact wording. His personal library was far away, probably sold off by Charles on Haight Street. Would have to consult the filthy Internet.

Cursing, Larry saved his 452 words – nearly half done – and looked outside. Getting ugly. He put on long pants and the Serbian coat and the war boots and walked across the dunes to plug in his phone. Lightning off the coast, a chilly mist, the first cold drops of rain. The restaurant was open, dining-room lights shining through the gloom. Strange, this late. Might best stop in, say hello to Ricky, just another dumb American local needing a nightcap. Cars in the lot, plenty of cars. Early weekenders, perhaps.

The sky shook with thunder, and Larry watched the lights of Ensenada go dark along the crescent bay shore, little clusters in a row, like fake pearls dropping off a necklace, and then the resort went black.

He relaxed. The laptop was dead for now. On the beach, a primal scene. Human figures, moving around a fire pit on the sand. In this darkness, it was a curious sight, some archetypical vision from the dawn of time. Or a bunch of New-Age idiots. As he crossed the final dune and the rain started pouring, a bunch of them ran south along the water, flashlight beams in the mist. Grunion running? That was a San Diego diversion. Run along the beach at night, grabbing the little grunion fish. Larry tried it once. They tasted horrible.

As he reached the restaurant doors, a candle lit inside, then another.

'Ricky?'

'Who's that?'

'Jerry ... Jerry Ramirez. What the hell?'

'Another goddamned power failure. Gotta start the generators.'

'Yeah, my power's out too. Let's have a drink first, and I'll help you with the machines. It's pouring out there.'

'Why not?'

Larry reached the bar and lowered himself to a stool.

'We're supposed to be closed to the public, but so what. Have a drink. Margarita?'

'Yeah, one of your famous margaritas.'

Ricky shook the drink by candlelight and opened a Pacifico for himself. Larry lifted his glass and took a sip. Excellent.

'What the hell are you closed for? You actually got cars here tonight.'

'Don't you know?'

'Don't I know what?'

'I thought you knew 'em.'

'Who?'

'These fat freaks.' He pointed to a crude banner on the restaurant wall. Larry couldn't quite make out the words, with the dark and all.

'What fat freaks?' Larry's jaw clenched.

'These fat-acceptance nudists, have their retreat down here every year. They run around naked, so we close the place while they're here. Gate's shut on the parking lot. Don't wanna scare anybody.'

Larry gulped half his drink.

'Ricky, why would *I* know about this?'

'They said you know 'em, they just left for your house.'

The grunion runners.

'I do something wrong? The one who runs the thing, Terry something, she just come in and asked where your place was, she knew the address …'

They both looked at the blank teevee.

'The kayak ad.'

'What's she, your ex-old lady or something?'

'Ricky, you wouldn't happen to have a gun around?'

'Oh shit. Oh I'm sorry, man – '

'Not your fault. Gun?'

'Can't have guns in Mexico, man, they – '

'Come on. These people want to kill me.'

Ricky reached under the bar and handed it to Larry.

'It's a nine millimetre – '

'Yeah,' Larry said, looking at the Glock in the candlelight. 'I know.'

He finished the drink and went for the door.

'Hey, Ramirez?'
'Yeah?'
'Should I call the cops?'
'Probably.'

45

Terry Texas shined the flashlight through the patio doors and saw the laptop, dark like the rest of the house. That was enough evidence for her.

'This is it!' She tried the door. Locked. She tried to slither between the houses to reach the front door. Impossible. Especially naked.

Some two dozen equally fat and naked people huddled under the eaves. The rain was hard and cold.

Terry stared at them. Weaklings. They hadn't suffered for the revolution. They hadn't spent a month in a Nevada crazy house. Some of them weren't even FLAVA members – in a non-profit sort of bankruptcy, FLAVA had merged with the Bay Area Fat Nudist Association. This was the BAFNA annual retreat, held for three consecutive years at Punta Gorda Beach Resort. This year's retreat had taken on a militaristic flavour. It had just grown more militaristic, when Terry – yelling to the kitchen for more food – saw a bulletin-board advertisement flash on the teevee. From one J. Ramirez, Casita #132 Strand.

Blissfully ignorant of the hundreds of Ramirez households around Ensenada, she cornered Ricky.

'Do you know Jesus Ramirez?'
'Jerry Ramirez?'
'Yeah, him. On the Internet.'

'I guess.'

'He's at 132 Strand, right?'

'I guess so.'

'Where is it?'

Ricky looked suspicious, and the Prozac told her to try a more subtle approach.

'I mean, I want to see him! He's an old friend!'

'Well, lady, one-thirty-two is just down the beach. It's got a number one-thirty-two on it, I guess.'

And off she went. The fat nudists were having a campfire sing-along, despite the foul weather.

'The racist?! The one who attacked our hero?!'

They looked up, confused.

'Tom Sanders, our hero! The racist who attacked him, I've found him! He's right here! He wants to kill Tom Sanders!'

Much muttering and confusion around the campfire. Tom Sanders – their keynote speaker in the morning. Somebody was trying to kill him?

'We have to stop him, now!'

With flashlights and much naked flesh, they trotted down the beach, seeking No. 132. The address numbers were on the street side of the houses, so they just stared into the dark patio windows, one house after another, until Terry found some evidence of the racist.

'We have to get inside!'

A voice under the eaves said, 'And do what?'

'And punish him!' She grabbed the barbecue from the patio and rammed it through the kitchen window.

46

'Tom, you shouldn't do this.'

The Bell executive chopper was being fueled. Thomas Sanders and Denisa Moss waited in the little lobby, the coffee table covered in copies of *Aviation Week*.

'Bullshit. These people want me to speak. You've never seen me, on a stage, people cheering. Until this punk ruined everything, I spoke everywhere, I had crowds! Stockholders, the damned media – '

'It's a parole violation. You get caught, they'll send you to prison.'

'Who the hell's gonna know?'

The fuel man returned and wrote a bill. Sanders paid in cash. They were at Brown Field, a little airport just north of the border.

'Getting nasty out there,' the fuel man said. 'Might be best to wait 'til morning.'

'Bullshit,' Sanders growled. 'Got a meeting.'

Denisa flinched. To her, he said, 'You'll see how I *was*.'

She didn't feel too good – the anti-depressants and the bumpy chopper ride and everything else.

The flight to Ensenada wasn't pleasant. Sanders could fly the thing, but the wind got stronger and the rain came in bursts, and just when they were coming around the bay, everything went black. Denisa gasped, but Sanders had GPS and a spotlight and all sorts of cop crap. BIPS had outfitted this helicopter.

His pig eyes blinked at the darkness below. 'Should be right here.' Then, lights filled the resort, but only the resort.

About a hundred yards over. He landed on the sand by the parking lot. Denisa opened her hatch and puked. Generators rumbled from behind the hotel.

The lobby was empty. Sanders stomped to the restaurant. Ricky was washing his hands.

'What's going on here?'

'Huh?'

'The lights?'

'Oh, we got generators. Power's out in Ensenada. You the guy in the chopper?'

'Yeah.'

'Hang on, lemme get your room keys. They all run off a minute ago.'

'Why?'

'Crazy. This dude staying on the beach, they're chasin' him or something.' Ricky saw the fat man squint and decided not to say anything else.

'Who?'

'I dunno.'

'Who?!'

Denisa grabbed Sanders' squishy upper arm. Ricky didn't answer. Sanders pulled a gun from his safari blazer.

'Tom!'

'Shut up.'

'What are ... you can't – '

'I'm on my goddamn own now. Who's watching out for me? Nobody.' To Ricky, he barked, 'I asked you who.'

'Just, ah, some dude, staying on the beach. Jerry, Jerry Ramirez.'

'Where'd they go?'

Ricky said nothing. He didn't like seeing a pistol aimed at his heart.

'Where?!'

'Man, just down the beach, I don't know nothin' about it.'

'Let's go. Where's your car?'

'My folks took it to town.'

Sanders grabbed Denisa's wrist and stomped back to the chopper. Really raining now. She was numb, number than she'd been in months of being numb. Sanders pulled the chopper up, thirty feet over the beach, and flicked on the spotlight. He landed on the sand when he saw the flashlight beams.

Larry didn't take the beach route home. He ran over the dunes, tripping and cursing, and reached the gravel roadway. Just as he unlocked the front door, a window crashed. Crouching in the dark, only a Mexican prayer candle burning on the table, he shouted, 'Don't move!' Somebody in there quit moving. On his knees, he moved past the guest bathroom, seeing vague shadows on the patio. What do people do in such situations, Larry wondered. Maybe a warning shot? He fired above the shadows, and missed as usual. It hit the ceiling fan, strange creatures gasped, and a fat naked woman smashed him over the head with a bottle of wine. He collapsed, knocking the candle onto a pile of old Mexican newspapers used to start the fireplace. The gun dropped from Larry's hand and slid beneath the big Mexican china cabinet.

Larry felt a little hazy when the nudists led him down the patio steps and onto the sand. There was something on the beach – a UFO? – lights glowing in the rain. A voice too close to his ear barked, 'Here's the racist, Mr Sanders.'

'Ramirez? You sure?'

Terry Texas walked to Sanders, a cultist smile on her face, and showed him the evidence: the wallet with the Social Security card, a notebook with Jesus' computer codes, some mail addressed to Ramirez in San Francisco, and the rental contract from the fridge door. She was sure the real evidence was on the laptop, but it wouldn't turn on.

'And it's a great pleasure to finally meet you, Mr Sanders.'

He grunted and grabbed Larry by his jacket.

'I've seen this guy before.'

Denisa coughed.

'This one, Denisa? This is the sonofabitch?'

She looked at the sand. A little seashell, reflecting the chopper's lights.

He pointed the Glock at Larry's chest – a spare pistol from BIPS, provided by Lindsey in case of emergency, before Sanders sent Lindsey to prison.

Larry's eyes began to focus. His head hurt.

'You stupid punk, I let you into my *house*. And you do this to me? You destroy my goddamned life?' Sanders clicked the safety off.

'Tom,' Denisa rasped. 'Don't.'

Sanders looked at the big faces lined around him. Terry was smiling; the rest looked very nervous. They were here to frolic in the sun, not kill people.

'Yeah. We'll take him … To the police.'

Terry yelled her approval. The others nodded, shivering in the rain. He took Larry by the neck and pushed him into the chopper's middle seat – the big Bell had plenty of room. Denisa didn't move until he grabbed her, too. He pressed the pistol into her shaking hand and said, 'Keep it on him.'

The helicopter rose. The noise helped Larry come around. Wine and blood streaming into his eyes, complicating his vision. He blinked and looked to his right. Denisa, shakily pointing a gun. And shaking on her lap, the left hand, a gruesome diamond ring on the engagement finger. No, the world wasn't *that* horrible, was it? He felt too hazy to make a pronouncement.

Then again, it wasn't a good time to be indifferent. The rotor noise and an open vent window impeded conversation.

He punched her in the mouth. A sloppy left-handed punch, due to the seating arrangements, but effective. She dropped the gun and gasped, not that anyone could hear it. He punched her again, hard this time. Her head slumped.

Sanders was watching the sky and his instruments, his ears covered by the pilot headset. Larry nudged it with the barrel.

Sanders glanced back and made a very ugly face.

'Down!' Larry shouted. 'Or you die.'

Larry made sure to mouth this. Couldn't hear a thing. Sanders' right hand spun toward Larry. Larry fired. And missed, as always, the slug lodging in the cockpit's shatter-proof glass. Sanders hunched over. His left hand dropped and crawled to his chest, his back jerking in spasms. Snorting, having a little trouble breathing. The long-overdue heart attack. His big head wilted against the instrument panel. The chopper tilted down.

They were only sixty feet above the water, but the plunge was violent. Larry's head hit the glass. When the ocean reached his mouth, he coughed and pushed the back door open. More water. Sanders' face was white, his eyes half-conscious and glassy. Larry swam away, heard Denisa's dull whine, and yanked her out behind him.

She dog-paddled listlessly, her face blank.

'Swim!'

'Help Tom …'

'Are you kidding? Swim.'

She couldn't swim so well. He grabbed her around the waist and towed her to the beach. When the water was knee high, he dropped her and stood.

Denisa stumbled, knocked down by a foot-high wave, her shoes lost in the bay. The sky was clearing to the northwest, the storm surge already fading. Down the beach, there were flames from his house and red lights from the Punta Banda volunteer fire department. He was sitting on the wet sand, watching a rotor blade sink.

She crawled the last few yards, coughing. 'Help me,' she said.

Larry didn't move. The tip of the blade didn't go under. The chopper had hit bottom. Shallow around here. The Hammerhead sharks would take care of Thomas Sanders. The bay was full of Hammerheads.

Denisa stopped crawling, the sea at her ankles.

He glanced over. 'Never had an editor try to kill me.'

'No.' The voice was weak and tired. 'No, no, I wasn't ... can't we do something?'

'He's dead. How far back does all this go?'

'You don't know.' She almost wept, hands on her face.

'Why don't you tell me?' Larry coughed out some salt water. 'Not much else to do tonight.'

'I knew you were behind that Web thing, that wasn't hard to figure out. But I never told him.'

'Sure. You two talked a lot?'

'I never told him! He had no idea you were down here, he came to speak to those naked people. I had no idea you were down here.' She looked up at him. '*What are* you doing down here?'

'I asked you the same thing.'

'We saw each other, okay? He was nice to me. I lost my job, not that you would care.' She watched Larry's eyes go to the fat diamond and added, 'It's just a gift, a stupid gift.'

He stood and reached for cigarettes. None. Reached for his lighter. Back in the kitchen with everything else. He watched the house burn for a moment and decided to walk the other direction.

She staggered up and said, 'Larry, please. Don't leave me ... here.'

'You'll survive.' He looked back and almost grinned. 'Got any money?'

She shook her head.

'Ah, so what? I know the bartender. Let's get a drink and make up your story.'

He waited for her and they walked toward the hotel's diesel-generated lights.

'And what's my story?'

'Whatever you like. Kidnapping, insanity, a tragic accident. Just keep me out of it. How's your Spanish?'

'I studied French.'

Along the bay, a cluster of lights blinked on, then another, then another.